It was like being drunk, but only faintly.
As the sensation grew stronger, Tal felt a sudden
flush of fear. His concentration broken, he felt
the cold steel bars of the cage pressing against him.
A cramping pain wrenched his lower back,
and he twisted onto his side with a groan.

TALBOT USKEVREN

He curled like a child as the pain rushed up
into his shoulders and down each leg. He cried out and
instantly prayed that neither Chaney nor Eckert would
heed him. Now the sound of rushing water filled his
head, almost deafening him to his own cries and
shouts. Hot rain pelted his brain, and a warm surge
filled his whole body, pushing it out in shapes it was
never meant to take. Lightning coursed through his
nerves, leaving agonizing spasms in its wake.

HIS CURSE IS HIS FAMILY'S SOLE HOPE

Despite the darkness, Tal saw a crimson wall rise
to surround him, closing in to press against his eyes,
then through them to his panicked brain. The red fury
penetrated his body, filled him to bursting,
and blasted his conscious thoughts to oblivion.

SEMBIA: GATEWAY TO THE REALMS

Book I
The Halls of Stormweather

EDITED BY Philip Athans

Book II
Shadow's Witness
Paul S. Kemp

Book III
The Shattered Mask
Richard Lee Byers

Book IV
Black Wolf
Dave Gross

Book V
Heirs of Prophecy
Lisa Smedman
October 2007

Book VI
Sands of the Soul
Voronica Whitney-Robinson
November 2007

Book VII
Lord of Stormweather
Dave Gross
February 2008

FORGOTTEN REALMS®

BLACK WOLF

SEMBIA
GATEWAY TO THE REALMS

BOOK
IV

DAVE GROSS

WIZARDS
OF THE COAST®

BLACK WOLF

Sembia: Gateway to the Realms, Book IV

©2001 Wizards of the Coast, Inc.

Cover art by Raymond Swanland
Map by Dennis Kauth
First Printing: November 2001
This Edition First Printing: August 2007

9 8 7 6 5 4 3 2 1

ISBN: 978-0-7869-4283-1
620-95949740-001-EN

U.S., CANADA,   EUROPEAN HEADQUARTERS
ASIA, PACIFIC, & LATIN AMERICA   Hasbro UK Ltd
Wizards of the Coast, Inc.   Caswell Way
P.O. Box 707   Newport, Gwent NP9 0YH
Renton, WA 98057-0707   GREAT BRITAIN
+1-800-324-6496   Save this address for your records.

Visit our web site at www.wizards.com

DEDICATION

For Chris Perkins,
Friend and comrade.

House Malveen

The River Hall
[Ground Floor]

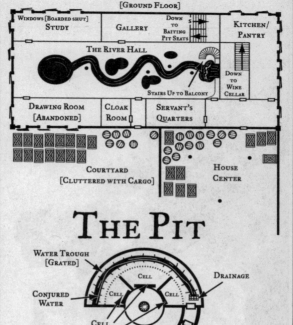

WINDOWS [BOARDED SHUT]
STUDY

GALLERY

DOWN TO BAITING PIT SEATS

KITCHEN/PANTRY

THE RIVER HALL

DOWN TO WINE CELLAR

STAIRS UP TO BALCONY

DRAWING ROOM [ABANDONED]

CLOAK ROOM

SERVANT'S QUARTERS

COURTYARD [CLUTTERED WITH CARGO]

HOUSE CENTER

The Pit

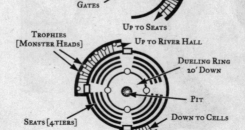

WATER TROUGH [GRATED]

CELL

CELL

CELL

DRAINAGE

CONJURED WATER

CELL GATES

UP TO SEATS

TROPHIES [MONSTER HEADS]

UP TO RIVER HALL

DUELING RING 20' DOWN

PIT

SEATS [4 TIERS]

DOWN TO CELLS

CHAPTER 1

OLD WOUNDS

Hammer, 1371 DR
The Year of the Unstrung Harp

Darrow slapped his arms against the cold and silently cursed his employer. Silently was the only way anyone ever cursed Radu Malveen. The finest swordsman in the city of Selgaunt was not one to suffer insults, especially not from his own carriage driver.

"Been in there a long time," observed Pons, the master's bodyguard. Twenty years older than Darrow, the old veteran had a voice full of smoke and pebbles. His breath turned to fog as it passed through his muffler.

Darrow looked up to spot the moon. Selûne was full and bright, a glittering trail of shards forming her wake against the dark winter sky. The black silhouette of House Malveen had only barely touched her silver body.

"Not so long," said Darrow. "Seems longer 'cause it's so damned cold."

The great black draft horse snorted and clapped its hooves on the cobblestones, as if to agree. Darrow pressed his hands against one of the copper lanterns that flanked the driver's perch. The frost on his mittens sizzled.

"Dark!" cursed Pons. "Seems long 'cause it *is* long."

"You want to go in and tell him to hurry? Here's the key."

Pons shot Darrow a dirty glance. He had been on duty the previous summer, when Souran Keel decided he didn't want to piss in the courtyard and went inside to find a garderobe. Radu Malveen emerged alone soon after and ordered Pons to drive home. No one dared to ask about Souran, and no one ever saw him again.

Darrow looked up at the slumping hulk of House Malveen. Even before it had been abandoned two decades earlier, the manor was the sole residence in an area increasingly overrun by salt houses and shipyards. In its day, it had been one of the premiere social landmarks of Selgaunt. Now, moldering crates and barrels spilled out of its sagging walls to fill the central courtyard. Even the once-fabulous fountain was piled with graying boxes, between which sad nereids and locathah yearned skyward on waves of verdigris.

He wondered only briefly what the interior looked like before thrusting the thoughts away. Radu entrusted his driver with the key to the north wing with strict instructions to enter with a warning only if the city guards approached. The Scepters were notorious for accepting bribes, and Darrow had little doubt they had been well paid to avoid House Malveen. He assumed his stewardship of the key was more a test of loyalty conducted by a man who enjoyed inflicting punishment on the disobedient. Radu Malveen was not intimidating for his swordsmanship alone. To his employers and peers alike, he gave the impression that he could do anything, without concern for the repercussions. Darrow admired that ability to live completely beyond fear of consequences. It seemed like power.

Pons blew into his mittens, then pressed them against the lantern beside Darrow's.

"Ever wonder why they don't just buy it back?" he asked. Behind him, strange gargoyles crouched as if to listen to their gossip. Moonshadows crawled slowly over their crustacean limbs, scaly hides, and blank, piscine eyes.

"Best not to talk about the master's business," said Darrow.

"The 'Skevren were broken for piracy, too," Pons said, oblivious to the warning. "The Old Owl's lord of Stormweather again and practically running the city. Why not the master and Pietro? What about Laskar? He's the eldest."

Darrow glared at Pons. Gossiping about the master's business was almost as stupid as disobeying his orders. Pons should have known better, having worked for the Malveens so long.

"So they do a little black business," said Pons, jerking a thumb over his shoulder to indicate the north wing. "They all do."

"Shut up, Pons."

"Don't you ever wonder what's going on in there?"

"No. Shut up."

"Don't tell me to shut up, boy. I'll—Wait, what's that?"

Darrow listened but heard only the distant shush of the surf crashing on the sea breaks around Selgaunt Bay. Straining his hearing, Darrow imagined he could also hear the hubbub of watermen and their families in the huddled community of their boats. No matter the season, the boaters lived on the water, lashing their rafts and barges together when the day's work was done. The proper folk of Selgaunt would have it no other way, since the alternative was to let the riffraff roam the streets.

Pons and Darrow peered into the courtyard, down the narrow alley formed between the north wing and a wall of crates. All they could see was a thin path of glistening cobblestones where the moon slanted down between the black shadows of crates and casks, the cargo that overflowed from the warehouse. Sometimes beggars would combine their efforts to push aside a few barrels to create a windbreak, but Darrow couldn't imagine anyone trying that tonight.

Without four walls and a fire, any beggar hiding here would have succumbed to the deadly cold long ago.

"I didn't hear anything," said Darrow at last.

"Don't make us come in there after you," Pons warned the unseen intruder. Darrow grimaced at the dark passage and pitied anyone foolish enough to make a shelter so close to the house. Pons didn't know when to hold his tongue, but he was ruthless and efficient when dealing with beggars. No vagrant who'd felt the wrong end of Pons's club came back for more.

Pons drew his short sword and stepped into the alley. Darrow did the same. Despite their caution, both men were caught flat-footed by the attack.

Something swept Darrow's legs from under him, and he hit the street hard. His boiled leather helmet spared his skull from cracking on the stones, but the impact blasted his breath away.

Where Pons had been, Darrow heard a low voice speaking but couldn't make out the words. He heard Pons's reply, "No! I can't!"

The answer was a savage roar and a rough shout, and a hot stream of liquid splashed Darrow's face, filling his open eyes.

For a second, he panicked, trying to scramble away on all fours. Behind him, a painful wheezing filled the alley. Pons needed help, so Darrow found his courage and turned, blinking away the blood. Then he heard a sound of butchery, a ripping and tearing worse than anything he'd experienced slaughtering sheep as a boy. In the darkness, something wet and heavy hit the cobblestones.

He stared, paralyzed with fright as a towering figure rose up from the shadows. It was a man who stood almost a head taller than Darrow. The full moon made a bright halo of his long white hair, and a beaded headband held a copper medallion of a ragged claw to the man's brow. Short gray whiskers bristled on his cheeks and chest, which was bare but for a thick woolen vest that hung loosely on his lanky, muscular body. The man's left shoulder was a bleeding stump, a few strips of pink flesh testament to an inadequate healing spell. In his right hand, the big man gripped Pons by the hair. The guard's eyes were wide and blank in death.

The stranger moved forward and put his face close to Darrow's. The man's teeth were white in the moonlight, and his canines were inhumanly long and sharp. His breath was hot and smelled of fresh blood.

"Can *you* open the door?" he rumbled.

Darrow thought about the master's displeasure. Then he thought about Pons's guts steaming on the ground nearby. Finally, he weighed his chances of killing or escaping this gigantic stranger who had eviscerated Pons in the time it took to blink.

"Yes," said Darrow, "I can."

Darrow stood in the antechamber, the one-armed man close behind him.

The hall before them was dark but for the tongues of continual flames licking from brass sconces set in the walls. Between them hung sea-colored tapestries. Darrow saw an oak door to his left, another one at the end of the hall, ten feet away. The wood of the far portal gleamed in the magical firelight. The whole room was surprisingly clean for an abandoned edifice.

"Go in," said the stranger.

Darrow complied. As he reached the middle of the hall, a painful spasm gripped his back. His breath caught in his chest, and for a terrifying moment he thought he was strangling. He tried to move, only to discover that he was completely paralyzed, and not by his own fear this time.

"Go," said the stranger. A moment later, he muttered, "Ah . . ."

Darrow heard the stranger chant a low, rhythmic song. He recognized only one word, the name of a dark god. Malar the Beastlord was no friend to city dwellers, nor to farmers like Darrow's father. The old man had sacrificed to Chauntea not only for bountiful crops but also for protection against the ravages of Malar and his wild hunts. The Beastlord's followers believed they were placed above all living creatures, and their favorite prey was the most cunning: humans and their ilk.

The magic that held him vanished, and Darrow slumped to one knee before recovering. He thought of the copper coin he wore on a chain around his neck, a symbol of the goddess Tymora, Lady Luck. He dared not touch it in sight of this cleric of Malar, but he framed a silent prayer in his mind: Lady Luck, please spare me from this monster.

Darrow's thoughts were interrupted. The cleric of the Beastlord was casting another spell. His fingers first pressed the medallion on his headband, then wiped his eyes, which flared briefly with unholy purple light.

The cleric looked up and down the hall. He chuckled as his eyes rested on the handle of the far door. "Open it," he said, stepping back.

Seeing the look in the stranger's eyes, Darrow realized the man saw something dangerous about the door. "It's trapped, isn't it?"

"That's why you are the one opening it," said the stranger. "Quickly, before you become more vexing than useful."

Another painful spasm of paralysis was preferable to Pons's fate. Darrow closed his eyes as he gripped the latch. When he touched the brass handle, a cold thrill coursed through his body, followed by a warm flush. He opened his eyes, expecting a column of fire or lances of ice, but there was nothing—no pain, no paralysis, no harm that he could discern. Slowly, he pushed the door open and entered.

Beyond the door was a vast hall of marble veined in blue and black. Rippling light rose from a long, winding stream that bisected the room, and the smell of salt water filled the air. The stream ran from a cascading fall in the north wall before winding its way through the grand hall to fill a large round pool in the south. Where the grand stream curved, smaller fountains nestled in its embrace, adding their lesser voices to the rushing flow. Each was ringed with coral seats carved in the likeness of creatures from an alien sea. Green pillars rose from the fountains, and from the stream itself, glistening with clear water that ran perversely up toward the ceiling over the half-visible fragments of crustacean eyes and invertebrate tendrils until it vanished in the darkness beyond the second-floor balconies.

Beyond the grand pool stood a wide pair of shelves and a cabinet of many tiny drawers, clearly out of place in the fabulous hall. They formed the borders of an island in the marble hall, a strange haven of books and papers. Between the shelves, on a richly woven carpet, stood a clerk's desk. The oil lamp on its corner still flickered as if disturbed by a fleeing ghost. Beside the lamp lay a stack of white vellum, an inkpot, and a stylus, still rolling across a page of figures. Even from forty feet away, Darrow spotted the fresh lines glistening wet and black. He crept closer for a better view but halted beside a pillar, afraid of attracting the attention of the room's hidden occupants.

The stranger shoved past Darrow and stamped toward the table.

"Show yourself, Malveen!" he roared. His voice echoed briefly before the sound of moving water devoured it. "I've come for the scrolls."

When no one answered his challenge, the stranger flipped the table over, scattering its contents across the marble floor. The inkpot shattered and sent a black spray across the marble floor beyond the carpet.

The cleric threw back his head and unleashed a terrific howl. The sound filled the vast hall and echoed in distant chambers. Darrow covered his ears and crouched beside the pillar, more afraid to be noticed than to remain still.

The room's guardians hissed in warning to the challenge. Against the far wall, three figures slunk out of the shadows. They were man-shaped, hairless, with glistening black skin. Their long, clawed fingers were webbed with translucent purple membranes. Long, needle-sharp teeth flashed in their impossibly wide mouths. They crept forward, crouching like ghouls.

Suddenly, one of the creatures turned its head and sucked in the air as if tasting it. Its fellows imitated its gesture. As one, they froze in place, then darted away from the illuminated water to find shelter in the darkness.

The light from the northern wall faded. Darrow saw the waterfall turn black, a great inky stain spreading in the tumult below. As the shadow moved along the stream, the light returned in its wake. The dark cloud flowed with the water, at last to reach the grand pool. The stranger looked down at it, then stepped back as the darkness surged up toward him.

The darkness rose to the surface, taking shape as it emerged from the water. What appeared looked like a muscular, hairless man except for a prominent dorsal ridge running from the top of its skull down its spine. Its skin was smooth and dark as an aubergine, slick and glistening. Golden rings pierced the creature's brow and the flaps where ears should be. From them hung a veil of fine chain links, obscuring the creature's face except for its golden eyes. The veil fell netlike over the creature's thick chest, ending in a thousand tiny hooks. Among them hung dozens of tiny arcane charms.

The creature gazed at the one-armed stranger briefly before turning to Darrow cowering by the pillar. Above its veil, the creature's eyes churned like boiling gold. It had no pupils, only black flecks that rose to the surface and sank away again. As those inhuman eyes turned on him, Darrow felt a surge of awe fill and warm his body. His fear vanished as he realized he was in the presence of a majestic, flawless power. Darrow sank to one knee and lowered his gaze.

The stranger was unimpressed both by the creature and Darrow's worship. He sneered at the kneeling driver and bellowed at the creature, "If you wish to live long enough to squirm back to the sewers, monster, summon your master."

From beneath the shadow creature's veil came a wet, choking sound. "I am master here."

"I want Stannis Malveen," said the stranger. "I want the scrolls he promised me."

Again the creature uttered that halting, coughing sound, and Darrow realized it was laughing. "It looks as though you want an arm, my old friend. Did you leave it with the boy you promised to bring me?"

"Stannis . . . ?"

"It has been a long time, Rusk. The years have been kinder to you than to me, as you can plainly see—except, of course, for the issue of your missing arm. Did you have an accident? No matter: You received my sending and agreed to my terms. Talbot Uskevren in return for the Black Wolf Scrolls."

"He's dead," said Rusk. "I gutted him before he cut me."

"I required him alive," hissed Stannis. "How bothersome of you to bungle it. Very well. Where is the body?"

"In the playhouse," said Rusk. He indicated Darrow with a toss of his head. "Your lackey can fetch it, if the clerics haven't dragged it away."

"Clerics, hmm?" Stannis pressed his rubbery fingers together. "Pray tell, who were these clerics in the playhouse? Do you mean real ones, with spells and halos and the rest? I hope you mean players in tall pointy hats, my dear Huntmaster. That is what you mean, isn't it?"

Rusk scowled.

"You simpleton! You're missing an arm, yet you healed yourself enough to come crawling before me with your petulant demands. What makes you think the boy was not healed as well?"

"I'll bring him to you alive or in pieces," shouted Rusk. "Just give me the damned, bloody scrolls so I can heal this wound!"

"I've seen the scrolls," said Stannis coyly. "In fact, I have read some singularly interesting passages in them. I did not, however, notice an extra arm among the leaves."

"This is your fault!" thundered Rusk, taking a step toward the pool. Blood from his half-healed stump spattered on the floor.

"Have a care, Huntmaster. You are soiling my favorite rug," cautioned Stannis. "Mulhorandi, and quite expensive."

Rusk lunged toward the water's edge.

Before he made it, a dark figure blurred toward him and spun Rusk aside. A long blade pierced his biceps and thrust him against a marble pillar. Rusk roared and thrashed, but he was pinned.

At the sword's other end stood a man with long, dark hair tied loosely at his neck. His pale skin was smooth and unblemished but for a trio of tiny moles beside his left eye. His plum-dark lips were impassively composed. A black silk shirt showed through the slashes of his dark purple doublet. Like the fitted leggings and thigh-length boots, they were precisely fitted to his body. The man's sword arm extended fully above a perfectly bent knee. His large black eyes looked calmly into Rusk's.

"My brother is rather protective of family," said Stannis. "May I suggest you exercise restraint?"

Rusk growled in response, but the sound gradually transformed into a deep chuckle. He glanced at the fresh wound in his remaining arm. Within seconds, the blood stopped trickling, and the flesh rejoined around the blade.

"You can't hurt me with mortal weapons," he said. "Mine is the Black Blood. I am a child of Malar."

"If Radu had intended to visit permanent harm upon you," said Stannis, "I would already be deprived of the novelty of your company."

Darrow never saw the motion, but suddenly Radu was leaning against the bigger man. His right hand held the pinioning sword in place, while the left pressed a slim white dagger against the cleric's throat. Rusk blanched at the weapon's touch.

Stannis clapped his rubbery hands and hooted. "Do you recognize it?"

"A bone blade," gasped Rusk, careful of moving his throat. "I told you about them when we were boys. "

"Can you feel its desire?" crooned Stannis. "Does it call to you, my old friend? Does it yearn for your spirit?"

Rusk's jaw barely moved. Darrow could see that it would take Radu only the barest motion to cut Rusk's throat.

"While Radu disdains the use of enchanted weapons,"

explained Stannis, "he understands the need for the proper tool—a tool for dealing with problems."

Rusk bristled as the dagger shifted slightly.

"You aren't a problem," said Stannis, "are you, Rusk?"

Rusk hesitated only briefly before responding. "No. No problem."

Radu withdrew before Rusk could counterattack. He returned the bone blade to its sheath at the small of his back, then wiped his long sword clean with a white handkerchief before returning the blade to its plain leather scabbard. He dropped the soiled cloth carelessly on the floor.

"You, too, are hurt only by enchanted weapons . . ." Stannis said, considering the vanishing wound on Rusk's arm. He turned to Radu. "Dear brother, did you not once say that Talbot Uskevren shares your affectation for plain steel?"

Radu looked loath to speak. "I did," he said. Darrow saw Radu's eyes narrow slightly as he looked at his inhuman brother. Whatever business Stannis had with Rusk, it was news to Radu.

"He had an enspelled blade in the playhouse," said Rusk. "After I released him from the cage, he dropped through a trapdoor and—"

"He was in a cage when you arrived?"

"He is . . . unusual," said Rusk. "I wished to learn—"

"He put *himself* in the cage? Did you send a messenger ahead with a request that he should bind and gag himself as well?" pressed Stannis.

"It's a common reaction among the reborn," said Rusk. His rough voice was becoming irritable, almost petulant. "He feared the change, so he—"

"Are you telling us," interrupted Stannis, "that you found Talbot Uskevren in a cage, released him, watched him escape through a trapdoor, and let him lop off your arm with a stage prop?"

Rusk glared at both Malveens, and Darrow saw the muscles in the Huntmaster's back tense.

"He *tricked* me," spat Rusk. "Besides, you didn't tell me he was dangerous."

"Dangerous?" Radu fixed his gaze on Stannis. "Talbot Uskevren?"

"You and he do have the same sword master," observed Stannis.

"He is a playhouse buffoon," said Radu.

"Perhaps," said Stannis. "But he's proven formidable in his way. To take off Rusk's arm like that . . . well, perhaps we've underestimated this boy."

"We?" said Radu, raising one eyebrow almost imperceptibly.

Stannis glided toward the center of the pool, his chain veil tinkling where it dragged in the water. "Perhaps the Huntmaster wishes to retire after his ordeal, hmm? Visiting the city can be a daunting experience for rural folk."

"What I want," said Rusk, "is what you promised me."

"We shall discuss it tomorrow evening," said Stannis, keeping his eyes on Radu, who looked back with a steady gaze. "Until then, please avail yourself of our humble accommodations—but not here, in the River Hall. You will find the other buildings are not warded—and I trust you will not continue to test the protections on this one. Not all of them are so forgiving as those you triggered."

Rusk hesitated, considering whether to repeat his demands. One more glance at Radu persuaded him to keep quiet. Reluctantly, he turned and left the way he came.

When Rusk was gone, Darrow expected his own dismissal—or worse—but the Malveen brothers spoke as if they were alone.

"How rude Rusk has become," said Stannis. "As a younger man he always—"

"What have you done?" said Radu. "Who was that monster?"

"I was so hoping to keep it a surprise," said Stannis with a sigh. "Rusk is an old friend of the family, one I had all but forgotten until Pietro encountered him last month."

"The hunting accident."

"Indeed. Our little brother would have been among the devoured had he not mentioned the family name in Rusk's hearing. Fortunately, the Huntmaster remembered his association with our great-uncle. It was his pack the boys encountered in the Arch Wood. Among the survivors was Talbot Uskevren, grandson of our old business partner, Aldimar."

"I told you to forget about Aldimar. The Uskevren are no threat to us."

"They are the very reason for our present state!" Stannis wheezed as he grew more agitated. "Thamalon could have saved mother from her persecutors, but he . . . he turned her away like a common criminal!"

"She *was* a criminal," said Radu, "and the Uskevren were recovering from their own scandal. They could ill afford to harbor a condemned pirate."

"They grew rich while she took the greater risks."

"That was Aldimar. The same people who persecuted our mother killed him."

"It isn't enough!" said Stannis. "We suffered far worse for our mother's crimes, while Thamalon escaped all harm. He has already regained everything the Uskevren lost, while you and I must cower in the shadows, scraping shoulders with the scum of Selgaunt just to keep Laskar and Pietro fed and clothed."

"It is precisely because of our brothers that we must walk the shadows," said Radu. "Nothing is more important than restoring them to their rightful place. Never forget that."

"It isn't fair," complained Stannis. The petulant tone sounded incongruous coming from such a huge, unearthly figure. "I remain a prisoner in the ruin of our family estate."

"You were reborn into darkness," said Radu, "and in darkness you will remain. Do not make the mistake of forcing me to choose between you and our brothers."

"Radu! Have I not been your good and faithful confidant? Have I not shared your own dark secrets with sympathy and fidelity?"

"You are my brother," said Radu, "but I will not permit you to endanger Laskar and Pietro. They have remained innocent of our business, and we must keep it that way."

"Why must the burden fall on us alone?" whined Stannis. "Surely we deserve some indulgence. All I desire is our deserved revenge against those who abandoned our mother."

"You cannot murder the son of Thamalon Uskevren," said Radu. "There's nothing to be gained from it, and far too much to lose."

"What of the men you have slain, dear brother? What's one Uskevren to a few dozen guild members?" Darrow was only slightly surprised at the implication that Radu had slain so many people, but Stannis said it so casually that he wondered whether the brothers even remembered they were not alone. "Besides, I said nothing about murdering the poor boy."

"What else would you do with him?"

"Our friend Rusk is not merely a cleric of the Beastlord," said Stannis. "He is a lycanthrope."

"What?"

"A nightwalker," said Stannis. "A skin-changer. A werewolf."

Radu stared at his inhuman brother. His features remained composed, but Darrow saw the faint line of a vein begin to form on his brow. When he spoke, his voice was cool and quiet. "You planned to turn him into a werewolf?"

"A delicious thought, is it not?" squealed Stannis. "But he is already a werewolf, I'm afraid. We can hardly call such a charming coincidence our own revenge. What we must do is take advantage of his condition, use Rusk to bend Talbot to our will."

"You will stop this mad scheme at once," said Radu. "Send Rusk away, and leave the Uskevren alone."

"But brother, it is—"

"I will hear no more of this," said Radu.

"What of your sparring partners?" asked Stannis. "If we are to cower in this hovel like frightened hares, not daring to attract the attention of the hounds, then I suppose I must stop fetching them for you."

Radu waved a hand dismissively. "Unlike you, I can deny myself if the risk is too great."

"What a pity," said Stannis. "Then you shan't be wanting the new arrivals. After all your talk of bladesingers . . ."

Radu raised an eyebrow, apparently intrigued by his brother's remarks but unwilling to inquire further. "As long as you acquire them outside the city, the risk is negligible."

Stannis pressed his fingers together, rising magically from the water to glide slowly toward his brother. Before he could rejoin the argument, however, Radu turned to Darrow as if noticing him for the first time. "Where is the other one?"

It took Darrow a moment to realize Radu was speaking of Pons. He bowed an apology and said, "He's dead, master."

"Put the body in the carriage," Radu said to Darrow.

"I could send my minions—" began Stannis.

"Keep your filthy spawn off the street," said Radu. "In the bay or within these walls, I do not care, but they are not to be seen outside."

"As you wish," said Stannis contritely. "Still, I would be only too glad to dispose of your problem personally. It would save you the trouble—nay, the risk—of taking it to Selgaunt Bay."

Radu's eyes narrowed, but he said, "Very well. Bring the body here, then wait for me by the carriage."

Darrow felt a chill that had nothing to do with the temperature. He knew he had seen and heard far too much. Radu would kill him rather than risk his gossip.

Salvation came from an unexpected source.

"I presume you intend to terminate this young man's employment, brother?" When Radu did not reply, Stannis said, "I have need of a servant."

"You have your creatures."

"Dull, tedious things," said Stannis. "They are good for fetching, but little else. Besides, they frighten our guests, your sparring partners. No doubt that accounts for their disappointing performances recently."

Whatever Stannis intimated made Radu scowl.

"Besides," persisted Stannis, "it is lonely here, and you visit so very rarely. Don't be so cruel as to deny my craving for . . . conversation."

"He is no courtier," said Radu. "His father was a sheep farmer."

"So long as he can speak in sentences and laugh at my jests, he will be an improvement. What do you say, my dear boy? Would you like to serve another Malveen?"

"I should like that very much, Lord Malveen." Darrow made the best bow he could muster, imitating the noblemen who greeted ladies disembarking from a carriage.

"Did you hear that, brother?" Stannis giggled and clapped. "Did you hear what the precious young man called me?"

"You mentioned new arrivals."

"A matched set," said Stannis. "I hope you will adore them as I do. They require some mending, I'm afraid. In a month, perhaps, they should prove entertaining."

"Very well," said Radu.

Cool relief washed through Darrow's body. A day ago he wouldn't have believed his good fortune. To serve such a one as Stannis was far more than he deserved.

"What are you called, my boy?" asked Stannis.

"Darrow, if it please my lord."

"It pleases him," said Stannis, wheezing with amusement. "It pleases him very much."

CHAPTER 2

NEGOTIATIONS

Hammer, 1371 DR

Talbot Uskevren stood in the parlor of his tall-house when the callers rapped at his front door. He turned slowly to check the room one last time before letting them in.

To his right, the door to the small dining room remained slightly ajar. The room beyond was dark, the draperies drawn against the afternoon light. Human eyes could not penetrate the gloom, but Tal nodded to himself as his increasingly keen sight detected the shape he expected there.

Behind him, tiny sconces of continual flames lit the hallway to the servants' quarters and the study. Between the sconces, the polished cherry doors gleamed above a rich camel-hair carpet.

Across from the kitchen, fresh logs rested in the fireplace. Above the unlighted hearth, twin cande-labra cast flickering light upon the high, arched ceiling. Above the mantle, a portrait of Perivel Uskevren gazed down at Tal. Perivel's hands were set firmly on the pommel of a gigantic sword. Tal shot a wink to the uncle he'd never known, wishing he felt as confident as Perivel looked.

Beside the front door stood a tall oaken wardrobe, a stand for walking sticks beside it. A pair of stuffed leather chairs, a velvet couch, and two small tables ringed the round Thayvian rug that lay in the center of the room. On one of the tables rested a delicate porcelain tea set.

"All right," said Tal to the room. "Here they come."

He opened the door just as the callers rapped a second time. One of them stumbled forward as the knocker was pulled from her hand, nearly falling into the room with a gust of cold winter air. Tal reached for her arm but checked the habitual gesture before he touched her. It took slightly more effort to restrain his smile at the woman's loss of composure. Beneath her woolen hood, she scowled.

Both visitors were almost a foot shorter than Tal. That wasn't unusual, but at first glance the women looked almost identical. Their deep blue cloaks were clasped with silver brooches in the form of a crescent moon. The woman who had stumbled was slightly more slender than the other, but their cornflower blue eyes were perfect reflections of each other.

"Feena, Maleva, come in," said Tal, a little too curtly to be polite. He covered his ungallant tone with a practiced smile. When the women complied, he shut the door against the bright, chilly day.

The women lowered their hoods, and Tal saw the most striking difference between them: Feena's flame-red hair might, in another thirty years, burn down to the same ash gray as her mother's. Despite the decades between them, Maleva did not look particularly old. The faint lines at the corners of her eyes and lips spoke more of laughter than they did of infirmity.

"Thank you, Tal," said Maleva. Tal noted her use of his shortened name. Most of his acquaintances called him "Talbot" or "Master Uskevren." He did not mind such familiarity, but usually only his friends called him "Tal." Despite the good they had done for him, he still did not trust Maleva or Feena enough to consider them friends.

As Tal took the women's cloaks, Maleva's eyes scanned the room, much as Tal's had earlier. When Tal draped the garments across the back of a chair rather than hanging them in the wardrobe, Maleva glanced again at the big cabinet. Tal stepped quickly in front of it, offering his visitors a seat beside the fireplace.

Beneath their cloaks, the women wore simple dresses of homespun wool. Feena's was embroidered with yellow thread at collar and cuff, but her mother's was plainly stitched. Their heavy woolen vests and rough leather boots were the sort of things Quickly would use as a costume for rustic fools in one of her plays. Had the women arrived at Stormweather Towers in such garments, they would have been turned away at the servants' door. Even the stable boy had finer apparel.

When the women were seated, Tal poured them each a cup of tea. It was rich, black, and expensive stuff reserved for those rare occasions on which Tal's mother visited his tallhouse. While Shamur Uskevren appreciated the fine quality of the tea, Tal expected it was lost on these women who were used to living in a cabin beside the Arch Wood, days away from the walled city of Selgaunt.

"It's dark in here," complained Feena, holding her cup in the palm of her hand. The ladies of Selgaunt would have shuddered to witness her awkwardness.

Maleva put a hand on her daughter's knee and squeezed gently. Feena wrinkled her nose in irritation, giving her a distinctly foxlike appearance. If she smiled once in a while, thought Tal, she would be very nearly pretty. But he had yet to see her smile.

Enough courtesies, thought Tal. He took a deep breath through his nose and smiled down at his visitors.

"I want to thank you both for all you've done," he said. "Despite our disagreements, I sincerely appreciate all you've done to help me since the 'hunting accident.' "

The words sounded anything but genuine, and Tal knew Quickly would berate him had he delivered such an unconvincing speech at the Wide Realms playhouse. He hoped Maleva and Feena had less discriminating ears.

Feena narrowed her eyes and somehow managed to look down at Tal, even though he towered above her. Tal knew she would not be satisfied by mere thanks, but that was all he planned to give them.

Maleva drank her tea without looking up at Tal, but he saw a faint, smile upon her lips. He realized that she knew what was coming.

"As you suggested, I've given my problem a lot of thought over the past month," Tal continued, "and as much as I appreciate your offer of assistance, I've decided to take care of it myself."

Feena put her teacup down hard enough to send it spinning in its saucer. "You can't," she said. Maleva squeezed her knee again, but Feena wouldn't be quieted. "You'll fail, and innocent people will pay for your stubborn pride."

A red veil fell across Tal's eyes, and he felt a sudden urge to slap Feena's face. That would shut her up.

She held his angry gaze unflinchingly. She might be arrogant and infuriating, but she was not easily cowed.

Almost as quickly as the fury came, it slipped away again. Tal had been uncharacteristically irritable all morning, even snapping at Eckert when the servant balked at his plans for this discussion. In a sudden flash of regret, Tal decided he must apologize later. The thought calmed him enough to keep his voice even and reasonable.

"Then give me another alternative," he said. "If the only way I can have this potion of yours is to swear obedience to your temple, then I'll find another way."

"Don't be a fool," said Feena, rising from the couch. "You need us. You need Selûne. The wolf is stronger than you."

Tal knew that was probably true, but he felt another stab of anger when she added, "More cunning, too."

He felt the heat on his face and saw Feena's faint smile of triumph when she saw that she'd stung him. That only made him angrier, and he hated the feeling. The only other people who could make him so furious were his parents, and he could always keep it off his face and out of his voice when facing them. For whatever reason, Feena could break his composure with a word.

Tal took a deep breath before responding, a trick Quickly had taught him when dealing with hecklers at the playhouse. It worked, and he made himself smile, trying not to sound too condescending in return.

"I have friends who will help," he said, "without trying to manipulate me into serving their ends."

"Your friends," said Feena, "know nothing about your curse. We do, and we can show you how to deal with it. You need our help."

"Whether I want it or not?" asked Tal.

Behind Tal, the wardrobe creaked, but Feena was too angry to notice. Maleva, however, could not suppress a smile. She said, "Don't you think your servant would be more comfortable out here, with us?"

Tal cleared his throat. "Actually, it's Chaney. Come on out, Chane."

The wardrobe latch clicked, and a narrow face peeked out. "What a relief! It was stuffy in there."

A short, boyish man slipped out and closed the wardrobe door, but not before Feena caught a glimpse of the hand crossbow he'd left inside.

"What, were you planning to kill us?" She sounded astonished and outraged.

"Of course not!" said Tal. "You're the one who said *I* would need killing if things didn't work out."

"Just a little sleepy juice on darts," explained Chaney, finger-combing his straight blond hair. "Little darts. They barely hurt."

Both women stared back at him, obviously displeased.

"In case you decided to put a whammy on Tal," added Chaney, "like you did to me and Quickly back at the playhouse."

He seemed oblivious to the twin glares from the women. While their gazes turned from him to Tal, Chaney smoothed the crushed velvet of his doublet. The fabric was old and worn, but it was finely cut and had obviously been quite expensive.

"After all we've done for you, you ungrateful—" Feena began.

Maleva put a hand on her daughter's arm. "We aren't here to force you into anything, Talbot," said Maleva. Tal winced at her formality and almost regretted asking Chaney to cover him as he did. "I realize it's hard to trust us, after all you've been through. We should have been more honest with you from the beginning."

"Should I come out now, too, master?" a tremulous voice called from the kitchen.

Tal slapped his forehead in disbelief. He had hoped to keep Eckert as a backup just in case. He sighed and said, "Why not?"

Eckert's tall, skinny figure emerged from the darkness of the kitchen doorway. His blue-and-yellow livery was impeccably arranged, the Uskevren family crest—the horse at anchor—embroidered over his breast.

"Because I thought you might prefer that I remain . . . oh," Eckert said.

He saw the expression on Tal's face and realized his blunder. Eckert wasn't usually so stupid, but he was easily flustered by danger. "I'm terribly sorry, sir."

Feena looked angrier than ever, but Maleva seemed to find the entire fiasco amusing.

"Is there anyone else hidden in the rafters?" she asked.

Tal hesitated only a moment before addressing the fireplace. "Lommy, it's all right to come out, now."

A fine sprinkling of soot heralded the arrival of a tiny green creature the size of a spider monkey. Lommy shook his coarse mane of black hair, sending up a cloud of fine black dust, then galloped across the room to leap up and perch on Tal's shoulder. He fixed his catlike eyes on the two women.

"No hurt Tal, or Lommy get help!" he snarled.

Tal had never heard the little creature sound so fierce. The tasloi was the Wide Realms' clown, evoking laughs with his pidgin Common and a subtle gift for mime comedy.

"Nobody's hurting anybody tonight," said Tal, with a pointed glance toward Feena. She was still angry, but she kept her mouth clamped tightly shut. "What we need is for everyone to calm down. Would you bring us some wine, Eckert?"

"Very good, master." The servant disappeared into the dark dining room, where the light of an uncovered lamp soon appeared.

"Mother, he doesn't know the first thing about riding the moon," complained Feena. "What's he going to do? Lock himself in the closet during the full moon?"

"The cellar, actually," offered Chaney. "Fortunately, he agreed to move the wine out first. Wouldn't want any drunken wolf antics, after all."

"What's 'riding the moon'?" asked Tal. He was genuinely curious, but Feena ignored him.

"See? They think it's funny," said Feena, turning to Maleva. "They haven't the first idea how to deal with the curse. We don't even know whether he's three-skinned."

"What's that?" asked Tal. "What's 'three-skinned'?"

Feena made a superior little smile and raised her chin.

"Some nightwalkers have three forms," explained Maleva. "The man, the wolf, and the beast between them. Feena saw you only as the wolf. If you take the half-form, you might be able to break out of rooms a wolf couldn't escape."

"Ha!" said Chaney, sinking down into one of the stuffed chairs and crossing his legs. "Not a problem. There's a cage in the cellar." He clicked his tongue and pointed a finger at his temple. "Smarter than you thought, eh?"

Tal considered the cleric's words, ignoring his friend's joke. He had witnessed the transformation in his nemesis, Rusk. Before he and the mad cleric of Malar had nearly slain each other, Tal watched Rusk begin to transform into a huge gray wolf. Tal wondered what else he did not know about the wolf inside himself, the big black monster that Feena reported seeing with Rusk.

"I don't care whether I have two or twenty skins," said Tal at last. "I'm not walking in any skin but my own. Like I said, I appreciate your concern, but you couldn't cure me before the first moon. You told me what I'm facing, and that's enough for me to keep it under control."

"You can't control it without help," said Feena. "Selûne can give you that help, through us."

"Rusk said something similar about his Beastlord."

"You would choose Malar over Our Lady in Silver?" Feena said, rising from her seat.

Lommy hissed at her, his rough nails clutching Tal's shoulder.

"Calm down!" said Tal. "It's nothing against your moon goddess. I just don't like the idea of anyone—Malar or Selûne—making my choices for me."

"That's just it," said Maleva, pulling at Feena's arm to make her sit again. "It is your choice, Talbot, the most important one you're likely to make."

"Those who die faithless spend eternity in the Wall of Tears, endlessly tormented for their selfishness," added Feena, returning to the couch. "Those who pledge themselves to Selûne spend the afterlife in grace and beauty. What are you smiling at?"

"That was a pretty speech. You could be a player at the Wide Realms."

Eckert returned from the dining room. On a serving tray rested four silver goblets and a bottle of Usk Fine Old, the precious family vintage favored by Tal's father, Thamalon. The servant set the tray down and began to pour the wine, scowling briefly when Chaney helped himself to the first one. Chaney winked back at the servant and shrugged himself more deeply into his seat, watching the conversation continue.

"It's no act to speak passionately about Our Lady in Silver."

"Rusk seemed equally 'passionate' about the Call of Malar," noted Tal. In fact, he thought the cleric was a reckless fanatic, if not a complete madman.

Feena's eyes flashed with anger. She thrust a scolding finger into Tal's chest. Lommy hissed at her again, but Feena ignored the tiny creature. "Haven't you heard anything we've told—?"

Tal held up his hands and stepped back. "I said I'm not choosing either one," he countered. "Both want nothing but my servitude. If I don't obey Rusk, I must obey you—that's what you keep suggesting, but it isn't true. I don't have to obey anyone."

"This isn't some trade negotiation," spat Feena. "You can't bargain for a better deal from one side or the other. If you try to contain this on your own, then you're dangerous to everyone. Eventually, someone will have to deal with you."

"Time for you to leave," said Tal. His patience was at an end. "Go back to keep watch over that pack in the woods."

"You'll regret turning us away," warned Feena. She and her mother rose from the couch and went to the door. Feena flung open the door and rushed out into the cold, but Maleva paused at the door.

"Come here, my boy," she said.

Tal plucked Lommy from his shoulder and set him on the floor before joining Maleva at the door.

"Come," she said, reaching up and beckoning to him to kneel before her. Feeling foolish, he descended to one knee. She took his face in her hands and looked into his gray eyes. For a long moment, she searched for something in them.

"Feena means well when she warns you of the danger," she said at last. "It is hard for her to understand why you refuse our help. But even she does not realize what you face. It is a thorny path, that of the nightwalker, and thornier for those like Rusk, and like you."

"Mother!" called Feena from the bottom of the stairs.

"What do you mean, like Rusk and me?" said Tal.

She did not answer. Instead, Maleva held Tal's face a little longer, then slapped him lightly on both cheeks. "Keep your good heart, Talbot Uskevren. It will guide you on the thorny path."

She turned and descended the steps to join Feena. Tal watched the two women walk down Alaspar Lane. As they moved farther away, he was surprised to hear their words, since they kept their voices low.

"I don't care how much you like him, mother. He is *not* the Black Wolf."

"Shush," said Maleva. "It is still considered heresy, whether we believe that or not."

Tal strained to hear them, but their voices grew fainter as they walked away. He briefly considered following them but realized there was nowhere to conceal himself on the snowy street.

"Then Talbot Uskevren is *not* the . . . you-know-what."

"Perhaps not, my dear," said Maleva. "But he *could* be."

"You used to say the same . . ."

Tal stepped out onto the landing, but the sound of the women's footsteps crunching in the snow obscured the rest of their conversation. He sighed and went back inside, closing the door against the cold.

They made an odd spectacle around the table: big Tal, small Chaney, and tiny Lommy. Eckert had tied a napkin around the little creature's neck as a bib, careful not to touch the tasloi as he did so. Even so, the fastidious servant could not conceal his disdain for serving the uncouth creature at the dinner table, and he appeared ready to faint when Tal stacked the collected histories of Selgaunt on Lommy's chair to help him reach the table.

What he lacked in warmth for Tal's friend, Eckert made up in culinary skill. Supper was oxtail soup followed by roast beef with carrots and onions, pickled asparagus in a spicy Turmish cream sauce, and a fried wheat cake smothered in jellied pears.

Tal ate twice as much as Chaney and Lommy combined, while Eckert dined alone in the kitchen. Tal had given up on inviting him to sit at the table. The very suggestion made Eckert nervous, for he had been a servant all his life and dared not overstep his station.

Aside from Eckert and the clerics of Selûne, the others who knew of Tal's condition were Chaney, Mistress Quickly, and the two tasloi. Tal hoped to keep it that way, even though it appeared that he would never be cured. After treating him with an almost lethal brew of herbs, Maleva had tried breaking the curse with powerful spells. For reasons she couldn't—or wouldn't—explain, all efforts had failed. Tal supposed he could go to one of the city temples, but he had a sinking feeling that they could do no better.

More puzzling was the fact that Rusk, the werewolf who had infected him, traveled far from his lair to bring Tal into his pack. Why was he so interested in Tal? He suspected that Maleva knew more than she was telling him.

After dinner, Lommy scampered back to the playhouse with a napkin full of meat for his brother, Otter. Unlike Lommy, Otter was shy of people. He rarely emerged from the rafters of the Wide Realms, where he controlled the trapdoors and other mechanical devices above and below the stage.

As Eckert cleared the table, Tal and Chaney descended into the cellar. The cellar entrance and the tiny window had both been barred and boarded, as had the door at the top of the stairs. Once the room had held an impressive collection of wine as well as some tools and packing crates. At Tal's command, Eckert had moved everything to the upper floor, leaving the cellar bare except for a single wooden chair and a huge steel cage. Fresh straw was strewn on the flagstones beneath. Reassembling the massive cage had taken the better part of a dark night and a flimsy story about Quickly wanting the cage out of the way backstage at the Wide Realms.

Tal pulled off his boots and stood up to unlace his shirt.

"That Feena is really something, eh?" Chaney nudged his friend with an elbow. He held an oil lamp in one hand, a big key ring in the other. "Do you miss her yet?"

"What are you talking about?" Tal draped the shirt across the back of the chair and unbuckled his belt.

"I've seen the way she looks at you, too." Chaney smiled, but only on one side. "All that fighting, it's just repressed desire. Believe me, I know about women. She's not here just because you turn into a cute puppy now and again."

"You're drunk," said Tal, knowing he was not. Neither of them had much to drink this night, though Tal had gorged himself intentionally. The last thing he wanted was for the wolf to spend the night hungry. "She's a religious fanatic."

"She was just disappointed she's not the one watching you undress."

"Don't be stupid." Tal laid his breeches on the chair and stepped out of his underclothes.

"It's a good thing she hasn't seen you naked recently," said Chaney. "Have you noticed how much hairier you've gotten?"

He had noticed. He'd had plentiful body hair before, but it had thickened everywhere, especially on his arms. The only place he was glad for more hair was over the ugly wound Rusk had given him. Thick, ropy scars crossed his belly like white roads in a black forest.

"Maybe I should have Eckert help me shave."

"Then he *would* quit," said Chaney. "Say, that's not a bad idea!"

"Take it easy on him," said Tal. "The only reason he keeps quiet about the wolf is that he's afraid my father would have me locked up in Stormweather, and he'd lose his job."

"I suppose you're right."

"Besides, I kind of like him."

"I thought he irritated you, too."

"Sure, but he's funny, and he's a great cook." Tal walked into the cage and closed the door behind him. It snapped shut with a resounding clang.

"That's true," said Chaney. With a moment's effort, he made a long, satisfied belch.

"I can't take you anywhere," said Tal, shaking his head in mock disapproval. "Lock the door."

"You *don't* take me anywhere, lately," said Chaney. He turned the big key until the lock clicked. "After the moon, we should celebrate the success of your cunning plan. The girls at the Black Stag have been asking after you since that hunting trip."

"Yeah? Which ones?"

"All of them," said Chaney. "You're more competition when you're gone than when you're there. Everyone loves a mystery. You want something to sit on in there?"

"No, just the straw's fine. You should probably go upstairs, now. The moon's coming."

"How can you tell? It's like a tomb in here."

"I can feel it." Tal patted his belly.

"It's those cakes," said Chaney. He belched again. "I'll see if there are any left."

"Don't forget to put the mattress against the door."

"Don't worry. Howl all you want. The neighbors won't hear a thing."

"Thanks."

Chaney spun the key ring around one finger and walked up the steps. He paused at the door. "You sure you don't want me to wait down here? At least let me leave the light."

"No. I'd rather be alone," said Tal. "But thanks."

"No problem, my friend."

"I mean it, Chane."

Chaney grinned, but his eyes looked sad. Despite his bluster, Tal could tell that his friend was worried. "See you in the morning."

" 'Night."

Tal sat cross-legged on the cage floor. The straw wasn't thick enough to make a comfortable seat over the steel bars. He'd have to ask Eckert to fetch more for tomorrow night. The full moon transformed him for three nights last month, and he expected it to do the same this month. He put the thought aside and concentrated on his breathing.

Under Master Ferrick's tutelage, Tal had learned to focus his mind before a fencing match, beginning with his breathing. Once the rhythm of his lungs was deep and steady, he imagined the concentric rings of the dueling floor. One had to keep one's eyes on his opponent, not the boundaries, but he had to know where the boundaries were without looking. Tonight, Tal's opponent was inside him, so he had to focus inward. That was a trick Master Ferrick had never taught him. Tal wished he had progressed further in his fighting studies. He was not a particularly good student, relying too much on his natural strength and speed and not enough on tactics.

His thoughts would not settle themselves, so Tal tried imagining himself on a warm, dark sea. It was something Maleva had said that gave him the idea. The seas were tied to the moon, and nightwalkers changed as the tides ebbed and flowed. Tal closed his eyes, and soon he imagined he could feel a distant force pulling at his body. He no longer felt the straw beneath him nor the cool air of the cellar. He felt only a vague and formless call, and he knew it was the moon. He had sensed it earlier, a vague attraction pulling at him. Not at his body, but at something inside. He tried to isolate the feeling. Was it pulling at his heart? At his guts?

He couldn't tell. The only sure feeling was a gentle wave-like motion, barely discernable. He could almost hear the sound of crashing surf, though Selgaunt Bay was much too far away for it to be real.

It was like being drunk, but only faintly. As the sensation grew stronger, Tal felt a sudden flush of fear. His concentration broken, he felt the cold steel bars of the cage pressing against his legs and buttocks. His arms were sweating where they pressed against his thighs. A cramping pain wrenched his lower back, and he twisted onto his side with a groan.

There he curled like a child as the pain rushed up into his shoulders and down each leg. He cried out and instantly prayed that neither Chaney nor Eckert would heed him. Now the sound of rushing water filled his head, almost deafening him to his own cries and shouts. Hot rain pelted his brain, and a warm surge filled his whole body, pushing it out in shapes it was never meant to take. Lightning coursed through his nerves, leaving agonizing spasms in its wake.

Despite the darkness, Tal saw a crimson wall rise to surround him, closing in to press against his eyes, then through them to his panicked brain. The red fury penetrated his body, filled him to bursting, and blasted his conscious thoughts to oblivion.

CHAPTER 3

CAGES

Alturiak, 1371 DR

Darrow began his new service with mingled hope and trepidation, yet working for Radu's strange brother was more agreeable than he could have expected. His awe of Stannis was mingled with dread, for he realized his new master was some sort of monster.

Unlike the monsters he had heard described in songs and tales, Stannis was talkative, even friendly, in stark contrast to his taciturn brother. His exaggerated charm soothed the horror Darrow felt in his new master's presence. As long as he avoided looking directly into those molten eyes, Darrow could address Stannis naturally, as if his master were a mere mortal.

After Radu's departure, Stannis showed Darrow the servants' quarters. There was even a butler's private chamber, but Darrow preferred the expanse of the main room and chose the bed that seemed most comfortable. He asked about fetching his clothes from Radu's tallhouse, but Stannis showed him a wardrobe full of old Malveen family livery. The black and purple garments were striking, if rather dusty. Darrow liked the Malveen crest as well: a crimson octopus holding a sword, a scepter, a scroll, and a set of scales.

In addition to forbidding him to leave the house, Stannis warned Darrow not to disturb the windows, which were boarded shut both from the inside and on the exterior. Darrow presumed they were warded similarly to the entrance, but he also realized his master must despise the daylight.

On the upper floors were drawing rooms, a barren library, and twin music galleries overlooking the main promenade, which Stannis called the River Hall. The creaking floors and spectral array of covered furnishings made Darrow glad to return to the ground floor, where he spent the rest of his first day uncovering furniture. He was not used to domestic chores, but the work kept him occupied until dusk, when he returned to the River Hall.

Beside the stream he found a wet basket of squirming eels and twitching fish on a bed of seaweed. Darrow noted the inhuman footprints that left a trail between the water and the basket. The delivery had come courtesy of one of Stannis's repellent minions. Unlike their master, the creatures had no fascinating hold over Darrow. They frightened and repelled him.

Stannis appeared soon after Darrow found the food, rising from the fabulous pool as he had the night before.

"Welcome home, my master," said Darrow. "Shall I prepare your dinner now?"

"Don't be foolish," said Stannis, not unkindly. "You realize I do not eat as you do."

"Of course, master," said Darrow. Shame warmed his face.

"You understand what I have become?"

"I . . . I don't know, master."

"Surely you do, child. Say it. Say the word."

Darrow hesitated, debating whether this was a test of his manners or of his honesty. He could feel his master's impatience grow as he wrestled with indecision. At last he sputtered out, "Vampire, my lord."

"Good. Now come." He took a jeweled goblet from the counting table. "Bring the food, and I will introduce you to your new charges."

He led Darrow to a gallery off the River Hall. Its carved door swung noisily open at their approach. Darrow glimpsed the dark, naked figure that held it open for them. It glistened even in the shadows, and it stank of rotting fish.

"Pay them no mind," said Stannis, gliding through the doorway. "Disgusting things. I don't know why I keep making them."

Inside the gallery, crushed velvet couches encircled four purple-veined marble pillars on a mosaic floor. Throughout the room, statues of jet and alabaster lionized long-dead sorcerers and sea captains, while long glass cabinets displayed smaller carvings, painted masks, bizarre fetishes, and a dozen ineffable relics of distant exploration. Dust dimmed every surface.

On every wall hung paintings of Malveen ancestors, most of them long faced and fair skinned, with hair that grew thin but not gray on the older men. The women shared a legacy of intelligent eyes and thin, taut lips.

"Here," said Malveen, floating gracefully toward one of the largest portraits. A thin line of seawater still trailed behind him.

The painting was a life-sized depiction of a dour old merchant with long mustaches and watery blue eyes. Darrow thought it looked like an older, weaker Radu. "My great uncle Vilsek," said Stannis. He held one finger up before his veil. "Shh! He keeps a secret for us."

Stannis lifted a part of the painting's dark metal frame. With a faint groan, the painting and the wall behind it moved outward to reveal a secret passage.

"Here," said Malveen. He spoke a few arcane words and sprinkled glittering red dust into the goblet he had brought.

Bright flames leaped from the cup and remained there, dancing. Stannis gave the chalice to Darrow, who was not surprised to feel that it remained cool.

Beyond the secret door was a wide, spiraling stairway. As they began the descent, Darrow sensed dark shapes looming above him. He looked up, fearful of what he might see.

Mounted to the stone walls were the preserved heads of great beasts. He saw the hooked face of an owlbear, the sleek head of a displacer beast, the hideous twin visages of a two-headed troll, and even more dangerous monsters. Griffin, manticore, dire wolf, wyvern, krenshar, and some beaked and tentacled horror of which Darrow had never heard all watched silently as they made their descent. The hides of some of them had turned yellow and waxy. Darrow wondered how long it had taken the Malveens to accumulate such a collection.

They continued to descend, spiraling down more than thirty feet below the ground floor. Darrow wondered how long before they reached sea level. The River Hall's stream must be linked to Selgaunt Bay, he thought.

At last they emerged into a wide arena. Four tiers of seats surrounded a sunken pit, thirty feet in diameter. Stone braziers cupped green perpetual flames at intervals along the encircling rail, from which irregular spikes jutted down. Varicolored sand covered the pit floor except in the very middle, where a black hole gaped eight feet wide. Around its mouth were blades stained with ragged bits of rotting matter.

"The baiting pit," explained Stannis. "My great uncle's passion has been neglected for over two decades. I like to think he would be pleased with our little revival."

Darrow smelled the faint odor of salt water. "Where does it lead?" he asked, looking down at the bladed pit. "The sewers?"

"Oh, no," said Stannis, amused. "Someplace worse. Someplace far worse. Now come."

Along the perimeter of the viewing stands, Darrow saw two more exits. One of them was a tarnished brass gate with a prominent lock. Stannis led the way and opened the portal with one of the dozen keys that hung from his chain veil. Darrow followed his master down another curving stairway, then along a passage that ringed the central pit. At last they came to a barbed portcullis.

"Watch," said Stannis, indicating a bar projecting from the wall. He inserted another key from his veil and twisted it twice widdershins. Then he pushed the bar up and quickly pulled it down again. The clangor of chains came from beyond the wall, and the portcullis rose steadily.

"How does it open?" asked Stannis. His tone was condescending but oddly gentle.

"Key twice around to the left, bar up, then down."

"What a clever child you are," cooed Stannis. He stroked Darrow's face with cool, moist fingers, then pressed the key into Darrow's hand. "It is important not to forget. There are many more doors to show you, many more secrets. See that you remember them all."

Darrow nodded. Stannis's touch had left cool, wet traces on his cheek.

"Now you must meet your charges."

The hall beyond the portcullis stank faintly of animal musk, but the odor of straw and filth was stronger. A wide passage curved around the perimeter of the baiting pit, and down its center ran a stream of water over which precisely cut stones formed a walkway. Dark stains showed that it was used as a sewage trough.

To each side of the passage were three cells. Each was the size of a horse's stall, with iron bars as thick as a man's forearm in the back and front. Beyond the rear bars was a slotted iron wall with tracks for gears. Darrow guessed they could be raised to allow entrance to the central pit.

All three of the cells were presently occupied.

In one, a massive troll squatted on the straw. A pair of buckets comprised the cell's only décor. Darrow was surprised to see that the monster wore fine leather breeches and a sleeveless shirt big enough to make a sail. The creature's rubbery green skin stretched tight over bulging muscles. As

Darrow and Stannis approached, it rose to its full height of over eight feet, the beads in its braided hair rattling gently.

"*Um brata nglath heem*, Malveen?"

"*Grata nglath heem weeta*," replied Stannis. His voice was smooth and graceful even when uttering the guttural words.

The troll nodded once and sat on the floor.

"His name is Voorla, Slayer of Eight Chiefs," Malveen told Darrow. "Quite a charming fellow, if you speak the language. You'll have no trouble with him, for he fancies himself a troll of honor and has given me his word of conduct. All the same, mind the bars when you leave his supper."

Two cells past Voorla, a pair of elves stood against the far wall, between a pair of cots. They looked like brothers, each with the same cream-colored skin and long black hair. They wore ill-fitting tunics and kilts, obviously not their own clothing. One touched the other's arm as they silently watched their captor glide past.

"Don't they just ooze arrogance? No idea what they call themselves," said Malveen. "If they weren't so exotic, I wouldn't bother saving them for Radu."

Darrow looked at the elves. They stared back at him. In their green eyes he saw patient loathing. It gave him an odd pang in his belly, and swallowing didn't help it. He looked away from them, but he could feel the reproach of the elves' eyes upon his neck. He hastened to follow Stannis to the next cell.

The woman was so short and muscular that Darrow mistook her for a shaved dwarf at first. She had a dwarf's scowling expression for them, but her face was startlingly pretty.

"Darrow, this our most cherished guest. Maelin, I trust you will find Darrow more agreeable than your former keepers."

Maelin's curses were as colorful as any Darrow had heard on the wharf.

"Your mastery of the language never ceases to inspire, my child," said Stannis. "And here I deluded myself into thinking you would be grateful."

"Just let me in the pit," she said, "where I can spit your damned brother and be free of this filthy hole."

"All in due time, my dear. I assure you that Radu would like nothing better, but you are still far too valuable to us alive."

"There's no ransom," she said. "How many times do I have to tell you that?"

"Oh, but there is, my dear. Did I forget to tell you? We discovered the one person in all Faerûn who cares whether you live or die."

She looked at him a long moment before speaking. "You're lying."

"Such directness is to be expected of one who fancies herself a swordswoman, I suppose," sighed Stannis. "Yet it is a habit you would do well to renounce, along with your predilection for a dockside vocabulary. One would have expected your father to have taught you better manners."

Maelin spat on the floor beneath Stannis, who pretended not to notice.

"Imagine our surprise when we found him within this very city. When Radu showed him your bracelet, he appeared most eager to secure your release."

"I want nothing to do with him," said Maelin. "He's got no money, anyway."

"Fortunately for you, my child," said Stannis, "he has much more to offer than money."

At night, Darrow listened to Stannis's tales and gossip, interjecting only rarely to ask a question. He wondered one night what had become of Rusk, the Huntmaster.

"Alas, my old friend rebuffs my hospitality, preferring to make his lair in the abandoned south wing. He finds my new form disquieting," said Malveen. "You don't find me repulsive, do you, dear boy?"

"No, my lord. You are the most majestic being I have ever seen," he said sincerely. Part of Darrow's mind knew and loathed Stannis for what he was, but another part was completely in thrall to his master. His servant mind was, by far, the stronger.

"Sadly," said Malveen, "few would agree with you. Most would prefer my previous appearance. I was more handsome than any of my brothers, you know. They were jealous of me, even when we were boys."

"How were you . . ." Darrow struggled to find the words. ". . . how did you . . ."

"Transcend my former self?"

"I meant no disrespect, my lord."

"Of course you didn't, dear boy. Your interest is flattering. You have heard of my mother's talent for magic, which I inherited?"

"Of course, my lord."

"And of her traffic with, shall we say, unsanctioned merchant vessels?"

"Pirates, master?"

"Just so. One of her allies in this venture was native to the sea. When the other Houses combined to ruin her, mother summoned him from the sunless depths. By dusk, when he could venture above the surface, our vessel had burned to the waterline, and the victors were finishing us off with crossbows. Our ally found me quite helpless in the water, but still alive. Knowing I had no means to survive in the open sea, he embraced me as I drowned, adding his powerful blood to my own."

"How strange!" said Darrow with enthusiasm—but not too much enthusiasm. He had learned that Stannis enjoyed such formal interjections and had practiced them. "But how did you return to Selgaunt?"

"You understand the nature of my condition, yes? You wonder why I did not remain in my sire's thrall?"

"My lord, I do."

"He grew curious about the contents of my mother's estate," said Malveen. "In short, he wished to add her plunder to his own. I could only obey, you understand. One cannot act against the desires of one's master. Fortunately, we arrived on the same evening Radu had chosen to visit the house alone. My brother was not pleased to see my new condition, so he severed me from my master's domination."

"He killed the vampire?"

"He did!" Malveen applauded his own story with a child-like clap of his flabby hands. "And in so doing freed me from my servitude. Now I am the master of Selgaunt Bay and House Malveen."

"But, my lord, this happened twenty years ago. How could your brother have slain a vampire? He must have been still a boy."

"Oh, my child," said Malveen. His voice lost its mirth as he confided, "Radu was never a boy."

Within a tenday, caring for the prisoners became routine. There was little to the task, since the captives threw their own slops into the hall, where the sewage trough washed most away. Darrow swept the rest into the stream, whose source was a wide, overflowing basin at the end of the passage that filled itself as mysteriously as did the waterfall in the River Hall. The water was fresh and clean before spilling into the trough. He wondered whether the water was conjured from another place or merely redirected and filtered from the bay.

The important chore was to feed the prisoners. They were used to raw fish or shellfish with seaweed. The elves disdained the meat, while Voorla devoured the fish and eels with relish. Maelin looked in her supper bucket with disgust.

"You could at least cook it," she said one day. "You know how to cook, don't you?"

"Yes," said Darrow.

"Then bring me a cooked meal."

"Why should I?"

She looked him up and down. "I could make it worth the effort."

Darrow considered her implied offer. Her face was not pretty in the usual sense, but there was a fierce energy in her eyes, and he liked the fine lines at the corners of her lips. Her body was firm and her hips curvaceous. She was strong, though, and probably a better fighter than he was. He could make her put on manacles before he entered the cell, he thought . . .

Before the fantasy could take root, Darrow thought of the master's displeasure should he find him in her cell.

"Forget it," he said.

"Please," she said. "It's little work to fry a fish."

There was a kitchen upstairs, which Darrow used for his own meals.

"I'll think about it," he said.

Four days later, Darrow returned with skewers filled with grilled prawns, bass, onions, and thick carrot slices. He was careful to remove the skewers before leaving the shallow bucket by Maelin's cell door.

"Great Chauntea!" Maelin exclaimed at the first smell of the cooked meal. "I can't believe it! Where'd you get the onions and carrots?"

"Lord Malveen sent me to the market yesterday," said Darrow.

The master had wanted the gallery cleaned, and Darrow needed a mop and a feather duster to do it properly. Since he needed supplies, he also asked permission to fill the larder for himself. He was still surprised at Stannis's generous allowance, and he was grateful for the display of trust.

As Maelin savored her meal, Darrow fed the others. The elves gazed at him suspiciously, and Voorla sniffed at his bucket. After a careful taste, the troll scooped handfuls of fish into his fanged mouth.

"*Meer ngla todu fosha,*" said the troll.

"You're welcome," said Darrow. He hadn't a clue what the troll had said.

After he'd swept the walkway and collected the dinner buckets, Darrow saw Maelin sitting on her cot. She looked at him with a calm expression.

"Are you coming in?" she asked.

For the past three nights, he had thought of nothing else but the touch of her hands, her mouth, her legs. He had never lain with a woman, and he wanted her; there was no question about that. But if it were a trick, or if Stannis should find out . . . he dared not take the chance.

"Maybe tomorrow."

He said the same thing the next day, and the next. Each time, his fear overcame his desire.

Nearly a month into Darrow's new servitude, Stannis announced a special occasion to be held in the secret arena. Darrow's stomach filled with cold dread, for he suspected the day spelled disaster for one of the prisoners. He busied himself with the day's chores to keep his mind from the evening's events.

When the appointed hour arrived, Radu appeared beside Stannis's pool. When the bloated, eel-like vampire rose from the water, Darrow was ready to drape his master's favorite mantle about his smooth shoulders.

"Be a darling and open the door for Rusk," Stannis said.

Darrow paused, momentarily surprised before he realized that Stannis must have sent the Huntmaster's invitation magically. He wondered why Rusk did not simply enter the hall, then realized that the cleric was wary of the wards. Stannis might have altered them to permit his servant to come and go, but obviously he did not fully trust his childhood friend.

He wondered why Rusk had not returned to his forest lair as he walked to the doorway. Sometimes he and Stannis would sit for an hour beside the grand stream. Stannis dismissed his servant after Darrow had served them their wine, so he did not know what passed between the two. They were both supernatural beings, he realized, yet somehow he still did not think of his master the same way he did of Rusk: as a beast.

Darrow thrust such thoughts away as he opened the door to the cluttered courtyard. The silver-haired cleric stood waiting for him just outside the door.

"Lord Malveen requests—" began Darrow

"I know," said the Huntmaster. "Lead on."

Darrow obeyed, and Rusk followed him exactly, careful to step only where he had seen Darrow safely pass.

They walked through the River Hall and into the portrait gallery, where Darrow opened the secret way. Rusk pushed past him and descended the spiral stairway. Darrow followed, noting that crimson lights now flickered in small braziers under the mounted heads of the trophy beasts.

Without waiting for an invitation, Rusk sat down in a chair beside Stannis's vast fainting couch. Darrow took his place at the vampire's side. Immediately he refilled his master's goblet with the earthy red wine Stannis favored. He looked to the eyes above the golden veil, but Stannis and Rusk both looked down into the baiting pit.

Radu Malveen stood on one side of the fanged pit inside the sunken ring. He held his slender long sword in its plain leather sheath in both hands. On the other side of the pit, a dozen weapons were thrust point-first into the sand. They ranged from a pair of Mulhorandi short swords to a giant's glaive, with all variety of blades and polearms between them.

In the stands above, Rusk sat brooding in a high-backed chair. Beside him, Stannis reclined on a vast fainting couch. Darrow stood nearby, attending his master's whim.

When Stannis reached out, Darrow ensured that his fingers closed on a crystal goblet of the finest vintage. Sometimes Darrow dreaded the seemingly inevitable request for a less savory beverage, but thus far he had been spared the responsibility of providing his master's baser requirements. Such tasks remained the duty of the master's other servants.

There were at least two of these minions, and Darrow suspected there was a third, perhaps even more. There was no way to tell them apart. Neither human nor wholly like the creature who had spawned them, the minions were naked, manlike figures with deep purple skin and grotesquely deformed limbs. They slipped out of the pools in the River Hall at night in answer to their master's unspoken summons.

Whatever he whispered to them, Darrow was never allowed to hear. Sometimes they returned with food for the captives. On occasion, as he passed through the hall on an errand, Darrow glimpsed baskets of wriggling eels or sea worms, only to note their absence on his return. Worst of all were the sounds of brief struggles that sometimes reached his quarters late in the morning, after his master had sent him away. He knew he was not welcome to attend such events, and he was grateful for the excuse.

Stannis drained the last of his wine and dropped the glass. Darrow barely caught it in time to save it from the floor.

"On to the entertainment!" he cried, slapping his rubbery hands together. "Would you like to inspect your gifts before we commence?"

Radu shrugged and closed his eyes. He drew his sword and cast away the scabbard.

With a twisting gesture, Stannis activated the switch to make the steel plates rise from the walls of the pit. Behind them stood the captives. Voorla paced impatiently, while the elves stood serenely in the middle of their cage. Maelin gripped the bars and stared straight across at Radu.

"Our uncle enjoyed watching bloodsport," Stannis volunteered. "He would release beasts from either side of the arena, and his friends would wager on the outcome. As you can see, my brother prefers an armed opponent. Which should we release? Hmm?"

"The troll," said Rusk.

"A formidable opponent to face without the benefit of fire," observed Darrow. "Is that your thinking?"

Rusk shrugged.

"Which would you select, dear boy?" asked Stannis.

Darrow hesitated before answering, "The elves, my lord."

"Because there are two of them?"

"No, my lord," said Darrow. "Because they were insolent."

"Excellent," said Stannis, practically purring his approval. "So shall it be."

Rusk snorted. Darrow glanced at him without turning his head. The Huntmaster sneered and shook his head.

Stannis gestured toward the elves, and the gate rose.

The elves turned to each other briefly. One touched the other's face for the barest second, and they ran toward the weapons.

Across the pit, Radu stood unmoving, his eyes still closed.

One elf took a short sword in hand. The other grabbed a rapier. Without hesitation, they ran lightly around the pit to flank their opponent. The one with the rapier held his weapon at full extension and charged. The point of his blade seemed to strike Radu before the man moved. He fell backward, rolling smoothly beneath and away from the rapier's thrust.

The elf with the short sword slashed at Radu, but the man came around too fast. One foot caught the elf in the ribs and knocked the breath from his lungs. Radu stood, opened his eyes, and parried the rapier's redoubled attack in one smooth motion, his blade cutting a perfect cone out of the air. With his opponent's blade out of line, Radu thrust the point of his sword through the elf's shoulder. He withdrew it just as quickly and stepped away.

The wounded elf made no sound, but his wide eyes signaled his surprise. He edged between Radu and the wall as his companion got on his feet and stalked the swordsman's other side, trying to flank him again.

Radu feinted toward short sword, then made a blinding series of cuts toward the rapier, beating the lighter blade out of line. He cut twice past the elf's failed defense, drawing blood at wrist and cheek. Then he turned his back mockingly and walked away, his sword held low by his side.

The elf with the short sword took the bait, slashing at Radu's calf. From the seats above, Darrow heard no warning of the attack, not even the shush of sand. But Radu heard something, for he leaped above the cut and stabbed down, pinning the elf's hand to the sandy floor. The elf choked back a cry.

The second elf struck at Radu's back, but the swordsman had already twisted aside. The thin blade pierced his short jacket, and Radu pinned the sword to his side with his left arm. Standing still, he slashed at the elf's face, cutting away one emerald eye and making a horror of the once-perfect face.

Now the elf screamed.

Radu released the elf with the rapier and darted away just in time to avoid a clumsy but powerful stab from the short sword. That elf screamed a string of sibilant words and charged recklessly toward Radu's exposed back. Radu whirled aside again, flicking his blade like a switch as his furious opponent rushed past. A hank of black hair floated away from the elf's head, and a bloody ear hit the sand.

That elf added his voice to the screaming.

Radu fell toward the elf with the rapier, his long sword catching the slenderer weapon in a crude parry. With his other hand, he grasped the elf's wrist and guided the slender blade into his brother's heart.

Radu released the surviving elf's wrist and walked away.

With his one eye, the elf stared into the face of his slain companion. He sagged to his knees, and his companion fell with him. The dying elf's last breath blew trails in the blood on the other's ruined face. The survivor embraced his dead companion.

Across the fanged pit, Radu produced a silk handkerchief and wiped the blood from his sword.

"Splendid!" cried Stannis, clapping.

Darrow added his applause, careful not to clap more loudly than did his master.

In the ring, Radu fetched his scabbard and sheathed his sword. Again he turned his back on the surviving elf, walking toward the exit. The elf rose slowly, drawing the rapier out of his companion's corpse. Radu showed no sign of noticing.

Darrow stepped forward involuntarily, opening his mouth to shout a warning. Stannis stopped him with a gesture.

Radu walked heedlessly past the armed elf, never glancing in his direction. Darrow stared in awe and horror as the elf braced the rapier's point against his breast, set the hilt upon the floor, and impaled himself.

"How delicious!" cried Stannis, opening the gate for his brother with a wave of his hand.

Darrow felt his gorge rise, and his mind whirled to imagine what passions could impel the elf to kill himself rather than seek revenge.

As Radu emerged from the stairway, Stannis turned to Darrow. "How did he know, you wonder?"

Darrow nodded mutely.

"Among my brothers many remarkable talents," said Stannis, "is a keen awareness of when he has won."

Darrow never asked Stannis about cooking for the prisoners, but after another month had passed, he simply assumed there was no objection. His master was far more interested in the state of the house, often praising Darrow for the good work he had done to clean the place.

Twice each tenday, Radu visited Stannis. The brothers made no effort to keep their conversations from Darrow, who brought his former master tea to drink while the Malveen brothers discussed the twin ledgers that detailed their public and their clandestine businesses. Laskar Malveen was head of the family, Darrow knew. From what he heard from Stannis and Radu, it seemed Laskar was only dimly aware that the family fortunes swelled as a result of the second set of books. Radu insisted on maintaining the obfuscation, while Stannis often complained about his isolation.

"Wouldn't it be lovely to have the whole family together again," said the master. "I do so miss my other brothers."

"You will abide by our agreement," snapped Radu. "Stay away from them. And whatever you are doing to Pietro, stop it."

"Whatever do you mean, dear brother?"

"The nightmares," said Radu.

"Merely inspiration for his paintings," said Stannis. "If I cannot enjoy his company, at least let me act as an anonymous patron of his burgeoning talent."

"They are becoming a scandal. You must stop it immediately."

Stannis sighed. "Very well. But you do a great disservice to the art community."

"If we are to recover our rightful position in Selgaunt, Laskar and Pietro must remain unsullied by the work we must do. Should we be caught, only you and I will take the blame."

"Yes, yes, I've heard it all before. It's all so dreadfully tedious. There's so little to do, confined as I am to the bay and the house." He made another exaggerated sigh and glided around the table to look over Radu's shoulder as his brother wrote. "I know, why don't you take your exercise tomorrow? It has been tendays since you last visited Ferrick's."

Radu ignored the suggestion. "I saw him on the docks yesterday," he said.

Darrow stood no more than six feet from him, yet Radu did not even nod in his direction.

"The market is closed at night," said Stannis. "And I can hardly rely on my creatures to fetch everything I require. Unless you would like to go to the market for me, of course."

"Someone will spot him coming in here." Radu laid his pen beside the inkpot and stood away from the desk.

"Darrow is careful not to be seen. Aren't you, my boy?"

"I am, master."

Radu turned to look directly at Darrow. His eyes were as black and as fathomless as a serpent's. Darrow found strange solace in the belief that he would be dead before he ever realized Radu had chosen to strike at him. He returned Radu's gaze without challenge.

Radu must have sensed something in Darrow's meek attitude. "You have refreshed the wards," he said. It was not quite a question.

"Yes, O my brother," said Stannis. At first Darrow thought he was mocking Radu, but the peculiar formality did not seem to irritate the swordsman.

"Alarm spells at the perimeter of the courtyard."

"As you wish, O my brother."

Radu looked from Stannis to Darrow in one last moment of consideration. "I will decide how we deal with Rusk. No arguments."

"But I need him for my plan to . . ." He saw the resolve in Radu's eyes and sighed heavily enough to move the golden links of his veil. "Alas, I shall miss him. Still, it is good enough that Talbot Uskevren is cursed as he is. With any luck, he will lose his temper and kill Thamalon. Or perhaps the older brother. Maybe we'll be lucky and he'll murder the whole wretched clan."

"Perhaps," said Radu, "but you will do nothing to endanger *our* family."

"Yes, O my brother," said Stannis. Darrow could almost hear him smile beneath the golden veil.

CHAPTER 4

PERIVEL'S SWORD

Alturiak, 1371 DR

In the pre-dawn darkness, Tal pushed through the bedroom window as quietly as he could. It was much harder than when he was a slim boy and could find his way into any nook of the great mansion. At nineteen, his broad frame was bigger than the narrow aperture, and he had to squeeze his shoulders as tight as he could bear to force his way through. The wooden panes creaked, and Tal paused to listen. Hearing no sound of approaching guards, he pressed his way through.

When he twisted around to brace his hands on the floor, his arm brushed against the toilet table, setting the porcelain washbowl into a looping dance.

From the sleigh bed across the room came the sounds of a sleeper stirring from troubled dreams. Tal froze again, but no sound came from beyond the bedroom door. When the occupant of the bed turned and lay still once more, Tal wriggled the rest of the way through the window, wincing at the pain the effort caused. His recent wounds were still tender, despite the healing he'd received.

He crouched beside the open window, then leaned out carefully to wave thanks to his accomplice below. The other, smaller man waved back, then vanished into the hedges. The Stormweather house guards were alert and efficient, but Tal knew his friend was clever enough to escape them. Together, they had years of practice evading guards and dogs alike.

Tal carefully closed the window and turned back to the room, his eyes quickly adjusting to the dim light. It was different from how he'd remembered it, though he hadn't been there in years. The room seemed more suited to their mother than to Thazienne. Solid furniture was decorated with fine lace and silk coverings, while the rough walls were painted in delicate but confident pastel patterns suggesting an unsullied seacoast at sunset.

The dolls were missing, he noticed, probably packed away in the attic. Not that Tazi had much use for dolls, even when the Uskevren children were so young. She preferred to run with the boys her age, climbing trees and rooftops, swimming and shouting and scrapping with the best of them. She was faster than either of her brothers, and more full of life.

Yet now she lay near death in her childhood bedroom.

Tal sat quietly on the chair left beside the bed. It still felt warm. Who had sat there so recently? he wondered. Probably it was his mother, Shamur, who always tried so hard to mold Tazi into her own image, the very model of a Sembian lady. Or perhaps it was Thamalon, his father, who tried so clumsily to do the same with Talbot and his brother, Tamlin. If half of what Tal had heard this evening was true, both Uskevren parents were likely exhausted and sleeping in their separate bedchambers. More likely, the chair had been left by one of the servants, perhaps the chief of them, Erevis Cale. In many ways, the tall, gaunt butler looked on the Uskevren children as his own offspring. He wasn't nearly old enough for the part, though his bald pate and gaunt appearance made him seem much older than he was.

Tal watched his sister. She seemed small and fragile under the heavy woolen blanket. Her skin was unusually pale in the half-light, especially in contrast to her black hair, cut short in the latest Cormyrian fashion. Tal wondered how much blood she had lost in the monstrous attack on Stormweather Towers, and he felt a sharp pang of guilt that he had not been present to help defend his home. At about the time Tazi had been hurt, he had been bleeding to death on the stage of the Wide Realms playhouse. Only the intercession of a pair of clerics of Selûne, the goddess of the moon, had saved his life. While he was grateful for his life, he now cursed those same women for preventing the news of Tazi's injury from reaching him sooner.

"Who's there?" Tazi blinked weakly. Tal knew just how she felt, for he had woken from a medicated stupor only a few tendays earlier, disoriented and confused. Again, those clerics had earned his resentment.

He took her hand. It seemed tiny in his big, gentle grip. "It's me," he said quietly.

"My big little brother," she murmured. "C'mere."

Tal leaned close, and she slipped her hand from his to tousle his hair. She grabbed a handful to tug his head playfully, but her grip was weak.

"What's Eckert putting in your hair?" she asked. Tal's man served as his butler, valet, cook, and barber.

"Nothing," he whispered back. "Why?"

"It feels thicker."

"Must be my winter coat," he smiled, then frowned at his own joke, which he couldn't explain to Tazi. Not yet.

"Why are we whispering?" she asked.

"I want to avoid—"

"Father," said Tazi with a knowing smile. "Don't worry. He and mother are probably both asleep. They took turns sitting up with me."

That was a relief. Slipping back out of Stormweather without another lecture might be easier than Tal had expected. "How're you feeling?"

"Not bad, considering the alternative."

"I would have come sooner."

"I figured you were doing the town with Chaney."

"No," he said, "I was . . . tied up for a few days."

"The jail again, was it? Not another brawl, I hope," said Tazi. "Not everyone's willing to leave it to fists, you know. You really should carry a sword."

"That's what Thamalon keeps saying."

"It's hard to believe, but sometimes Father knows what he's talking about."

"You're right," said Tal. "That *is* hard to believe."

They both chuckled, then they both winced at the pain. When they'd recovered, Thazienne said, "I heard you two had a 'discussion' about fraternizing with the help."

"Larajin . . ." said Tal, realizing that he hadn't returned to explain his odd behavior to the young housemaid.

Larajin had asked for Tal's help on a peculiar task that reminded him of the games they'd played as children. Unfortunately, their jaunt took them down into the steaming sewers of Selgaunt, and Tal began to fear he had misjudged the daylight. When he felt the first pangs of his affliction, Tal fled in a panic rather than risk hurting his friend, for whom he felt an abiding and—recently—confusing love.

Later, he tried to apologize and explain his odd behavior to Larajin when his father interrupted them. Mistaking the situation, as the Old Owl always did when it came to Tal, Thamalon led Tal off to hear a scolding lecture on the responsibilities of the upper class to their servants. At the time, Tal failed to recognize his father's exceptional anger for anything other than his usual self-righteousness. As Tazi reminded him of the cause of his father's lecture, Tal's face grew hot with a new realization.

Thamalon was keeping Larajin as his mistress.

There was no better explanation. Suddenly, all the years of cool civility between Tal's parents made sense, not to mention Thamalon's harsh separation of Tal and Larajin as the children grew into adults.

"Tal?" asked Tazi, snapping him out of his reverie. "It wasn't as bad as all that, was it?"

Tal blinked, then forced a smile. It might have convinced an audience at the playhouse, but he knew Tazi would see through it. "Sorry. I'm just a little tense being here. If I stay too long, someone's bound to spot me and summon Thamalon."

"You know," said Tazi, "he'd probably prefer it if you called him 'Father.'"

"Oh, I know," said Tal, his smile turning wicked.

"Tamlin irritates Father because he just doesn't care," said Tazi, "but you seem to go out of your way to make him angry."

"I'm not trying . . ." began Tal. It was pointless to lie to Tazi. She knew him better than anyone else, except perhaps Chaney. "Well, maybe sometimes. I just hate hearing all the things he thinks I ought to be doing, all the things he thinks I ought to *be*."

"So, what do *you* want to be?"

"That's not the point," said Tal, more loudly than he'd intended.

"You didn't answer the question," Tazi pointed out.

"You really are starting to sound just like him," he said. She poked him in the ribs. "Ow!" he winced, only half-jokingly.

"Sorry," said Tazi. "You don't look so hurt. What happened, exactly?"

"It's hard to explain," said Tal. The wounds from his recent ordeal had healed, but his second transformation had left his ribs and joints aching. Perhaps the wolf had thrown itself against the cage the night before, or maybe changing shape left him tender. Either way, Tal couldn't think of a way to explain it without making Tazi afraid for—or of—him.

"Want to talk about it?"

Tal thought about it for a moment, then decided, "Maybe later."

"You've got Chaney watching your back, I hope." Tazi glanced at the window. "He's out there playing lookout, isn't he?"

"Actually, I told him to slip away as soon as I got in. I don't want him to get into the habit of loitering beneath your bedchamber. He's still sweet on you."

"I know," said Tazi with a sigh, "but I'd hoped you'd put that notion out of his head. He's a disgusting braggart about women, and so fickle!"

"He's not a bad fellow," said Tal, "and I thought you'd fancy him, since Mother so obviously disapproves of him."

"Maybe I fancy someone else," she replied. She glanced away mysteriously.

"Aha! So that's how it is. Want to talk about it?'

"Maybe later," she said. Now they were even.

"Fair enough," said Tal, patting her hand gently. "I'd better get out of here before someone tells Thamalon I'm here."

"Visit me again soon."

"I'll try."

"Promise."

"I promise I'll try," he said, kissing her on the forehead.

He walked to the door. Before he could touch the handle, however, it opened so quickly that he had no time to hide. A dark figure whipped into the room to stand between Tal and the bed. Tal tensed for an attack as the intruder crouched with hands curled at his sides, ready to strike. The morning light showed the clean silhouette of his shaved head but left a shadow across his face.

"Cale?" said Tal. He had never seen his father's butler move with such speed, nor appear so dangerous.

"Master Talbot," replied the tall, gangly man, relaxing slightly.

Even as the light revealed his face, a peculiarity in the shadows left a brief domino across his eyes. Tal had always thought of Cale as dangerous but not in the physical sense. Something about the recent attack on Stormweather had changed him. Tal considered what that might be as Cale remained protectively beside Tazi's bed.

"It is good to see you've finally arrived."

"Finally" sounded like a reprimand, and Tal bristled. He realized he was clenching his fists and released them with an effort.

"Tal came as soon as he could," said Tazi.

"Of course," said the butler. "Scaling the wall must have required a considerable delay."

"Erevis!" said Tazi, plucking at his loose sleeve.

Tal raised an eyebrow at her use of Cale's first name. Only recently, the Uskevren siblings referred to the gaunt butler as "Mister Pale" when they were sure he wasn't within hearing.

"I mean only to point out that your brother's undetected entry points to a failing in house security. No doubt Lord Uskevren will want to discuss it personally with Master Talbot."

"That's my cue," said Tal, heading toward the door.

"Your father left strict instructions," said Cale, "that you were not to leave the house without a blade and an escort. It was clear that he wished to speak with you as well."

"I brought my own escort," said Tal. "He's waiting outside."

"Foxmantle?" Cale frowned. "Your father would not approve."

"My father can kiss my—"

"Tal!" said Tazi. She sat up with an effort. "Both of you, be nice. Tal, you take a sword from the armory before you go. Cale, you wait until Father wakes before telling him Tal was here."

Both men stared at the young woman.

"Understood?"

"Yes, Tazi," they said in unison.

Tal arched an eyebrow at the servant's use of his sister's familiar name. If Cale noticed, he pretended otherwise.

Tal and Chaney stood with Cale within the Stormweather armory and dueling circle, where Tal had his earliest fencing lessons. Set in the floor were concentric rings of alternately light and dark hardwood forming the dueling circle. A mute row of practice dummies stood at attention beside a rack of wood and bone practice weapons. Wicker fencing masks hung on a tree nearby, along with worn suits of padded armor. On the opposite wall hung real weapons, mostly long swords and spears.

"You have ten minutes before I wake your father," said Cale. His attitude had softened since the encounter in Tazi's bedroom, but he still seemed different from the servant Tal had come to know over the past seven years.

"Sorry about the window," said Tal. "Since we were children, none of us ever thought of someone else breaking in that way."

"No," said Cale, his voice tinged with bitter recrimination, "but I should have."

Tal let the comment sink in for a moment. Cale's duty was the administration of the house, not its defense, but Tal knew that Cale felt more than an employee's responsibility to Thamalon Uskevren. He never understood the bond between the two men, but only a fool would fail to see it.

Thinking of his father reminded Tal of their last confrontation. Thamalon had warned Tal to stay away from Larajin, intimating quite strongly that there was to be no impropriety between the family and their lesser. Tal never thought of the servants as anything other than family—with the possible exception of Larajin, whose friendship was even more important to him. Thamalon had never cautioned Tal about being familiar with any of the other servants, and Tal finally realized why he had been warned away from Larajin. His father was keeping her as a concubine.

Thinking of Thamalon's hypocrisy, Tal muttered an obscenity.

"I beg your pardon," said Cale. Chaney did his best impression of a second coat of paint. He was always quiet around Cale.

"Not you," said Tal. "Sorry. I was thinking of someone else."

Cale looked straight ahead. "There are more swords in the armory, but the dueling room contains the better blades."

"Thanks, Cale."

The gaunt man merely nodded.

"So," said Tal, trying to lighten the tone, "can you make that twenty minutes before waking the Old Owl?"

Was that the shadow of a smile on Cale's lips? Tal decided he would think so.

"The kitchen staff could use a visit," the butler allowed. "It might take as long as half an hour."

"Thanks, Erevis," said Tal. He held his breath while awaiting a reaction.

Fortunately, Cale did not object to the use of his familiar name, though his eyes narrowed slightly.

"Good day, Master Talbot," he said. Then he was gone.

Chaney waited until the gaunt man was out of sight. "Erevis, is it? Whatever happened to 'Mister Pale'?"

"Shut up, Chane," said Tal. "He might hear you."

Tal walked along the wall of blades with a purpose. While there were dozens from which to choose, only one held any interest to him.

When he was ten, Tal worshiped his uncle Perivel, whom he had never met. Thamalon's older brother had perished the night the Uskevren's rivals tore down the original Stormweather Towers. He died defending the house against other members of the Old Chauncel, who had come to punish Aldimar Uskevren for trafficking with pirates. In a nation of powerful merchants, there was no greater form of treason than to steal from your neighbors.

Among his other youthful glories, Perivel had ridden out after bandits in his day. After one foray, he returned with the head and sword of a notorious ogre chieftain whose forces had virtually halted commerce from the Dalelands. He often carried the monstrous blade for show, but it was too big for even the Great Bear to employ.

Two thick iron bolts held the big sword up on the dueling hall's southern wall. At its broadest, the blade was wider than Tal's hand was long. The dull gray metal never rusted nor did it gleam with an ever bright enchantment. It had a place of honor, away from the other swords. To each side, big kite shields bearing the horse at anchor guarded its flanks.

"You can't be serious," said Chaney when he saw where Tal's eyes came to rest. "Thamalon will *kill* you."

"Nobody else uses it," said Tal.

"Nobody else can lift the damned thing."

Ignoring his friend, Tal took the huge weapon into his hands. It was every bit as heavy as it looked. He liked the feeling. Its grip was too short for a bastard sword, at least for someone with Tal's big hands, yet it was much heavier than any long sword he'd ever held.

"That's not a sword," said Chaney. "It's a plough with airs above its station."

"Hmm," grunted Tal. He hefted the blade in one hand, then extended it toward the heart of an imaginary foe. The point dipped, causing Tal to drop his shoulder to compensate.

"Imperfect!" quipped Chaney in a poor imitation of Master Ferrick, their sword instructor.

Tal grinned. "A little more weight in the pommel would do the trick." He handed the big sword to Chaney, who wilted under its weight.

"Great gods!" said Chaney. "Why not just use a lamppost?"

"I like it," said Tal, taking the blade back.

He turned to one of the practice dummies, its surface marred by thousands of cuts, and whirled backward to deal a mighty slash to the target. To his surprise, the blade cleaved through both the sturdy wicker exterior and the iron post that held it up. The mutilated dummy listed heavily to one side, its spine severed.

"Nine Hells!" cursed Chaney. "Remind me never to piss you off when you've got that thing."

Tal gazed appreciatively at the sword and made a low whistle. "Must be enchanted after all," he said.

"Or maybe the wolf has made you a lot stronger." He seemed to like that thought and considered it further. "You have been looking rather buff lately, and your beard shows up by noon each day. That has to be something to do with the wolf. In fact, maybe it's taking over your body a little bit every night, and eventually you'll—"

"Chaney?" said Tal.

"Yes?"

"Remember never to piss me off when I have this thing."

"Right, right. But think about it! When that lunatic comes back, you can lop off his other arm."

"What makes you think he'll come back?"

"I don't know. Whatever made him come after you in the first place, I suppose."

Tal grunted. "Well, you're right, but I'm not going to wait until he comes looking for me. It's about time we organized another hunting trip."

He adjusted his grip and flipped the blade. It made a low *whoosh* as the blade whirled in a nearly perfect circle. Tal caught the grip neatly, bending at knee and elbow.

"Be careful with that thing!" protested Chaney. "You might be nigh invulnerable, but I might get cut in half."

"Don't worry," said Tal. He wrapped Perivel's sword in an old padded practice jacket and tied the sleeves to form a crude handle. "I'd never cut you by accident."

"That's reassuring," said Chaney.

Tal clapped Chaney affectionately on the shoulder. He had never so much as slapped his smaller friend in jest. Since they met as boys, Tal had designated himself Chaney's chief protector, defending him whenever the smaller man's sharp tongue got them both into trouble.

"Let's get out of here," said Tal. "I'm ready for a nap." He strode out of the dueling hall.

"You've been up only an hour or so . . ." said Chaney, following him. "Oh, I guess you didn't sleep well, huh?"

Tal nodded. "It's weird. It's like I'm dreaming, but I wake up feeling like I've been running all night."

"Maybe you have."

"In that little cage? There's no room."

"I mean, maybe you've been pacing all night, trying to get out."

"Not me, remember," insisted Tal. "The wolf."

"Right, the wolf." Chaney's tone revealed that he wasn't as convinced as Tal was about the division between man and beast.

They turned onto the grand hall and saw the house guards posted at the main entrance. Tal gave Chaney a look that meant no more wolf talk. The guards gave Chaney an altogether different look, but they stood aside as Tal and Chaney donned their cloaks and stepped out into the cold winter air. They remained silent until they emerged from the courtyard of Stormweather Towers and stepped onto Sarn Street, heading west.

"You serious about going after Rusk?" asked Chaney, glancing back to make sure they were out of earshot from the Uskevren guards.

"Of course," said Tal. "Why wouldn't I be?"

"I was just thinking of the last hunting trip," said Chaney glumly.

He was one of only a few of the young nobles who had escaped in time when Rusk and his pack attacked their camp. Tal had not been so fortunate, but at least he survived. Nearly a dozen other minor nobles and servants had never emerged from the Arch Wood after that night.

"This time I know what I'm facing," said Tal. "Besides, I almost beat him last time."

"You would have bled to death if Maleva hadn't woken when she did. A few seconds longer, and no healing spell in the world would have saved you."

"You could be more encouraging, you know," complained Tal.

"I could, if I wanted you dead. Don't forget that Rusk isn't the only werewolf out there. He had a whole pack with him."

"True," said Tal reluctantly, "but he seemed to want me to join his pack, not just to kill me. I want to know more about that."

"Maybe he changed his mind after you cut off his arm," said Chaney. "I know I would."

Tal frowned and nodded. "All right, so hunting for him

in the woods might not be the best idea. I still want to know what he wanted with me. Maleva won't tell me anything."

"You really think she knows more than she's telling?"

"I'd bet on it," said Tal.

"Then why don't you take her up on her offer?"

Tal squinted down at him. "Join her temple and become some sort of candle-lighting acolyte?"

"Just for a little while," said Chaney. "Just until they give you the stuff that lets you control when you change."

"I don't think it's that easy," said Tal. "Besides, it's one thing to refuse to join a following. It's a different business to join one under false pretenses. I've already got one curse to deal with."

"So what are you going to do about it?"

"Maybe . . ." Tal stopped and looked back toward his family's home. The tallest spires were just barely visible over the other manors they had passed since leaving Stormweather. For a moment he thought about going back, but he knew Thamalon would be looking for him. "Maybe I should learn a little more about Malar and Selûne before I do anything else."

"Your father's library?" guessed Chaney.

Tal nodded. "Of course, getting in there without a lecture is the trick. Want to help me slip in again in a few days? He'll be out of town."

"Can I be the one to climb through your sister's window this time?" Chaney darted away, but Tal just sighed.

He made it a point never to beat Chaney, no matter how much his friend deserved it.

CHAPTER 5

THE WINE CELLAR

Tarsakh, 1371 DR

As Darrow's leash grew longer, he spent more and more time outside of House Malveen. Aside from shopping at the market and listening for gossip at alehouses, Darrow sometimes attended plays to memorize and repeat to his inhuman master. At first Stannis had thought to send him to the opera, which the master preferred. While Darrow was an apt enough conversationalist, especially compared to his master's other creatures, describing music was beyond his meager talents. The stories and even some speeches from the plays were much easier to learn. More importantly, the plays occurred during the day, making it much less likely that Radu would arrive to find Darrow roaming from House Malveen.

Even Stannis did not like the thought of Radu's displeasure.

As an added benefit to his visits to the Wide Realms play-house, Darrow was able to observe Talbot Uskevren. The young man was a far more imposing figure than Darrow had expected. All of the players seemed larger than life on the stage, but Talbot was deceptively tall. Seen alone, from a distance, he looked like any other muscular youth. When he stood beside another man, however, his true size became obvious.

Only one or two of the other players came close to his size, and one of them looked more like an ogre than a man. The other was the notorious head of the troupe, the playwright and chief owner of the playhouse. She was a vulgar, pipe-smoking woman whose name, Quickly, was the punch line for half the jokes among the working class. Darrow was not surprised to hear in his eavesdropping that Talbot's parents did not approve of his involvement with the players.

Most surprising, Darrow discovered that Talbot Uskevren was an appealing fellow, at least on stage. Even when he played the unscrupulous moneylender in *Favors and Fivestars*, he pleased the audience with his character's unintentional mockery of his own profession.

Darrow lingered after each performance, watching the players mingle with the audience. Talbot seemed popular among the groundlings, though Darrow noticed that he artfully avoided the overtures of his fellow nobles when they inquired about the health of his family or invited him to meet their eligible daughters. It wasn't hard for Talbot to escape, for very few nobles attended the plays, and those who did paid extra to sit in the gentleman's gallery, delaying them long enough for Talbot to see them coming. In any event, the young man seemed far more comfortable with the common folk, much more than could be affected by a noble who practiced slumming as a mildly dangerous diversion.

Sometimes Darrow followed Uskevren and his friends after they left the playhouse. Invariably they arrived not at some exclusive salon or festhall but the public alehouses.

Darrow remembered the names and faces of Talbot's most frequent companions, notably Chaney Foxmantle.

Stannis asked about all the gossip Darrow had overheard each night, even that which had nothing to do with Talbot Uskevren. Darrow tried to remember everything said near him in the playhouse itself and in the taverns afterward. He knew his master was much less interested in common clack than he was in any hint of scandal among the Old Chauncel. Unfortunately, relatively few of the upper class would stoop to being seen at the playhouse. Fortunately, most of their servants were frequent visitors.

The vampire had been absent from Selgauntan society for two decades, but he had an uncanny knack for identifying the children of his contemporaries by Darrow's reports of the servant's descriptions. Their scandals delighted Stannis to no end.

"Rilsa Soargyl," he chortled, enjoying the sound of her voice on his tongue—or whatever it was he had beneath that golden veil. "Every bit the slut her mother was. What else did you hear?"

Darrow relayed the gossip as many times as Stannis commanded, pouring him goblet after goblet of deep red wine. When he was especially pleased with Darrow's report, Stannis insisted his servant enjoy a drink for himself. The wine was old, dry, and sour, and Darrow did not much like it. He thought at first he lacked the refined tastes of a noble, but later he decided the Malveen cellars were simply long past their prime. Whatever dire magic had transformed Stannis's dying body had, perhaps, altered or even dulled his once refined palate.

One night Darrow noted that the wire rack that held the bottles was nearly empty. When he informed Lord Malveen, Stannis said, "Fetch us some more from the cellar, beneath the pantry. You will need this." He removed a tarnished key from his golden veil and laid it on the table. "But first tell me again what you heard about Tamlin Uskevren today. Did you say the girl was pregnant or indignant? I was laughing too hard to hear, I'm afraid."

As Darrow finished repeating the most recent rumor about Talbot's older brother, Stannis waved at his veil as his head tipped back in a yawn.

"It is nearly morning, my pet. Let us resume tomorrow."

Darrow stood and bowed. He had been practicing the bow after observing gentlemen meeting on the street. The gesture still felt clumsy, but it seemed to please his master.

Stannis rose gracefully from the broad couch to glide over and into the grand pool. Once submerged, his dark body broke into a black cloud and sank down to the bottom of the pool. There it gradually faded, oozing through unseen vents and passages to the vampire's hidden lair.

Darrow assumed that his master slept in the murky depths of Selgaunt Bay during the daylight, rising to feed off the boaters who lashed their vessels together and huddled against the darkness. He also assumed that the master's spawn were taken from the same source. Should he displease Stannis, Darrow feared, his fate would be the same as the boaters. As he left the River Hall, Darrow touched the coin of Tymora where it lay beneath his livery and whispered a prayer for the goddess to spare him such a fate.

He briefly considered putting off the trip to the wine cellar, for he loathed the thought of entering the pantry. While he had restored the kitchen more or less to working condition soon after his arrival, he had taken one look inside the pantry and shut the door again.

Darrow lit a lamp and approached the door. Rats had gnawed ragged passages at the bottom, letting a faint and earthy stench of decay waft out. Darrow braced himself and opened the door.

He looked in, holding the lamp high. Twenty years ago, no one had taken the trouble to clear out the stores once House Malveen was abandoned. Rats scurried from the light to crouch in the black shadows. From the surrounding shelves, moldering lumps spilled over onto the floor, where rilled fungus grew on twisted furrows of accumulated dirt and gods only knew what else.

Wincing at the sight, Darrow moved the lantern this way and that, daring not step into the room until he had found his destination. The cellar door was all the way in the back. Darrow approached timidly, grimacing at the thought of stepping on a rat or something worse. He fumbled briefly with the lock, then pulled at the door. It moved grudgingly, opening only a foot or so before the scraped filth held it firm. Darrow tried to kick away the blockage, but his nerve broke as the rats scurried over to investigate the new avenue. Darrow retreated before them, pushing through the narrow opening.

His first step slipped away, and Darrow grabbed the door handle to keep from tumbling down the stone stairs. Dark slime had formed on the steps, and there was no railing to hold. For an instant Darrow considered fleeing, but one thought of his master's burning eyes made him press on. He descended with painful caution, half-crouching over the precious light.

The sound of dripping water greeted him at the bottom, where the stairs ended in a long cellar. Beads of moisture crawled slowly down the walls. Those that did not vanish into the thousand ragged cracks in the stone pooled in the corners or in a great sagging depression near the middle of the room.

All along the left wall stood rusted iron racks. Those nearest the stairs were barren. Darrow raised the lamp to see beyond, but all he could see was the shifting shadows of a thousand empty sockets. He walked farther into the cellar, avoiding the pooling water where he could. Beyond the center racks, he glimpsed the shattered remains of wooden crates. He moved closer to examine them.

Something hissed above him. Darrow spun around, holding the lamp up like a warding talisman. An oily black shape oozed across the ceiling to merge once more with the shadows. Before his eyes could follow it, something else rushed across the floor toward him. It was far bigger than a rat.

Frantically, Darrow raised the lamp, but a heavy blow struck it from his hands. It crashed against the floor, oil spreading in a dark crescent beneath the broken glass as the fire fluttered on the wick. In the dying light, Darrow was nearly blind. Clammy hands clutched his arms and a cold tongue pressed against his cheek, searching. The smell of dead fish and seawater—

Darrow threw himself backward, knocking his head hard against the stone wall. He slid to the floor and felt shards of the broken lamp cut into his elbow. The same motion pushed the feeble wick into the escaping lamp oil.

Three horrid faces leered at Darrow, gradually moving closer after the surprising return of the flame. Their skin gleamed like black oil, reflecting colors where the light fled at its touch. Dull black tongues writhed between long yellow teeth in anticipation of the hot spurt of living blood. Their talons raked out to tear at Darrow's tunic.

Darrow could not hear his own scream. It was drowned in the thundering drumming of his pulse as he flailed uselessly against the attacks. He turned to get away on hands and knees, but an irresistible grip held his legs. One of the spawn flipped him onto his back. The third pinned him to the floor by straddling his chest. It reached out with long, half-webbed fingers and ripped away the last remnants of fabric to reach Darrow's naked throat.

A shriek of agony joined Darrow's terrified screams. Suddenly the weight was gone from his chest. Darrow opened his eyes and saw that the nearest spawn had vanished. The others still held his limbs, but their fishy eyes stared at his throat, where the coin of Tymora lay glimmering.

Darrow snatched the disk and held it forth. The spawn squealed and hissed, flinching from the sight of a holy icon.

Instantly, Darrow scrambled across the wet floor toward the steps. Heedless of the slime, he fled up the stairs, pushed through the slender opening at the top, and slammed the cellar door shut. Only after the key had turned twice in the lock did he realize he had never ceased screaming.

He stopped then and staggered out of the filthy pantry, where he slowly crumbled onto the floor. There he lay panting until sleep mercifully took him.

"Sometimes I feel . . ." said Darrow.

From her cot, Maelin looked up at Darrow. His conspiratorial attitude piqued her curiosity.

"What?" she said. "What do you sometimes feel?"

"Sometimes I feel as though I'm as much a prisoner as you are."

Maelin snorted and turned her eyes up to the ceiling.

"It's true," he said.

"Pardon me if I don't weep openly," she said. "Maybe if you took me to a tragedy at the playhouse, I could squeeze out a tear or two."

"Look what they did to me," said Darrow, pulling open the collar of his tunic to reveal the scratches on his neck.

"Then run away," said Maelin. "Buy a pair of balls next time you go to the market. Maybe then you'll have the courage to drop an anonymous note to the Scepters that there's a miniature slave trade going on down here."

Darrow gaped at her. He had hoped for some understanding, maybe even some sympathy. Now he realized that her earlier overtures were what he originally suspected them to be: a trick.

"I thought you'd understand," he said bitterly.

Maelin left the cot and crouched beside Darrow. Only a few inches of air separated them. That and the bars.

"I'd be a lot more understanding if we talked about it somewhere else," she said. "You've got the keys. Everyone else is asleep during the day. What's stopping you from opening this gate and leading me out of here? We could catch a ship before dark and be on our way to Westgate before that levitating slug even knows you're gone."

"There's Radu," said Darrow.

"He's never here! You said so yourself."

"He'd find us," moaned Darrow.

"Dark and empty, you jellyfish!"

Darrow only hung his head in response to Maelin's words. Suddenly, she grabbed his tunic and jerked him into the bars, hard.

"Give me the sodding keys!" Spittle sprayed Darrow's face.

Darrow grabbed her wrists and tried to pull her hands away, but as he feared she was stronger than he.

"Give them to me!" she demanded, slamming his face against the bars again.

"I can't!" shouted Darrow, his eyes welled with shame and anger. "They're over there." He jerked his head back toward the closed portcullis.

"Bloody, bloody bugger-all!" She pushed him away and threw herself down on the cot.

Darrow straightened his tunic and wiped the spit and tears off his face with a sleeve. He hoped Maelin saw only the spit.

"I'm not stupid, you know." He knew as he said the words how pathetic they sounded.

"No," said Maelin. "Just weak."

Darrow cursed himself again when he stepped outside. He'd wasted too much time sulking in the baiting pit gallery after the humiliating encounter with Maelin. The sun's edge had already touched the highest spires of central Selgaunt, casting them in grand silhouette. The warm red light of the western clouds belied the cold evening air.

There was no time to reach the market and return before Stannis awoke. Darrow did not look forward to explaining his encounter in the cellar, and he needed some way to soothe his master's displeasure at his failure to fetch the wine. Then he remembered a fancy shop on Sarn Street, one that he had never before thought to enter. If he pooled his own savings with what remained of his master's allowance, he might afford a bottle or two of wine fit for a noble.

Darrow returned breathless and shivering from the cold. Despite his worries, he had plenty of time to compose himself and await his master's return. Stannis emerged as usual from the pool in the River Hall. He seemed sleepy and indifferent to conversation until Darrow presented him with a goblet.

"What is this?" sniffed Stannis. He lifted his golden veil and brought the cup to his mouth. Darrow had yet to see his master's entire face. He took pains not to peer too closely when Stannis drank.

"The wine seller recommended this one highly," said Darrow. "It is not commonly available."

"How nice," said Stannis. He slurped at the wine. "Hmm. It is very sweet, is it not?"

"It is a dessert wine," said Darrow. "Storm Ruby, it is called."

"You are a thoughtful boy," said Stannis. "You must have a reward."

Stannis gestured toward the bottle and another goblet. Darrow bowed his thanks and poured himself a glass. He made a show of sampling the bouquet, for sometimes Stannis asked him his opinion, reaffirming Darrow's guess that his master's own senses were dulled with age and death.

The wine tasted faintly of cherries, with a slight, indescribable tartness that balanced the sweetness. Darrow momentarily forgot about the morning's ordeal, and a smile crossed his lips.

"Excellent," murmured Stannis, gazing at Darrow's face. Something he saw there made his eyes narrow. "But have we depleted the cellars so soon?"

"No, master," said Darrow. He felt a cold presence in the room, something that had not been there a moment earlier. "I thought you might like to sample some of the more recent vintages."

His eyes flicked unconsciously toward the shadows across the room. He knew that somewhere in that darkness crouched the spawn who had attacked him. Stannis noticed the glance and moved toward him. He reached out to touch a scratch on Darrow's cheek.

"Have my minions been interfering with you?"

Darrow hesitated before answering. He knew the spawn would retaliate if he complained, but he dared not lie. "Yes, my lord."

"Jealous creatures," hissed Stannis.

His great body shot up to hover eight feet above the floor. He turned with imperial grace to gaze upon the darkness that covered his spawn. With a gesture he summoned them forth.

The spawn shuffled out of the shadows, shivering in anticipation of their master's displeasure. It came with the utterance of arcane syllables and a flourish of the master's hand.

"Disobedient wretches!"

The unseen threads of magic plucked at the spawn's limbs. They twitched and moaned as pain filled their limbs and minds.

"Why must I repeat myself?" said Stannis.

The spawn babbled and hugged themselves, writhing under the pangs of invisible wounds. They fell to their knees and begged forgiveness with their inarticulate tongues.

Stannis spat his words at them. "The boy . . . is not . . . to be . . . touched. Not by you!"

Darrow had not heard such anger from Stannis before. He could not bring himself to pity the creatures who had tormented him, but he shrank from the sight of their punishment. He felt their seething hatred even though their eyes avoided him. They looked like beasts, he knew, but they were cunning and mean. They would remember.

"Begone," spat Stannis, "and be grateful for such a gentle reminder. I shan't be so forgiving again."

Chastised, the spawn fled like dead leaves before a winter blast.

"There, now," said Stannis, descending once more. "Distasteful task, that, but they shall not trouble you again."

"I thank you, master," said Darrow, bowing. At last, fate was rewarding him for enduring the day's earlier indignities. Tymora's coin was turning in his favor.

"It appears I've spilled my wine," said Stannis.

He set his goblet beside the bottle and held up his hand. Darrow quickly fetched a towel and gently wiped the wine from his master's wrist. Stannis watched him all the while, his eyes half-lidded with approving affection.

"What is this charming discovery you have made?" he asked, indicating the wine bottle. "You say it is a local vintage?"

"Yes, master," said Darrow.

He lifted the bottle to show off the vintner's stamp. He had not noticed it before, the seal of a horse's head beneath a slender anchor. He realized his mistake just as Stannis recognized the device.

"The horse at anchor . . . The horse at anchor!" he rasped, choking. He dashed the bottle out of Darrow's hand. It flew across the carpet to crash against a nearby pillar.

"You seek to poison me with the milk of my enemy?" Stannis moved closer to loom over Darrow.

"No, master!" Darrow pleaded. He dropped to his hands and knees, averting his gaze from the dread presence. "I didn't know."

Stannis spoke the words Darrow feared, though he could not understand them. Then he felt the agony he saw on the faces of the spawn moments before. Every sinew felt like a copper wire stretched thin and fragile over a raging fire. He thrashed and convulsed, but no effort could save him from the sorcerous pain.

As the spell subsided, Darrow tried to smother his sobs with his fist. He felt his master's dark presence draw close, and he knew Stannis was looking down at him. Humiliated beyond all endurance, he pulled the holy symbol of Tymora from beneath his tunic and held it up toward Stannis.

Darrow heard the sudden intake of breath, a gasp quite unlike the vampire's usual sighs and hisses. He looked up to see that Stannis had recoiled, his bulky form bobbing in the air five or six feet away.

"Stop . . ." said Darrow. Even the brief look at Stannis Malveen's inhuman form melted his resolve. The vampire's eyes surged and tumbled with infernal energy. "Please," sobbed Darrow, dropping the coin to his chest.

"Throw it in the pool," commanded Stannis.

Darrow obeyed at once, snapping the leather cord that held the talisman and dropping the holy symbol into the water. There it sank to the curved bottom and slipped out of sight through one of the long oval drains.

"Master," he said, turning back to Stannis without standing. "I beg you, it was a mistake."

"It was indeed," concurred Stannis, floating down to peer into Darrow's eyes. "It was a very grave mistake."

That night, Darrow learned just how many screams he had in him.

CHAPTER 6

MOONSHADOW HALL

Tarsakh, 1371 DR

Tal endured the self-imposed captivity of another moon before winter began loosening its icy grip on Selgaunt. Frost still bit those who overslept their hearthfires, and some mornings revealed a light sheet of snow on the streets, but by noon the sun and traffic had cleared the cobblestone streets, and the smell of freshly turned earth rose from every garden in the city.

Before trying to slip unnoticed into the library at Stormweather, Tal and Chaney visited the booksellers at the market and in the city's shops. They searched for anything to do with werewolves, Selûne, and the phrase that continued to trouble his thoughts: the Black Wolf. Eventually Tal found a few volumes that dealt with lycanthropes, or nightwalkers as Feena had called them.

When he bought more than one book at a shop, the package came back across the counter with some curious looks from the seller.

"It's research for a play," Tal explained. He made a claw and menaced Chaney. "*Grr!*"

"*Help!*" cried Chaney in a credible falsetto.

The shopkeepers laughed politely, but the querulous looks vanished into smiling nods.

Once he was sure that Thamalon was away from home, Tal visited his father's library. It was one of the most eclectic in Selgaunt. If the Old Owl kept an entire shelf of tomes on elven lore, Tal figured he was bound to have a few volumes on religion. He discovered volumes ranging from *The Speculum of Selûne* to *The Visage of the Beast*, yet none explained the overheard reference that Feena refused to discuss. Worse yet, they were all written in the elliptical manner of sages who fancied themselves poets. Tal briefly considered taking some of it back to the Wide Realms for a dramatic reading the next time the company needed a few laughs.

"It's pretty boring stuff," he told Chaney later. They had found a quiet corner at the Black Stag, a tavern close to the playhouse.

"But useful, right?" Chaney sat with his back to the wall, scanning the room each time newcomers arrived. Whenever Tal teased him for his paranoid habits, Chaney reminded that twice he'd spied a pickpocket creeping up on Tal. "The Black Wolf is another name for Malar."

"Maybe," said Tal. He'd known only a little about Malar before his recent studies, and what he'd learned since was little help.

The god of hunters was worshiped more widely in the country, especially the farthest wilderness. Like sailors who prayed to cruel Umberlee to spare them from her mighty wrath, farmers and herdsman made offerings to the Beastlord so that he might spare them from wild animals and monsters. City dwellers had little use for the ancient god. Among urban churches, the Beastlord was considered a primitive god. Powerful, to be sure, and older than most of the other dark gods, Malar's name was rarely spoken in civilized places. When it was uttered, it was by the lips of huntsmen who wished only for a fine trophy to bring home from their jaunt in the country.

Tal thought back to the night of his own hunting trip, when beasts raged out of the darkness to scatter the young men and women from Selgaunt. He had thought they were owlbears at first, but later he learned it was Rusk and his pack who had slain his fellows and inflicted him with their curse. What monsters they must be, to hunt humans like mere animals, to eat their kill.

They were cannibals.

More than any other aspect of his curse, it was that thought that most horrified Tal. It was a dire thing to kill a man, but the thought of preying on other humans was repellant to Tal. He loved fencing, and yet during the brief period in which he thought he'd killed a man, he considered putting an end to his own life lest he murder again.

The thought gave Tal pause. He could kill, if need be. He was sure of that. Should someone threaten his friends or family—even, gods help him, his annoying brother or overbearing father—he'd feel no qualms about cutting the offender into parts.

At least, that was his theory. Except for maiming Rusk in self-defense, Tal had yet to prove he could kill. He knew it was too much to hope that the silverback werewolf had crawled away to die. He must have made it back to his lair in the Arch Wood by now. Chaney's warning about going after him when Rusk was surrounded by his pack carried weight with Tal, but he hated the idea of just waiting to learn whether Rusk would return to trouble him.

Tal had learned this much through his readings, and they had discussed it before.

"Anyway, they call him a lot of things," said Tal. "Especially different kinds of dangerous animals: big cats, wolves, bears—you name it. Most often it's the Beastlord or the Black-Blooded Pard. The way Feena said it, though, I don't think all this necessarily has to do with Malar."

"But Rusk is a priest of Malar. What else could it mean?" Chaney looked sadly into his empty mug. Tal took the hint and raised a finger to the barkeeper, who nodded back.

"I don't know," admitted Tal. "It has to be something that wasn't in the books I found, probably something to do with Selûne."

"Just because Maleva worships Selûne doesn't mean this Black Wolf heresy comes from her sect," said Chaney. "Selûne and Malar both figure in those werewolf stories, right?"

The conversation paused long enough for the skinny young barmaid to replace Chaney's ale and receive four pennies, a penny tip, and a half-hearted wink in return. As she sauntered away, Chaney peered into his purse before cinching the strings and tucking it back into his green jacket.

"Spend all your allowance already?" Tal took a sip of his own ale, still nursing his first mug.

Chaney looked up at him, an odd quirk on his narrow lips, as if Tal had made a joke but blundered the punch line. "Yeah," he said, plucking at his well-worn jacket. It was a once-fine garment of worsted silk, but it had seen far better days. The piping at cuff and collar was slightly frayed, and the patch on one elbow was slightly too dark. "Shouldn't have bought that new wardrobe."

"You really ought to retire that thing," suggested Tal.

"What, my lucky jacket?" said Chaney. He took a long drink of his ale and clapped the half-empty mug on the table. "So, you were saying something about Selûne. If this Black Wolf business is to do with the moon goddess, then why didn't Maleva tell you more about it?"

"Aha!" said Tal, "That I can answer. If it is a heresy, you wouldn't expect it to be published anywhere, would you? The temple would suppress it."

Chaney nodded thoughtfully. "All right, that makes sense. So where do you find out what it means? Go back to Maleva?"

"No good," said Tal. "If she was willing to tell me, she

would have done it already, but she said something about the high priestess of Selûne in Yhaunn."

"Dhauna Myritar," said Chaney, "the one who gave her the moonfire potion."

"Right. Maybe she'll be willing to tell me things that Maleva held back."

"Maleva and Feena living so close to the Arch Woods," said Chaney, sitting up straight, "it makes me think they've got some special grudge against Rusk and his pack."

Tal nodded. The same thought had occurred to him.

"If that's true, then wouldn't they be experts on werewolves?"

"Say 'nightwalkers,'" said Tal, looking around. "And keep your voice down."

" 'Nightwalker' and 'lycanthrope' sound pretentious," said Chaney. "I don't know why you're so defensive about the word."

"I'm not defensive."

Chaney arched a dubious eyebrow.

Tal held up his palms and shrugged. "All right, maybe a little defensive."

"If Maleva's some *werewolf* expert, maybe she knows something this Dhauna Myritar doesn't. Or maybe Maleva lied about getting the moonfire from Myritar. Or maybe Maleva's the one who put all the conditions on giving it to you."

"Maybe Myritar would sell it to me," said Tal. He did not feel hopeful, but he was curious about this high priestess. "There's only one way to find out," said Tal. "You talked me out of *werewolf* hunting, but how about a short trip to Yhaunn?"

"You haven't been there before, have you?" asked Chaney.

"Once, when I was really young," said Tal, "but I don't remember it well. There are bridges and ladders and things all between the buildings by the docks, right."

"That would be the stiltways," said Chaney. "The whole place is a little seedier than Selgaunt."

"Sounds great to me," said Tal. "Want to come with me? I bet the nightlife is something else."

"I don't know," said Chaney. "It's kind of a bad time for me to run off. You've got plenty of time on your hands until the spring productions start up, but I've got some things—"

"That's all right," said Tal, waving away his friend's excuses. Chaney went on the ill-fated hunting trip under protest, feeling far more at home in the city than out in the wild. It was asking a lot to invite him back out on the road so soon afterward. Tal would have felt better with Chaney to watch his back, but he didn't want to twist his arm. "It's probably best that I go alone anyway."

"Thamalon will have a fit if you go without a guard."

"Only if you tell him that I went," said Tal.

"You don't think he'll send someone to look for you if you're gone that long?"

"You can imitate my handwriting, can't you?"

"I haven't done that in years," said Chaney. "I'd need to practice."

"Fine, I'll leave you some samples. Check in with Eckert every couple of days. If there's an invitation from Stormweather, just write an excuse. If it's Mother, write that I have a previous social engagement. If it's Thamalon, say I'm meeting a merchant from Turmish about importing musical instruments."

"They believe that crap?"

"Works every time," said Tal. "Well, maybe they don't believe it, but they leave me alone if I make the effort to concoct an excuse."

"How are you going to keep Eckert quiet? He can tell the Old Owl that you left town without mentioning the werewolf business."

"I'll deal with Eckert," said Tal, "but there is something else you can do for me."

Two days later, Tal was ready for his journey. Traveling to Yhaunn and back would take no more than a tenday. That left Tal a comfortable margin before the next full moon, when he would need to confine himself to the cage once more. If he needed more time, he could ride hard and make the return trip in only three days.

He wore a heavy woolen jacket over a simple blue tunic and his leather riding breeches and long boots. Over it all he threw a heavy gray cloak with ties rather than an expensive clasp. With Perivel's big long sword in a simple leather scabbard and a plain bundle of clothes and rations slung over his shoulder, he looked more like one of the Hulorn's outriders than a young noble of one of Selgaunt's richest families.

He said his farewells to Eckert and left the tallhouse at dawn. Chaney awaited him outside.

"Ugh," said Chaney by way of greeting.

"I thought I'd have to go looking for you," said Tal. "Sorry to get you up so early."

"You didn't," said Chaney. "Long night. Don't ask."

Tal suppressed a laugh but honored his friend's request. Chaney had probably drunk too much, gambled too much, or dallied too long with one of the tavern wenches he favored—probably all three. A few months before, Tal would have been at his side, indulging in the same wild behavior and providing the muscle to back up Chaney's barbed witticisms.

They walked up Alaspar Lane, turned west on Densar's Alley, and snaked around side streets before heading north on Galorgar's Ride. Passing beneath the fabulous water horses carved on the Klaroun Gate, they stepped onto the High Bridge. The wide span joined Selgaunt with Overwater, on the far bank of the Elzimmer River. To each side of the road were crammed tiny shops and ramshackle alehouses, the first and last effort by the petty merchants to separate travelers from their coins. Even at this early hour, the bridge was noisy with haggling voices and the rumble of cartwheels.

Beyond the High Bridge lay Overwater, a bustling staging ground for caravans and passenger carriages to the capital city of Ordulin. Tal had briefly considered booking such passage, but the convenience was outweighed by two other concerns. It was simple enough to give a false name when hiring a carriage, but there was always a chance that one of the other passengers would recognize an Uskevren. Moreover, the carriages traveled at a leisurely pace, taking five days for a journey that would take a lone rider only two.

Halfway across the High Bridge, Tal smelled grilled sausages and fresh bread as he and Chaney passed a tiny bakery beside the eastern rail. Far below, boatmen poled their barges across the Elzimmer, ferrying goods and passengers to the caravan staging area in Overwater or out into Selgaunt Bay.

"You want something to eat before setting off?" asked Chaney. He eyed the sausages greedily.

"Eckert made breakfast," said Tal, "but you go ahead."

"Ah . . ." Chaney made a show of searching for his purse.

"Don't you have any change left?" The day before, Tal had given his friend a big leather purse containing more than a hundred gold fivestars.

"You said you wanted a really good horse."

"For that much, it had better have wings," warned Tal. Still, he chuckled and put a pair of silver ravens in Chaney's hand. "Get me one of those little loaves with the cheese inside."

"Um, why don't you get the food?" said Chaney, returning the triangular coins and looking over Tal's shoulder.

Tal followed his glance and spied a short, pot-bellied man standing beside a shallow alley between a fishmonger's shop and a cartwright's shack. The man was shorter than Chaney but with fish-white skin and thinning hair that formed a laurel around his head. He ignored Tal and impatiently crooked his finger at Chaney.

Tal turned back to Chaney. "Trouble?"

"No," said Chaney, but he glanced at Perivel's sword over Tal's shoulder. "I just need a word or two with this fellow."

"I hope she was worth it," joked Tal.

"Believe me," said Chaney, "she wasn't."

Tal sighed. He knew it was more likely a gambling debt than an offended brother or husband. "Need some money?" he offered.

"It's not that," said Chaney. "Don't worry. Won't be a minute."

He hurried across the cobbled street and disappeared into the alley with the short man, who put his arm around Chaney's slim shoulders in a patronizing gesture that Tal instantly disliked. He strained to hear what was happening, but the din of the traffic was too great.

He looked at the triangular silver coins in his hand, then slipped them into his jacket pocket and strode over to the cartwright's. He stood as close as he could without revealing himself to the alley's occupants. While he wanted to respect Chaney's privacy, he knew that some of the boaters lingered near the bridge to collect the reward for murdered bodies dropped from the High Bridge. It was already daylight, but Tal did not like the look of the man who had summoned his friend.

He cocked his head to listen and could barely make out some murmured words. Then he heard a painful gasp followed by hoarse coughing and retching.

Tal ran around the corner.

The space between the two little buildings was cluttered with junk. Stinking pots of fish heads and offal lined the wall of the fishmonger's. At the far end was the stone bridge railing, rising three feet above street level.

Chaney was pressed up against the cartwright's shack. Two big men held his arms fast. One of them was bald, with an elaborate web of gold hoops and chains linking his left ear with his left nostril. It was the latest fetish among Selgaunt's elite, but Tal doubted this bruiser had bought it originally. More likely, some foolish young nobleman was walking around with a torn earlobe and nostril. The other big man was a hairy brute whose patchy beard barely concealed the network of scars that had ruined his face.

In the hammy grip of his captors, Chaney looked more thin and fragile than ever. The pot-bellied man dealt the beating. His eyes never left Chaney's as he spoke in a harsh whisper.

". . . too late," he was saying. He grunted as he delivered another punch to Chaney's gut. Around his hands he wore hard leather strips studded with iron. "What made you think—?"

The man's rough voice cracked as he felt himself suddenly lifted from the slick cobblestones and hurled six feet away, where he smashed into the fishmonger's waste pots.

The men holding Chaney released him and took a step toward Tal, hesitating when they saw the big sword in his pack. Tal grinned back at them and tossed the sword and pack aside. The bald man raised his fists and stepped forward.

Tal was faster, stepping into the attack and batting away the man's guard with his left arm. His right fist flattened the man's nose and snapped his head back against the shack wall. Stunned, the big man sank to one knee. He shook his head, sending streamers of blood across both cheeks. The nose-ring fell away to dangle from his ear alone.

The other bruiser stepped between Tal and the pot-bellied leader, who shook fish guts from his arms.

"Stay out of this," he warned, glowering at Tal. "It's nothing to do with you."

"Go back, Tal," said Chaney. He remained where the brutes had held him and looked shaken but not seriously hurt.

The scar-faced man gave his boss a hand up, but he slapped it away and struggled back to his feet on his own. He was soaked from the waist down. "Listen to your friend."

"Chane," said Tal, "you know I can't just stand by and let—"

"Please, Tal," pleaded Chaney. "We're just going to talk."

"That's right," agreed Potbelly. "We're just having a little philosophical discussion."

Tal hesitated. He knew he was making things worse for Chaney, but he couldn't stand the thought of letting him suffer a beating.

"Then talk," said Tal, "but touch him again, and we'll find out whether you can swim."

"On second thought, maybe this does involve you," sneered the man. He glanced at his henchman and nodded at Tal. When they hesitated, he shouted, "Get him!"

By the wall, Chaney slapped a hand over his eyes.

Tal made a quick feint toward Baldy. When the bald man obligingly flinched, Tal turned quickly and kicked

Scarface in the stomach. The man doubled over with a whoosh of breath.

Baldy threw his meaty arms around Tal's shoulders. He was even stronger than he looked, lifting Tal off the street. Tal shot an elbow into his gut, and the man relaxed his grip for an instant, only to shift it into a choke hold. Tal felt his eyes bulge from the sudden, crushing pressure. He shifted his weight to pull the man forward, but Baldy had his feet firmly planted and kept his hold.

Scarface staggered forward, still winded but recovered enough to slam his fist into Tal's sternum. He raised his fist for another blow, then fell over backward to reveal Chaney standing behind him, a heavy wooden spoke clutched in both hands.

Tal shoved Baldy backward, forcing him against the fishmonger's wall. The bruiser kept his hold, but then Tal jerked his head backward. The man's head cracked against the wall once, twice, and finally a third time before he sank to the street.

Tal staggered away, rubbing his throat and gasping. He looked for Potbelly, but the pale little man had made his escape. Near the street, Chaney peered back toward the city before turning back to Tal.

"We had better get out of here before the Scepters show up," he said.

He tossed his improvised club aside and threw Tal his pack. They emerged from the alley and headed north. Only a few questioning glances from the nearest merchants followed them.

"Listen, Chane," said Tal. "I'm sorry—"

"Couldn't be helped," said Chaney. "After all, I can't expect my bodyguard to stand aside while some creep roughs me up, can I?"

Tal made a weak smile. Chaney had called him his bodyguard since Tal first defended him against bullies some ten years before, when they were boys.

"Of course, I can hardly stroll back through town unattended now," said Chaney. "You got enough money for another horse?"

Four days later, Tal and Chaney rode past the high walls of Castle Narnbra and descended into the port of Yhaunn. The midday sun shone through a light shower of rain, but it was still clear enough for a grand view of the city. It was set within a vast rock quarry whose gray cliff walls rose up to the encircling walls.

From the vantage of the castle entrance, Tal could see some of the city's most famous buildings, including the graceful spires of Glassgrafter's Hall and the four domes of Ordulin's Manshion, a huge and famous rooming house. Not far from Orgulin's was a tall, round tower that could only be Moonshadow Hall. Its soaring walls were adorned with bas-reliefs of graceful winged devas and other celestial beings. They were miniscule at this distance, but Tal thought he recognized the shapes of owls in place of gargoyles above the seven gates to the temple. The building reminded Tal of an overgrown playhouse, with its multiple entrances and a central courtyard open to the sky.

Elsewhere, the city seemed impossibly crowded by small houses. Some of them were so narrow that two could fit into Tal's Selgaunt tallhouse, which he considered rather cozy. The buildings were especially dense near the harbor, where the stiltways rose four stories above the street. The bustling market district was a dizzying conglomeration of shops and alehouses linked by rope bridges, ladders, swings, ramps, and even more improbable connections above street level. The waterfront was open to Yhauntan Bay, a gray expanse filled with trading cogs and barges.

After they secured lodging at Orgulin's, Tal immediately ordered hot baths and refreshments brought to their room. While waiting for the tubs, Tal composed a brief note of introduction and paid one of the inn's boys to deliver it to Moonshadow Hall.

Within an hour, two pairs of house boys arrived and set a couple of deep wooden bathtubs before the fireplace. With precise economy, they filled the tubs with hot water from the cauldron above the fire. As the boys worked, a maid set out a warm jug of brandy with two small cups, as well as dishes of candied fruit, spiced lamb, seeded bread, and pickled onions. Then she arrayed the clean clothes neatly while Tal and Chaney stripped off their travel-sodden garments and handed them over for laundering. The servants left with the dirty laundry and a coin for each of them.

Tal and Chaney stepped into the hot water with hisses, then sank down to their chins with sighs of contentment. For a long time, they let the heat dissolve the knotted muscles and cold aches of the journey while they sipped warm liquor and nibbled from the tray between them in contented silence. Only after Chaney had refilled their cups for the second time did Tal broach the subject that had been troubling his mind since they left Selgaunt.

"Who were those men on the bridge?" he asked. He was surprised that Chaney hesitated before answering, since he'd had the past three days to formulate an excuse for his latest predicament.

Chaney slowly slipped under the surface of the water. He remained submerged so long that a faint, irrational anxiety plucked at Tal's imagination. Before he became concerned enough to grab his friend by the hair and pull him out, Chaney raised his head out of the water. Rather than answer the question, he grabbed a bar of soap and began lathering his hair.

Vexation paced along the back of Tal's mind, but he did not repeat himself. Instead he followed Chaney's example and scrubbed himself clean with a lavender-scented bar before leaning back to soak up the heat again. The warmth gradually reached his bones as he tried to empty his mind as Master Ferrick had taught. The meditation was much easier while sitting in a hot bath, he soon discovered. He had almost pushed away the question of Chaney's trouble when a house boy returned with his reply.

Tal gave him a penny and broke the wax seal to read the note.

"That was quick," said Chaney. "Will she see you?"

"It doesn't say," said Tal. "But I have an audience tonight with someone, if I want it."

"You probably have to impress some functionary first."

"Probably," said Tal.

"Want me to go with you?"

"No," said Tal.

He folded the vellum sheet and exchanged it for his glass on the small table between the bathtubs. Both he and Chaney sipped their drinks and settled back into the silence that had fallen over them since the fight at the High Bridge. Tal wanted to know more about Chaney's problem, and he felt it was only fair to tell him since he had confided everything in his friend. Still, while he felt compelled to intervene when it came to blows, he would not stoop to nagging Chaney.

While he waited for Chaney to share his secret, however, Tal would drag his friend no further into his own private affairs. Maybe it was petty, he realized, but maybe it was prudent. If Chaney were mixed up with hard criminals, not just a few cheated gamblers or a gentleman's loan gone sour, then Tal had to consider how to limit his own involvement. Despite his relative independence from Thamalon and the rest of his family, he knew better than to invite real trouble back to Stormweather.

He only hoped Chaney was not in real trouble, and he wouldn't know until Chaney confided in him.

Tal was surprised to find that Dhauna Myritar was a short, plump woman of perhaps sixty or as many as eighty years. She had brown skin and eyes of no particular color, with laugh lines that reminded Tal of Mistress Quickly and perhaps also Maleva.

The high priestess wore her fine blue and silver gown as comfortably as a fishwife would an old shawl. It was all bustles and lace with a fantastical collar that rose high above the top of her head. In her coifed hair she wore a silver tiara of six crescent moons surrounding one perfect disk in the center. It should have looked ridiculous on her, but somehow it did not.

"May Selûne guide your steps in the night and bring them to the new dawn," she greeted him. She had an air of comfortable formality, as though she'd said the words a hundred thousand times but still meant them honestly.

She handed the bright ceremonial scepter to one of the three young novices attending her before dismissing them from the room. It was a small, comfortable antechamber, thickly carpeted and appointed with furnishings that looked more appropriate for a gentleman's lounge than a temple. The servants had left a decanter of wine so white it was nearly silver, and the high priestess gestured for Tal to pour her a glass.

He obliged with practiced grace learned more from the stage than a courtier's habit, careful to hand it to her delicately and say, "Your grace."

"Thank you, Talbot," she said. She sat back and put her slippered feet up on a stuffed footstool. "You may call me 'Dhauna' when we're alone. Why, I feel as though I know you already. Oh, don't look so surprised. You are not stupid, and you needn't pretend to be."

"No," said Tal. "Of course Maleva told you about my problem."

"Oh, much more than that," she said.

She drained half of the wine from her glass in one smooth motion. Far from seeming crude, the gesture was natural and homey. Tal thought more than ever that she reminded him of Maleva.

"I see," said Tal, not knowing what else to say.

"To be honest, I expected you much sooner. Or else I expected you to go rushing off in search of Rusk. Revenge!" She lifted her glass like a sword.

Tal just stared at her. Each time she opened her mouth, she flabbergasted him anew.

"Actually," he admitted, "a friend of mine talked me out of that."

"Good friend," she said, finishing her glass and raising it for a refill. Tal poured again. "You'll need good friends if you plan to keep your curse a secret. But you can't keep it that way forever, you know."

"Yes," said Tal. "That's why I'm here. I want to know more about—"

"You want to know more about moonfire and why you can't buy any," she said. This time he was not surprised. "That part is simple. It won't work for you. You could drink a barrel of the stuff—if it weren't a sacrilege, that is—and the best it might do is cure your sniffles or maybe make you glow in the dark for a while."

"But Maleva said—"

"Maleva said it would control your shapechanging for seven moons."

"Right."

"But only if you worship Selûne."

"Yes, that was the deal."

"It wasn't a deal, Talbot. Mind if I call you Tal?" She was sipping on her wine now, but her cheeks were already pleasantly flushed. "She was explaining how it works. It suppresses the call of the moon *if* you are a worshiper of Selûne."

"Oh," said Tal. "That's not exactly the way she put it."

"That *is* exactly the way she put it," said Dhauna. "It's just not exactly the way you heard it. Drink some wine. You look confused."

"Thank you," he said, following her example and draining half his glass in one smooth draught. He frowned to think he'd come all this way only to hear the high priestess of Selûne tell him the same thing Maleva had already told him.

"Now you look sad. I like you the other way better. Drink some more."

At that, Tal laughed softly. Dhauna's banter took the edge off his disappointment far better than more wine could ever do.

"You're welcome among the faithful," she said in a less frivolous tone. "You truly are, and not just because the ratio of women to men is approaching eight to one. In fact, I think you will find eventually that your place is among us."

Tal shook his head gently, but she spoke again before he could comment.

"Just not yet," she said gently, reaching over to pat him on the knee. The gesture seemed far more friendly than patronizing.

"No," Tal agreed. "It's not that I mean any disrespect."

"I know," said Dhauna. "You're just a bit of a hot-head, a little too young, a little too wild. Our job is to see that you have a chance to grow out of it."

Tal wasn't sure whether he liked the sound of "our job," but he already knew he liked Dhauna Myritar and wanted to hear what she had to say. He had not done a particularly good job of listening to advice from Maleva and Feena.

"I do need help," said Tal.

"Then I'll send you someone," said Dhauna. "It will take some time to arrange, but soon. In return, you must provide room and board, and you must listen and take what she says seriously."

"She?"

"One of our initiates," said Dhauna. "As you might have noticed, most of our clergy are women."

"Chaney would like it here," said Tal.

"So would you," said Dhauna. Before he could protest, she added, "Just not yet."

They smiled at each other.

"There is one thing that Maleva didn't tell me," he said as she sipped some more wine. "I overheard her daughter say something about a Black Wolf heresy."

Wine spurted from Dhauna's nose. She caught most of it in the glass, which she set aside.

"Your grace, I didn't mean—"

"It's all right," she said, mopping her chin with a handkerchief drawn from her sleeve. "I should have expected that. Just don't mention it openly, not here. After all, it is a heresy."

"Of course."

"You know what heresy means? It means it's untrue. Still, it's a big lie that comes from some little truths. Did you tell Maleva when you were born?"

"Yes, she asked me that. The time, too."

"Were you born during a new moon?"

"I don't know. She didn't say anything more about it."

Dhauna sighed.

"What does that mean?"

"Well, it means either you were born under a black moon or you weren't. We don't know, since Maleva enjoys being mysterious. That works well with the people where she lives, but it's annoying to civilized people like you and me."

Tal chuckled.

"That wasn't a joke," she said, frowning.

Tal wiped the smile from his face, but he felt a blush rise to his cheeks.

"But that was," said Dhauna, shaking her head mirthfully. "Don't be so gullible."

"You don't seem very much like a high priestess," said Tal.

"You don't seem very much like a werewolf," she replied. "Not tonight, at any rate."

"About the Black . . . thing . . . business," he prompted.

"If you were born during a black moon, a new moon, then it might be easier for you to learn how to ride the moon. That's our poetic and mysterious way of saying, learn how to control the change."

"Why didn't Maleva tell me about that?"

"Well," said Dhauna, "perhaps she was trying too hard to persuade you to join the temple."

"That can't be it. She was really trying to help me. I can't believe she would just leave out telling me that I can control the change."

"You haven't proven that you can," said Dhauna. "Not everyone succeeds at it, especially those bitten by wolves, boars, and the other savage beasts. Those who suffer the benign lycanthropy have it much easier."

"Benign lycanthropy?"

"Werebears, for instance," said Dhauna. "They are not as susceptible to the call of the Huntmaster."

"You mean Malar, don't you?"

She nodded.

"He's also called the Black Wolf, isn't he?"

"Sometimes my attendants listen at the door," she said. "Don't embarrass me."

"Sorry."

"The temple of Selûne does not actively oppose the Beastlord," she said. "We're not friendly with his followers, and some of our clerics take it upon themselves to defend folk against lycanthropes—with our blessing, naturally—but we concern ourselves primarily with other evils."

"Like Shar and Mask," suggested Tal. He had read that the clerics of Selûne were especial enemies of the goddess of darkness and the god of thieves.

"Exactly," she agreed. "There are so many dark gods, and we of Selûne's faithful must devote our energies to thwarting the minions of her foes."

"And Malar is not one of her foes."

"No," said Dhauna. "Not in the same way."

Tal had a glimmer of insight, a half-formed idea that dissolved even as he tried to make it take shape. Somehow he realized that he had almost grasped a hidden truth, but it had slipped away. Its passing left another, lesser question.

"Maleva is not in good standing with the temple, is she?"

"No," allowed Dhauna. "Even though we are old friends, she has chosen a different path."

"Because she wants to oppose Malar."

This time Dhauna's sigh was full of weary resignation. "The matter is more complicated than you know, for reasons that I won't share with you."

Tal thought about what she had said. "You said 'won't.' "

"I did."

"One of the Old Chauncel—the old families who run Selgaunt—one of them would have said 'can't.' "

"But that would have been a lie, Tal."

He smiled. Perhaps he had not found all the answers he had hoped for, but he trusted this Dhauna Myritar, and through her he trusted Maleva more than ever, despite her mysterious ways.

"Thank you," he said, standing up to bow to the cleric. "May I visit you again some day?"

She rose and offered him her hand, raising one sly eyebrow. "Are you already considering joining us?"

"No," he said, "but perhaps we could sit and drink some wine."

CHAPTER 7

THE ARCH WOOD

Tarsakh, 1371 DR

Darrow turned the key and paused to listen. He heard nothing from the other side of the door, so he carefully pushed it open.

Inside, shafts of daylight slanted from the ceiling thirty feet above. The intervening floors had been torn away except for a wide ledge on each side, forming a crude double balcony in the vast room. Perhaps once these had been receiving halls and parlors, bedchambers and libraries. Long ago, the Malveens lived here. Since then, it had been cut open to serve as a catacomb for unwanted cargo.

The upper ledges were filled with shipping crates and pallets of barrels, as was most of the ground floor, where they formed a twisting maze. Built upon the huge central beam was a peculiar double crane for raising and lowering the stores.

Its intricate design spoke of gnome craftsmanship, and Darrow guessed it still worked, even after years of neglect. In the dim light, it looked like a lightning-struck tree, one half leaning to rest on the southern ledge.

Darrow raised the cup of continual flames and stepped inside. He stepped on something that crunched under his foot. He kicked it into the light and saw the desiccated body of a rat.

"Huntmaster," called Darrow, mindful to call the Malveens's guest by his title. "My lord Malveen wishes to see you."

He waited a moment for a reply before venturing farther into the warehouse, among the ruined treasures of the waterfront. Some of the wares were stamped with the Harbormaster's seal of confiscation. Others were damaged or otherwise imperfect, like a pallet full of dusty bolts of Shou Lung silk, stinking of smoke and mold.

"Huntmaster!" called Darrow. "Rusk!"

No answer came, but Darrow caught the scent of roasting meat. Following it, he heard the crackle of Rusk's cooking fire and worried briefly about the danger of an open flame amid so much dust and wood. At last, he spied Rusk's lair in the far corner of the warehouse.

The big man had lost weight in the four months since his injury, but the stump of his left arm was completely healed. He sat cross-legged before his fire and watched Darrow approach, making no move to rise.

"Lord Malveen summons you to the baiting pit," said Darrow.

"Summons me?" snarled Rusk. He tore a rib from what appeared to be a roast dog and sucked the meat from the bone. He offered some to Darrow, who blanched and politely waved it away. "I'm ready to return to the lodge. I should be summoning Radu here. Still," said the Huntmaster, "it would be something to see the place again."

"You've been there before?" said Darrow. "The arena?"

"Who do you think stocked the place?" Rusk said gruffly. He wiped his greasy hand on one leg and stood up.

"I assumed Lord Malveen," Darrow said, "or perhaps his mother, the Lady Velanna, had ensorcelled the beasts."

"Twenty years ago, 'Lord' Malveen could barely light a candle with a brand."

"My lord is the most powerful sorcerer in Sembia," said Darrow.

"You pathetic sycophant!" Rusk laughed heartily. "He's charmed you, hasn't he? That's what the second ward did when we broke in."

"No," said Darrow, but he wondered whether it was true. He had been so grateful that Stannis spared his life since his indiscretion about the wine that he never considered the possibility that his master was anything but a kind and merciful lord.

"Stand still," commanded Rusk. With a touch of the talisman on his brow, he chanted a spell.

"No!" Darrow ran to hide behind a stack of crates. Before he made it, he felt a faint tingling sensation, and he heard Rusk's mocking laughter.

"Come out, you foolish lamb!"

"My master won't let you—" A sensation of gentle, cold fingers touching his skin came over Darrow. It felt like standing naked in a light snowfall. Whatever magic Rusk had cast, it was done.

"Be silent," said Rusk. "Your bleating annoys me. Let's go see what you think of your master now."

As Rusk had promised, Darrow saw his master in a new light as they entered the arena. It was all he could do to hide the revulsion he felt when he saw the blubbery folds of the monster's body lapping over the couch. His piscine stench was overpowering, but worse was the stink of death just beneath it, insinuating itself into Darrow's nostrils, into his very pores.

Stammering fear replaced the awe he once felt in his master's presence. Try as he did to hide it, it must have shown on his face. Stannis observed him with growing interest.

"Have you been interfering with my servant, Huntmaster?"

Rusk shrugged, barely suppressing his own mischievous smile.

"Look at me, Darrow," snapped Stannis. "Look at me now!"

Fearfully, Darrow obeyed. An instant's glance into the roiling depths of his master's eyes restored his faith. His moment of doubt and horror became a confusing memory. He knew only that Rusk had tempted him to some beastly offense against his glorious master.

"That's better, is it not?"

"Thank you, Master," said Darrow. "I crave pardon for my . . . confusion."

"Think no more about it, dear boy. Now, to the duel."

As before, Radu stood patiently on one side of the fanged pit. He held his sheathed sword lightly in both hands, and his eyes were closed.

Voorla stood near the bars of his prison without touching them. With a slow twist of his head, the troll cracked the bones in his neck. He stretched his huge green arms and flexed the muscles in his shoulders. Voorla was ready to fight.

Two cells away, Maelin sat on her bunk and watched dispassionately. Darrow had already told her of the match, so she knew it was Voorla who would be released into the ring. In the months of her imprisonment, she had become resolved to the fact that she would receive no chance to win her freedom.

When Stannis raised the gate, Voorla surged forward. He snatched a cutlass from the row of weapons and hurled it across the pit.

Radu opened his eyes at the sound and turned just far enough to avoid the sword. He drew his own blade and cast away the scabbard as the cutlass struck the wall hard and snapped in half. Before the broken halves could hit the ground, Voorla hurled a spear after it.

Again, Radu moved just far enough to let the spear pass harmlessly by. He strolled around the pit, seemingly unconcerned at the continuing stream of missiles.

The third was a short sword, tumbling end over end like a showman's knife. Radu deflected it with his long sword, using both hands to brace his sword against Voorla's powerful throw.

"I had expected a more courageous display," said Rusk. "A true hunter does not kill from afar."

"He calls himself a warrior," said Stannis, "not a hunter."

"Is that what your brother calls himself?" said Rusk. "A warrior?"

"Not at all," said Stannis. "He does not speak of his talents at all, but I suspect he would be succinct if put to the question. Radu is a killer."

In the pit below, Radu began to demonstrate the veracity of his brother's definition. He closed with the troll. With a quick lunge, he pierced the monster through the calf. Dark blood appeared on Radu's blade, but the wound closed as quickly as it was made.

Voorla hefted a glaive and swung it one-handed. Radu tumbled past the troll's tree-trunk legs, springing up back-to-back with the monster. Without turning, he reversed his grip on the long sword and shoved it back into the troll's thigh.

Voorla wailed. Blood poured from the wound, then trickled and oozed until it stopped.

"He won't get anywhere that way," observed Rusk.

"Indeed," said Stannis, "but watch."

Voorla chased his opponent around the ring. Radu did not flee so much as lead the raging troll, narrowly avoiding each savage chop of the glaive. At last, the troll's blade sliced a hank of silk from Radu's jacket.

"Oh, my," said Stannis, reaching out for another glass of wine. Darrow was so transfixed by the battle that he missed his cue. He fumbled with the crystal decanter and placed the goblet in his master's flabby hand.

"Are you worried at last?" asked Rusk.

"Dear me, no," said Stannis. "I think our entertainment is almost finished. That was his favorite jacket, a gift from Pietro, our youngest brother. How Radu dotes on the boy."

Rusk grunted dubiously, but the master's words proved prophetic. Radu reversed his retreat and whirled effortlessly inside Voorla's guard. With a wide, two-handed cut, he swept the troll's left hand from its arm.

Voorla howled and scrambled after the severed limb. If he could touch it, hand and limb would rejoin in a matter of seconds.

Radu reached the hand first, spearing it on the tip of his long sword and flicking it into the fanged pit.

Voorla screamed, chopping wildly with the glaive. Radu skipped aside but gave no ground. He was done taunting his foe.

When the glaive struck the sand where he had stood, Radu leaped over it and drew a bloody line across Voorla's brow. The brief flow poured into the troll's eyes.

As Voorla blinked, Radu struck another two-handed blow into the troll's forearm, but not far enough to sever the troll's heavy thews. Voorla jerked back before Radu could withdraw his blade, pulling the swordsman close and pushing him to the ground.

Voorla shouted triumphantly as he pinned Radu with one heavy foot, then raised his arm for the killing blow. Radu's face remained impassive as he held onto his sword, twisting it to the side to cut through the remaining sinews of the troll's arm. Before the muscles could repair themselves, the glaive fell from Voorla's twitching fingers.

Voorla kicked Radu away then tried to grasp his maimed arm with his missing hand. Unable to grip his wound, the troll fell to its knees and cradled his ruined limbs, desperately whispering to them. Darrow imagined he was praying for them to rebind themselves faster. For the first time since meeting the troll, Darrow felt something other than fear of it: Voorla looked piteous.

Radu stood and stabbed his sword into the sand. He paused to slap the sand from his breeches before walking toward the fumbling troll.

On his knees, the troll was the same height as his opponent.

"Voorla gnagt veek nogu, Malveen."

"Voorla acknowledges your superior skill, my brother," translated Stannis.

"Eent moku ngla foma," said the troll.

"He humbly requests your mercy."

Radu nodded, walking behind the troll. Voorla sank to his haunches. He stared at the pit, perhaps longing for his hand. As the bone blade entered the back of his skull, white light burst from Voorla's eyes and mouth. His green flesh turned ashy gray then dull white as his life and body alike were consumed by an insatiable, unholy power. Within seconds, his body withered to the barest, crumbling skeleton, which then collapsed into powder that mingled with the stained sand of the pit.

In Radu's hand, the bone blade had turned black as sin.

Darrow wrenched his gaze from the awful scene to look at the others. There was no way to discern Stannis's reaction under his golden veil, though his glowing eyes were fixed on Rusk. The Huntmaster tried maintaining an aloof indifference, but he could not disguise his revulsion at the effects of the bone blade.

Stannis began the applause, which Darrow obediently joined. In the pit, Radu watched as the bone blade slowly returned to its original white as its smooth surface absorbed the dark stain. With a gesture, Stannis opened the baiting pit gate for his brother, who joined them in the gallery.

"Well done, my brother," said Stannis. "Not only do you thrill us with your skill, but you set my heart at ease upon your journey far from home." He turned to Rusk. "Not that he should have need of self defense while in your company, Huntmaster."

"No," agreed Rusk, his eyes fixed upon the white dagger.

"Good," said Stannis. "Then I will not worry about his traveling alone."

"I am not traveling alone," said Radu. He indicated Darrow with a slight nod of his head. "He will come with me."

"What? But how shall I get along without him?" protested Stannis. "I have become quite dependent on his company.

Despite a few . . . human flaws . . . I need him for those tasks that prove too subtle for my minions."

"All the more reason he should come with me."

"You gave him to me," said Stannis petulantly. "You called him unreliable."

"All the more reason he should not remain here, where he might draw suspicion to the house."

Stannis paused, then tried another tack. "What possible use do you have for him in the woods?"

"He will set camp, prepare my meals. . . ."

Stannis sighed. "You are determined, I see. I suppose there is nothing more to be said."

"No," said Radu.

No one said another word as they left the arena.

Spring rains had left the ground soft, and Darrow wished again that they had stayed to the roads. Their horses left a trail of black divots, and the effort was sure to tire the beasts soon. Before it did, they came to the edge of the Arch Wood. There a carpet of fir needles and the deep clutch of roots made the ground firm. Rusk led Radu and Darrow slowly into the forest.

"How far?" asked Radu.

During the past three days, Radu Malveen had not spoken a word. Darrow had considered making conversation with Rusk, but the cleric was brooding about his severed arm. His healing spells had sealed over the raw stump but left it ugly. Something other than his wound was troubling him. Several times he had halted their progress, dismounted, and sniffed the air. Each time, he turned to scowl back the way they came, as if someone were following them. None of them saw any sign of pursuit, so they continued on their journey.

To Radu's question, Rusk grunted and dismounted. Darrow's roan shied away from the big savage. Even Radu's Calishite stallion tossed its head until the swordsman mastered it with the barest tightening of his legs. None of the horses liked Rusk until he had cast a spell to befriend the muddy brown dray horse that would bear him.

Rusk moved away from the horses, holding his head high to snuffle for a scent. His hairy jaws worked as if he were drinking the wind, tasting it.

"You don't know where they are," said Radu.

Darrow heard the impatience in his master's voice. He remained still and kept his eyes from Radu.

Rusk scowled at the accusation. "They're roaming," he said. "If we go to the lodge, we might have to wait tendays for their return. You don't want to wait tendays out here. Give me the scrolls now, and I'll hunt for them alone."

Radu did not answer at first. Darrow knew that Radu and his hideous brother were suspicious of Rusk's claims. Even if he had a pack at his command, would they still obey a maimed leader?

Finally, Radu said, "Take us to the lodge now."

Darrow saw the tension coil in Rusk's shoulders. It made the thick gray hair on his arm ridge up. Without another word, Rusk mounted his horse and grudgingly led them northwest. Radu followed, and Darrow knew better than to break the silence.

They traveled until dusk, when the fat horns of the waning moon appeared beyond the dappling canopy. Behind them trailed the shards, tiny motes said to be Selûne's handmaidens.

Darrow looked to Radu for a sign that it was time to erect the master's tent. It was the master's habit to leave all the menial tasks to Darrow, who was now driver, cook, drudge, and fetch. In the months since Darrow had stumbled upon the Malveen family secret, he was grateful enough for his life that he did not complain. The thought of revealing the truth about Stannis Malveen never crossed his mind, nor did hope of escape. Besides, when he was honest with himself, Darrow realized that he enjoyed being in the service of a man so powerful and dangerous. If he stayed loyal and kept his wits about him, Darrow could profit very well indeed.

Despite the growing darkness, Radu did not seem ready to camp. He looked to Rusk, who cocked his head in an attitude of concentrated listening. Darrow followed his example but heard nothing except the hush of the gentle evening breeze.

Then he realized the forest had become quiet.

Rusk jumped from his horse, slapped its flank, and crouched low over the ground. All the while he intoned a low chant.

Darrow looked to Radu, but the master was gone. His stallion pawed the forest floor. Without a lead to follow, Darrow slipped as quietly as he could to the ground and put his back against a big tree. His horse needed no encouragement to trot away.

Rusk finished his spell with a brief touch of the holy symbol on his brow. His muscles bulged and rippled as infernal strength flowed through his limbs. Throughout the incantation, he never took his eyes from the northeastern shadows.

Darrow drew his long sword and stared at those shadows. Something was approaching, he knew, even though he saw and heard nothing. Maybe Rusk smelled it, but all Darrow smelled was moist loam and tree bark.

The attack came from above, slamming Darrow to the ground and knocking his sword away. A hard root cut into his cheek as nails raked his back. Hot breath spilled over the back of his neck as a living weight pressed him to the ground. He tensed for the pain of teeth tearing into his flesh, but then the weight was gone.

Darrow scrambled for his sword, but bright motes danced in his vision, and his fingers clutched only cool soil and thistles. Then a sound like a dozen angry dogs dropped from a tower exploded around him.

Blinking his eyes clear, Darrow saw Rusk standing amid a boiling mass of dark wolves. He held one by the throat, far above the others. The animal thrashed and struggled to get its mouth around Rusk's arm. With terrible ease, the cleric hurled it away. The wolf smashed into a tree with a sickening crack. It fell to the ground whining, its hind legs useless.

"Back!" roared Rusk, kicking a wolf that darted at his legs. "I am the Bloodmaster. Obey me!"

Most of them shied away at his words and the demonstration of his strength, but one bold wolf stalked forward, growling at Rusk.

Rusk touched the talisman on his brow, then thrust a finger toward the wolf. "Submit," he said.

His voice was low, but its effect instantaneous. The rebellious wolf rolled onto its back, exposing its throat and belly.

All the other wolves gazed at Rusk and the defeated challenger. Darrow took the opportunity to find his sword. When he turned to where it had fallen, however, he saw a slim white wolf sitting between him and the weapon. Its icy blue eyes were fixed not on Rusk but on Darrow. The wolf turned its head from side to side in an eerily human gesture. No, it seemed to tell him, before its gaze returned to the central conflict.

Rusk stood amid the wolves, looking from face to face as if seeking any signs of further defiance. Where his gaze went, wolf heads dipped or turned away. Only when he turned to the white wolf did his inquisition meet with a steady return gaze. Rusk's eyes moved on, seeking something they had not yet found.

Where is Radu? wondered Darrow. He hoped his master had not fled. Somehow, he knew the man was nearby, as invisible as on the night Rusk had first invaded House Malveen. He prayed to Mask, the Lord of Shadows, to keep him hidden from the beasts until he chose to strike. He prayed to Tymora, Lady Luck, to give him the chance to save himself as well.

"Bloodmaster . . ." called a weak voice. The wolf Rusk had thrown away was now a naked young man. Blood bubbled from one nostril, and his ruptured lungs wheezed as he spoke. Like the wolf he had been, his back was twisted halfway around, his legs lying useless below him. "Grant mercy, please . . . heal me."

Rusk went to him and knelt, placing his hand on the young man's head. "Fraelan," he said, "why did you attack your master?"

"We didn't know . . . it was you."

"You beg mercy and lie to me? I'll leave you for the scavengers!"

"You do smell like the city, Rusk," said a sweet voice. Darrow looked where the white wolf guarded his sword. Now the wolf was an elf who sat careless of her nakedness. Except for her dirty hands and feet, her skin was ghostly. Her faintly blue eyes were almost white except for the startling black pupils.

Rusk ignored the elf and took Fraelan's face in one hand.

"Who was it?"

Tears made trails on the young man's dirty face. He hesitated only a few seconds. "Balin," he whispered.

Rusk nodded, as if it were the answer he wanted to hear. "Now you have earned mercy," he said, pressing his forehead against Fraelan's. "I grant you mercy. Malar grants you mercy."

"No," gasped Fraelan. "Please . . . heal—"

Rusk's whiskery mouth covered the younger man's. Fraelan clutched weakly at Rusk, but the big man held him firm and drew out the crippled man's last breath. Darrow felt a chill watching the deadly kiss. As Fraelan's strength waned and vanished, Rusk lowered him gently to the ground. He rose to face the pack then. Darrow saw new power in the cleric's face. The scratches his pack had caused him were gone, and his muscles rippled with new strength. The symbol of Malar gleamed red in the twilight shadows.

"Now," said Rusk, "where is Balin?"

The wolves all turned in the same direction. The forest trembled, and the saplings parted as the monster approached.

Growing up a farmer's son, Darrow was not surprised by large pigs. They were dangerous animals, even when raised as livestock. One had killed his cousin and had begun eating the boy before Darrow's uncle could fend him off with a spear. He'd summoned help from his neighbors before slaughtering the beast that night. The wild boars hunted for festivals often dwarfed their domestic cousins, and Darrow had seen some large enough for a big man to ride, if he dared. When he came to Selgaunt and saw the colossal boar's head mounted above the bar in the Black Stag inn, he thought it must be the biggest boar in all Faerûn. They called it Demon and said it had killed more than a hundred and thirty men who dared to hunt it, including all but two of the twenty who had finally brought it down with spears and magic. Its long tusks were as thick as a dock worker's forearm. They curled awry, giving the vast red face a mad expression. Its eyes were tiny black stones, almost invisible in the expanse of bristling red fur. A man could put a fist in one of Demon's flaring nostrils, and its mouth was big enough for a man's head, as the city gallants sometimes proved after a few pints of ale. Darrow wouldn't have done that for a hundred fivestars.

The boar that came out of the Arch Wood that night could have been Demon's big brother.

It walked toward Rusk, stopping only a few feet away. As Darrow watched, the giant boar transformed. Its flesh rippled and contorted, reforming into the figure of a man even taller and much heavier than Rusk. His prominent tusks and low brow betrayed his orc parentage.

"A coward hides behind the pack," said Rusk. "A challenger stands alone against the Bloodmaster."

"I am the Bloodmaster now," said the half-orc. "You stayed too long in the pen, Rusk. You've become one of the sheep."

"Malar speaks to *me*," shouted Rusk, "not you. I was Huntmaster before you were born, and I'll be the Bloodmaster long after you're dead."

"Malar pisses on old cripples," Balin said, pointing at Rusk's stump. "I am the strongest hunter now, and I lead the People of the Black Blood where we belong, in the wild. Run now, and I'll let you live with your sheep."

"Malar tests me, yes, but I need only one hand to slaughter a pig."

Darrow couldn't tell who moved first. Balin lunged for Rusk, but the cleric leaped to the side, leaving the half-orc skidding in the dirt. Walking almost casually away from

Balin, Rusk sang another prayer. It drew the power of his god into his hand, which grew to nearly twice its size and sprouted wicked talons.

Across the clearing, Balin rose slowly to his feet. His form shifted again, this time halting halfway between boar and half-orc. His previously massive limbs were now as thick as battering rams, his fists like the heads of sledgehammers.

The pack watched but did not interfere. Those in the clearing moved aside for the combatants.

Balin charged. Rusk waited until the last instant, then dropped low and kicked hard at the wereboar's left leg. There was no satisfying crack, but Balin crashed into the brush instead of his enemy. Rusk slashed Balin's exposed buttocks with his monstrous hand. While the wereboar recovered, Rusk strode into the center of the clearing again and waited.

"You are slow and stupid," he said. "My only mistake has been to let you live among us."

Balin's reply was rough snorting and another charge. This time, he kept his body low to avoid a trip. Rusk vaulted over Balin, but not before the wereboar lifted his tusks to tear a deep gash in the cleric's leg. The wound made him stumble and fall in Balin's wake. Before Rusk could recover, Balin turned to charge again.

This time, Balin threw himself on Rusk, who couldn't get away in time. Rusk's howl was cut off as the bigger man's weight crushed him, but Balin screamed too. They rolled together on the ground, leaving a trail of blood.

Like a bear, Balin hugged his opponent, trying to squeeze his breath away. Rusk's arm was pinned between them, but he jerked and pushed as if reaching *into* his enemy. Soon they were both smeared in blood, and Balin's screams turned to squeals. Still his arms continued to crush the cleric, who had no breath to scream.

Rusk transformed, his body shifting from man to half-man to silver-gray wolf. His half-tunic was pinned beneath Balin's massive arms, but his boots and trousers fell away, tangling his legs.

Balin's hug pinned the slender foreleg of Rusk's wolf form helplessly, but now Rusk's long jaws were at the wereboar's throat. They snapped once and caught, and there they held. Blood gushed down the gray wolf's muzzle. Together, Balin's two wounds drained away his life. In death, the wereboar's body shifted one last time to leave a huge boar's corpse on the ground. The wolf rolled away from it, more red than gray.

The white elf ran to Rusk and began licking at the blood. Darrow turned away, disgusted, but a perverse fascination made him look again. Two wolves joined the elf, whining sympathetically as they tried to soothe their master's wounds.

As his breathing slowed, Rusk shifted back into his human shape. He cuffed the nearest sycophants. "Get away," he barked.

All obeyed except the elf, who pressed herself against Rusk, laying her head against his bruised ribs. Rusk grabbed her by the hair, jerking her head back and forcing her to look up at him.

"Balin was a simpleton and a coward," Rusk said. "I wonder who encouraged his ambition."

The elf's face remained impassive. She did not struggle in her master's grip.

Rusk stared into her face a little longer, then shoved her away. "Bah," he said. "The challenge is done. I am the Bloodmaster. Does any deny it?"

He did not deign to look around. Every member of the pack looked to the ground. Darrow noticed the elf glancing up at Rusk, a faint smile on her lips.

"Impressive," said Radu. He stood at the edge of the clearing, holding the reins of his stallion. The other two horses were nowhere to be seen. "Impressive, yet puzzling."

"What do you mean?" said Rusk.

"You defeated this brute," said Radu, gesturing at Balin's bloody corpse, "yet you say Talbot Uskevren sliced off your arm."

Rusk's eyes blazed at the reminder. He worked his jaw but said nothing.

"Was that the name of your prey in the city, Bloodmaster?" The elf's tone was humble, thought Darrow. A trifle too humble.

"Silence, Sorcia," said Rusk.

"Yes, Bloodmaster," said Sorcia contritely.

Her eyes turned to the ground until Rusk looked away, then they turned to Radu. Darrow took the opportunity to collect his sword, sheathing it as quietly as he could to avoid attracting the attention of the monsters that surrounded him.

"Our guests have brought us a gift," said Rusk, "a gift from the Beastlord himself. We have the scrolls of Malar."

Darrow glanced at Radu, hoping his master would not correct Rusk before his followers. Stannis had permitted Rusk to bring only a fraction of the Black Wolf Scrolls. Rusk had howled when he saw the torn fragment, but he dared not challenge the Malveens in their home. Now, with his pack looking on, Rusk might not take another humiliation so mildly. Probably Radu could kill any one of them, maybe even most of them. But he'd never kill them all before one of them tore Darrow to pieces. Of that he was sure.

Perhaps Tymora smiled on Darrow then, for Radu merely gestured for Darrow to take the reins of his horse. Darrow obeyed, grateful to stand apart from the werewolves.

"To the lodge," commanded Rusk. At last the Bloodmaster permitted himself a smile at his victory. After his dangerous quest in the city, he was home among his people. He gestured to Balin's corpse and added, "Don't forget the meat."

CHAPTER 8

THE AUDITION

Tarsakh, 1371 DR

Impious shadow of the king who was," bellowed Presbart as the baron. His soldiers pointed their swords at Tal's heart. "Release the scepter stolen from his tomb!"

"I wear the crown by acclamation true," replied Tal, leaping back onto the crenellated wall. "Deny my claim and hasten your own doom." On the rhyming syllable, he struck a guard's blade from his hand.

The weapon skittered across the stage and shot through the surrounding rails, sending Sivana and Ennis diving out of the way. Ennis managed to flatten himself, causing even more laughter among the other players.

Tal winced at the accident and smiled a weak apology. The distraction almost caused him to miss the incoming attacks. He parried one blade and leaped over the other. When the guard swung again, he leaped up to stamp on the blade, trapping it on the wall. His kick missed the guard's face by less than an inch, and the man flipped backward to lay still.

"Your reign was not ordained, O faithless prince," declared Presbart, brandishing his own sword.

The first guard grabbed a spear from the back wall and thrust at Tal's head. Tal parried easily, then bound the spear's shaft with his sword and thrust it into the baron's sword, blocking them both.

Tal leaped from the battlement to arch over both men. He twisted gracefully to land facing them from behind. Still distracted by his earlier blunder, he neglected to bend his knees to cushion the blow. The impact of his body sent a booming echo through the trapdoor room below.

Before his foes could turn around, Tal thrust his blade under the arm of the guard, who cried out, clutched his heart, and fell to the floor. The baron dropped his sword and ran to hide behind the stage right pillar. Tal followed, slashing first on one side, then the other, as the cowardly baron dodged.

"In faith, I am a prince no more than thou," said Tal, "As this, my final answer to your base demands will . . . oh, dark and empty. What's the line?"

"That's enough," said Quickly from the floor. Her big arms were crossed over her chest, and she gnawed on the stem of her unlit pipe.

"I almost had it," said Tal, walking to the edge of the stage. "The sword going off the stage threw me. We should probably reverse that so it goes backstage."

Quickly nodded. "Right. Show Mallion what to do."

"You're giving the part to him?"

Mallion was the most beautiful man in the Wide Realms troupe, and he knew it. Even at nearly thirty, he looked only a few years older than Tal and the other young players. They all teased him for spending so much money on skin creams, hair tonics, and eye cosmetics, but his flawless complexion and rich black curls garnered him a flock of adoring admirers after each performance. Worse yet, in Tal's opinion, he really was a fine actor with tremendous range. His elocution was second only to Presbart's rolling phrases, and he was one of Tal's few rivals for physical scenes.

Behind Quickly, Mallion buffed his nails on his chest. Beside him, Sivana flicked his ear and shot Tal a sympathetic wink. With Mallion and Tal, she was one of the most accomplished stage fencers in the company. Of them, only Tal had any real weapons training, but Sivana's lithe, androgynous figure made her a better foil for the slender Mallion. Both of them squeezed together would barely make one Tal.

"He's better for it, Tal. You know that." Quickly beckoned him down from the stage. He leaped the rail and landed heavily on the ground. Walnut shells left by last night's groundling's crunched under his feet. "Besides, one more vault like that one and you'll go straight through to the Nine Hells."

"I can fall into a roll, instead," he said. "Or we could move the wall to curve around there, and . . ."

"I've made up my mind, Tal, my lad. You're good, especially at the swordplay, but Mallion makes the better villain."

As if to prove the point, the handsome actor leered menacingly behind Quickly. Without looking, she poked him in the chest with a beefy elbow.

"*Oof*," he said with exaggerated injury. Then he smoothed his neat beard in a gesture that made Tal think of a cat cleaning itself.

"What about me?" said Tal. Hearing the whining in his own voice made everything that much worse.

"I was thinking of Maeroven," said Quickly.

Tal rolled his eyes. He didn't want to play the bumbling cook. "But I played the nurse in *The Curse of Brynwater Abbey*," he complained. "People will start expecting me to wear a dress every time I get on stage."

"You should have thought about that before you perfected her voice," said Quickly.

Tal wasn't so distracted that he didn't catch the change in her tone. He was about to suffer a tweaked nose.

"What voice is that?" he asked innocently.

Both Mallion and Sivana were hiding their faces. They'd told her about Tal's Mistress Quickly imitation, which he was careful to do only well out of the troupe leader's hearing.

"You know the one," said the brawny woman, slapping him on the bottom. " 'No, no, that's all wrong! Say it with guts. *With guts!*' "

Now the entire company broke into laughter. Sivana actually fell onto her back, kicking the empty air. She shook her head back and forth, sweeping the hard packed ground with her hair, which was black this month. No one could agree on its natural color, which was the source of speculation even among the majority of the company, whom she'd taken to bed.

"That's not it," said Tal. "It's more like, 'What's the matter with you street buskers? Leave your spines backstage? Stand up straight and tell me that!' "

The laughter turned to wails and gasps, and even Quickly herself was fanning herself with one meaty hand.

"You're a good play, Tal," said Quickly with another sharp swat to his buttock. "Glad you understand about the part."

He did understand, but Tal still felt a strong pang of disappointment. For months he'd been pestering Quickly to give him a role in which he could show off all he'd learned at Master Ferrick's. Despite all his auditions, he always ended up with a supporting role, usually a comic foil or a character with a peculiar voice. He had no one to blame but himself for the latter, since he'd been mimicking the butts of his jokes since he was a small boy.

Quickly turned to address the company at large. "All right, you bunch of street buskers . . ." She paused for the laugh. "Back here tomorrow, in costume by noon. Don't forget your wands for the jig."

Half the company moaned at the reminder. Since last summer, Quickly began adding a jig to the end of the tragedies. She said it was to give people a lift after all the death and despair. Sivana joked that it was to scare the audience out of the playhouse so the players had a fair chance to get a seat at the alehouses before the places were filled. Tal liked the absurdity of showing the dead princes and queens dancing merrily after their death scenes, shaking their skull-topped wands for the audience. It was a reminder that nothing was real on the stage.

"Hey!" called a voice from the first balcony. Chaney hoisted a pair of leather tankards and set them on the railing. "I brought you something from the ale cart."

Tal scrambled up a beam to the middle gallery. He was nowhere as nimble as Lommy, but he was becoming quite the climber thanks to all the time he spent helping Quickly repair the thatched roof after the winter storms. It gave him a workout as well as an excuse to avoid the tallhouse, where Thamalon had been sending him messages. Tal refused to read them. He was still angry about Thamalon's lecture about Larajin.

"Thanks," he said to Chaney, taking the tankard and draining it in one long draught.

"Nice one! I thought you were taking it easier these days."

"Special occasion," said Tal, wiping the foam from his upper lip.

"So I see. You were pretty good up there, but I did worry you'd go right through that floor."

"That's ridiculous. It's an excellent floor. I reinforced it myself only last month."

"Well, there was that business with the sword, too."

"Nobody was hurt."

"And it might have helped if you'd remembered your lines."

"All right," sighed Tal. "That part *was* a problem."

"Want another drink? I think I've got a few fivestars left."

"No, thanks. Let's get out of here."

As they rose to leave, Chaney spotted someone on the far side of the gallery. "What's she doing here?"

Tal followed Chaney's gaze until it came to Feena, sitting alone in the gentlemen's gallery. She wore a simple blue dress over a cream blouse, without the night-blue cloak she usually wore. Someone had embroidered the dress with bright green and yellow leaf patterns, and Tal wondered whether Feena had done the work herself.

Despite the efforts, she still looked like a country girl, but more like one visiting the city to see the sights. Tal almost expected her to dart away, as she did when she first began spying on him last winter. Instead, she walked up to the railing dividing the gentleman's gallery from the common seats.

Tal considered whether he should just walk away. He was in no mood for her arrogant preaching, even though she and Maleva had saved his life twice. Still, his feelings toward the clergy of Selûne had mellowed since his meeting with Dhauna Myritar, and he was curious why Feena had returned. He met her at the rail.

"Well met," he said, hoping the common greeting would hold true this time.

"Well again," she said, glancing at his face only briefly before casting her eyes down at the rail. She did not seem shy so much as uncomfortable, and Tal was pleased to know he wasn't alone in that. "Sorry you didn't get the part you wanted."

Her reminder of his failure annoyed him, especially since he found it hard to believe she was truly sympathetic. "It's good not to get everything you want," he said. "We spoiled rich children have trouble with that."

"I didn't say a thing!" said Feena. She turned to Chaney for corroboration. "Did I say a thing?"

"She didn't say a thing. I'm pretty sure she didn't."

Tal took another of the deep breaths that were becoming the punctuation marks of his life. As he let it out, he said, "You're right. I'm sorry. I must be a little more disappointed about the audition than I thought."

"That's no reason to be sarcastic."

"No," he agreed. "It's no reason at all."

"All right, then," she said.

"All right."

"This could be a long conversation," observed Chaney, "if the two of you keep repeating each other."

They both turned to glare at him.

"Of course, I could help by butting out, couldn't I?"

"Are you hungry?" asked Tal. "Care to join us for dinner?"

Feena shook her head and opened her mouth to decline, but then she changed her mind. Perhaps it was as difficult for her to be civil as it was for Tal. "Yes, please. I would like that."

They made an unusual spectacle as they strolled west down Sarn Street, two of Selgaunt's most eligible bachelors on either side of an uncultured young woman who might have fallen off a milk wagon. Tal wore Perivel's sword at his side, and even Chaney went armed with a slender blade. After the fight on the High Bridge, they were both more careful not to travel alone. Going armed made them look like bravos, especially when they swaggered down the streets in mockery of their more popular peers.

After a whispering group of Soargyl girls sniggered at them as they passed by, Chaney gallantly offered Feena his arm. He was always quick to defy the mores of his class. Feena looked at his crooked arm and shook her head. Chaney looked hurt, and Tal could tell his reaction wasn't just in jest.

"I thought you and Maleva had gone home," he said to her.

"We did," she replied. "Mother wanted to see whether there was any sign of Rusk near the wood. Besides, the people there count on her for help."

"Was there?" asked Tal. When Feena looked at him blankly, he added, "Any sign of Rusk."

"No," said Feena. "Not for certain, at least. His pack still roams the forest, but one of the other nightwalkers might be leading them."

"Are they all nightwalkers?"

"Yes, but Rusk also leads a wider congregation on festival days. Even the good folk are afraid to turn him out of their villages at festival."

"I don't understand that," said Chaney. He crooked his fingers above his head and capered like a goblin. " 'I'm the great bloody monster of an animal god, here to devour your children. Please come to my ceremony, and don't be stingy at the offering box.' "

"You have no idea what you're talking about," said Feena.

"No," agreed Chaney, "you're right. I might be ignorant in the ways of rural beast gods, but it seems ludicrous to invite some barking madman into town when you know his people turn into wolves and eat folk."

"That's not all they do," said Feena. "They're hunters, and they don't prey on the villagers."

"Why are you defending them?" asked Tal.

"I'm not defending them," said Feena. "I'm explaining why the people pay their respects to their god. You live in a port city. Don't your sailors pray to Umberlee?"

"Sure," said Chaney. "They pay tribute so the Sea Queen doesn't sink their ships."

"Ye-es?" drawled Feena, encouraging Chaney to make the connection.

"They're warding off evil," said Tal. "Like paying off bandits to leave your caravans alone."

"Ha! You sound like Thamalon when you put it that way," said Chaney.

"You take that back!" said Tal, capturing his friend in a headlock. They wrestled in mock combat for a moment before realizing that Feena was staring at them impatiently.

"How old are you two?"

"I'm one-and-twenty," said Chaney, squirming out of Tal's hold. "This big lout's the baby, though you wouldn't think it to look at him."

"You're both behaving like ten-year-old boys."

"We were just having a bit of fun," said Chaney. "You could stand to have a little fun yourself. In a few years, they'll be calling you an old maid."

Tal winced at Chaney's crass remark. Feena was probably still a few years shy of thirty, but she was in no danger of appearing past her prime. True, her round hips and unrestrained breasts were not noble Selgaunt's feminine ideal, but Tal doubted she cared about city ideals.

"I'm not here for fun," she said, turning her back on Chaney and stabbing a finger at Tal. "I'm here to look after you."

"I don't need looking after."

"Besides, that's my job," said Chaney, puffing out his chest. "I watch his back."

Feena snorted derisively. "Why do I have the feeling you're the one who gets him into trouble?"

"Hey!" protested Chaney.

"Hm," observed Tal. Remembrance of the attack on the High Bridge darkened his thoughts, but he was too pleased that Feena had turned her sharp tongue back on Chaney to dwell on it. "She's more perceptive than she looks."

"Hey!"

"Let me guess," said Tal, voicing a thought he had been considering since the moment of Feena's return. "You're the one Dhauna Myritar sent to help me."

Feena lifted her chin. "That's right," she said, "and she also told me you promised to cooperate."

Tal laughed. "We'll see about that," he said. "Now come on. Here's the place."

He nodded at a small shop whose sign depicted a pie through which poked the heads of three singing blackbirds, and through its door came the savory odor of chicken pies. They went inside and found a vacant table, where the proprietor took their orders and left them with a steaming pot of the hot black tea Sembians favored.

"Mother says she's sure Rusk is alive," said Feena. She poured for Chaney and Tal before filling her own cup.

"How does she know?" asked Tal.

"I don't know," Feena answered. "Sometimes she just knows things, and it does no good to ask how."

She looked down at the table, and Tal realized she must be as frustrated with her mother as he had been with Chaney.

"If that ambulatory carpet comes back here," said Chaney brightly, "Tal's going to lop off his other arm." The table rocked as Tal kicked him in the shins. "*Ow!* Well, you said so yourself, didn't you?"

"You were lucky last time," said Feena, fixing Tal's eyes with her own. "You realize that, don't you?"

"Maybe," said Tal.

Feena's face flushed as she raised a finger to berate him.

"Yes, I was lucky," Tal added before she could speak. "I know, but I also didn't know he was coming. Now I'm better prepared."

"With what? That great ridiculous beam you call a sword? Rusk can stop you with a word. The only reason he didn't do it last time was because he was seducing you."

"*Seducing* me?" said Tal, grimacing at the word. "He didn't even buy me dinner."

"Can you be serious for once and listen to what I'm telling you?"

"We're quarreling again, aren't we?" said Chaney. "You two should just rent a room and get it out of your systems." He pushed back from the table before Tal could land another kick.

"All I'm saying is that you need a plan if you want to be ready for Rusk." Feena tossed back her tea and slammed the ceramic cup on the table. Tal refilled it.

"Wait a moment," said Tal. "Rusk hasn't gone back to his lair, right?"

"Right, as far as we can tell."

"So where in the Nine Hells has he been hiding all this time?"

"Perhaps somewhere in Selgaunt," suggested Feena.

"He's not exactly inconspicuous," said Chaney. "He'd have to have someplace to hide for those two or three months."

"Somehow, I don't see Rusk spending that time at an inn," said Tal. "He must have friends in the city. What do you think, Feena?"

She thought for a moment before answering. "It's possible," she said. "Rusk is older than he looks. Mother said he roamed all over Sembia when he was young."

"If he was interested in you the whole time," said Chaney, "then it all started with that hunting trip. Whose idea was that?"

"I don't remember," said Tal. "One of the Soargyls, maybe."

"Wasn't it Alale who actually invited you?"

"Maybe," said Tal with a frown. "Dark and empty! I think it was."

"Why don't you ask him?" said Feena. "Maybe he has some connection to Rusk."

"He does," said Tal. "Or rather, he did. He's the one Rusk killed in my tallhouse last winter."

Tal's appetite vanished as he remembered waking up to find the man's mutilated body in his own bedroom. At first he feared he'd done the killing himself. Later, Feena assured him that she'd seen Rusk commit the murder in an effort to inflame Tal's bloodlust. Tal remembered none of it, for he remained completely unconscious of what occurred while he was in wolf form.

"That means Alale can't have been the one hiding him all this time," said Chaney. "If he has a friend in the city, it's someone else."

"Good thinking," said Feena.

Chaney missed her sarcastic tone and basked in the compliment.

"We can work on figuring out who Rusk's city friends are," said Tal, "but I'm more interested in finding out what he wants with me. Dhauna was very nice, but she didn't tell me anything about that."

" 'Dhauna,' is it?"

"Yes," said Tal. "We hit it off. You could say we're friends."

"She's the high priestess of Selûne!"

Tal smiled over his teacup. "She likes me."

Feena turned away but glanced back at him out of the corner of her eyes. Rather than rise to the bait, she returned to the subject at hand. "Mother will give us a sending if someone spots Rusk."

"Isn't it dangerous for her to stay so close to the pack?"

asked Tal. "Even with two of you there, aren't you horribly outnumbered?"

"She can take care of herself," said Feena. "Selûne grants strong powers against shapechangers."

"They didn't stop Rusk last time," said Tal.

"That wasn't our fault," protested Feena. "He surprised us. It didn't help that you'd locked yourself inside a cage and were no help in the beginning."

"I was only in the cage to keep from hurting—"

"Girls, girls," said Chaney. "You're both pretty."

"You stay out of this," said Feena.

"He'll probably come during a full moon, won't he?" said Tal, pouring more tea.

"Not necessarily," said Feena. "Unlike you, he can change shape whenever he likes. So can most of his pack."

"You're going to teach me how to do that, aren't you?" said Tal.

"Maybe," said Feena. "It all depends on you. Not everyone can manage to ride the moon."

"It won't matter if he just wants to kill you this time," suggested Chaney. "You did cut off his arm, after all. I'd be pissed about that. Wouldn't you, Feena?"

Feena ignored the remark. "Rusk is a proud man. You wounded his pride as much as his body, but I don't think he wants you dead."

"Because he thinks I'm this Black Wolf?"

"Where did you hear that?" demanded Feena. Her voice was tinged with alarm. "Did Rusk say it to you?"

"Actually, I heard it from you," Tal smiled, "when you and Maleva left my tallhouse." When Feena looked perplexed, Tal added, "My hearing has been getting keener. I wasn't trying to spy on you."

Feena frowned. "Never mind the Black Wolf prophecy. It's nothing to do with you anyway."

"It's a prophecy? I thought you said 'heresy.' That's what Dhauna called it."

Feena looked to the heavens in exasperation. "Stop calling her that! It gives me the creeps."

"So tell me about the prophecy."

"It's something Rusk believed. The temple of Selûne declared it heretical back in the Eighth Century."

"Why?"

"Because it *is* heresy. It combines legends from the cult of Malar with philosophical discourses from sages devoted to Selûne. Besides, it's a load of rubbish that's been the cause of no end of trouble since Rusk first heard about it."

"Because Rusk thinks *I'm* the Black Wolf? Or because he thinks he is?"

"It's nothing to do with you *or* Rusk, and it's bollocks anyway!"

The shop owner returned with a platter of steaming pies, setting them before each of his guests before hastening back to the kitchen. He looked glad to escape his bickering patrons.

For a while they ate in silence, blowing on the molten spoonfuls of thick gravy filled with chunks of meat and vegetables before tasting them. Chaney managed to burn his tongue and flapped his hands helplessly until one of the cooks ran to him with a cup of cold water.

Eventually, Tal broke the silence.

"All right, so you don't want to talk about the Black Wolf, whatever that is. How are you planning to help me learn to 'ride the moon'?"

"Is that another country euphemism like 'roll in the hay'?" asked Chaney. Feena flicked a glob of hot gravy at him, and it stuck on his cheek. Chaney wiped it off with his thumb and sucked it clean.

"It means controlling your change, making it happen when you choose. It's hard, and not everyone can do it."

"How do you know how to do it?" said Tal.

"It's something the clerics of Selûne have been teaching for years. It's a discipline, a kind of meditation. It would have been a lot easier if you were one of us, because then you could take the moonfire. It'll be even harder for you, since you have the attention span of a toddler."

"She's got you there," said Chaney. "Master Ferrick was always calling Tal 'unteachable.' "

"I've been doing very well lately, thank you. I've won a challenge almost every meet these past two months. You could've watched me whip Mervyn Elzimmer next time if you hadn't dropped out."

"Too expensive," said Chaney. Before Tal could offer to pay his tuition, Chaney added, "Besides, I'm a lover, not a fighter."

Feena appraised him again, shaking her head in disbelief. When Chaney saw that she was looking down on him, he sat up straight.

"I guess everyone moved up a rank when Malveen quit," said Chaney.

"He didn't quit," said Tal. "Pietro sold Arryn Kessel one of those weird paintings of his and said Radu was just out of town on business."

Like most others in Selgaunt, Tal had little use for the peculiar Pietro Malveen, but he admired Pietro's older brother and hoped one day to challenge him to a match at Ferrick's. First he would have to earn that right, however, and the prospect of testing his skill against that of Ferrick's best student drove him more than any other force to hone his skill.

He had little hope of besting Radu Malveen at the blade, he knew, but Tal consciously tried to imitate the older man's cool grace. Some might consider him aloof, but most of the other students were young and shallow in comparison, a good fifteen years younger than Radu.

"Can you two save the gossip for another time?" said Feena impatiently. "It's not as if I know anything about your little social circles."

"Sorry," said Chaney.

Tal nodded. "All right, when do we begin learning to ride the moon?"

"The next full moon," said Feena. "But there are things I can show you before then. Breathing's the first thing."

"I think he's got that one licked," said Chaney. This time

it was Feena who kicked him under the table. "*Ow!* Between the two of you, I won't have a leg to stand on."

"Actually," said Tal, "Breathing is one of the first things Master Ferrick taught us. Breathing and balance."

"That's good," said Feena. "It's probably similar to what we'll be doing."

Chaney opened his mouth to make another jest, but one dire glance from Feena shut it again.

"What are the two halves of balance?" asked Feena.

"The red and the white," said Tal. "Aggression and passivity, anger and calm, force and acceptance."

Feena looked impressed. "Then you understand that Malar is the red, Selûne the white."

"Motion and stillness," said Tal, nodding.

"Good and evil," offered Chaney.

"No," said Feena and Tal at once.

"Malar *is* evil," corrected Feena. "That is, evil in the sense that we understand it. His followers are cruel and often wicked. But for what we're discussing, it's not a question of good or evil. It's the light and the darkness, the moon and the shadow."

"And you want both of them inside of you," said Tal. "Right?"

Feena nodded, not in response to his question but in silent appraisal of all he had said. "I think this just might work," she said.

"I hope so," said Tal, "because otherwise I'm going to have to charge you for the room and board."

CHAPTER 9

THE HIGH HUNT

Greengrass, 1371 DR

They reached Rusk's lair the next morning. There was no sign of the lodge at first. Instead, Darrow saw thirteen colossal stone fangs curving inward to form a wide circle among the trees. Most of the fangs were twice the height of a man, but three had broken off at various points. On all of them were carvings of wolves, wildcats, boars, and other predators— including spear-wielding human hunters.

At the center of the ring was a ragged pit filled with cinders and bone fragments. Beside the fire was a low stone altar, its scarred face stained with blood. All around its edge was carved the symbol of Malar: a ragged claw. At its base were scattered weathered skulls of every sort of prey, including humans and elves.

They had walked around the lodge without noticing it, leading their horses along an old, worn path. It had been built in the side of a low hill in the Arch Wood, reinforced with stones and timbers, and covered with a sod roof, now overgrown with thistles and a few young trees. The only sign of its location was its entrance, a heavy leather flap painted with images of men and wolves hunting stags through a great forest.

The hunters left Balin's carcass near one of the great stone fangs and retired to their lodge to sleep away the daylight. Darrow noticed that some of them had never transformed into humans and wondered whether they were true wolves. They were much larger than the animals he'd seen testing the borders of his father's farm. Dire wolves, they called such beasts. One alone could take down a steer, while a pack could destroy a herd.

Radu chose a place for his tent and left Darrow to set camp while he searched for a nearby stream. Before he finished his work, Darrow spied an intruder. An old man emerged from the forest bearing a bundle of twigs under his arm and a crude rake over his shoulder. When he spotted Darrow, he nodded affably but did not approach. Instead, he set the twigs near the fire pit and began clearing the winter's detritus from the circle.

Radu returned from his ablutions and retired to his tent without a glance at the old man. Curious about the newcomer but too tired to pester him, Darrow followed his master's example and slept at the foot of the tent.

He awoke hours later to the sound of more new arrivals. Foresters and hunters, farmers from the edge of the Arch Wood or the outskirts of Highmoon, and far travelers who arrived wearing backpacks and an inch of road dust—they trickled in throughout the day to make camp around the lodge. Some set up fires and cooked dumplings or cakes to trade with other visitors. Others brought hares to roast or hedgehogs to bake in the banked coals. A minstrel strummed the yartar while her companion chanted the chronicle of Yarmilla the Huntress. Someone produced a small keg of ale and three wooden tankards, which the people passed from hand to hand.

As the sun descended behind the trees, the hunters emerged from the lodge to greet the visitors as the dire wolves padded around the edges, sniffing at them. The hunters clasped arms with the visitors, but Darrow saw that the newcomers held the hunters in high regard. After the friendly greetings, most of the hunters slipped into the woods singly or in pairs or trios. The rest remained to listen to news of births and deaths and the hardships of the past winter.

Darrow guessed that Radu was inside the lodge, so he went for a look. Before he could peer inside, a big bearded man came out and shoved him away from the door. Darrow stepped aside to let him pass, but the man pushed him again, forcing him onto the ground.

The man stepped close to loom over Darrow. He smelled of animal musk and wood smoke. He wore only leather breeches, and his bare feet were dirty and heavily callused. Dark red hair covered his body so thickly that it formed tufts on his forearms.

Darrow kept his eyes on the ground. The aggressor sniffed, spat on the ground near Darrow's hand, then kicked some dirt on him before walking away. Darrow heard laughter but did not look up.

Instead, he got up and slapped the dust from his trousers. Suddenly he realized the white elf was standing just behind him. She had clothed herself in fringed leather breeches and a beaded vest that did little to conceal her supple body.

"Welcome to the lodge," she said. Her tone held just enough irony that Darrow couldn't tell whether she was mocking him or sympathizing. "Looking for your master?"

"Yes." Darrow glanced once more inside the open lodge door, then strolled away. He felt the eyes of the nightwalkers and their pilgrims upon him as he walked with Sorcia.

"They've been talking all afternoon," Sorcia said. "What little I overheard was . . . intriguing."

Darrow shrugged, unwilling to discuss his master's business with a stranger. Sorcia's blue eyes sought his own, and he looked back with what he hoped was confidence rather than defiance. She had tied back her white hair with a leather thong, and Darrow saw that her flesh was not completely white after all. Her long, tapering ears were faintly pink, as was the translucent flesh of her wide eyelids. Faint blue veins showed through her skin at her throat and between her white breasts.

"Is it frightening to be outside your pen?" she asked, arching a pale eyebrow.

Darrow ignored the bait. "Who are all these people?" he asked, indicating the newcomers.

"They are the Huntmaster's followers," said Sorcia, "pilgrims for the High Hunt. We hunt for them in winter, so they pay homage to the Lord of the Hunt each season."

"So they aren't . . ." Darrow struggled to find the polite word.

"They are not People of the Black Blood. They are not nightwalkers," said Sorcia, "but they are as loyal to Rusk as any of us."

Darrow raised an eyebrow but didn't ask the next obvious question. Sorcia saw it in his face and answered anyway.

"Strength breeds loyalty," she said, "and strength must be tested." She looked into Darrow's face. "That's one of the first lessons Rusk teaches his followers, whether they are mere followers or People."

"Is that why Balin took over?"

"He was the strongest in Rusk's absence. Even before then, Balin was restless. It was only a matter of time before he tried again."

"You make it sound as though this happens all the time."

"Rusk has been Bloodmaster for longer than most nightwalkers live. It is only natural that the younger wolves would try their strength against his."

"It's a wonder there is anyone left to follow," said Darrow.

"He doesn't kill every challenger," said Sorcia, "only those who won't submit when he proves his strength. You know how to submit, I see."

Darrow frowned at her but did not comment. Instead, he stole a glance at the nightwalker who had bullied him. The man was drinking a cup of ale while listening to a few of the visitors.

"Ronan likes to test newcomers," said Sorcia. "He almost beat Rusk last summer."

"But Rusk spared him?"

"Even the strong must submit to greater strength," said Sorcia. "Rusk smiles on those who want to test their strength. Ronan is likely to become his favorite now that Balin is dead."

"I had the impression you were his favorite," said Darrow. He expected a blush or at least a scolding glance, but Sorcia was nonplussed by his suggestion.

Sorcia walked around him once, slowly. Darrow felt the hairs on the back of his neck rise as she came back to face him, smiling up into his face. She said nothing.

"Rusk must spend all of his time watching his back," Darrow concluded.

"The pack is only as strong as its chief. Is it not the same in the city?"

Darrow reflected on the backstabbing politics of the Old Chauncel, which he couldn't even pretend to fathom. Just hearing one of Stannis's tales of subversions, bluffs, and betrayals with such intangible weapons as import taxes and trade concessions was enough to make him dizzy. The disease of cutthroat rivalry was not limited to the merchant class in Selgaunt. Even the other guardsmen he knew were always competing with each other and their superiors for advancement and recognition. He could not disagree with Sorcia's assertion that the city and the wild were both dangerous and uncertain places.

"At least in the city there are laws," said Darrow. "The powerful can't do anything they want."

"Can't they?" laughed Sorcia. "The laws are just another kind of power. We know something of them here, too. Rusk's power comes from Malar as well as himself. The People might follow him just for his strength, but the pilgrims come because Rusk speaks the law of the wild."

"Isn't that just another kind of strength?" said Darrow. "The kind all clerics have over their followers?"

"Indeed," said Sorcia. "There are many kinds of strength. In the city or the wild, strength is the only law. All must bow before strength."

Within an hour, the first hunters returned with their prey. Karnek carried a lean buck over his shoulders, while Brigid strutted beside him. When Karnek lay the deer upon the ground for all to see, the sight of the clean kill earned them praise.

"You are truly a child of Malar, sister wolf," said the old man who had been gathering firewood earlier. Brigid nipped at his ear, evoking a chorus of hoots from pilgrims and night-walkers alike.

Wanting to appear useful, Darrow helped gut and skin the carcass and set it on a fresh spit. Soon the smell of roast venison filled the air, summoning the remaining hunters from their lodge. Radu appeared last, with orders for Darrow to break camp and pack the horses.

"Are we leaving before the feast?" asked Darrow.

"No," said Radu. His tone invited no further inquiry.

As Darrow finished with the horses, Rusk emerged from the lodge to walk among his people and their followers. He wore the skull of an enormous owlbear upon his head, the creature's glossy pelt spilling across the big man's shoulders to drag upon the ground. The beast's clawed hands were tied across Rusk's chest, concealing his missing left arm.

The Huntmaster's arrival was the signal for all to gather within the fanged temple. Darrow followed but stopped just outside the ring of stones, unsure whether he was welcome inside. He saw Radu standing on the other side, leaning casually against one of the giant gray fangs.

Rusk took his place between the altar and the blazing bonfire. Some of the pilgrims produced hand drums. Without prompting, they began to beat a simple rhythm. The sound chased the sparrows from the nearby trees and echoed off the great stone fangs.

Sorcia danced around the fire, her pale limbs licking the air like flames. As she circled the bonfire, the rhythm increased to a fluttering heartbeat. Sorcia danced faster, her lithe body whipping the others into a frenzy of cheers and howls.

Ronan joined in on the other side of the fire, his own movements quick and aggressive. He stamped the ground with both feet, then darted forward as lightly as the wind. When he caught up with Sorcia, he raked at her with clawed fingers. She flung herself to the ground, the wounded doe. As Ronan raised his hands in triumph, she leaped back to life and stalked around the circle, the hunted becoming the hunter.

The rest of the pack joined the dance one-by-one, until all of the nightwalkers stalked and leaped around the rising bonfire. Some had flung off their clothes, and their naked bodies glistened with sweat in the heat of the fire. All around them, the pilgrims chanted and wailed as the drummers beat an increasingly frantic rhythm.

Darrow's heart pounded with the drums. He felt an urge to run away before the dance was done, but one look at the dire wolves pacing outside the fanged temple put that thought from his mind. He looked for Radu, but his master was gone from his earlier place.

The pilgrims began joining the wild dance, even the old twig-gatherer. Soon there were none left to beat the drums, but the rhythm lived on in the dancers' shrieks and howls. At last, someone pulled Darrow into the dance.

It was easier than he expected. His thumping heart had already taught his feet the rhythm, and an exultant scream flew unbidden from his chest. He pantomimed throwing a spear at a barrel-chested pilgrim, who threw himself to the ground and thrashed like a wounded boar before rolling back up to his feat to stalk his own prey.

How long they danced, Darrow could not say. It stopped abruptly, as a deafening howl rose among the dancers. Rusk stood atop the altar by the fire, his head thrown back as he pointed. All heads turned to see the first horn of the crescent moon rising above the black horizon. The dancers added their voices to the Huntmaster's, heralding the moon's arrival. They howled for long minutes, until at last Rusk lowered his pointing arm.

"We welcome the moon, which lights the path," he chanted.

Pilgrim and hunter alike repeated the invocation, as did Darrow. His voice was hoarse from howling, but he had never felt so free and natural. When Rusk raised his hand again, everyone sat on the ground to receive his benediction.

"Give thanks to the Great Black Wolf, who chases the moon across the sky," chanted Rusk. "Let him fill our limbs with strength."

"We hunt for our strength," replied the congregation.

"Give thanks to the creatures of the wild, for the meat they yield to the skillful hunter. Let them nourish our bodies."

"We hunt for our nourishment."

The prayer was long and repetitive, so Darrow could join in and say the words with the rest of the worshipers. At last, Rusk welcomed the newcomers to the Lodge. He promised that the People of the Black Blood would continue to feed them in times of famine, so long as they kept faith with Malar, the Black Wolf, Master of the Hunt.

After the prayers, the congregation fell silent to listen to their Huntmaster. Darrow heard only the crackling of the bonfire and the susurrus of the wind until Rusk filled the temple with his powerful voice.

"Tonight, as spring gives way to summer, we celebrate the High Hunt," said Rusk. He put his hand on something concealed beneath his cloak. "This year's Greengrass feast is most auspicious, for with it comes the result of my own long hunt. The Black Wolf Scrolls are returned to their rightful place!"

Rusk lifted a bone scroll case above his head for all to see. It was carved from the femur of some enormous beast and capped at each end with golden images, one a leopard, the other a wolf. In the firelight, its surface wriggled with glyphs and carvings.

After a moment of stunned silence, the congregation whooped and howled.

"Now the unsullied words of the hunter-prophets shall be revealed to me, and I shall master the forgotten wisdom of our forebears and teach it all to you, my hunters, my followers, my pack!"

The cheering grew deafening, and Darrow wished he understood what it meant. He thought the Malveens refused to give Rusk the scrolls and wondered why they had changed their minds. If the scrolls were false, he prayed silently that he would be far away by the time Rusk discovered the forgery.

"What better way to celebrate this momentous event than with a High Hunt?" thundered Rusk. Still excited by his proclamation, the crowd quieted just enough to hear his words. He spoke again, half-chanting the words, "Who shall hunt our prey?"

"We will!"

All of the People of the Black Blood rose to their feet, as did a few young men and women among the pilgrims. Those who still wore clothing flung it away. Half of them stretched and bent, their limbs twisting and reshaping themselves. Thick fur sprung from their flesh, until a dozen wolves hunkered among the seated pilgrims.

"You are the foremost, the natural hunters," called Rusk. "Lead the way for those who have yet to master their skills."

Rusk barked out a string of ancient words, an infernal invocation to Malar. His eyes blazed red, and flames leaped from the bonfire to enshroud him in ruddy light. With a violent gesture, he flung the magical energy toward the People who remained in human form.

They screamed as the red power entered their ears and mouths. Their bodies jerked and transformed until they, too, stood as wolves among the pilgrims.

Only four pilgrims remained standing. At a nod from Rusk, other pack members handed them long spears.

"I see a mighty host of hunters before me," called Rusk. "What prey is fit and worthy of their prowess?"

"A great boar," called a woman among the pilgrims, "with his long tusks and strong shoulders." The rhythm of her words told Darrow that the response was canon.

"No," said Rusk. "These hunters are stronger, and their teeth sharper."

"A stag," called a man, "with his great horns and swift legs."

"My hunters are swifter still. You must choose better."

"The owlbears, with their sharp beaks and talons."

"The claws of my hunters are more keen. Is there no prey worthy of my hunters?"

"A man," called Radu from outside the circle, "with his weapons and his wits."

Darrow turned to see his master already mounted, the lead to his own horse secured to his saddle. Then he realized what Radu had been discussing with Rusk when he saw his own horse tethered to Radu's saddle. Without Stannis present to object, Radu had finally disposed of him.

"That prey is fit and worthy of my hunters," responded Rusk. He turned his eyes to Darrow, and the entire congregation rose to form their own circle among the stone teeth, blocking his escape.

"The prey may take whatever weapons he desires," declared Rusk. He pointed directly up. "The hunt begins when the moon touches the highest vault of heaven. It ends when the land has swallowed her up again."

"Wait!" cried Darrow. He realized his words were useless, but he could not stop himself. "I'm not worthy of your Hunt, but he's the greatest swordsman in Selgaunt." He pointed at Radu, then immediately dropped his hand as their eyes met. He was desperate indeed to draw the ire of Radu Malveen.

"The prey has been chosen," declared Rusk.

"No," called a deep voice from the congregation.

A man with a big, solid belly stood forth, his muscles round and hard as stones. The silver in his black hair and beard marked him as a veteran, if not one of Rusk's generation. Darrow saw that his objection carried weight among the other pack members.

"The lamb is right, Rusk. The other city man is far worthier prey than this cringing whelp. Show us that your city dealings are truly over."

Among the pack rumbled murmurs of assent.

Ronan stepped forth from the pack. "Bloodmaster, your return brings us great joy. It is an occasion deserving of great honor and sport. Listen to Gorland. Let the hunt be of worthier prey."

Rusk looked down at Ronan, then back toward Gorland who had first spoken. "Is this how you honor my return?"

Neither of the men replied, but the crowd stirred restlessly, watching for any sign of weakness. Darrow realized that they could easily turn on Rusk.

"If you prefer to hunt that man," he said to Gorland, "then bring him before me."

The big man smiled and nodded to the Huntmaster. He had the look of a man who knew he'd just won much respect among his fellows. The smile remained as he walked over toward Radu.

The swordsman removed his gloves as he watched Gorland approach. He wore the expression of a man tired of waiting for his driver to open the carriage door.

Gorland raised his arm to take Radu by the shoulder. To Darrow's eyes, Radu merely stepped backward while flicking one hand toward the big fellow. Everyone heard the rasp of steel, once as it left the scabbard, then again as it returned. The sounds were so close together as to seem like one prolonged sigh.

"Ah!" said Gorland.

He stopped and stood still, his arm still raised to grasp a shoulder that had suddenly moved six feet away. He shook his head as though perplexed or stunned, then clutched at his face. His hands came away slick with blood. Twin torrents descended from his ruined eye sockets, filling his gaping mouth.

The horses stood calmly by, unaware of the violence so close to them.

"Does anyone else question my selection?" From the advantage of the stone altar, Rusk looked over his followers. His gaze lingered on Ronan, who lowered his face and stepped back. When he was satisfied of no further challenges, Rusk called out to Radu. "Go, now."

He watched Radu Malveen ride slowly out of the firelight and into the dark forest. Then he leaped from the altar and strode over to Darrow.

"Give us a good hunt," Rusk said. "Elude us until dawn, and all honor is yours. You may ask any boon, and it shall be granted."

"But if you catch me?" asked Darrow. He tried to compose a brave face before the assemblage of hunters, but fear cracked his voice.

"Then we will honor you another way," said Rusk with a toothy smile.

CHAPTER 10

RIDING THE MOON

Kythorn, 1371 DR

Tal sat cross-legged in his cage. The cool basement air raised goosebumps on his flesh, for he wore only a kilt borrowed from the playhouse wardrobe. It was loose enough to fall away when his hips grew long and narrow, but for now it provided a slight modesty. His hands lay open upon his thighs, and his head drooped slightly as he held his eyes closed and listened.

"Now lean back and float. Let the water hold you up. You can still hear the surf as the waves gently carry you deeper."

Feena sat on a stool near the cage. He had asked her to stay farther back, but she had ignored his request. Whatever else she might be, the cleric was not afraid of him in any form.

Tal tried to let his mind drift with the imaginary currents. Feena had decided that water was the best focus for him after listening to his descriptions of his previous transformations.

"The sea is a reflection of the moon," she explained, "moving with Selûne's own passage, just as you do, just as everyone does."

"Every nightwalker, you mean."

"No, every living creature responds to the moon in some way. Men are simply less sensitive to her passing. That makes it harder for you to learn to ride the moon."

Tal began to object, but then he realized the truth of what she was saying.

"Is that why most clerics of Selûne are women?" he asked.

"Part of the reason," Feena answered, nodding. "It's easier for a woman to learn how to ride the moon. For you, who haven't felt the passage of the moon all your life, it helps to think of something like the tide. Imagine yourself as part of the sea, ebbing and flowing with the moon."

And so he tried exactly that as he and Feena sat in the basement of his tallhouse, but he found it far harder than he had expected. Troubling thoughts continued to intrude on his meditation. Some of them were the lingering suspicions he harbored about Feena's motives for helping him, and Dhauna Myritar's for sending her to Selgaunt when she and Maleva lived so far away. It made sense to send someone who had fought against nightwalkers for so long, but he suspected the greater appeal was the opportunity to study one closely.

The thought made him feel paranoid and ungrateful at the same time, but it was hard to set aside his doubts.

Even worse were his concerns about Chaney, who had had become increasingly scarce since the journey to Moonshadow Hall and Feena's subsequent return to Selgaunt. Feena joked that he was jealous that Tal had given her the guest room that Chaney had occupied so frequently before. Tal suspected the truth involved Chaney's criminal associates. He no longer deluded himself into thinking that his friend's problems were confined to a gentleman's wager or a social dispute. Somehow he had gotten himself into real trouble with Selgaunt's underworld, and Tal's interference had only made things worse. Finally, Tal's persistent questions had driven off his only close friend.

"You aren't focusing," said Feena. "You'll drown if you let yourself become distracted."

"Drowning" was the word Tal used to explain the helpless sensation he felt the first several times he underwent the change. It was an apt description, agreed Feena, but the trick was not to resist the sensation of an intruding force. It was the draw of the moon, and it was as much a lure as an invasion. Those who let it pull them only so far from their own minds could establish equilibrium. They could remain conscious during the transformation and afterward, and with training retain control of their animal selves.

"When the waves wash over you, don't struggle. The goal is not to swim but to float. Try not to listen to my words, just hear them and imagine floating on the sea. Think of the vast, dark water gently rocking you."

With an effort not to make an effort, Tal finally relaxed enough to hear her words without thinking about them. It was a state of mind he reached only while fencing, when for brief moments he could obey Master Ferrick's instructions without knowing he'd heard them. Soon Feena's words dissolved into the images he had practiced forming.

He felt himself floating in warm water, the tide gently tugging him first away from and toward a shore he could sense but not see. Each wave that pulled him farther from land was stronger than the one that pushed him back, and each time he felt slightly farther from his surroundings, even his own body.

Gradually he floated out to sea, the distant shush of the surf growing fainter as he went. The waves grew stronger, raising him high before dropping him back below the surface. He tried to remain calm as he rose back to the surface, but he felt smothered and restrained. A sharp pain twisted his back. He gasped for air but felt no relief.

Opening his eyes, he saw only a dim yellow light on the other side of the bars. A human voice spoke to him from beyond the lamp, but he could not understand its words. Standing, he felt the clothing fall away from his transformed body, rough straw and hard iron bars beneath his paws. A hundred strange smells competed for his attention. They were all familiar, but he could not think of their names. One in particular called to him, a musky odor similar to the smell of his own body but far more alluring.

"Tal," said the voice.

It was a sound he should recognize, he thought briefly, but he was more interested in the scent. He moved toward it and found the bars. He was too big to press between them, so he turned to find another path. He turned and turned again, finding nothing but the narrow spaces.

The other animal kept speaking, low and urgent. He felt the sounds should mean something, but they were unimportant. It was the borders that vexed him. He could not stay trapped. He *would* not stay trapped.

He called out for help, and a voice answered. It told him to stay, to remain calm, but it was not trapped as he was, and it would not help him.

He forced his head between the bars and pushed. They would not yield. He leaped up upon them, shouting to frighten them away. They did not run. Instead, the blood roared in his ears, and a red cloud filled his eyes. Rather than blind him, it gave him the hunter's sight—he could sense every movement in the room, despite the bright spot of light.

The other animal was out there, and it was keeping him confined. He wanted to get at it, to tear and bite at it, to kill it for holding him here.

Again and again he threw himself against the barrier, raging and howling in the darkness.

"Halt!"

Tal remained utterly still as Master Ferrick strolled among the four ranks of students. At just over five and a half feet, he was shorter than his reputation led most to believe, though his hawkish nose and imperial gaze gave him an air of authority. More than sixty years had left their trails across his tanned face, but his compact body was that of a man half as old. He moved with a quiet grace, never hurrying.

When he first joined the school eight years earlier, Tal found these slow, deliberate inspections excruciating. His twelve-year-old arms could not hold even a foil steady for so long, and he dreaded attracting Ferrick's attention. Fortunately, he had earned Ferrick's correction only rarely in recent months. The man's keen eyes spied every imperfection, and he noted them in terse syllables as he passed each offender.

"Overextended," he told one student. "Grip," he said to another.

Silence as he passed was all the approval he was likely to give. Tal accepted his gratefully, keeping his eyes on his imaginary opponent as Ferrick passed. The instructor completed his inspection and stood beside Radu Malveen. Even in his peripheral vision, Tal detected Ferrick's faint nod. The instructor's foremost student was the only one worthy of acknowledgement. Despite frequent absences, Radu retained the mantle of first student. He had never lost a challenge.

It was no longer a secret that Tal wanted to change that standing.

Ferrick snapped out another string of commands.

"Return. Cross left. Advance. Retreat. Half advance! Cut four! Parry eight! Recover!"

The words never formed completely in Tal's brain. Instead, his body moved before he could think, but always in the right direction. Action without thought was one of the best things about fencing drills, and he had become much better at it since Feena's arrival. Learning to ride the moon was a difficult and often disturbing process, for each morning after he remembered more and more what it was like to have been a wolf. The rage he felt at confinement was frightening, but he knew it meant he was gradually asserting his own will over the wolf's mind.

Sword drills had become Tal's greatest pleasure. He was beginning to spend as much time at Ferrick's studio in the Warehouse District as he did at the Wide Realms, though it was in the playhouse that he choreographed endless fight scenes in anticipation that Quickly would put them in one of her plays. His creations were equal parts fighting and fancy, and his fellow students would surely sneer to see them.

While he did not share the scrupulous ideals of his fellows, Tal tried to ensure that the stage fencing was as plausible as possible. Sometimes he went too far, and Quickly chided him for making it so realistic that it was boring to watch. What was exciting to do, he realized, was not always exciting to show.

The students who had seen his performances at the Wide Realms used to scoff at Tal's showy technique, but fewer were scoffing lately. Since the month of Ches Tal had challenged his way out of the middle ranks and into fourth place among Ferrick's students. His three-month rise won him both admirers and rivals, and he reveled in the praise and scorn alike. In truth, he had never much liked most of his peers. Like his brother, Tamlin, most young nobles were more concerned with fashion and gossip than skill at arms.

One of the few exceptions was Radu Malveen. He rarely spoke to the other students, a reticence usually attributed to his family's questionable past. Tal thought of him as self-sufficient rather than haughty, though he sympathized with the family history.

The Malveens were still on the recovery after their involvement with pirates cost them the head of the household, Velanna Malveen, as well as her eldest son. A similar catastrophe would have obliterated House Uskevren but for Thamalon's tireless efforts to restore both the wealth and the reputation of his family. Even so, all of the Uskevren had been subjected to subtle reminders from their peers that theirs was a lineage on which the shadow of villainy still fell.

How much worse would it have been for Radu, had he dared to engage his peers socially. Far better to remain apart from them, thought Tal, who had his own reasons for avoiding his peers.

Tal imagined that he and Radu were similar in other ways. Radu's younger brother was a notorious wastrel, not entirely unlike Tamlin except for his reputation as an eccentric artist. His bizarre paintings were notorious for their unsettling abstractions, which naturally put them in high demand among the art-conscious nobles of Selgaunt. Laskar, the eldest of the Malveen brothers, had a reputation for integrity and fair dealing that rivaled that of Tal's father. Tal imagined that he must be equally insufferable to Radu.

"Armor and masks," commanded Master Ferrick. As his students complied, he clasped his bronzed hands behind his back and gazed out the window toward the bay.

Tal grabbed a pair of towels and tossed one to Radu, who caught it neatly and without acknowledgement.

"Did you have a good journey?" said Tal.

Radu raised an eyebrow.

"You were away on business, I heard," said Tal, hoping to strike up a conversation. "I hope it went well."

Radu pressed the towel to the back of his neck, where his long black hair descended in a simple braid. Tal noticed that Radu perspired very little.

"It is concluded," said Radu.

"Say," ventured Tal, "I've been meaning to thank you for your advice."

Radu raised one eyebrow and awaited an explanation.

"About my fencing," said Tal. "You remember, last winter. I was clowning around with Chaney, and you reminded me of the difference between stage fencing and real fighting."

Radu said nothing while he donned a thin white tunic and his padded armor, but Tal could see that he remembered the conversation. At the time, Radu refused even to practice with him until Tal demonstrated more respect for the dueling circle.

"Well," said Tal, his easy manner faltering in the face of Radu's indifference, "I took it to heart, and it's helped—both here and at the playhouse." He shrugged on his own armor.

"Good," said Radu.

Without invitation, Tal secured the straps on the back of Radu's armor, then turned to receive the same help.

"Who knows?" said Tal. "If I win today, maybe I'll be ready to challenge you in a month or two?"

"Who knows?" said Radu. He made a brief smile, but it never reached his eyes.

Master Ferrick called the students to the circle for the challenges. There were sixteen in this, the most advanced class. While they sometimes drilled with the less experienced fencers, challenges were the exclusive province of those who had proven themselves.

"First challenge," called Ferrick. "Talbot Uskevren and Perron Karn."

Tal stood on the outer ring, while the defender took the center. Perron was Tal's second cousin on his mother's side, a stout man of thirty-four years. His reddish beard curled up on all sides, giving him the appearance of a man caught in a sudden gust of wind.

The swordsmen bowed to Master Ferrick, then saluted each other before donning their masks.

"Begin!"

Both advanced at once, Tal shifting left while Perron cut at his legs. Tal parried and feigned a high thrusting riposte. Perron ignored the bogus attack and cut at Tal's wrist, forcing Tal to open his upper right guard. Perron's blade darted toward Tal's shoulder, but Tal let his knees sag and rapped Perron on the elbow.

"Challenger's point," announced Ferrick.

Perron rubbed his elbow. It had been a smart blow, harder than necessary. Beneath his mask, Tal smiled.

"Mind your control, Talbot," warned Ferrick.

Tal's grin vanished, and his face flushed hot. He already knew he could defeat Perron. What he wanted now was to make the man concede or to win a perfect round, but all he had managed was to earn a rebuke in front of the entire class. Worst of all, he'd done it in front of Radu Malveen, whom he'd wanted to impress.

"Begin!"

Tal's mind had drifted, and he was not prepared for the second pass. Perron's vertical cut forced Tal's blade down against his mask and pressed hard. As Tal pushed back with all his strength, Perron stepped back and executed a perfect horizontal stroke across Tal's padded chest.

"Two points defender," declared Ferrick, holding one finger toward Tal and two toward Perron. A growl rose from Tal's chest, causing Ferrick to give him a questioning glance. Tal set his jaw and took his place, focusing on his opponent.

"Begin!"

Tal rushed forward and beat Perron's weapon aside, then smashed it again as Perron brought it back in line. He made no attempt to move beyond Perron's guard, only to batter it from all directions. At last, Perron saw the flaw in Tal's attack—there was no attempt to guard low. He faded back and slashed at Tal's knees.

Which was exactly what Tal had been expecting.

Tal leaped over the sweeping blade and struck the top of Perron's mask. The blow made a resounding crack.

The other students stifled their laughter, but Tal saw hands fly up to cover smiles. Only Radu and Master Ferrick seemed unimpressed.

Perron was already in position on the middle ring. Tal took his place. Ferrick pointed his fingers, three and two. "Begin!"

Tal expected Perron to be more cautious this time, but the older man surprised him with a quick, feinting advance. Tal parried and retreated, concentrating on defense. Perron persisted with a steady stream of careful thrusts at Tal's wrist and arm. As long as Perron's attacks remained so modest, Tal had to maintain his own defense.

Perron suddenly shifted to a flurry of high cuts. When Tal deflected them and riposted with a thrust, Perron beat

Tal's blade so hard it struck the floor. His own sword nearly found its target before Tal recovered with an awkward full-center parry.

Tal nearly laughed. Perron wasn't a small man, but he couldn't beat Tal in a contest of strength. Still, if that was how he wanted it . . .

Tal met the next attack with his own, lunging forward even as Perron came at him. The wooden blades cracked as they came together. The top foot of Tal's snapped away, and the splintered remainder ran through Perron's guard and into his mask. Tal felt the thick, sickening impact as his shattered blade passed through the wicker bands and into his cousin's face.

Horrified, Tal let go of the blade. It stuck fast through the mask.

Perron fell to his knees and clawed at his mask, but it wouldn't come off. A trickle of blood ran out from under his bib, down the front of his white armor.

Tal reached out to help, but someone got in the way. He couldn't see who it was, because all the faces in the room whirled about more quickly than he could recognize them. An oceanic roaring filled his ears, and he heard distant voices shouting his name and "get away!" Then he felt hands pulling him, and he had no more strength to resist them.

Later, they called it an accident. In the hours after the event, Tal heard Master Ferrick's opinion. He knelt as the swordmaster lectured him for nearly two hours after the others had left. Tal's knees hurt, and his legs turned numb, but he did not complain. He deserved far worse and knew it would come later.

When he was dismissed, Tal bowed one last time to the master, recovered Perivel's sword from where he'd left it in the dressing room, and walked quietly down the stairs for the last time.

It was an hour after noon. The street was hot, and the Warehouse District stank of fish and tar. Tal headed west on Larawkan, stamping his feet to force some feeling back into them. The rhythm of hitting the cobblestones soon became hypnotic as Tal imagined the punishments he had yet to face.

There was no way Thamalon would protect him from whatever just retribution the Karns demanded. Even his mother was unlikely to stand long between him and the righteous anger of her family. Even after paying the temple for healing Perron's mangled face, there was the matter of the eye. Regenerative magic was neither common nor cheap. This would mean the end of Tal's relative freedom in the tall-house. It was just the excuse Thamalon needed to cut off his stipend and force him back to live at Stormweather Towers, where they could keep an eye on him.

Tal noticed that people where scurrying out of his path. He looked back, expecting to see a drover trying to regain control of a panicked ox or perhaps a captive griffin breaking out of its chains on its way to the Hulorn's Palace, but there was nothing frightening back there. The people were avoiding the huge thundering dolt who was muttering to himself.

"Wonderful," he said aloud. "Let's frighten everyone in Selgaunt."

He tried to relax and walk in a way that didn't suggest he was on his way to a murder. Once he even forced a smile at a pair of young women, but they took one look at him and crossed to the other side of the street.

As he turned onto Alaspar Lane, Tal heard a whistle from an ivy-laden trellis. Crouched behind it was Chaney Foxmantle.

"Over here!" hissed Chaney. "Hurry!"

Tal hurried to join his friend, and together they peered around the foliage to look toward Tal's residence.

Standing a block away from the tallhouse were two men in Uskevren livery. Tal did not recognize them, but he was becoming increasingly unfamiliar with the house guard since he visited Stormweather so rarely. They stood a respectable distance from the tallhouse, but their frequent glances left no question about their business. They were waiting for Tal.

"I deduced from their arrival that the Old Owl wanted a word," said Chaney, "and I thought maybe you'd like the option to postpone it."

"You are a gentleman and a scholar," said Tal.

Despite his black mood, he was happy to see Chaney. Only now that they saw each other only a few times a month did he realize how inseparable they had once been.

"Don't forget devilishly handsome and irresistible to women."

"Let's get out of here," said Tal. "I should check in at the Realms."

After Ferrick's blistering lecture, Tal was not ready to hear more of the same from Thamalon. They faded from Alaspar Lane and headed for the anonymity of streets less traveled. Winding their way through lanes and alleys, they eventually came to the Wide Realms Playhouse.

From a distance, the Wide Realms looked like part of a larger structure. It was surrounded by other businesses, including a bath house, a scribner's, and several buildings shared by artisans who could not afford their own establishments. Some of them worked on commission for Quickly, making costumes or props for the players. In return, they were some of the Wide Realms's most frequent customers.

Unlike the opera audiences on the other side of town, the playhouse crowd didn't mind mingling with the common folk. Most of them were laborers and tradesmen, gaining admittance to the grounds for a mere five pennies. For a silver raven, they could sit in one of the galleries, sheltered from the sun. Those willing to part with more silver or even a golden fivestar could sit in the balconies behind the actors or on the stage itself, to be seen by all. Some of the more dissolute young nobles were becoming regular attendees, though they were apt to fall asleep when they weren't heckling the players for the amusement of their companions. Tal's brother, Tamlin, was one of these. Thankfully, he had not yet appeared at one of this season's productions, and Tal was hopeful that his brief interest was now a past fancy.

They walked past the main entrance to find the stage door open. They crossed through the backstage clutter, following the sound of voices from the stage beyond.

"Let me play the prince," cried a muffled voice, "or I'll cut off your other head!"

Waving Chaney back, Tal peered around the corner to see what was happening.

The idiot half of the grotesque ettin's mask rested on Sivana's shoulder, Lommy's slender green legs poking out beneath the neck. On the floor by Sivana's feet was the vicious head, growling up at the heavens. Sivana swung a ridiculously large spiked ball and chain while lurching toward their opponent.

The other actor was obviously Ennis Lurvin, a big man usually cast as a fool or a warrior. He was about Tal's size, so they were often cast as guards to stand on each side of a king's throne or given the same simple part to play alternately. He brandished a glowing sword, the favorite prop of all the actors. Upon command it would light up, burst into flame, or ring with celestial music. It was also kept quite sharp since the previous winter and not to be used recklessly. Tal was not concerned about the sword, however. What attracted his attention was the mask Ennis wore, a fresh creation of papier-mâché that Tal had never seen before.

It was the gigantic head of a savage wolf.

"Grulok not afeared of werewolf of Selgaunt!" yelled Sivana in a deep, silly voice. She stalked forward as Lommy pulled the handle that made the mask's eyes roll and the tongue loll.

Tal could bear no more. He rushed forward and knocked the wolf's head off Ennis. "What in the Nine Hells are you doing?"

Lommy peeked out from the ettin's gaping mouth and peeped in surprise, his tiny voice muffled by the mask. Sivana smiled nonchalantly and lifted the ettin's head off of the tasloi, who scampered up the back wall to disappear into the balcony. "Just goofing off, Tal. We were thinking of doing a children's play next month."

"Who told you?" demanded Tal. "Was it Quickly?"

"Told us what?" said Sivana. Ennis's face had turned from a shocked pale to a deep scarlet. Tal knew Sivana was lying.

"It was supposed to be a secret!" Tal shook the big wolf mask at her.

"It's *still* a secret," said Sivana, abandoning the pretense. "Nobody outside the playhouse knows."

"Nobody inside the playhouse was meant to know, either."

"You told Quickly, Otter, and Lommy, but not the rest of us?"

"I needed the cage, so I had to tell Quickly. Lommy and Otter live here." Tal let out an enormous sigh. "I can't believe she told you."

"Don't blame her," said Sivana. "She let it slip one night. You know how she talks in her sleep."

"I *knew* it!" said Chaney, storming onto the stage. When everyone looked blankly at him, he explained, "You know, the stories about all you players sleeping with all the other players." Still, everyone just stared at him. At last he shrugged. "I felt left out."

"I just haven't gotten to you yet, darling," said Sivana, patting Chaney on the bottom. He brightened at once.

Tal would not let them change the subject. "Quickly had no right to tell you."

"It's not as if we wouldn't have figured it out. You're missing only when the moon is full, and you're *always* missing when the moon is full. There's one coming up soon, isn't there? I can tell, because you're always cranky a few days before."

"You don't know what you're talking about," growled Tal. "I thought you were my friends."

"We *are* your friends," said Ennis. The big man's voice cracked, and he looked near to crying. His childlike fear of confrontation made the other players teasingly call him Quickly's Puppy. "Come on, Tal," he pleaded. "You know you can trust everyone here. We're like family."

Tal choked on his reply.

"Maybe not the best analogy you could have picked," said Chaney, grimacing.

"What are you children carrying on about?" Quickly emerged from one of the trapdoors to the Abyss below the stage. She held a bulging sack in both hands while clamping her pipe between her teeth. "If you've got so much energy, you can help repaint the rest of these masks."

All eyes turned to Quickly, then back to Tal to see how he'd react. He crushed the wolf's head mask in his hands and flung the fragments on the floor at Quickly's feet.

The pipe fell from Quickly's mouth, and she let the sack of masks slip through her hands onto the stage floor. "Tal . . ." she began.

Tal whipped around and stalked off the stage. He had thrown open the back door by the time Chaney caught up with him. He let the little man through before slamming the door behind them.

Chaney took one look at Tal's face and shut his mouth tight. They walked quickly and in silence for several blocks before Tal cooled off enough to speak.

"I might as well go to Stormweather and get it over with."

"You want me to come along?" asked Chaney.

"No, there's no telling how long Thamalon will want to bellow at me this time. Besides, you annoy him."

"Want to meet up later? I'll fetch Feena, and we . . ."

"No!" said Tal. "The day's been bad enough without another lecture."

"What makes you think she'll lecture you? Maybe she can—"

"Dark and empty, I said no!"

"Take it easy, Tal. It's me. I'm just trying to help."

"You can help by leaving me alone," snapped Tal.

"Sure, sure," said Chaney, holding up his hands and retreating. "Whatever you say."

Tal seethed, furious at . . . he didn't know what. Thamalon, Quickly, Rusk, maybe—or himself. By the time he realized he owed Chaney an apology, his friend was gone. After all of the day's reversals, he hoped at least that Chaney would remain his friend.

Tal pinched the bridge of his nose and sighed. Then he turned west and headed to Stormweather alone.

CHAPTER 11

BLACK BLOOD

Summer, 1371 DR

Darrow did not escape the People of the Black Blood. He had run less than five miles from the lodge before the wolves dragged him to the ground. In the panic that seized him upon first seeing his pursuers, he dropped his useless sword and begged for his life. His screams for mercy did nothing to save him from the ripping claws of the werewolves. Nor did his blubbering pleas stop the hungry mouths from feasting on his body. Only as his lifeblood seeped into the soft ground of the Arch Wood did salvation arrive.

It came in the form of a silver wolf.

The three-legged beast chased the other predators from the kill, then sat beside Darrow's dying body and looked down into his face. As Darrow looked up at the big wolf, it shifted back into the form of Rusk, the Huntmaster.

"The Hunt is over," he declared. Then with a chant to Malar, he pressed his burning hands on Darrow's gaping wounds and sealed them. He cast spell after spell, until at last Darrow could breathe.

"Why?" Darrow whispered. "Why did you save me?"

Rusk chuckled deep in his chest. "Because I have use for you."

👁 👁 👁 👁 👁

During his first month among the People of the Black Blood, Darrow was everyone's servant. He fetched wood and water, cleared the fanged circle, and scraped the hides of deer and boars for crude tanning. If someone told him to do a task, he made himself useful.

At night he huddled in a corner of the lodge while most of the pack roamed their territory. A simple smoke hole served as a chimney for the fire pit, which was flanked by two rows of rough-hewn timbers supporting the sod roof. Various pack members had carved their names or marks in the wood over the years. Others with some talent had engraved scenes of humans and wolves hunting together. One depicted a passionate embrace between a dire wolf and a woman. Darrow found the image at once revolting and compelling.

The Huntmaster's inner sanctum was divided from the rest by an old tapestry depicting scenes of wolves and humans hunting and living together as an antlered god held his cloak to form the night sky above them. Even when Rusk was away, Darrow did not dare part the fabric to peer inside.

When the werewolves returned to sleep away the daylight, Darrow went outside to perform his chores alone. He hated the smell of the lodge when the pack was there. The smoke stung his eyes, and the odor of so many dirty bodies reminded him of his father's pigsty. Even as a boy he knew he wanted nothing to do with farm life, and this was far worse. He was living among monsters.

Soon he learned that he had become one of them.

After his first transformation, Darrow was sick for days. He remembered little of what occurred those three nights, but the days were full of exhausted cramps and bloody retching. No one tended to him in his misery, not even Rusk, who had saved his life. He was too afraid to ask questions, and no one offered any answers.

"At least I'm still alive," he told himself. But he did not know why or for how long.

A few days after his change, Rusk answered one of those questions. He led Darrow a short distance from the lodge, where they sat on a grassy knoll.

"Tell me about the Malveens," he said.

Darrow nodded, eager to be useful. "What would you like to know?"

"Everything," said Rusk. "Start with what they want with Talbot Uskevren."

Despite Rusk's interest in Darrow, the other werewolves did not accept him as one of their own. Even as the days grew long and the nights warm, the pack spoke to him when necessary, but never in anything approaching the rough camaraderie they enjoyed among themselves. They were a community unto themselves, albeit a savage one. Among the men and women were a few children. They frightened Darrow more than any others, for they had never known a life apart from the Hunt. How much more monstrous than their parents would they become?

"What do you and Rusk talk about?" asked Sorcia one day.

Rusk had not forbidden him to tell, but Darrow sensed it was best not to reveal too much. "The city," he said.

Sorcia must have detected his reluctance, for she let the subject drop. "Rusk usually leads us throughout the forest this time of year," she said, "but now all he does is talk with you and pore over those scrolls. What's in them, I wonder?"

"I wouldn't know," said Darrow.

That was the truth. Rusk had never shown them to him, and he had never asked about them. Unless Rusk was secretly illiterate, Darrow could not imagine what was taking him so long to finish them. Perhaps they contained spells the Huntmaster could not comprehend, or maybe he did not like what he read in the scrolls.

Sometimes Rusk spent hours watching the night sky through the clearing above the fanged temple. He rose before dusk to observe the long shadows that fell from the teeth, comparing their patterns to drawings in the Black Wolf Scrolls. Whatever he saw there often sent him into a quiet rage. The other People could smell his displeasure and avoided him at those times, and Darrow soon learned to discern the almost imperceptible sourness. Before his transformation, Darrow would never have detected such a faint odor. Now it was almost overpowering, a warning to stay clear of the Huntmaster.

It was increasingly clear that Darrow's submissive behavior had planted him firmly at the bottom of the pack hierarchy. Ronan's bullying the night he was transformed was only a harbinger of the abuses that followed. They pushed past him at the lodge entrance and stared him down around the fire when he dared to speak.

Sometimes Darrow looked up to see Rusk watching him after another member of the pack had cowed him, and he felt ashamed. Other times, Sorcia shook her head as Darrow stepped aside for Ronan or one of the other big nightwalkers.

Despite the hazing, Darrow tried to feel like one of the pack. His routine shifted gradually from day to night, when he would sit around the fire working leather and fur, cutting tough strips for laces, and sewing his own rough clothes. The lodge held communal tools for cutting firewood and repairing the building itself, but the People had few personal belongings.

The exceptions were weapons and mates. Most of the females chose a single male companion, though a few remained independent or concealed their affairs. At first, Darrow assumed that Sorcia was Rusk's mate, but she never entered his sanctum, and he never saw them go off alone.

If they had been partners, it would have soon become obvious, for there was no modesty among the People. As many as four or five pairs would copulate among the sleeping pack some mornings. Darrow turned his back when it happened, but the lovers' moans made him restless and keenly uncomfortable. When at last he fell asleep, he dreamed of stealing into House Malveen, taking the key, and opening the gate to Maelin's cell. When they escaped together, she could prove her gratitude without the coercion of a cell.

He knew it was unrealistic to dream about rescuing Maelin. He realized Radu would have slain her the day he returned from disposing of him among Rusk's pack. Still, he held her image and the thought of her rescue as a sort of talisman against despair. If he could dream about a selfless act, then surely he had not become like the monsters that surrounded him.

After another month of learning to stalk his prey and throw a spear, Darrow brought down his first stag. When Morrel slung the carcass over his own shoulders, Darrow thought it was a friendly gesture, but the werewolf carried it back to the lodge and claimed it as his own. When Darrow protested, Morrel sent him spinning to the ground with a powerful backhanded blow.

Darrow bristled but stayed down. He kept his eyes low, and Morrel ate the steaming heart when it came off the fire.

Afterward, Darrow grew sullen and sat far from the fire pit. Sorcia was the only one who would come near him.

"How am I supposed to act?" he complained to her. "I do what they say, but they take it away."

"Should a sheep complain of its stolen fleece?"

"I am not a sheep," said Darrow.

"Then act like a wolf," said Sorcia.

Six days later, as four of them were stalking a wounded boar, Karnek cuffed Darrow for making too much noise. Darrow balled a fist and punched Karnek in the face. The lean man laughed and licked the blood from his lip.

Then he proceeded to beat Darrow half to death.

When Darrow could stand again, they resumed the stalk without a word about the fight. That night, after they roasted the boar, Brigid handed Darrow a hunter's portion.

"But I lost," he complained to Sorcia later.

She shrugged. "Yet you fought, little wolf."

Later, she led him out into the woods, running ahead until he chased her. They ran until Darrow's breath came hard and ragged, and she let him catch her. When he grabbed her around the waist, she twisted in his grasp and struck him across the mouth.

He tasted blood and felt a growl rise in his chest. He released her and raised a hand to strike back, but Sorcia swept his legs out from under him, and he fell to the ground. Before she could dart away, he grabbed her ankle and pulled her down beside him.

She rolled atop him and grabbed his hair with both hands, holding his head against the forest floor. Her naked thighs were hot against his chest. He gripped her legs and would not let her go. She opened his mouth with her tongue, and their kiss exploded in his brain. Pleasure arched his back and filled his body with liquid fire.

Her body was incandescent in the moonlight, her beauty almost painfully unreal. Darrow closed his eyes and imagined her with Maelin's dark hair and heart-shaped face. The image galvanized his body, contracting every muscle.

Darrow imagined they lay on the straw floor of a dark cell, the door open beside them. He felt her fingers run over his perspiring skin, scratching lightly over his stomach before peeling away his breeches.

He kept his eyes closed as she tossed aside her own clothes before settling back atop him. Their bodies joined slowly, and she guided him with practiced hands. Breathless, he followed her lead without question.

Afterward, they lay a while upon the ground, watching the sky grow lighter through the trees. When Darrow opened his mouth to speak, she stopped it with a savage kiss. They gathered their clothes and walked back to the lodge, where

Sorcia walked away to take her place among the sleeping bodies. There was no question of his joining her. He curled up alone by the wall. He didn't mind it. In his dreams, he was not sleeping alone.

When the High Hunt was less crowded at Midsummer, Darrow thought little of it. It bothered those closest to Rusk the most. Ronan, Karnek, and Brigid wore dour faces for days afterward. They were the closest Rusk had to disciples, and their moods often reflected his.

More worrisome than the lightly attended feast were the rumors that arose in the tendays that followed. Hunters returned from their ranging with stories of an unseen watcher in the woods. Even as they stalked their prey, the People felt the presence of something stalking *them*. Those who doubled back or laid ambushes found their efforts futile. Morrel joked that it was a ghost from a hunting party the pack had destroyed last winter. The other People repeated the joke until Rusk cuffed one of them for it. Why it offended him, no one understood.

Darrow began spending more time away from the lodge, ranging with two or three other hunters. When they found signs of human intrusion in their territory, they tracked the source. Those they recognized or who showed a symbol of the Beastlord were friends, and the hunters asked if they wanted for meat. If so, the hunters tarried long enough to bring down a stag or a wild boar.

Those who did not revere the Beastlord were given an hour's lead before the hunters followed. Darrow was present for three such intrusions, and none of them escaped the pack.

Any qualms Darrow felt about killing human prey were outweighed by his joy to be alive. Better still, he was a member of the pack, no longer a lackey to the monstrous Stannis Malveen. Best of all, his muscles were becoming lean and hard from ranging the woods. His senses grew keener still, and he could hear every sound in the forest if he remained still. The other hunters taught him what all the new smells meant. Now he could tell when prey was sick or with child, and he left them for more suitable quarry.

Even so, for nights after helping pull down a human trespasser, Darrow dreamed of fleeing down dark corridors. Shadows flew after him, curling around the torches until there was only darkness. Maelin's voice cried out for help, but long before he could reach her, a hideous wheezing sound came up behind him. He fumbled with the key, almost losing it in the darkness. If he could only release her from her horrid captors, his own guilt would be absolved. Before he could put the key in the lock, he felt clammy hands upon his shoulders before falling through the veil of sleep to wake panting and cold with sweat.

He felt the same way after the nights of the moon, when the beast emerged to take command of his body, reshaping Darrow to its own carnal desires. In the mornings, Darrow could barely remember running with the pack, though faint smells and dim images clouded his memory.

"How do you change when you will?" he asked Sorcia.

Some of the nightwalkers could change only during the full moon, or when Rusk evoked their transformation through the power of Malar. Darrow was among the latter, and he envied the others.

"Some were born with the gift," said Sorcia. "They are true nightwalkers. For them, it is as natural as speaking their mother tongue. They learned it so long ago that they can't remember not having it."

"But you can learn a language," said Darrow.

"Just so," she agreed. "And you can learn to change shape when you will."

"Teach me," he said.

And so she did. The lessons began with words but soon left them behind.

The beast was always inside a nightwalker, no matter whether proud Selûne rode the sky or veiled her face. Lured out with rage or desire, it would come to the right call. When

Sorcia slapped him, Darrow felt the beast snarl. When they ran naked through the forest, he heard it panting in the back of his mind. And when they lay together, even when he closed his eyes to see Maelin's face, Darrow heard the distant howling of his other self deep inside.

By the end of the month of Flamerule, Darrow no longer forgot the nights of four-legged hunting. When autumn came, he could change whenever Selûne showed more than half her face. By the Feast of the Moon, he hoped, he would stand as a wolf before Rusk used his infernal spells to impel the change in the weak.

Even fewer people made the pilgrimage to the lodge at Harvestide. All the worshipers from the northern woods arrived, but there were only two from the south. A scowling Rusk emerged from the lodge after receiving them in private.

To lift the mood, Rusk spoke to the People and their worshipers after his opening prayers.

"My journey to the city was not in vain," he said from the altar, "nor was my sacrifice for naught. The Black Wolf Scrolls contain the words of Malar, the Great Hunter. In them I have found the truths the moon worshipers tried to conceal from us. In them, I have found the path to our destiny.

"Our birthright is not limited to the wild. We are the children of the natural world, including the cities shaped by the misguided followers of the weakling gods. The day of our retribution draws near, when the Black Wolf will lead us on the hunt that reclaims our rightful territory from the herd.

"Hear me well, my faithful children, for I speak the words of Malar, and mine is the honor of leading the last wild hunt to break down the pens and fences of the city dwellers. Those who prove strong enough may join us, while the weak we will hunt for our sustenance and our pleasure."

That night, the chosen prey ran fast and far, but in the end he did not join the pack. He cried for Mielikki, Daughter of the Forest. If she heard his plea, it was far too late. Ronan tore out his throat, and the whole pack feasted on his flesh.

Three tendays later, in late Eleasias, Rusk took Darrow and Sorcia ranging to the southwestern reaches of the Arch Wood. They walked in human form, though Darrow had wished for a chance to prove he could transform at will. He had become much better at it recently. It took him less than a minute to enrage the beast and let it come over him.

When they reached the southwestern woods, they found the first signs of human habitation. First they smelled the wood smoke and the unmistakable odor of human kitchens. Soon they spied lone cottages and small clusters of sod houses appeared just within or beyond the tree line.

"Why do they live so far from a town?" asked Darrow. At least in the northern woods, the foresters were within a day's walk of Moonwater.

"No lords to tax them," explained Rusk. "No laws to bind them. Most of them are strong. That is why they make good prey and sometimes good People."

Contrary to Rusk's endorsement, the forest dwellers seemed weak and frightened. They barred their doors at the sight of the strangers and peered at them through the shutters.

"Something turns them against us," grumbled Rusk. "They cannot have forgotten the winters when we fed them."

"You know who it is, Huntmaster," said Sorcia.

Rusk frowned and increased his pace, leaving Darrow and Sorcia behind.

"Who is it?" asked Darrow quietly.

"Maleva," said Sorcia. "A cleric of Selûne."

"One cleric?" said Darrow. "Why don't we drive her away or kill her?"

"Her home is protected by a forbiddance," said Sorcia. "And Rusk has long decreed that none but he shall take her life."

"A matter of honor?" asked Darrow.

"No," said Sorcia, "a matter of weakness."

They found Maleva's cottage the next night. It stood atop a low hill near the forest's edge. One square window glowed with yellow light, and a thin ribbon of smoke rose into the dark blue sky. Even from fifty yards away, Darrow smelled rabbit stew and wood smoke, as well as the dog lying beside the front door.

"See how close you can get," said Rusk. Sorcia and Darrow looked at him in surprise. "Both of you, from different directions."

"You said she had a forbiddance on the place," said Sorcia.

"That's why he's sending us first," said Darrow, who remembered all too well the way Rusk used him as a trap-springer back at House Malveen. He didn't like it, but he knew Rusk would not tolerate an argument.

Sorcia felt otherwise. "You called Balin a coward for leading from behind," she said.

Darrow blinked and stepped back, expecting Rusk to strike her down. Instead, he merely fixed his eyes on hers and asked, "Which of you will free me from paralysis or heal me if I am struck down?"

Sorcia had no retort for that argument.

"When you wield the power of Malar, perhaps we will discuss my decisions. Until then, you will do well to obey them."

Darrow had already turned away to skirt the hill and approach from the north, where the tree line would prevent him from making a silhouette against the sky. The stars shone in the cloudless sky, and the crescent moon was bright and high.

From this side, Darrow could see neither the dog nor the window. Darrow crept close, expecting trouble only when he reached the building. Thus, he was unprepared when he triggered the ward when still thirty yards away.

Brilliant silver light suffused his body, and an invisible force thrust him away from the cottage. He fell sprawling on the ground, twitching and breathless. The force that pushed him back felt like fire and lightning combined. He couldn't smell or taste, and all his flesh felt numb and useless.

He rolled to his feet and felt briefly dizzy. His vision blurred, then cleared. He looked for Darrow and Sorcia but saw neither of them.

From around the cottage came the dog, barking furiously. It was a big wolfhound with a mottled gray coat. Darrow heard the sound of the door opening, and a woman's voice called out, "Who's there?"

Darrow turned and ran, the wolfhound close behind.

"Call back your dog, Maleva," boomed Rusk's voice. Darrow veered toward the sound, seeking the protection of numbers, as well as Rusk's magic. His body stung and ached from his expulsion.

After a moment's hesitation, Maleva called out, "Here, Shard! Come here, boy!"

The dog broke off its pursuit just as Darrow reached Rusk. Sorcia was already with him, looking no worse for testing the Selûnite's ward. Maybe she had simply waited to see what happened to Darrow, first.

Maleva let Shard inside the cottage then closed the door before approaching the three werewolves. She wore a dark blue cloak with the hood thrown back to reveal white hair bound in a long braid. She stopped inside the ward around her cottage, about twenty yards away.

"I see you brought a pair of your own dogs," she said.

"Bitch," muttered Sorcia. Darrow noted she said it quietly.

"Won't you come embrace your old friend, Maleva?" Rusk walked halfway toward her but stopped well beyond the magical boundary.

"Go back to your lodge, Rusk. Hunt the animals, and leave the people alone."

"You could come with us," he said. "You could run with

me as we did so long ago. There is still great strength in each of us."

"You are wasting your breath, Rusk. If you want to turn away from Malar, I'll go with you to Moonshadow Hall. Otherwise, I'll stay here until one of your pups tears you down."

"But you won't kill me, will you, Maleva?"

"I will if you don't keep away," she said. "Stay in the woods, Rusk."

"Where is Feena? Why does she not come out to greet me?"

"In Yhaunn," said Maleva. "With Dhauna Myritar, well beyond your reach."

"The Mistress of Moonshadow Hall taking your acolyte under her wing? I think not. She never forgave you for your heresy."

"Think what you will," she replied.

"Perhaps you left her in Selgaunt to look after the boy."

"Think whatever you will. Just stay in your woods."

"You think he is the Black Wolf, don't you?"

"The Black Wolf is a myth," she said. "We are too old to believe in such stories."

"You once believed it enough to run with me," said Rusk.

"We were young then. I was a foolish young girl, and you were a much better man than you are today. Stay in your woods, Rusk."

"Perhaps I'll pay them a visit," he said. "There are so many things I would like to tell them both, Feena and this young wolf. But not too soon, I think. Perhaps next summer would be a good time."

Maleva's eyes flashed bright blue, and she raised her hands in prayer to the moon. White light formed on the medallion around her neck.

Rusk pressed the back of his hand against the talisman on his forehead, chanting his own invocation. When he thrust his open hand toward Maleva, a burst of red light surrounded her. For an instant, Darrow could see the smooth, curving border of the invisible field surrounding her home.

Rusk cursed. Whatever the spell was meant to achieve, it had failed.

Simultaneously, a cone of silver light shot from Maleva's palm and covered all three werewolves. Every muscle in Darrow's body cramped at once, and he was forced low to the ground. Before he realized he was transforming, he was in wolf form.

Nearby, Rusk snarled but seemed otherwise unaffected. Beside him stood the white wolf, her vicious teeth bared.

"Go back to the woods, before you lose one of your pups."

She raised her arms toward the moon and called again on Selûne's power. Rusk hesitated, then turned to leave. He walked at first then moved more quickly as he willed his own transformation into wolf form. Soon they entered the dark forest, where neither Maleva nor her spells followed them.

CHAPTER 12

MASKS

Marpenoth, 1371 DR

In the months since his expulsion from Master Ferrick's, Tal began his own sword practice. There was no room in the tallhouse, so he used the backstage area at the Wide Realms.

At first he came in the mornings, when the building was deserted except for Lommy and the reclusive Otter. Within a tenday, Mistress Quickly complained that Lommy was missing his cues for opening the trapdoors or lowering the sun and moon from the heavens. One look at the bleary-eyed tasloi made Tal realize his mistake. The arboreal creatures were nocturnal by nature, and Tal had been disturbing their sleep.

He changed his schedule, returning to the playhouse a few hours after a performance. He practiced by himself while Lommy and Otter scampered about the mechanical works in the rafters.

He didn't know what the tasloi were doing up there—maybe just chasing each other in play, or perhaps building new gods and comets to drop and swing from the ropes—but he liked the sound of them nearby. He liked to think they were glad of his presence, too.

Often he would stay until dawn, having exhausted himself with drilling, then hours of working out new fight scenes for plays that had yet to be written. Soon he found himself most alert at night, sleeping away the mornings before rising to a quick breakfast and a return to the Realms for rehearsals.

On full moons, Tal's routine was always the same. He ate a big dinner then had Chaney lock him in the cellar. During the transformation, Tal did his best to remain calm, meditating as Master Ferrick had taught him until the tidal dreams swept him out to oblivion. An hour after dawn, Chaney and Eckert would let him out. He stayed in the tallhouse for all three days, bidding Eckert to tell callers he was out carousing with Chaney in an alehouse somewhere.

In truth, Tal no longer frequented alehouses. He'd drink a cup of wine or a tankard of ale with Chaney in the tallhouse, but he wouldn't drink more, and he wouldn't go anywhere where he might get into a quarrel. He didn't want to hurt anyone else.

Word of the accident at Master Ferrick's eventually reached the players. Mallion and Sivana were uncharacteristically sympathetic. Instead of the expected jokes, Tal received a surprising request one day in the cold month of Uktar.

The three actors stood among the vendors outside the playhouse. Most of them sold food and drink to the audience as they arrived. The smells of roast meat and baked dumplings mingled with the sweet autumn air. Brown leaves scratched along the cobblestones.

The three actors clutched cups of hot cider to warm their hands. The autumn air was still comfortable, but the playhouse doors were already open.

"Let's go back inside," suggested Tal.

"Actually," said Sivana, "we wanted a word with you alone."

That sounded ominous. Tal braced himself for some admonishment about recent rehearsals. Quickly had cast him as the mad king, a role most of the players—including Tal—thought should go to one of the more experienced actors. Quickly said the role demanded a voice by turns thunderous and frail, and that Tal had proven he had the range. That was true enough, thought Tal, who had been expanding his repertoire of mimicry mostly through his mocking representations of the Hulorn and members of the Old Chauncel. On the other hand, Tal was far too young to express the emotional depth of a man driven mad by his children's betrayal.

At least, that was Tal's fear.

"We heard you weren't going to Master Ferrick's these days," said Mallion.

The sly, handsome actor was the one who usually got the roles Tal wanted. He rarely passed up an opportunity to point out Tal's shortcomings, usually in front of the other players. He did it in a tone of genial humor, but there was no doubt in Tal's mind that he also did it to make sure everyone realized that Mallion was the better actor.

Tal nodded, then sipped his cider. It was spicy and almost too hot to drink.

"You probably want to stay in practice, though," added Sivana. This month, her hair was blue and short. In *The Wizard's Exile* she played both sprite and ship captain, the latter with a false beard and a silk scarf on her head.

"So we were thinking," said Mallion, "maybe you could teach us what you know."

"Me?" said Tal, coughing on his cider. "I'm no teacher."

"You're the one who stages all the fight scenes these days," said Sivana.

"That's not the same as real fighting," Tal said. "I mean, I hope it looks convincing, but it's not the same at all."

"Wouldn't it look better if we all knew how to fight for real?" said Mallion.

"Maybe," Tal allowed. Then his suspicions arose again. "And maybe it would give you an advantage when Quickly casts *Waterdeep* next season."

"Please," said Mallion. "Sivana and I are getting those parts anyway."

"Don't be so sure about that," said Tal. "The four duels are the most important scenes."

"And who would believe either of us could beat an ogre like you?" said Sivana. She and Mallion together barely weighed more than Tal. "They've got to be the same size."

"Maybe she'll pick Ennis and me," said Tal.

It was a feeble argument, since big Ennis was both portly and homely, hardly a good choice for one of the romantic rivals. He usually played the foolish counselor or the cuckolded husband.

"Fat chance," said Mallion.

"We really want to learn," said Sivana.

"Why not go to Ferrick's yourself? You're both good enough to get in."

While neither of them had had proper training, they'd learned enough in the playhouse that their greatest challenge would be to break the bad habits they'd formed.

"We'd rather learn from you," she said.

Tal looked from Sivana's face to Mallion's, expecting to see one of them crack a smile and reveal the joke before they'd had their fun with him.

"Really?"

"Really," said Mallion. Sivana nodded.

"I'll have to think about it," said Tal. He liked the idea of having fencing partners, but the fear that he'd hurt someone again still turned restlessly in his belly. "When would you want to do it?"

"Right before rehearsals," said Sivana, "to warm up."

"I'll think about it," said Tal.

He didn't have to think for long. Within a few days, Mallion and Sivana had already learned the basic footwork and followed Tal's lead for an hour of vigorous exercise. When Chaney learned about it, he insisted on coming along. His lazy efforts provided the perfect bad example for the actors, yet he could get it right when Tal corrected him. Best of all, he didn't mind the criticism.

As Tal expected, the hardest part was breaking them of habitual posing and fancy but ineffective flourishes. Deep down, Tal knew that those were some of his own failings as a swordsman, but it was easier to see it in others. He corrected, gently at first, then with an increasing scolding he knew came from long familiarity with Master Ferrick's sharp, imperious commands. When Mallion complained that he worked them too hard, Tal knew he was starting to do a good job.

"Why don't you practice with us?" Sivana asked one afternoon. Chaney had just given Mallion the thrashing of his life, even through the padded armor and masks Tal insisted they wear. Now both men complained they were too tired to go on.

"Because you're not good enough yet," said Tal. It might have been true, but Sivana's eyes narrowed. She suspected the real reason.

"You're not going to hurt us, Tal."

"I'm not worried about hurting you," he lied.

"Then show me that parry you say I botched," said Mallion.

That sounded reasonable. There was no danger in demonstrating a parry. Tal agreed, inviting Sivana's attack and catching her blade, binding it, and parrying just barely outside her line of attack.

"You don't want to go too far," he said. "Otherwise, you have to move too far for the counterattack.

"Show me the counterattack," said Sivana.

"Not today," said Tal.

Despite his reticence, Tal wanted nothing more than to fence. More honestly, he wanted to fight. He loved the contest, the trick of outthinking his opponent, then driving home the determining thrust.

He just couldn't be sure he'd hold that thrust in check.

The feeling was strongest just before the full moon. Sometimes his arms craved impact and his legs wanted only to run after a foe and catch him. Sometimes he wished Rusk were not only alive but back in the city, rushing toward him. He felt his jaw clench and bite, wanting to feel a hot rush . . .

When such thoughts took hold, Tal shook his head so hard his hair stung his face. He stretched his arms as far as they would go, then let them hang loose at his sides, his fingers stirring in an invisible current.

Tal practiced with Perivel's blade only alone, at night. If Lommy was watching, he'd use one of the practice swords instead. But when the tasloi ran off to join his brother, Tal took the monstrous sword out of its canvas bag and fought imaginary foes with lusty abandon until he noted and corrected his own mistakes. Much as he chided Mallion and Sivana, he berated himself when he caught himself blurring the lines between real fighting and choreography. Perivel's sword should be used only for fighting, he decided. Not only was it too dangerous for play but it seemed made for killing. It had a purpose.

Tal found that he could wield the weapon with increasing ease, and he noted with satisfaction that his muscles had grown not only harder but sharper. The scars of Rusk's attack had flattened with his stomach. They were still visible through his thick body hair, but perhaps they were not so ugly anymore.

One night, Tal paused in his drill to stand before the mirror to admire himself, stripped to the waist and gleaming with sweat. He liked the way he looked and considered telling Quickly that he was willing go shirtless on stage again. Rehearsing the conversation in his mind, he realized how truly vain he had become—or how vain he had always been.

Even though he was alone, Tal flushed with shame. He didn't like to face his own failings, especially those that he despised in Tamlin, his conceited older brother. In some ways, the brothers were not so different.

One night in late Uktar, just before the Feast of the Moon, Tal paused in his solitary practice. Something he couldn't identify seemed out of place. He couldn't hear Lommy and Otter, but that was not unusual. Sometimes they were quiet, even at night. Then Tal realized he had just felt a brief coolness on his naked back and caught a fresh whiff of the pre-dawn air. A glance told him that both stage doors were still closed, but he realized that one of them had been open seconds earlier. An intruder had entered the playhouse.

To his relief, Tal saw Perivel's sword on the makeup table, where he'd left it. An assassin would have removed the weapon first, so maybe the intruder was merely a burglar. He would be a disappointed burglar, since Quickly removed the admission funds to a vault in her tallhouse each night. He'd be a regretful one, too, since Tal intended to find him.

Tal saw no one backstage, and he heard nothing unusual. His sense of smell had grown keen over the past ten months. When he sniffed the air, he detected only the usual odors of the Wide Realms: water reeds, lime, and horsehair from the thatched roof, oak beams and plaster from the walls, powder, greasepaint, and linen from the dressing tables, even nuts and orange rinds from the ground beyond the stage doors.

Despite the evidence of his senses, Tal was certain someone besides him and the tasloi was in the playhouse. Sword in hand, he stalked the unseen intruder, pausing every few moments to listen and sniff. He peered into the shadows between the larger props and scenery that lined the walls. Not even a rat emerged.

Tal looked over the backstage area again, hoping his threat would make the burglar nervous enough to break and run. No such luck.

Then Tal noticed one of the royal guards staring at him. Mallion always put the practice masks over the heads of the guards when practice was over. And now, four masks and a barefaced guardsman stood motionless against the wall.

The ruse amused Tal even as he pretended not to notice it. He feigned interest in the costume hampers while observing the masks out of the corner of his eye. None of them moved as he poked the baskets with the tip of his sword. He prepared to rush the intruder. He needed just a few more steps . . .

"Wait," said a muffled voice from the fourth mask. It was a woman. "I know you can see me."

Tal moved to stand between the intruder and the nearest outside door. "Show yourself," he said.

The woman came out from behind the mannequins. Beneath the practice mask, her clothes were all dark gray, from gloves to tightly laced boots. Tal could see nothing else about her except that she walked with a confident grace. Awfully sure of herself for a captured burglar, he thought.

"Who are you?" he said.

"An admirer," she said.

"A secret admirer, it would seem."

The woman inclined her head. Tal wondered whether the gesture came with a smile under the wicker mask. "I've been coming to the plays lately," she said. "You are very talented."

"Thank you," he said. "And you are very mysterious."

She made an elegant curtsey. Charmed by the gesture, Tal bowed in return.

"I'm fairly sure you're not here to kill me," he said, "and there's nothing worth stealing. But you know that, don't you? Why are you here?"

"I mean you no harm, Talbot."

"That's not an answer."

"I'm just here to watch you for a while, to make sure you are all right."

"Thamalon sent you, didn't he?"

She didn't answer. Perhaps Tal's guess was wrong, or perhaps Cale was involved. His father's butler was as mysterious as they come, and Tal had often suspected that the man had some sort of criminal connections.

"Perhaps I merely wanted to learn why you've disappeared from the rest of the city. You spend all your time here these days."

That was true. Except during the full moon, Tal went to his tallhouse to eat, bathe, and sleep before returning to the playhouse. His absences had begun to irritate Eckert, whose fussy reminders had been replaced by a moody silence. Perhaps this stranger had been sent to spy on him because Eckert had too little to report to Tal's father.

"I've been busy," he said.

"Busy fencing alone at night? Are you expecting a fight?"

That was a question Tal hadn't seriously considered before. Chances were good that Rusk wasn't dead, but Tal didn't expect him to come back to the city.

"It's best to be prepared if one comes unexpectedly," he said. "After all, you came to me, didn't you?" He nodded toward the practice swords and raised his own to point at the woman's head.

She put a hand on the hilt of one of the wooden swords. It was little more than a slightly curved staff with a cross-guard, its length marred with thousands of dents and scratches. "What will you give me if I hit you?"

Tal laughed, not just because he thought the woman couldn't hit him but because he admired her attitude. "You came to learn how I'm doing. I'll answer a question for each touch."

"Done!" said the woman. Before Tal realized she had the sword in hand, she lunged forward and stabbed at his foot. He withdrew it, but not before she grazed the tip of his boot.

"That was a touch!" she cried. She neglected to disguise her voice, but Tal still couldn't place it.

Annoyed by his own carelessness, Tal snapped at her. "Ask your damned question."

"Why are you so angry?"

"Because I should have been ready for you—"

"No," she said. "Why are you so angry all the time?"

"I'm not . . ." he began.

He kept up his guard as he considered both the question and the woman who asked it. For a moment he thought it might be his sister, Tazi, but she wouldn't disguise herself. Even more than Chaney, she could talk to Tal about anything. He decided there was no harm in answering, no matter who she was.

"I hate other people deciding my life for me," he said at last.

The woman beat Tal's sword lightly then cut over it and feinted. He withdrew out of range, keeping the tip of his blade near hers.

"Who does that?" She cut under Tal's blade, then again as he followed. "Your father?" Tal reversed and feinted, cutting under to attack her leg as she parried the false thrust. She barely managed to parry the real attack.

"You're good," Tal said, "but that's another question. I bet you won't hit me again."

He attacked her blade in a flurry of beats interspersed with feints. She retreated and he followed, crossing over to put her back in the corner. She saw what he was doing and dived to the ground, tumbling away from the trap.

Tal nearly struck her as she escaped, but he hesitated to hit her in the back. As she turned, she saw that she had been vulnerable.

"How gallant," she said, "not to strike a lady in the back."

"How do I know you're a lady?"

"You'll have to take my word for it," she said with a sudden attack at his wrist. Now his blood was up, and Tal's blade moved with time to spare.

"I think it's my turn for an answer." Tal stamped, but the ruse failed to shake her guard.

He tried a binding glide, but she caught it and withdrew as she parried, circling past the royal guards. She shoved one toward Tal and darted to the side, but he anticipated the trick and was already there. He rapped her lightly on the calf.

"Who are you?" he demanded.

"I didn't agree to answers."

"It's only fair," he said, moving closer. "Besides, that's my mask. I think I'll take it back now."

"No!" she said, putting both hands on the sword in an earnest guard.

This time Tal didn't hold back, attacking her blade with his full strength. Feeling the power of his blows, his opponent retreated and dodged to avoid taking his attack on her blade. She was as quick as he, but not nearly so strong.

When he came too close, she attacked his exposed head to make him parry. As he did, she threw her sword between his legs, almost tripping him as he lunged to follow. By the time he recovered his balance, she had the door open.

She was almost out of the playhouse when Tal caught the back of her tunic and pulled back hard, lifting her feet off the ground. She twisted around and kicked his knee hard, but he took it and snarled at the pain. He dropped the wooden sword, grabbed the front of her mask, and turned her to face him.

She punched him in the stomach. He didn't even grunt. She shot a knee at his groin, but he blocked it with his thigh.

"Don't," she said. Her voice was strong, not pleading.

"You owe me an answer, and I intend—" Tal stopped.

With his face so close to her mask, he could smell the woman's skin. She was very clean, as if she'd bathed just before coming out to spy on him. Tal smelled the ghost of bathing oils and beauty creams, and a more familiar scent beneath them.

He released the woman, leaving her mask in place. Even so close to its narrow slits, he saw only the vaguest image of her gray eyes looking back at him. Her lower face was obscured by the same cloth that muffled her voice.

An apology formed in his throat, but he swallowed it. Instead, he said, "You can keep the mask."

She stepped away, making sure the door was open and the way clear before she turned back to speak again.

"Thank you," she said. She seemed about to say something else, but then she turned and ran away.

"You can keep yours, too," she said when she thought she was out of range.

Now that he had the answer to his question, a hundred more bloomed in his mind as he listened to his mother go.

CHAPTER 13

THE MOONLION

Winter, 1372 DR
The Year of Wild Magic

The pack settled in for the winter. The snow limited their ranging, but they continued to hunt in all but the most violent weather. In case game was scarce, they also had plenty of salted meat and vegetable stores from the northern communities. It was both tribute and thanks for the hunting they had done for the northern settlements in the tendays before the Feast of the Stag.

The werewolves remained in the lodge most days. They tended chores for only a few hours each day, stitching clothes, mending weapons, and repairing the lodge itself.

The pack included only six children under thirteen. They ran with the adults soon after they could walk, and few of them survived to make their rites of adulthood at thirteen. Those who did were strong and cunning. Despite his growing acceptance by the pack, Darrow knew he was still less dangerous than some of these cubs of ten years or younger.

The pack spent less time on work than they did amusing themselves with simple games and stories. Darrow earned more esteem among the pack by teaching them a game of stones he learned as a boy. He carved the triangular grid on several planks to pass around, and soon everyone was playing "Darrow's Stones."

He also found himself a popular storyteller. Even though he had no gift for it, he could reconstruct bards' tales the others had never heard before, and he remembered a few plays he had seen in Selgaunt. He even recalled seeing Talbot Uskevren perform on one or two occasions, though he didn't find the young man remarkable at the time.

"Why did Rusk not bring him back to us?" asked Morrel.

"Have you seen him clap lately?" remarked Sorcia. Since their ignoble retreat from Maleva's cottage, the white elf disparaged the Huntmaster at every opportunity.

Morrel ignored Sorcia. "More importantly, why did he want him in the first place? I know it has to do with the Black Wolf prophecy, but what the hell is that?"

"Don't you listen?" said Brigid. She lowered her voice and mimicked Rusk's resonant baritone. "The Black Wolf will lead us in the wild hunt across all the land to reclaim our rightful territory."

"Enough of that," snapped Morrel.

"Afraid he might hear you?" asked Sorcia.

"I'm not the one mocking the word of Malar," he said. "Rusk knows something he can't tell us yet. It's a test of our faith in him, and in the Beastlord."

Sorcia raised her eyes toward the ceiling.

"What is the Black Wolf?" asked Darrow. "The way he says it it sounds like it's something everyone knows about."

"You know how you learn to change without the moon?" said Brigid.

Darrow nodded.

"That's part of it," she said. "You learn to control your transformations even when the moon is completely dark; you're one step closer to the Black Wolf."

"It's also part of who we are," added Morrel. "Some nightwalkers are really just beasts. They have no code, no community. Most of them are slaves to the moon—they don't have the Black Blood like us. Others are tamed to join the herd. That's what the Selûnites do. They cut off your balls to make you gentle."

Darrow was surprised by this news. "They don't actually—"

"No," laughed Brigid, "but the result's the same. You do what they say, and they put your beast to sleep, so you don't chase the other sheep around the pen."

"What they don't realize is that the Black Blood sets us above the herd," said Morrel. "We're the hunters, and we have no lords among men. The Black Wolf is a state of being, when you have no master but Malar."

"So Rusk is the Black Wolf?" asked Darrow.

"Maybe," said Morrel.

Sorcia snorted and walked away.

"It depends whether you mean he's reached that state or whether he's the Black Wolf of prophecy. Not everyone believes the Black Wolf Scrolls are the word of Malar."

"But Rusk does."

"Yeah, I think he does."

A draft came into the lodge, right over the place where Darrow usually slept. He tried to ignore it for a few nights, but it grew stronger. He peered up at the root-tangled ceiling but saw no hole. He felt the incoming air with his hands and guessed where it originated outside. Bundling himself in furs, he went outside to patch it.

After sweeping away the snow in several places, Darrow finally heard a murmuring sound through the sod roof. A glimmer of red light shone through a hole. He was nowhere near the fire pit, so he peered inside.

He was above Rusk's sanctum.

The sound he heard was Rusk's voice, chanting low and steady. Darrow smelled smoke and tasted incense in the air. He knew he should cover the hole and go away, but curiosity overcame his fear. He put his face right against the hole and shielded it from the light with his arms.

Below him, Rusk sat cross-legged on the floor, illuminated only by the glowing coals of a black iron brazier. His naked body gleamed with animal fat, though his silver hair fell loose about his shoulders. Where he had lost his arm, an ugly worm of flesh clung to his shoulder.

A congregation of skulls looked down on the ritual from their places on the walls. In the darkness, the skulls seemed to float around the Huntmaster. Darrow noted the skulls of deer, wildcats, boars, owlbears, and other monstrous beasts of the Arch Wood—there were even the skulls of humans and elves.

"Great hunter," intoned Rusk, "hear my plea. Great Malar, show me your wisdom and will."

As his prayer ended, flames rose from the brazier's coals. Rusk thrust his hand above flames, clutching a scrap of parchment.

"This is the path of the moon and its shadow. Show me a sign, if it marks truly the night of the Black Wolf."

The flames rose, and licked around his fist leaving parchment and skin unburned. When they subsided, Rusk set the parchment aside before holding his hand once more above the fire.

"Do I remain your fit and worthy vessel?"

The flames surged up again, but this time Rusk howled in pain. Every muscle of his body stood out in his struggled to keep his hand within the fiery oracle. Darrow imagined that the consequences otherwise must be fell indeed.

When the flames withdrew into the brazier's bowl, Rusk gnashed his teeth and shook his head against the pain. Tears streaked his face as he glared down at the ruin of his left arm.

After a moment's reflection, he asked again, "Am I no longer the Black Wolf?"

Again the oracle's fire burned him. Darrow watched as the hair on Rusk's arm wilted and the skin turned angry red.

Again Rusk thrashed against the pain, his hair forming a wild halo around his agonized face. His eyes were closed tight for many seconds, but then they snapped open in sudden realization.

Still, Rusk hesitated before asking the next question. Darrow guessed that only negative answers came with punishment.

"Mine remains the chosen spirit of the Black Wolf?"

The oracle crackled, but the fire remained in the bowl.

"Yet another is now the vessel?"

Yes, the fire hissed.

Rusk paused again before asking the next question. Judging from his tone, Darrow imagined he hated to give voice to the question more than he feared a burning no.

"Has my infirmity made me an unworthy vessel?"

The oracle said, *Yes*.

Rusk sat quietly for a moment. Then his body began to tremble, imperceptibly at first, then more and more furiously until he risked taking his arm from its place before concluding his spell.

At last his fury subsided, and Rusk invoked the name of Malar, thanking the Beastlord for his oracle and chanting the words that returned the brazier's flames to dull red coals.

He spun to face the darkness. Darrow could no longer see his face, but he continued to listen. Eventually, Rusk spoke.

"He took my arm," he growled. "He stole my fate!"

He sat silently so long that Darrow was about to slip away when he heard another voice in the room below. It was even deeper than Rusk's, but with a hollow sound of dry stones.

"You allowed him to defile the chosen vessel," said the sepulchral voice. Darrow could not identify its source.

After a few breaths, Rusk replied. "Mine is still the chosen spirit. The flames ordained it so."

Again, the voice paused before answering. "Without a fit and worthy vessel, the spirit is powerless in the world."

"How can I heal this wound? The scrolls do not say."

"It is beyond your power," said the voice. "Your body is forever despoiled in the eyes of Malar. That is the price of your foolishness."

"There must be a way," insisted Rusk.

"There is," whispered the voice. "You hold the power already. The secret lies within the scrolls."

"Where?" said Rusk. "Tell me—"

A lump of snow fell past Darrow's cheek and through the hole. It barely made a sound as it hit the floor of Rusk's sanctum, but it was enough. Rusk turned to look where it struck. Before his gaze turned to the ceiling, Darrow scrambled away from the hole. He ran down the sloping roof to the woodpile and filled his arms with split timbers.

He entered the lodge and took the wood to the fire. When Rusk pushed aside the tapestry and emerged from his sanctum, Darrow looked up as nonchalantly as possible. Rusk watched him place the logs on the fire, then returned to his sanctum.

Darrow breathed a sigh of relief until he felt the melting snow run down his leg. His furs were caked in snow from where he had lain on the ground.

"Tell us all about Talbot Uskevren," said Rusk in the tone of one asking a cleric to read a sacred fable.

The lodge fell silent, and all eyes turned to Darrow. In private he had told Rusk everything he knew about the object of Stannis Malveen's revenge, but he had not expected the Huntmaster to ask him to repeat it to the entire pack.

He took a deep breath, hoping this was not the prelude to punishment for his spying tendays earlier.

"I watched him only in public, usually at the playhouse," he said. "Everything else I heard from Stannis Malveen, who learned it from someone close to Talbot Uskevren."

This claim of sources was a ritual among the People. The legend of Yarmilla the Huntress, who went out hunting bears with a switch, began with such a long citation of bards who had passed the story down throughout the years that many made a jest of it by singing the names as quickly as possible.

"He performs in the playhouse and practices swordplay," began Darrow.

"We have heard these things before," said Rusk. "Tell us about how he guards his secret. Tell us the gossip your master shared with you."

Darrow was surprised, but he could hardly refuse. Much of what he'd heard from Stannis was so trivial that he would never think to repeat it. He composed his thoughts before going on.

"He quarrels with his family, especially his father. So does the older brother, whose name is Tamlin. There is a sister, too. Her name is Thazienne."

"Tell us more about these quarrels," said Rusk. "Leave nothing out, and everyone listen well. We will have a new High Hunt this summer, and we must learn all we can about our prey."

"Why go to the city to hunt?" asked Ronan.

"Because it is the will of Malar," said Rusk.

From her place across the fire, Sorcia snorted. A few of the others nodded. They, too, doubted the wisdom of ranging not only far from home but also into the walled confines of Selgaunt.

Rusk counted the disapproving voices with flicks of his eyes before speaking again. "On the night of the Black Wolf, we shall hold a High Hunt for a new Huntmaster."

The rest of the pack murmured and shifted uncomfortably.

"That is all you must know for now."

"We have faith in you, Huntmaster," said Morrel, standing, "but we are too few to venture into the city. Even you, our mightiest hunter, did not return unscathed. Perhaps we should gather the other People."

Darrow had heard tales of other convocations of People of the Black Blood scattered throughout the world. Not all of them wore the form of wolves when they hunted, but all could change shape, and all embraced the truth of the Black Blood. They were the Hunter's chosen, set above the other creatures of the world.

"The honor is for our pack alone," Rusk said. "Malar spoke to me, not to the other pack leaders. His will is clear to me. We will go to the city on the moon after Greengrass, and there we will hold the High Hunt among the gathered herd. But our prey will be no lamb—it will be the Black Wolf himself."

"But . . ." Morrel stood, struggling for the words. "Are you not the Black Wolf?"

"I was," said Rusk, "and I am. Mine is the spirit of the Black Wolf, but the vessel runs apart from us. We must fetch it back when Malar casts his cloak against the sky."

"But how . . . ?"

"All will be revealed in time," said Rusk. "For now, let us hear more of the new Black Wolf, for soon he shall be our prey."

☙ ☙ ☙ ☙ ☙

On the appointed day, Rusk led them south. He took only the best hunters, leaving behind a half dozen adults to defend the children at the lodge.

They made no effort to avoid Maleva's territory. Darrow considered asking the Huntmaster whether he intended to force a confrontation, but he decided it was better not to remind Rusk of their retreat last time they encountered the cleric of Selûne. Darrow would be glad never to see her again, but he had a sinking suspicion that Rusk wanted her to face the full strength of the pack.

They took wolf form for speed. Darrow was proud to be among those who did not require Rusk's magical compulsion to transform. It was easier at night, especially under the gibbous moon. He joined the cluster of strongest wolves around Rusk, half expecting one of Rusk's favorites to warn him off. None of them did.

Sorcia ran nearby, as did Ronan, Morrel, Brigid, and a few more of the best hunters. Darrow thought Rusk continued to favor him in part to counteract Sorcia's influence. Whatever the white wolf whispered among the rest of the People, Darrow reported to Rusk. Sometimes he worried whether the other pack members suspected his role in keeping the Huntmaster apprised of such gossip. He was certain Sorcia suspected him, but that did not stop her from continuing her subtle efforts at subversion.

They traveled fast, resisting the lure of game trails and fresh scents. Those who traveled out of sight called out their positions. The mournful sound would once have terrified Darrow, but now he found it comforting. It meant friends were nearby. His own voice joined the reply when it was their turn to howl.

By midnight they neared the edge of the wood, running along a wide clearing that ended in a thin screen of trees. Beyond them, Darrow remembered, lay the first of the farmsteads. The muscles in his back and shoulders began to tense, and his mane bristled in anticipation of an attack.

He did not have long to wait.

A huge bird descended silently toward the pack, blotting out the moon and the stars with its passage. It was a gigantic owl with a wingspan over three times Darrow's height. The wolves flinched as they sensed its presence then turned to look at it as it screeched, passing them.

It was the perfect distraction.

A shower of arrows fell among the pack, many sprouting from the wolves' bodies. Darrow felt fire crease his ribs and tried to dance away from it. The arrow had only grazed him, but the pain was sharp and persistent.

"Silver!" he wanted to yell, but all he could do was bark a general warning. It was redundant, as all the wolves could now smell the human scent nearby.

A second volley fell on the nearest cluster of wolves. A wolf called Corvus yelped and thrashed on the ground, then lay still.

Rusk ran for the edge of the wood with four wolves following close behind. Darrow ran after them in time to see five archers retreating from the tree line. They did not panic, nor did they fall back far, for they had an ally.

A lion the size of a cottage covered their retreat.

Its pelt was incandescent, as white as the swollen moon. The moonlion's mane was a brilliant corona, and its eyes were blue flames. Its open mouth looked like a cavern full of swords. With a thunderous roar, it ran toward the oncoming wolves.

Darrow hesitated, cowed by the sight of the colossal beast. Ahead of him, Rusk paused only long enough to see that a dozen more wolves had emerged from the forest. Then he rushed toward the lion. At first he looked awkward on his three legs, but he was still nimble enough to dart away to avoid the monstrous lion's pounce. Even from his safe distance, Darrow felt the vibration as the lion's immense mass hit the ground.

The wolves ringed the giant lion, darting in to bite at its flanks when they dared. Ronan's teeth caught the lion's thigh, and the creature roared as it whirled around to slash at him. Ronan barely escaped the scythelike claws, leaping away as they formed deep furrows in the earth where he had crouched an instant earlier.

Rusk and Morrel took advantage of the lion's distraction, wetting their fangs before retreating. The lion's blood was black under the moonlight. Darrow saw that its tiny wounds closed almost as quickly as they appeared.

Rusk must have noticed it as well, for he broke off to leave the rest of the pack harrying their foe. The great silverback rose up on his hind legs, smoothly transforming into human form. He stood naked except for the bronze talisman of Malar.

Pointing at the archers, he chanted a prayer to Malar. Red light flashed from his hand to strike the men. Three of them loosed their arrows, while two stood paralyzed by Rusk's magic.

"You," he shouted at the wolves nearest him, including Darrow. "Kill them all."

Eight nightwalkers and dire wolves broke off at his command, but the archers also heard. They adjusted their aim and shot at their attackers. Two wolves went down, and Brigid shied away with an arrow through her hind leg.

Darrow ran under the legs of one of the men, knocking him to the ground. Before he turned back to bite the man, Sorcia was already at the archer's throat. Her muzzle was dark with blood.

The other wolves had already dispatched the moving archers. Darrow and Sorcia leaped on the paralyzed archers, knocking their rigid bodies to the ground.

"Get away from them!" snapped a woman's voice.

Without daring to look toward the woman, Darrow sprinted out of the way just in time to avoid the searing ray of silver light that washed over the other wolves. Two of them vanished in a red mist, while the other three yelped and ran for the woods.

Like Darrow, Sorcia had not hesitated to flee at the sound of Maleva's voice. After avoiding the initial attack, she turned toward the cleric. Darrow wanted nothing to do with the terrible magic she cast, but he couldn't leave Sorcia to face her alone. He ran close behind, cursing her silently.

They would have hit her before she could invoke her goddess again, but a powerful compulsion made Darrow veer away at the last moment. He saw that the magic had the same effect on Sorcia.

Seeing that her spell worked, Maleva ignored the were-wolves and knelt to tend one of the fallen archers. Darrow saw that she was bleeding, but he had seen no one strike her. In the instant before he turned to run away, he saw a gash appear on her cheek. At the same time, he heard the moon-lion roar in pain.

Darrow ran back to Rusk. Sorcia followed his lead this time.

The bodies of two dire wolves lay torn apart on the ground beneath the moonlion, as did the broken human figure of a werewolf called Mandor. Darrow knew that a dead nightwalker always reverted to the form of his birth, but the sight still shocked him.

The surviving wolves continued to harry the moonlion, as Rusk sang more prayers to Malar. Magical power surged into the Huntmaster, and his body rippled with unholy strength. His remaining hand had grown huge and clawed. Razor sharp talons curved from his thick fingers.

Darrow needed his human shape to warn Rusk of what he'd seen. With a searing effort, he willed himself to transform. It was much harder when he was frightened, but his message couldn't wait. The pain left him on hands and knees, even after he had a human mouth.

"Maleva is here," he said, pointing back to the archers. "She's taking the lion's wounds on herself."

Rusk spied his nemesis, who was healing herself after reviving the archers who had survived. The foresters fled now, leaving the cleric alone to support the moonlion.

"Then give her some of her own," growled Rusk. "Don't be a coward!"

"We tried," said Darrow. "She is warded."

Rusk nodded almost absently. "Let's see what we can do about that."

He cast his own spell, jabbing his hand toward Maleva. Darrow saw no effects of the spell. Maleva continued with her own chanting, and her wounds vanished under the white glow of her palms.

With a curse, Rusk tried again. This time his spell caused Maleva to start and raise her hands to defend her face. She took a cautious step back and turned her head from side to side. The spell had taken her sight.

Rusk laughed with cruel satisfaction. "That should make things more interesting."

He cast another spell upon himself before running toward the blinded cleric.

"Follow me," he said.

Darrow obeyed, and Sorcia followed also.

By the time Rusk reached Maleva, the cleric had dispelled the blindness, but now her clothes were steeped in blood.

She reeled from the effects of her sympathetic wounds, and a glance back at the melee confirmed for Darrow that the battle was finally turning against the gigantic moonlion.

When Maleva saw Rusk charging her, she raised one hand and held her holy symbol in the other. It was the same gesture she had made before destroying the other werewolves.

"Selûne, send—" Rusk's clawed hand gripped her throat. He lifted her as easily as he might a ceremonial cup before a valediction.

"Oh, Maleva, the years have not been kind."

The cleric struggled in the werewolf's grasp.

"No, do not speak. I will remember you as you were, with your fiery hair and unquenchable passions." He sighed. "You believed in me, once."

Maleva's struggles grew weaker as Rusk maintained his grip. Her lips formed the words, but she had no breath to sound them.

"What is that?" asked Rusk, cocking his head. "How shall I treat with the Black Wolf? Alas, Maleva, you were right about my failings. It took me years to accept the truth. Now I realize your young favorite is Malar's chosen vessel—but he will not take my place. No, he is the very implement of my redemption!"

Maleva's head lolled, her eyes seeking the moon. Selûne rode high behind her, swelling near to fullness. Rusk turned her head to face him, lowering her body to the ground and relaxing his stranglehold just enough to listen for her dying breath.

"How can it be?" he said. "I knew you would ask. The answer came only recently, in a vision from the Beastlord. Yet our time is fleeting. It would be better if I showed you."

As Maleva's eyelids fluttered and closed, Rusk bent to kiss her, whispering obscene invocations to his god. Where their lips met, silver light welled from Maleva's mouth. Rusk sucked it forth, drawing it into his own mouth, where it congealed and dulled into a sooty cloud.

Sorcia and Darrow watched as their master drank the cleric's life. As they had witnessed at the death of Fraelan,

Rusk's body surged with stolen power. His already exaggerated muscles swelled and ripped with unholy strength as the last wisps of energy trickled down his throat.

For a moment, Rusk gazed tenderly at the lifeless body beneath him. Then he rose and turned toward the battle.

Six ruined bodies lay beneath the moonlion, and more limped away or slumped on the ground beyond the melee. The remaining wolves circled from a more respectful distance. They were growing tired.

"Now we finish this," he said.

He rushed the moonlion, only this time it was no feint. As the lion's jaws gaped wide, Rusk thrust his monstrously clawed hand up under its chin. His arm sank deep into the lion's throat, and hot blood gushed down over his body.

The lion shook its head violently and smashed him with a monstrous paw, tearing long strips down Rusks's back, but Rusk dug deeper still into the lion's throat.

Heartened by Rusk's lead, the pack swarmed over the moonlion's body to support their leader. Darrow leaped into the fray, but he was too late. The giant beast vanished in a flash of silver light. The period of its summoning had ended, depriving them of their kill.

Darrow resumed his human form and sat on the ground. He watched Rusk walk among the wounded and the dead, granting healing where he could, a quick death where he must. When Rusk was finished, Darrow counted fifteen survivors and seven dead.

Those who were still fit to hunt ran off to track the archers to their homes. Without their cleric, they were sheep for the slaughter.

"He's culling the weak," whispered Sorcia in Darrow's ear. As usual, she had crept up silently. "How was it that you were not among them?"

"I could ask the same of you," said Darrow. "You do a good job of running just behind the leader."

Even as the words left his mouth, he realized the danger of angering Sorcia. She might be smaller than he, but he was certain she was far more dangerous in every way.

To his surprise, she smiled as if at a child who had just learned a simple lesson. "You are becoming good at that yourself," she said. "It's a good place to be when the leader makes a mistake."

"We won, did we not?" Darrow indicated the fallen cleric.

In the distance, he could hear the howls of the pack as they brought down their prey. Their revenge would go on for hours.

"What did we win?" asked Sorcia.

"Territory," said Darrow. "The cleric can no longer turn the woods folk against us."

"But weren't we going to the city?"

"Of course," said Darrow. "Anywhere we roam will be our territory, once the night of the Black Wolf has come."

"I think a parrot bit you. Your mouth is moving, but all I hear are Rusk's words."

"Don't you believe the prophecy?"

"I know you don't," she said. Darrow gave her a dark look, but she was not cowed. "Except for Morrel and perhaps Karnek, none of the strong has any illusions about this so-called prophecy. It's just an excuse for whatever mad scheme Rusk really has in mind."

"That's not a very loyal thing to say," observed Darrow.

"I wouldn't say it if I thought you didn't already know," she said. "He talks to you more than anyone these days. What does he expect us to accomplish in the city?"

Darrow hesitated before answering, unsure how much he should say to Sorcia. "I'm not sure," he said. "I know he wants to find Talbot Uskevren."

"To kill him?"

"I don't think so," said Darrow. It felt good to voice his misgivings. He never dared question Rusk about his plans. "Maybe he wants to win him over."

"Last time he tried that, he came back short-handed."

"Keep your voice down. You've got to stop saying that."

"What about the Malveens? I thought they were done with Rusk."

"Only Radu," said Darrow. "He doesn't like anything that

might threaten the family business. It's Stannis who wants to hurt the Uskevren."

"They sound unreliable," said Sorcia. "What do we need from them?"

"I think Rusk plans for us to take shelter there," said Darrow. "And Stannis knows more about the Uskevren. He has a spy among them. At least, he had one. Radu probably killed her last year. He doesn't like loose ends. He prefers to cut them off."

"Aren't you one of those?" said Sorcia. "A loose end?"

Darrow didn't answer, but fear made a knot in his throat until he swallowed.

Sorcia looked at him and smiled.

CHAPTER 14

OPENING NIGHT

Alturiak, 1372 DR

Despite the enchantments that kept snow and cold outside the Wide Realms in winter, the players usually spent the season rehearsing the spring productions and performing for private audiences. Since the strange attack on the playhouse the previous autumn, audiences were practically beating on the gates for more. Ever the businesswoman, Quickly wasted no time obliging them.

The house was packed on the opening night of *The Cormyrian Cousins*. The play was another of Quickly's broad comedies, full of mistaken identity, physical humor, and cross-dressing. While he was glad to help research Cormyrian history and customs from two centuries ago, Tal was disappointed to see that most of his hard work was demonstrated in the costumes, not the dialogue. It was hard to complain, however, since Quickly gave him the role he wanted—as well as all the fencing.

Tal was proud of the fight scenes, which he had been developing since Ches with Mallion and Sivana—who played both twin sisters except during the revelation, when hulking Ennis would wear the swordswoman's gown for the wedding dance.

Only one of the fights took place on the stage, while the others ranged from the balconies to the gallery railings. Most took place right on the ground, among the audience. Quickly had concerns about safety and ordered Presbart to monitor the gate carefully, admitting only a hundred groundlings to leave room for the fencers. It was all very well to capitalize on Marance Tallendar's attack last winter, but she didn't want to make a habit of maiming the audience.

The galleries were packed, heightening the nervousness all the players felt when unveiling a new production. Quickly puffed on her pipe and stalked the backstage area. Tal wished she would find some detail to correct—someone in the wrong costume or missing a wig. After fixing a problem, she might stop worrying that she'd forgotten something.

When she called time, Tal donned a heavy cloak and circled around the outside of the building to take his mark near the front entrance. There he winked at Presbart and handed over the cloak as he stepped inside. Together, they peered over the edge of the gallery rail to see who had come.

Among the usual crowd of artisans and laborers were many young merchant nobles, conspicuous in their fine doublets and gowns. There was a brief scuffle in the lower gallery as a man refused to doff his tall, feathered hat while a round-shouldered bricklayer kept swatting it off his head from behind. At last the peacock chose another seat, and all was well.

"Psst!"

Tal turned at the sound, smiling as he spotted Chaney leaning on the rails of the lower gallery. He had an arm around a buxom brunette who craned her neck to see someone on the other side of the yard. Tal thought he recognized the woman as a barmaid from the Green Gauntlet, but it had been so long since he'd been there that he couldn't be sure.

Lommy leaned out of the tiny window in the peaked roof directly above the stage. With an explosive puff of his green cheeks, he blew a brassy fanfare on a curled gloon. Once the crowd's chatter had subsided, the tasloi crossed his arms and leaned upon the window's edge. Whenever he spied someone pointing or staring at him, he made a grotesque face or thumbed his nose.

Ennis strode onto the stage in the stately gown of a royal herald. He set the scene in a windy series of obvious anachronisms and malapropisms, which the audience corrected by shouting back at him. Before the pompous character could bore the audience, Lommy descended from the heavens dressed as the world's ugliest messenger of Sune, goddess of love and beauty. Rather than bless the herald's exposition as the blustery man prayed, the messenger chased him off the stage with a heart-tipped wand.

That was Tal's cue. The audience parted before him as he strode through the yard. Simultaneously, Mallion emerged from backstage. Dressed in a lord's nightgown, he also wore a scabbard at his hip.

"What bird is this that wakes me from my sleep?" he blinked up at the heavens, too late to see Lommy vanish into the trapdoor.

"The herald of my retribution calls," cried Tal from the center of the yard. "Stand forth and face your rightful punishment!"

Mallion fumbled for his sword, feigning sleepy confusion so well that the audience already began to chuckle. "Come no closer, knave, or I shall call the dogs."

"The dog stands before me, or else—" Tal choked as someone jerked his cape.

For an instant, he imagined he was back in the Arch Wood, fleeing from Rusk and his pack when he had felt a similar tug at his throat. He whirled around to face the offender, but he saw no likely suspect.

"Mind the hedges," said Mallion, descending the stairs to the sound of laughter.

Such a smooth cover for Tal's mishap was one of the many reasons Mallion continued to garner the best parts. Tal was too grateful to hold it against him.

"I'll trim them when I've finished shaving you," said Tal with a cut at Mallion's head.

Mallion parried neatly. "Not once I've cut you down to human size."

"That won't hide his bastard's blood!" cried a voice from the crowd. The audience tittered nervously. Feeble as it was, Tal sensed that the insult was directed at him, not his character.

"Don't blame the boy," called another voice in the yard. "It's the mother's fault!"

Lightning flashed in his brain, and Tal turned his head toward the speaker. Expecting Tal's parry, Mallion checked his cut too late, and the point of his sword cut Tal's cheek. Tal barely felt the cut as his eyes sought his rude accuser. Before he could spot a likely source, another voice called from the second gallery.

"She must have fancied Perivel's ogre."

Tal looked up to see a big bearded man pointing at him as he laughed. More shocking still was the sight of an elf sitting on the rail beside the mocking man. Her cloak was two sizes too big for her slender form, and her pale skin stood out even among the powdered faces of the gallery. If more of the audience spotted her, she would regret it. Most Sembians loathed elves, and the rest were sure to avoid their company for fear of sharing the stigma of the hated outsiders.

The laughter was even more uncomfortable this time, except for a dozen loud voices throughout the yard. Tal had not heard such dirty gossip since his early teens, when his unusual size made him the object of childish jibes about his real parentage.

Someone in the yard shouted, "That's enough! We came to hear a play, not—" The voice cut off suddenly as someone pulled the man down. Tal could barely see the scuffle, but it looked as though two men had pushed the speaker to the floor.

"That's not why he was kicked out of the house, though," called a big red-bearded man with a broken nose. He stood where Tal had seen the scuffle a moment earlier, one meaty hand on his hip. His tone was insolent, inviting a quarrel. "His father won't share his concubine!"

"Right," growled Tal, dropping his sword. "That's it."

"Don't do it!" warned Mallion, lowering his sword and reaching for Tal. He was much too slow.

Tal was already halfway to the redbearded man, the audience scattering in his wake. Red was ready for the attack. Their fists struck home simultaneously, each cracking the other's jaw. The crowd went momentarily silent at the sickening collisions. Tal tasted blood and felt loose teeth in his jaw.

"Help him!" yelled Quickly from the stage door.

Instead, most of the groundlings scattered. Those few who tried to interpose themselves between the fighters soon regretted it and stepped back holding a bloody nose or bruised ribs.

Tal grabbed his opponent's beard and smashed his nose flat with a head-butt. Hot blood sprayed his face as the man shot a knee into Tal's stomach. Breathless, Tal let go and staggered back.

All around him, people were shouting, grabbing, or fleeing. The actors poured out onto the stage and into the yard. Quickly kept bellowing for order, but more brawlers joined the fray every second.

"Look out!" Chaney shouted from nearby.

Tal ducked just in time to let another big man fly over him, into the crowd. Despite the chaos, Tal smelled something on his new assailant that reminded him of the bearded man. They both had the same musky odor almost hidden by a faint smell of smoke. It seemed familiar, but Tal had no time to ponder it. Redbeard and his friend easily shrugged off the hands that tried to restrain them.

"Not bad," spat Red, grinning madly at Tal. Blood poured

over his mouth and soaked his beard. "Maybe he is a hunter after all."

Rusk, thought Tal. Before he could ponder the idea, Red's companion was upon him.

Long brown sideburns flared from the man's cheeks, emphasizing his lupine features. He snarled as his long fingers encircled Tal's neck and thrust his thumbs into Tal's throat.

Tal tried to rip the hands away, but the man was far stronger than he looked. His fingers dug into Tal's throat, even as Tal strained to pull them away.

"This is how Rusk killed the old woman," said the strangler. "Maybe I'll do the same for you."

Maleva, thought Tal. Could they have killed Maleva?

Tal punched the man and felt ribs crack, but Red kept his inhuman grip. Tal punched again, feeling his own strength wane as his lungs ached.

The strangler gasped suddenly and loosed his grip. Tal pushed him away and caught his breath as his assailant turned to face his new opponent. Chaney darted away, unwilling to face the big man after his sneak attack. The big fellow clutched his back and pursued him.

Tal went after him, but Red stepped in the way. "Not so fast, Black Wolf."

"Who the hell are you?" growled Tal. Confusion and anger swirled in his mind. "You killed Maleva?"

"Oh, no," said Red. "She was the Huntmaster's. But maybe I'll get to do the daughter."

Tal's eyes flashed red, and heat surged in his brain. He acted without thought, lashing out and feeling flesh part under his suddenly clawed fingers. He lunged to bite out the man's throat, but Red blocked him with an arm. Tal's teeth sank deep into the man's flesh—far deeper than he imagined possible.

Red howled in pain, and Tal felt something buffet his back. Heedless, he slashed over and over at Red, tearing his arms to ribbons with huge claws. His mouth opened wide to scream at the man, but only an incoherent snarl came out.

"Get away!" shouted a woman.

Tal glimpsed a muscular woman pulling at Red, trying to lead him into the crowd. The strangler was at her side, staring at Tal in alarm and confusion.

"Look at him!" said the strangler.

Tal's vision blurred. He could see no clear details, but his eyes picked out the slightest movement: the pulse in the strangler's neck, the muscles in the woman's hands as she clutched the wounded man.

"Help me," said the woman, shouldering the wounded man.

The strangler obeyed, only too glad to flee from whatever he saw when he looked at Tal. His reaction stunned Tal more than the fight. What was happening to him?

The yard was a maelstrom of sounds, but Tal could pick out every voice. Chaney was shouting his name, as were most of the players. The man who'd taunted him from the gallery was yelling, "Get away! Get the hells away from him!"

A hundred other voices shrieked or panted for breath as players and spectators alike fled the scene of mayhem.

"Tal!" shouted Chaney again.

His voice was coming closer, and Tal turned to spot him. As their eyes met, Chaney stopped dead, staring at Tal's face.

Chaney, Tal tried to say. Again, no words took form. His mouth felt all wrong.

"Tal?" Chaney said. His eyes fell to Tal's hands.

Tal looked down to see two enormous claws where his hands had been. Even as he watched, the black hairs and claws shrank away, leaving only his own human hands.

"It's too soon," muttered Tal. "It's still light, and the moon—"

"No time for that," said Chaney. "We've got to get out of here."

He took a step toward Tal, then hesitated, afraid to come closer. The look of fear on his friend's face was even more horrible than the blood on his hands.

The yard was almost empty now, except for the players who stood well away from Tal and Chaney. Their faces were masks of fear and revulsion. Mallion bit his knuckle to stop a scream, while Sivana kept her eyes on the stage floor. Ennis gaped like a blowfish.

"Let's go," said Chaney. "This way, before the Scepters get here."

Dumbly, Tal nodded and followed Chaney onto the stage. All the other players moved away as they passed. Tal held his bloodied hands away from his body as if afraid they might turn on him at any moment.

Outside, the crowd had spread nervously around the playhouse. As Chaney and Tal emerged, someone cried, "They're the ones!"

Four city Scepters stepped forth, batons in hand. After one look at the blood on Tal's hands and face, they dropped the clubs and drew their swords.

"Get on the ground!" shouted one of them. In a lower voice, he ordered one of his men to summon help. That Scepter sheathed his sword and ran for reinforcements.

"Run for it," said Chaney.

Even as he spoke, another quartet of Scepters arrived from the opposite direction. There was no way to escape without a fight.

"No," said Tal. "It's over."

He put himself down on the street. Reluctantly, Chaney lay down beside him as the Scepters cautiously approached.

CHAPTER 15

DOUBLE DEALING

Tarsakh, 1372 DR

Ronan's face was lily pale. Brigid and Karnek supported him on either side, practically carrying him along the street. Darrow led the way, while Sorcia lagged behind to watch for any sign that the Scepters were following.

"We're going the wrong way," said Karnek. "I thought you knew this city."

"In there," said Darrow, indicating a vacant alley as they approached the Oxblood Quarter. "We'll wait until sunset, then circle back."

"He's still bleeding," protested Brigid.

"You want to draw a big red line between us and the playhouse?" asked Darrow. "Here, lay him down, behind that pile of skins."

"Who put you in charge?" demanded Karnek. He and Brigid lowered Ronan to the ground.

"Rusk did," said Sorcia.

It wasn't strictly true, but Darrow was glad she had said it. Then he wondered why. Sorcia did nothing without a reason.

"He said nothing about leading the hunt," said Brigid. "He told you only to lead us to Uskevren."

She pulled the bloody tunic away from Ronan's ruined abdomen. Through the ragged wounds, Darrow glimpsed Ronan's glistening intestines. The sight would have made him retch a year earlier, but he had seen far worse since he'd started running with the pack.

"It wasn't a hunt," said Darrow. "Rusk said nothing about fighting him. Great Malar! Uskevren is the one who took off Rusk's arm. What were you trying to do down there?"

"Rusk said to test him," said Karnek. His tone changed from defiant to defensive.

He surrendered his own tunic to Brigid, who folded it before pressing it against Ronan's abdomen. Ronan gasped.

"He said 'take his measure,'" said Darrow, "not provoke him into eviscerating you."

"What were we supposed to learn by watching him strut about and play at fighting?" Brigid had lost none of her anger, but she sounded uncertain.

"Keep your voice down," hissed Sorcia, watching the alley entrance.

"Don't tell me what to do, bitch," said Brigid.

The big blonde woman was almost twice the size of the pale elf. Darrow had little doubt of which one would win in a straight fight.

"Stop it, both of you," he said. "What's important is to get back without being seen. The last thing we need is to cross Lord Malveen."

"I'm not afraid of Malveen," said Karnek.

He had never even seen the strange vampire whose home they claimed as their lair in the city. Rusk planned to face him after sunset, which was soon approaching. The rest of the pack awaited their return in the abandoned warehouse.

"Then you're more stupid than I thought," said Darrow.

When darkness came, they crept out of the alley. Ronan was too weak to walk, but his bleeding had subsided. The trauma left him muttering and confused, but he might survive the night if Rusk could heal him in time.

They kept to side streets when possible, but Darrow abandoned stealth for the broader avenues when traffic seemed light. When passing other pedestrians was unavoidable, Darrow raised his voice in slurred song, hoping observers would mistake them for a group of drunks carrying their friend home. It was a thin ruse, but Karnek joined him in it, and at least Brigid stopped complaining until they reached the warehouse district. There they fell silent and crept through the shadows until they reached House Malveen.

The looming edifice was much as Darrow remembered it. The shape of the piled cargo had changed, but there was still so much that the inner court was completely obscured from the street. They wound their way through the narrow alleys of crates and barrels to the main building.

Inside, the rest of the pack awaited them.

"Where's Rusk?" demanded Brigid. Beside her, Karnek carried the unconscious Ronan in his arms.

Several fingers pointed to the west door. Only Darrow had been beyond it, and even he had been forbidden to enter. Rusk did not want the rest of the pack within the bounds of Stannis's wards.

"We have to wait," said Sorcia.

"He'll die," protested Brigid.

"Then he dies," said Sorcia. "He did it to himself."

"I'll go," said Darrow. "Lord Malveen's minions might let me pass."

"And if they don't?" asked Sorcia.

"Then I'll have to kill them, won't I?"

Sorcia was unimpressed by his bravado, but Brigid and Karnek both gave him a long look. He saw something resembling respect in their eyes.

Darrow did not tell them that he was betting Stannis had not changed the wards that allowed his servant access. Even if Rusk told the vampire that Darrow still lived, Lord Malveen would hardly consider Darrow a threat worth refreshing the wards for.

At least, that was his gamble. He walked through the door to the River Hall before he could change his mind.

To his relief, Darrow set off no wards while passing into the outer reaches of the River Hall, but Stannis had not left the door unattended. Two dark figures crawled down from the ceiling, where they had been lurking in the shadows. One hissed at him.

"I bring tidings for Lord Malveen," said Darrow.

He hoped the monsters recognized him and assumed he was still one of the master's servants. The vampire spawn stared at him through slitted eyes, but they slunk back toward the promenade. Darrow followed. Soon he heard Rusk's low voice and the familiar, breathless sound of Stannis Malveen. Their conversation paused when they heard him approach. Darrow joined them at the end of the grand pool.

"What a pleasant surprise!" cooed Stannis.

The vampire had not changed in the year since Darrow left his service, though there were a few new additions to the furnishings in the River Hall. Stannis draped himself in a damp crimson cloak the size of a tapestry, and he reclined on a new, larger fainting couch whose legs bowed under his weight.

Stannis rolled onto his back and pressed his rubbery fingers together. The tip of his brown-black tail switched back and forth.

"My brother let me believe you met with an unfortunate accident when you escorted him to the Arch Wood last spring."

"It was no accident, my lord," said Darrow with a bow. Such gestures made it easier for him to disguise his revulsion at his former master's appearance.

"However have you kept such splendid manners while living amongst the beasts, my dear boy?"

Stannis dipped a hand into a large basin beside the couch and withdrew a writhing sea worm. He slipped it through his veil of golden chains. With an awful sucking sound, the worm vanished like a pink tongue.

In the past year, Darrow had done many things that would have horrified him before. Still, Stannis made his blood run cold.

"Where are my manners?" Stannis said. "Here I am, basking in the pleasure of your company when I am not the only one who would enjoy it. I believe another of our guests would be most eager to see you again, my courteous boy. You recall Maelin?"

"I thought . . ."

Darrow only now realized how much he had hoped against reason that she was still alive. The sudden joy was muddied by the realization that she remained a captive. The guilt Darrow felt at leaving her behind returned as an overwhelming pressure on his chest. Again his emotions shifted, and a frail hope occurred to him. If he could free her, perhaps he would deserve freedom also.

"I mean," Darrow continued, "I presumed she was meant to be one of your brother's sparring partners."

"Oh, yes," said Stannis, "she was indeed. But after he was so careless with my favorite servant, I decided to keep her for myself. Petty of me, I know, but Radu must be reminded that he is not the only one who can be cruel. Besides, I knew she might prove useful once again, as your new master's return proves."

"That's what I wish to discuss," said Rusk.

"As well as the matter of my permission for your 'People' to lair within my property," said Stannis. His tone indicated he did not take the uninvited arrival of more than a dozen werewolves lightly.

"You were the one who sent—" began Rusk.

"Of course, Lord Malveen," interrupted Darrow. He made his apology to Rusk with a quick glance. "We did not wish to disturb you during the day, yet we also did not wish to draw attention to your home. So we took shelter where you were so gracious as to house our Huntmaster last year, counting on your generosity to forgive our presumption."

"You haven't been in the woods all this time, have you? I think you spent the winter at court in Ordulin, practicing your courtesies for all the fine ladies." Stannis waved toward a cabinet, and one of his spawn emerged from the shadows to fetch a decanter and goblets.

"What happened at the playhouse?" asked Rusk at last.

"Ronan is hurt and needs your help," said Darrow.

Rusk glowered at him, awaiting an explanation. Darrow decided to leave the details for the others to explain.

Rusk rose ominously from his chair to tower over Darrow. "Where is the Black Wolf?"

Darrow realized his mistake at once. He should never have returned without locating Talbot Uskevren after the fight.

"The Scepters were summoned," said Darrow. "He was probably arrested."

A vein pulsed in the center of Rusk's brow. "Find him."

"If I might suggest an alternative," said Stannis, raising one finger. The digit swayed like the tendril of an anemone in the current. "There is a much more expedient way to determine whether young Uskevren is in the local jail."

"Very well," said Rusk. "I want to know before dusk tomorrow. The night of the Black Wolf is almost upon us. I want him flushed out, not locked up. Come, Darrow. Let's see what our friend has done to Ronan."

"Might I detain your young friend for a while?" asked Stannis. His emphasis on the word "your" held just a hint of bitterness. His golden eyes fell upon Darrow.

When Rusk hesitated, he added, "I promise not to do anything unseemly to him."

"Very well," said Rusk with only the barest hint of reluctance.

Perhaps he thought it fitting punishment for Darrow's bungled scouting mission. He stalked back to the warehouse, growling at the spawn who did not get out of his way quickly enough.

"You have pleased me," Stannis said to Darrow, "and you shall have a reward. Go down and have your visit. No doubt you have many tales to share. You do remember the way?"

"I do, my lord," said Darrow.

Stannis made a show of removing the prison key and handing it over.

"Be sure to leave enough time to come back and repeat them all for me. I have been so dreadfully lonely."

Maelin was the only occupant of the cells beside the baiting pit. Her confinement had transformed her every bit as much as Darrow's year in the woods had changed him. Where once her face was flush with life, blanched flesh now stretched taut over hollow cheeks. Her hair had grown to touch her shoulders, but it was limp and dirty. Even her eyes seemed to have faded in the darkness, and she looked at Darrow for long seconds before recognition filled them.

"So you aren't dead after all."

"Nor you," said Darrow. Her listless greeting was disappointing, but he knew it was because she was on the brink of despair. "I thought you'd have faced Radu by now."

"Stannis wouldn't let him," said Maelin. "I begged him to let me fight back when I still had a chance."

"You never had a chance," said Darrow. "Even if you could beat Radu, Stannis would never let you go. He needs you to get to the Uskevren."

"Don't say that," said Maelin. "I can't bear to believe it. At least if there was a chance . . ."

She tried to raise her hands, but even the simple gesture was too much. Her arms hung lamely at her sides as she leaned against the back wall of the cell. It seemed much bigger than Darrow remembered, but so did her cot, her clothes, and everything else around her shriveled body. Whoever—or whatever—had tended her in his absence had obviously taken no pains to keep her well fed.

"I'm going to get you out of here," he said. He watched her face, knowing the promise would give her hope.

She raised her head to look at him. Her mouth widened, and her body convulsed. It was all the strength she had to laugh.

"I'll help you," he said. "The whole pack will help you."

Maelin's silent laughter continued until it turned into a wracking cough. When she had recovered, she asked, "Pack of what?"

Darrow told her.

When Darrow returned from the baiting pit cells, Stannis was nowhere to be seen. Briefly he debated waiting, knowing that Stannis would be displeased if he crept away without sharing the "gossip" of his past year. Then he realized he still had the key to the cells. He clutched it tightly and returned to the warehouse.

The vast, cluttered room was filled with angry voices. The pack stood around Ronan's body.

"All goes as planned," bellowed Rusk. His body surged with magical strength, and Darrow realized at once how he had dealt with the disobedient Ronan.

"What do you mean?" said Brigid. "Was Ronan's death *as planned*? He worshiped you, and you took his life!"

"He threw his life away!" thundered Rusk. Then he lowered his voice. "Ronan was a good hunter, but he should not have tried to face the Black Wolf. None shall face him but I. There can be no mistakes."

"Ronan was the strongest!" shouted Brigid.

Several others nodded at her words. Darrow caught Sorcia's eye. The white wolf had avoided Rusk since their first encounter with Maleva, but he was certain she was still sowing discord among the pack.

"You sent him to die while you hid in this filthy vampire's lair," Brigid accused.

Rusk stepped toward the defiant nightwalker. "You were sent to scatter the herd from their pen," he thundered.

"Ronan almost ruined everything when he forgot there was a wolf among the sheep."

"Is that what happened when he cut off your arm?" she spat. Despite her defiance, she flinched in anticipation of a physical rebuke.

Rusk surprised them all by not lashing out. "Yes, I too was hasty," he admitted. He turned, raising his voice and gesturing toward his missing arm. "And Malar demanded a sacrifice from me as well. That sacrifice brought us the Black Wolf Scrolls, and from them we know the night of our triumph is nigh. Ronan has made his own sacrifice, as will all who jeopardize the fulfillment of the prophecy."

"You keep telling us about this prophecy," said Morrel. He and Sorcia had been whispering earlier, but Darrow noticed she was nowhere near him when he stepped forward now. "What if it's only a myth? What if you have the time wrong? We are far from our own territory."

"This *is* our territory," said Rusk, "and so is all of the land, the wild and the city alike. I shall face the Black Wolf on the appointed night. Only then will the will of Malar be revealed."

"You mean the will of Rusk, don't you?" said Morrel.

"I speak the words of Malar," he said. "Do you doubt it?"

Morrel met the Huntmaster's eyes only briefly before he turned his face away. Before Rusk could continue, the warehouse door opened. One of Stannis's ghastly minions beckoned for Rusk to follow.

"We will speak more of this later. Come with me," Rusk said to Darrow. Sorcia began to follow him also. "Not you," he told her.

As they left the warehouse, Darrow glanced back at the pack. All of them watched Sorcia as they waited for Rusk to depart.

Inside the great hall, Darrow was not surprised to find Rusk and Stannis arguing, and only slightly surprised to find that Radu had joined them. He knew it was only a matter of time before the younger Malveen became involved, but he had not looked forward to meeting him again. No matter how much stronger Darrow had become in his year of ranging with the pack, he knew he stood no chance if Radu decided to correct the error of his survival.

"We shall all benefit from this endeavor," said Stannis. "Perhaps when all is done, you will let me provide you with sparring partners once more. Perhaps Talbot Uskevren could be the first—"

"No," said Rusk. "After the night of the Black Moon, no one will harm Talbot."

"Then he will be in your control?" inquired Stannis.

"Completely," said Rusk.

From the tiny crinkling at his eyes and the corners of his lips, Darrow sensed the Huntmaster was harboring a secret he had yet to reveal to the pack.

"That is what you promised the first time," observed Radu. He looked pointedly at Darrow. "And it is not the only promise you have broken."

"I agreed that Darrow would be the prey at the High Hunt," said Rusk. He smiled like a chess player who had just made a surprising move. "And so he was. We hunted him, and we caught him."

"We should put an end to all of this," said Radu.

"Two more days," promised Rusk. "When the Black Moon comes, the prophecy shall be fulfilled."

"It occurs to me," said Stannis, "that you have not entirely explained the ultimate outcome of this so-called prophecy."

"You had the scrolls for years," said Rusk. "Did you not read them?"

"Of course I did," said Stannis. "To be blunt, I found them tedious and vague. Naturally, I skimmed all that business with the star charts and the tidal foofaraw. Even so, I wonder that you derive a prophecy from it all. Please, enlighten us as to the particulars."

"The Beastlord is not to be mocked," growled Rusk. "He has revealed his will unto me, and that is enough."

"Give us a hint. Will there be earthquakes and firestorms? I suppose that's really more the domain of Talos the Destroyer. Perhaps Umberlee will donate a tidal wave. I do hope you would warn us if that were the case. What catastrophe would the Beastlord unleash upon a city? A rain of frogs, perhaps?"

"Enough!" roared Rusk.

"Please forgive my *beastly* manners," said Stannis. "The gods have laughed at me for so long, it only seems fair that I laugh back. What are they without the promise of paradise after death. And what is 'after death,' to me?"

While Stannis baited Rusk, Darrow watched Radu's face. His expression became increasingly calm as he watched his brother the vampire talk with his ally the werewolf. For a moment, Darrow felt sympathy for Radu's preposterous circumstance. He was the only human being in the room.

"What will it take to end this?" Radu said.

"I must face Talbot Uskevren," said Rusk. "Tomorrow night, under the open sky."

"Not here," said Radu. "Nowhere near us."

"Agreed," said Rusk. "I have another location in mind."

"And afterward, your pack leaves Selgaunt forever," said Radu.

"Agreed," said Rusk, to Darrow's surprise.

Were his promises of claiming the city as the People's territory lies? Or was he lying now? Darrow realized he had deluded himself into thinking Rusk had taken him into his confidence. He was just as much a servant as he was when he served the Malveens.

"One more thing," said Stannis. "Whatever happens when you face Talbot, it will be unpleasant for him? It will hurt his father?"

"You can consider him dead," said Rusk.

"That isn't as good as tormented," complained Stannis, "but it is something. Very well. He is indeed in the city jail. I have made arrangements for his petition for bail to be delayed until you wish him freed."

"Excellent," said Rusk. "Then all that is left is to flush him out of hiding tomorrow night."

" 'Too bold to hide,' " quoted Darrow. When the others looked at him, he explained, "The Uskevren family motto."

Rusk laughed. "Indeed," he said. "Let us pray it proves a part of the greater prophecy."

He turned to leave, beckoning Darrow to follow.

"Tut!" clucked Stannis. "Are you not forgetting something, dear Darrow?"

Darrow froze, fearing the worst. He was nearly right.

"You forgot to return my key."

"Of course, Lord Malveen." Darrow produced the key and returned it to the vampire, careful to avoid touching his cold, black fingers. "How forgetful of me."

"Indeed," agreed Stannis, gazing thoughtfully at him.

Darrow held his tongue until he and Rusk were out of the Malveen brothers' hearing. Before they returned to the warehouse, he stopped and sniffed for any scent of the spawn before daring to speak.

"Huntmaster," he said, "I have a boon to ask."

Rusk raised an eyebrow.

"Their hostage," he said. "They'll have no more use for her once you've dealt with Uskevren. Let her join the pack."

"What have you done to earn this favor?" demanded Rusk.

"I have been loyal," said Darrow.

"Do you suggest that others have not?" His tone hinted at a test. Darrow knew he must not fail it.

"Sorcia," he said. "She is trying to turn the others against you. She says you are mad."

Rusk nodded. "She is not the only one, is she?"

"She's the only one who says it," said Darrow, "but others are beginning to believe her. They are beginning to doubt you."

"Do you doubt me?" He fixed his eyes on Darrow's face.

Darrow took a breath before answering. He could not lie, but he feared telling the truth. "I sometimes . . . doubt the prophecy, Huntmaster, but I will follow you through it, no matter what happens."

"You betray the others to me, yet you swear you remain loyal when they will not." A smile slowly formed on Rusk's face. "I will consider your boon. First, however, I have a task for you. I do not trust your former masters, yet I know how much you fear them. Do you have the courage to turn against them?"

Darrow thought of Maelin and her gratitude upon her rescue. "I do, Huntmaster."

Tracking by scent was virtually impossible in the city. Chimney smoke, nightsoil, cooking fires, and a thousand other pungent odors foiled Darrow's senses. Darrow could never have discerned his own footsteps among the clamor of voices and the rattling carriages that passed along the street. He relied solely on sight to follow Radu through the streets of Selgaunt.

Fortunately, Radu made no effort to hide himself as he left House Malveen and took Larawkan Street out of the Warehouse District. He turned onto Vandallan Lane soon after entering central Selgaunt. It was less congested than the main thoroughfare but still provided ample cover for Darrow, who stayed well behind Radu, matching speed with carts or small clusters of pedestrians whenever possible. They provided even better cover than the brush in woods, since they moved with him. Darrow saw more clearly than ever how much the city and the wild had in common.

Darrow followed Radu west through the Central District, then north, skirting the eastern border of the Oxblood Quarter. The streets narrowed and the crowds thickened, as did the smell of livestock, tanning acids, and dyes.

As they crossed into the Oxblood Quarter, Darrow lost sight of Radu. He approached the spot where he'd last seen Radu, careful not to blunder into an ambush. He knew better than anyone that his former master was not to be underestimated. From that point, there were three likely places for Radu to have disappeared: a leather goods store, a butcher's shop, and the alley between them.

Darrow walked past the alley with his face turned away, toward the street. He turned at the next alley. The other side opened into a filthy yard shared by the nearby shops. The mingled chemical and animal smells made Darrow's head pound, but the walls muted the clamor of the streets. He cocked his head and listened. At first he heard nothing and wished he could take wolf form before the moon rose. Then he heard a stifled cry from another alley across the yard. Keeping low, he crept nearer.

". . . see you there," said a wavering male voice.

"Who gave you the money?" asked Radu.

Darrow heard the clink of heavy coins in a bag. He peeked around the corner. A slender, balding man of forty or fifty years stood in the middle of the alley. His long, thin face was pale with fright, and his hands trembled as he gripped a big leather satchel.

His resemblance to Maelin was slight. They had the same prominent eyelids and narrow nose, but her mother must have contributed everything else, including her strong will. If his personality matched his looks, Darrow understood why fiery Maelin could not bear to acknowledge her father.

"Lady Shamur," said Eckert. "She also sent a message to Lord Uskevren in Ordulin. He should return tomorrow."

Radu nodded. Darrow couldn't see his face but knew from experience that it betrayed no emotion.

"What of the cleric?"

"She came to the tallhouse. She seemed agitated about something, but she wouldn't say what. I told her nothing about the arrest. When she asked after Master Talbot, I said he was spending the evening at Stormweather Towers."

"Very good," said Radu. "Give me the money."

"Where is Maelin?" said Eckert. He clutched the bag of coins against his chest.

"You will see her soon."

"The sending said this would be the last task."

"It will be," promised Radu, drawing his sword.

"Wait!" the thin man dropped the satchel.

Radu struck before it hit the ground, and Eckert gasped. Before he could touch the wound beneath his heart, Radu's sword licked out again, piercing him high on the left breast.

The third stroke cut through Eckert's hand and pierced his heart.

Radu plucked a handkerchief from his sleeve and used it to wipe his blade clean as Eckert stood silent and gaping. Radu dropped the bloodied cloth as he watched the man sink to his knees. At last he sheathed the weapon and picked up the bag.

Darrow ducked into a cellar stairwell. When he heard the faint jingling of the coins recede across the yard, he peeked out and saw that Radu was gone. He hurried to the dying man's side, but a woman was hurrying toward him from the street side of the alley.

"Get away from him!" snapped the woman. She flung open her blue cloak and put a hand on the silver talisman that hung from a chain around her neck.

"Don't!" said Darrow. He kept his hands away from his sword, snatched Radu's discarded handkerchief, and pressed it against the thin man's bloody chest. "I didn't do this."

"Maelin . . ." gasped Eckert. A sickening wheezing came from the man's chest, and a mist of blood sprayed from the sucking wound. Blood pooled on the ground beneath him, soaking Darrow's breeches at the knees.

"Get away, I said!" She pushed Darrow away, intoning a prayer to Selûne as she pressed her bare hand against the thin man's chest.

Silver light surged within her hand, then spread across the thin man's chest. Darrow watched as she said the prayer again, and more radiant energy passed from the cleric to the wounded man. At last, the blood stopped pouring from the man, and his breathing became steady.

"Will he live?" asked Darrow.

"Depends on what he has to tell me about what we just saw," said the woman angrily. She fixed her blue eyes on Darrow. "The same goes for you, nightwalker."

"How did you know—?"

The woman cast another spell, this time summoning a blade of white light to her empty hand. "Where is Rusk?" she demanded.

"Listen," he said, backing up and holding up his hands in a gesture of peace. "We can help each other."

"I'm listening," she said. "Make it good, and make it quick. I'll probably kill you anyway."

"You don't need to kill me. I—"

"Maybe not," interrupted the woman, "but I might *want* to. Now talk."

CHAPTER 16

BEHIND BARS

Tarsakh, 1372 DR

Even before Tal became accustomed to locking himself into a cage three nights of every month, he was no stranger to barred cells. He needed the fingers of both hands to count the number of times he and Chaney had been hauled into jail for public disorder.

Usually it was Chaney's fault. When faced with a belligerent drunk who disliked nobles slumming in his tavern, Tal usually responded by buying the man another tankard of ale. After a few repetitions of the trick, the drunk usually passed out harmlessly or staggered out to be sick in the alley. Sometimes a match of arm wrestling would do, and once Tal won over an entire crew of rowdy Chessentan sailors by winning a contest in which he and their strongman took turns lifting a barmaid-laden table, adding a new girl to the load with each attempt.

Unable to respond with feats of strength, Chaney relied on his sharp tongue when challenged. He especially liked insulting the other young nobles who frequented the cheap alehouses, since they were more likely to provide fair sport for his quick wit. They were also less likely to turn to fisticuffs, at least when Tal was nearby. Given enough ale, however, and even men smaller than Chaney would resort to violence. Even though he never threw the first punch, Tal was always ready for it. When he was honest with himself, he had to admit that he liked the thrill of combat, especially the admiration of the bystanders when he won against a fair opponent—or six lesser challengers.

He missed those brawling days over the past year. Since the wolf emerged, Tal had stayed out of taverns for two reasons: to avoid another "accident" like the one that maimed Perron and to avoid finding himself in jail when the moon was full.

As it would be tonight.

Chaney paced, turning sharply at each corner of the cell. Even with his short legs, it took him only four steps in each direction.

Tal rested his chin against his folded arms, staring out through the barred window that slanted up to the narrow alley outside. Street-filtered runoff still trickled down the short shaft to pool on the stone floor. Despite the dirty water, Tal was grateful for the relatively fresh air. The previous occupant of the cell had left a noisome puddle of vomit beneath the cot.

The only other occupant in this block of the jail was an old man with a long wispy beard. Tal recognized him as one of the homeless drunks who begged for coppers in the Oxblood Quarter. There was less money there but more charity than in Central Selgaunt, where the Scepters were poised to run off beggars and thieves alike.

"I never thought I'd say this," Chaney said without breaking his stride, "but I can't wait to see Eckert."

"You always say that when we're waiting for bail."

"Sure, but I never *expect* to say it. Hm?"

Before this past year, Tal's servant made a habit of checking the jail when Tal hadn't returned home in the morning. If the tallhouse funds were insufficient for bail, it meant a trip to Stormweather to fetch a larger amount from Lord Uskevren. For the first time in his life, Tal dreaded his father's not being told of his predicament more than another night in jail.

"Let's hope he didn't choose last night to run off with the silver to marry a widow," said Chaney.

His banter did nothing to cheer Tal. Their recent arrest was far worse than any of their previous visits to the city jail. If Tal's attacker died last night, there was no chance a magistrate would allow bail, even if Thamalon were willing to pay it. Even if the charge was short of murder or attempted murder, Tal was sure the Old Owl would wash his hands of his wayward son this time.

"At least this time it wasn't your fault," said Tal, trying lamely to respond with a jest.

"Everyone will think it was anyway." Chaney sounded genuinely regretful.

"I thought you liked being thought a scoundrel."

"Only when it impresses the ladies," said Chaney with a smile.

"Let's hope it impresses the magistrate enough to get us out of here before dark."

"That's right," said Chaney, as if he had not yet considered the problem of the moon. "We've got to get you home before curfew."

Tal realized that Chaney was making a great effort to put on a brave face. As bad as it was for Tal to transform while in jail, it would be far worse for anyone locked up with him. Tal glanced at the other prisoner before speaking again in a quiet voice. "I'll get them to put me in another cell."

"How? You think they'll fall for the old 'I'm sick' routine?"

"Not likely, all things considered."

"We could stage a fight," suggested Chaney.

"We . . . could," said Tal slowly. He looked at Chaney and worried about hurting his smaller friend. "We'd have to make it look real."

"Or you could just let me have it once or twice," said Chaney. "I might not be a big strapping lad like you, but I won't break."

"I just don't like the idea of hitting you. Usually, I'm fighting other people who're trying to hit you."

"Hard for me to complain about that," said Chaney.

"Besides, there's what happened last night. Punching you once or twice is one thing . . ."

". . . and pulling my guts out is quite another," Chaney finished for him. He kept his eyes on the floor and continued his circuit of the cell.

They were both silent for a while.

"Maybe we can break out," said Tal. He gripped the bars and pulled with all his might.

The old drunk saw his efforts and hooted. "Have to be a lot stronger'n you look to bend those bars, me lord."

Tal sneered at the old man and kept pulling. The drunk laughed until he coughed, pointing at the ludicrous sight. The laughter stopped with a sudden hiccup when the old fellow saw the bars bend, ever so slightly.

Encouraged, Tal pulled harder. No matter how he strained, the iron bars would bend no farther. When it felt like he would tear a ligament, Tal let go. The bars flexed back into their original positions, looking as straight as ever.

"I know you've been getting stronger," said Chaney, "but dark and empty, Tal! Those are almost as thick as the bars on Quickly's cage."

"Been practicing, have you?" The old man scratched under his beard and whistled through a gap in his brown teeth.

"I hate being in here," said Tal, lowering his voice and turning his back on the old drunk.

"I thought you'd be used to that by now, with all the time you've been spending in the cage at home."

"It's not the same," said Tal. "When I lock myself up, it's my choice. I can't stand it when someone else decides for me."

"Oh, please," said Chaney. "I thought you were done with all that everybody-wants-me-to-be-what-they-want-me-to-be whining."

"Whining?"

"Yeah, whining, crying, belly-aching . . . whatever. I've put up with it ever since we met, but I don't want to hear it now—not when we're both locked in this stinking cell and you're about to turn all teeth and claws and fur and all kinds of horrible man-eating things."

"I don't whine," said Tal, trying not to think about the other part of what Chaney said.

"Of course you do," persisted Chaney. "That's why Sivana and Ennis were making fun of you with the wolf mask. All you saw was the wolf bit, because you were so afraid of your secret getting out. Well, that's not going to be a problem after tonight, is it? What's really ridiculous is all your complaining about not getting your way all the time."

"You don't know what it's like," said Tal. "Everything I do, Thamalon criticizes because it's not what he would do. Even after everything that happened this winter, Mother still looks down her nose at the playhouse. And don't get me started about Tamlin and—"

"Oh, spare me. You have more freedom than anyone I know," said Chaney. "Thamalon let you have the tallhouse, didn't he? And no matter what she says about the playhouse, your mother hasn't stopped you from acting. You can't say they're making you do what they want. All you can do is complain that they don't approve of the choices that they let you make for yourself."

"How's that any different from you?" said Tal. "You don't even talk about your family, and I've never seen you spend any time at the house."

Chaney stared at Tal, incredulous. "There's a reason for that, you lunkhead."

"And I suppose it's better than my reasons for avoiding Thamalon."

Chaney laughed at him. "You could say that."

"What are you talking about?"

"You know how I'm always saying my father disowned me?"

Tal nodded.

"I wasn't speaking metaphorically."

Tal cocked his head, confused.

"He threw me out three years ago," said Chaney. "Drew up legal documents to make sure I never have any claim on the family money. He had the Scepters drag me out of the house and into the street, where a magistrate read the pronouncement."

"What are you talking about? I thought—I mean, where do you get your money?"

Chaney laughed. "Mostly from you. You're pretty quick to pay wherever we go or to let me stay at the tallhouse when we've been out late."

"But I don't always pay," said Tal, "and you haven't been wearing the same set of clothes for three years, that lucky jacket aside. You've got money coming from somewhere, right?"

"Well," said Chaney, "for a while my Aunt Verula was slipping me a little now and again, but the old man found out, and there was a big row. I've been totally cut off for about two years."

"I can't believe you didn't tell me."

"I must have told you a hundred times. You laughed, like it was a joke."

"I thought it *was* a joke."

"Did you now?" said Chaney dubiously.

"Of course I did. What else?"

Chaney shrugged and plucked a long straw from the cot. "I figured you didn't want to hear about my problems," he said. "You've always been so wrapped up in your own."

"What are you saying?" demanded Tal. "That I'm so self-centered I don't care about what's happening to my friends?"

"No," said Chaney. "You care all right. You just care more about yourself."

"That's a rotten thing to say about someone who's supported you over the past three years."

"You didn't even know you were doing it! Besides, I don't need your charity. I can get by on my own, thanks very much."

"Sure, that's why you've leeched off me instead of getting a proper job. At least I work at the playhouse. What do you do?"

"I don't think you want to hear what I do," said Chaney. "It might offend your honorable sensibilities. After all, you didn't ask too many questions when I took care of the little problem with Alale Soargyl last year, did you?"

"I didn't ask because . . . well, because . . ."

"Because you didn't want to get your own hands dirty," said Chaney. "You like to talk about how you're different from the rest of the Old Chauncel, but when it comes to getting your hands dirty, you're glad to leave it to others. You're just like your father."

Before he knew what he'd done, Tal backhanded Chaney, knocking him into the cell bars.

Shame burned his face, but anger still buzzed in Tal's head. He stepped close and grabbed a handful of Chaney's shirt, easily lifting the smaller man off the floor.

Chaney remained limp, and Tal hesitated. Before Tal realized the ruse, Chaney shot his knee into Tal's groin. The pain shot flares through Tal's already spinning head. He glared through a red haze and growled at Chaney before slamming him against the bars. He both felt and heard the cracking of ribs.

"What's going on in there?" yelled a guard through the cellblock gate.

"Help!" cried Chaney. "He's gone berserk—he'll kill me!"

Tal felt dizzy and confused. What was he doing? Murdering his best friend for a few criticisms? He had to calm himself, or else what happened at the theater might make the moonrise redundant.

"Nice try, Foxmantle," called the guard. "I been to the playhouse once or twice." He slammed the shutter closed.

Tal gently lowered Chaney to the floor, then helped him to the cot.

"Great gods," said Tal. "I'm sorry, Chane."

"Just my luck," gasped Chaney, gingerly lying down on the straw tick mattress, "the guard thinks you're a great actor."

"You were baiting me on purpose, you idiot! Weren't you?"

Chaney grimaced through the pain. "Maybe."

"You really had me fooled," said Tal. "Not that it's any excuse . . ."

"Yeah," said Chaney. "Tricked you real good."

"It was very realistic," said the old drunk from across the aisle. "Especially the rib cracking."

"You shut up," said Tal.

"Why should I?" said the old man. "Until you manage to bend those bars, I'll say anything I like. Ratbreath. Maggot-eater. Arse-licking son of a—"

Tal showed his teeth and growled. The old man shut up.

"Here," said Tal, rolling his shirt into a pillow. "Let's get you comfortable."

"Just let me rest," said Chaney. He waved his hand at the other side of the cell. "Go, over there. Leave me alone a while."

"I can't tell you how sorry I am," said Tal.

"Yeah," said Chaney. "Me neither."

Chaney remained quiet for the rest of the afternoon. Tal spent his time brooding by the narrow window. Several times he resolved to apologize again, but when he started to speak, Chaney turned his face away.

"Lover's spat" cackled the drunk. "Always the worst. Ye'll be sleepin' on the floor tonight."

Tal no longer answered the taunts. The old man nattered on without encouragement, secure in the safety of his own cell.

Tal reached through the barred window. With a stretch, he could barely put his fingers on the cobblestones of the alley. There was plenty of room for Chaney to slip through, if Tal could pull out two of the bars. Unfortunately, they were set deeply into the stone casement, not just bolted to the wall. Tal put both hands on one, then walked up the wall on his knees. Firmly braced, he pulled outward with all his strength.

The bars did not even bend. After a few minutes, Tal dropped back down to the floor.

"It's getting dark," he observed after catching his breath. Chaney didn't answer. It was hard to tell by looking into the alley just how close it was to dusk. Tal began to pace, just as Chaney had done earlier. With his longer stride, he could take only three steps in each direction.

"Would you stop that?" asked Chaney at last.

"Sure," said Tal. He tested the cell door for the hundredth time, hoping it would prove weaker than the window bars.

"You can stop that, too," said Chaney. "I've got a headache."

Tal sighed and let go of the door. Then he cocked his head. "Did you hear that?"

"What?" said Chaney. He rose from the cot and gently felt his back with both hands.

"Someone just called my name," he said, moving to the window. He heard it again.

"Here!" he shouted through the barred window. "I'm over here!"

Feena dropped to her hands and knees beside the low opening.

"There's no bail coming," she said breathlessly.

"I know," said Tal. "I didn't expect the magistrate to allow it."

"But he did," said Feena. "Eckert got money from your mother—but we'll discuss that later. First, we get you out of here."

"There's no time," said Tal. "Go to the guards and make them let Chaney out of this cell."

"No time for that, either. Stand back," said Feena.

"But—" Tal thought better of protesting and took a step back. Behind him, Chaney began muttering a string of prayers to Tymora, goddess of luck.

Feena grasped a bar in both hands and pushed. Tal expected to see her cast a spell for inhuman strength or to turn the metal bars molten hot. But instead of invoking Selûne, Feena shook her head violently, like a horse tossing its mane. She grimaced and stretched her neck as if it hurt.

"It's no good," said Tal. "I've tried that—"

Feena's eyes flashed red.

"Look out!" cried Chaney, but Tal was transfixed by the sight. Feena's fair freckled skin was now covered in downy russet fur. Her bared teeth were growing long and narrow in her elongating jaws.

"Get back," warned Chaney. "It's a werewolf disguised as Feena!"

"No," said Tal. He put his hands on either side of Feena's and pulled as she pushed. "It's her, all right. I can smell her."

"But if she's changing, then when will you—?" He stopped as he saw Tal's face, which was covered with fine black fur.

"Pull!" said Feena. Her voice had fallen half a register. "But concentrate on the bar. Don't think about anything else, Tal. Listen to me! Pull the bar. I'll help you break the bar."

"Dark and empty!" said Chaney. "Am I the only one here who doesn't turn into a wolf?"

"I don't," offered the drunk from across the aisle.

"Shut up, both of you," snarled Feena.

They obeyed, watching as the transforming werewolves strained to break the window bars. Tal and Feena bristled with fur, and rough claws jutted from their fingers. Tal's legs were changing shape, bending back in wolf fashion to end in clawed pads. He kicked away his useless boots, and his trousers fell after them.

"The bar, Tal!" roared Feena. "Pull the bar!"

Tal tried to answer, but his words became an inarticulate growl. His upper body was still human except for a thickening black pelt, but it was growing broader by the second. Tremendous muscles twitched and wriggled beneath his skin, still transforming as they struggled to break the bars.

The bar came away with a clatter of stone. Before Tal could put his hands on the next, Feena was already pushing. Her face was more wolf than woman now, but she could still speak.

"Pull!"

Together, they ripped the second bar from the wall. There was still too little space for Tal's big form to pass through. Feena grabbed the third bar, but Tal turned toward Chaney.

His face was almost completely unrecognizable now, with a long lupine snout and blazing red eyes. His own long hair formed a shaggy mane that blended with the fur of his sloping shoulders. Panting, he reached toward Chaney.

"The bars, Tal! You have to pull at the bars!" Feena repeated. "Come back to the window!"

With a yelp, Chaney tried to dart away. He was too slow, and the werewolf's clawed hands gripped him by the arms.

"Help me, Feena!" Chaney called.

"Tal!"

Chaney struggled but could not resist the powerful hands that lifted him from the floor and swung him around to the window. In one graceful gesture, Tal shoved Chaney through the narrow aperture and into the alley with Feena.

Behind him, Tal heard the guards calling out. The drumming pulse in his head scrambled the meaning of their words, but the clinking of their keys told him they were coming through the door. His shirt had torn, but it twisted uncomfortably at his shoulders. He ripped it away as easily as he might shred a leaf.

Outside, Chaney scrambled to his feet. He cradled his injured ribs, then turned to try to help with the bars.

"Run," said Tal. His voice was barely understandable, deep and stony as a dry well. *"Ruuun!"*

"Go!" said Feena.

She put her hands on the next bar, and Tal's joined hers. As they struggled with the bars, Chaney limped to the end of the alley. He paused only until he saw them break away the third bar. At the sound of guards running toward the alley, he bolted at last, finding cover in the twilight shadows.

The guards were inside the jail block now. "Get the cross-bows!" shouted one as his companion fumbled with the key to Tal's cell.

"Silver bolts!" ordered another from the relative safety of the outer door.

At last, Tal and Feena broke the fourth bar away. Wielding it like a baton, Tal banged it against the cell door. The guards leaped back, and the one with the keys dropped them as he shouted in alarm. Tal threw the window bar at them, then jumped up into the open window.

Feena grasped his arms and pulled, but Tal's broad shoulders could not pass through the window. He struggled to squeeze himself through the narrow gap. The ragged holes left by the bars scraped at his flesh, cutting him even through his fur.

Tal wriggled and twisted, gaining only a few inches before the twang of a crossbow sounded behind him. He felt something slap his thigh and fought harder to push through the cell window.

Tal's struggling caused Feena to lose her grip. She fell back onto the alley floor. As her shadow fell away from Tal, moonlight spilled onto his face. It felt like cool water, washing him from head to feet. As the sensation ran through his body, he felt all his flesh shift and remold itself. His hands became paws scratching for traction on the stone alley floor, and his slenderer trunk barely slipped through the window, leaving wet patches of bloody fur behind.

As a wolf on four legs, Tal stood nearly as tall as Feena in her half-wolf form. She bowed her head and shifted completely back to human shape just as the reinforcements blocked the alley's mouth.

Tal turned to snarl a warning at the guards. There were four of them, three aiming crossbows with silver-tipped bolts. Feena was talking to them, but Tal could not understand her words. He perceived the barest motion of the Scepters' weapons and smelled the sour fear in their sweat. Then he smelled something strange, a clean white energy emanating from Feena. It blew like a cool breeze to engulf the bowmen. As it washed over them, they stood stock still.

Feena said a word to Tal, and though he could not understand it, he thought the command was "run." Human language was strange to his ears, but it was becoming clearer as his blood slowed. Then Feena crouched low, transforming from woman to half-wolf to full wolf in a matter of moments. She wriggled out of her fallen clothes. Only the silver talisman of Selûne remained secure on a chain around her neck.

When she stood on four paws, Feena butted Tal's flank with her narrow head before rushing out the alley through the legs of the paralyzed guards. The gesture said more clearly than words, "Run with me."

Together, they fled the alley. Pedestrians scattered at the sight of two wolves—all but one.

A man gazed at them from the street corner. Tall and broad-shouldered, he wore the rough woolen breeches and leather jerkin of a laborer. Thick mutton-chop whiskers gave the man a wild appearance, but Tal smelled a familiar scent on him. It was more than an animal scent. There was a familiar aura about the man, and Tal knew immediately he was like Tal and Feena—a werewolf.

Tal moved toward the man, growling. The stranger backed away, but Feena butted Tal again before he could close.

No, she was saying. *This way.*

Tal wanted to pursue the strange werewolf, to chase him off or fight him—he wasn't sure which. He ignored Feena and rushed forward. The stranger turned to flee, but two legs would never outrun four. Tal was almost upon him when Feena bit his flank.

Irritation more than anger spun him around to bite back, but the russet wolf was nimble. She slipped away before his teeth could catch her. Tal paused, torn between pursuing the stranger and chastising Feena. He turned toward the stranger, who was almost a street away.

Feena nipped him again, then ran away before he could bite back. This time he pursued her.

She was fast, but his legs were longer. He was almost upon her when she turned suddenly to run down a side street. His claws scraped on the cobblestones as he skidded to a halt before rejoining the pursuit.

People scattered before the wolves, and twice they ran past startled clusters of city Scepters. Once a bolt pierced Tal's shoulder, and he yelped as he rolled to break it loose. It came away easily, leaving an angry mark that soon healed over. It was no more harm than a mosquito bite.

Feena called to him in the wolf's voice, and he followed. His desire to punish her distracting attacks had faded, but he felt an urgent need to escape all the motion in the city. Dimly he knew that those crossbows could do more than sting, but even more he wanted wide spaces. In the city there were walls and buildings at every turn. He felt confined by the boundaries, harried by all the commotion wherever they ran.

At last, Feena led them to the city gates. The guards took one look at the running wolves and pushed open the gates, as one might open the shutters to free a bat caught in the house. Tal could smell their fear subside as he and Feena ran through the opening, leaving the city behind.

Beyond the walls of Selgaunt, they ran through grassy fields, heedless of the road. Feena nipped at Tal again, more playfully than before. He chased her again, but not for retribution. His anger and confusion were gone now, and he felt only joy at the wide freedom of the open land and the cool light of the radiant moon.

The chase continued until they were far out of sight and scent of the city. Still Feena led Tal along, nipping or butting him, or just feinting an approach before dashing away. Before long he learned the patterns of her play, and at last Tal caught her by the scruff of her neck. He held her tightly but without drawing blood, bearing her down to the ground.

Feena stopped struggling, at last laying her head down between her paws. Her scent was a strange blend of her human odor and animal musk. The combination evoked an uncomfortable but pleasant sensation in Tal. He released his grip and snuffled at her, drinking the smell of her. Rather than quench his desire, it inflamed him all the more.

Feena nuzzled him and licked his face. Their scents mingled, forming a heady blend of odors both male and female, human and wolf . . .

Tal's sudden passion was equal parts panic and desire. He wanted Feena, more than he'd ever wanted a woman—but not like this, not as wolves. Thoughts wrestled with emotions in a confusing tumble. He turned and walked away from Feena, trying not to look back.

He sat and listened for the sea, less than a mile away. It was but a black line on the horizon, discernable only by the reflection of the moon. Tal's ears pricked up to hear the faint susurrus of the waves. The constant rhythm soothed him, and gradually his racing heart slowed. He imagined himself floating gently on those waves, the water carrying him without filling his lungs. Slowly, slowly, he felt the wind in his fur become the breeze on his skin.

He looked down to see human hands, human legs. He looked up to see Selûne shining full and bright above him. Behind her trailed the shards, sparking fragments of light. Feena had told him they were the goddess's servants, forever attending their Lady of Silver.

Warm hands touched Tal's shoulders. He turned to see Feena kneeling behind him. The moonlight washed away all but a few of her freckles and left her eyes big and dark.

"We're safe out here," she said. "No one will find us."

The warmth of her hands was thrilling and comforting at once. She stroked his shoulders gently, then pressed her hands against his back, leaning close. Tal could feel the warmth of her body only inches from his own skin.

"Thank you," he said. The words sounded feeble even as they left his lips.

"Are you cold?" she asked. Her lips were close to his ear, and he smelled her breath. Before he could answer, she added, "I am."

He turned and opened his arms to her. She nestled against his chest as if they were familiar lovers. Her artless gesture stole away his breath.

"I didn't want . . . I didn't know . . ."

He never finished whatever he was about to say. Feena pulled his face down to hers and stopped his lips with a long, warm kiss. It set his heart running once again, and he feared the wolf would overcome him once again. When their lips parted, their twined bodies were still human.

"I want," she said. "And I know."

She looked into Tal's eyes for assent, but he gave it with his lips.

They said no more that night, and when Selûne passed her greatest height and descended gracefully to the far horizon, they fell asleep on the soft grass, their human bodies twined together.

CHAPTER 17

BETRAYALS

Tarsakh, 1372 DR

Uskevren is still in the city," Darrow told the cleric. "Exactly where, I don't know."

"Don't know or won't say?" she demanded.

Something about her blue eyes seemed disturbingly familiar. Suddenly he realized that this had to be Maleva's daughter, sent to Selgaunt to watch over Talbot Uskevren. If she had not yet learned of her mother's death, Darrow didn't want to be the one to tell her. After witnessing Maleva's powers, Darrow would have feared her daughter even if she weren't wielding a blade of holy light.

"What I do know is that Stannis Malveen has this man's daughter locked up," Darrow told her. "He's been blackmailing him for information on Talbot Uskevren."

"To what end?" asked the cleric.

"I'm not sure," said Darrow. She raised her weapon. "He changes his mind! At first it sounded like he wanted revenge because of some old quarrel with Thamalon Uskevren. Later, he was making a deal with Rusk to get at Talbot."

"You're coming with me," she said. "You can explain all this to Talbot yourself."

"I can't," he said. "If I'm gone too long, they might kill her. Besides, I think Talbot is in jail."

"What?"

"That's why this one was meeting Radu, I think. They were going to make it look like he was robbed of the bail money."

"Tonight's the full moon," said the cleric, looking at the sky.

"I know," said Darrow. "You have to get your friend out of his cell."

"First you will help me carry Eckert back to the tallhouse."

Darrow considered the likelihood of escaping once the cleric had brought him back to the tallhouse, where Uskevren family guards would no doubt keep him for questioning. While he had little doubt the cleric could reduce him to a tidy pile of ashes if she desired, he would never have a better chance to escape her than now, when she was concerned for Eckert's life.

He turned and ran.

"Hold it!" she yelled after him.

He clenched his teeth and kept on running, fearing with every step that he would feel the first pangs of paralysis or the searing heat of divine fire.

Darrow hastened back to House Malveen. His mind was filled with conflicting hopes and schemes. He did not trust Rusk to follow through on his promise of demanding Maelin's freedom. Even if he asked, and even if Stannis consented, there was still Radu to consider. The calculating swordsman would never permit such a loose end to dangle from these mad schemes he had opposed from the start. If he could slay them all, he would no doubt kill every member of the pack to keep his brother's plots secret.

He thought about defecting to the side of Talbot and his allies, but Maleva's daughter would be unlikely to trust a werewolf after learning of her mother's death, much less help him. There was no guarantee that Talbot would lift a finger to help the daughter of his faithless servant, either.

Most confusing of all was the question Darrow had never dared to ask himself over the past year. Why did he care at all whether Maelin lived? Her only overtures to him had been coerced by her situation, and they could hardly be genuine. She was not the most beautiful woman Darrow had ever seen and definitely not the most charming. The closest he could come to answering his own question was to say he did not like to see her confined. He wanted to meet her outside of her captivity, to hear her thank him for placing himself in such danger on her behalf. Beyond this vague fantasy, Darrow's obsession remained a confounding mystery.

The pack was listless in the confines of the Malveen warehouse. Some of them had cleared a place for Ronan's corpse to lie. They would take it back to the Arch Wood, where they would leave it exposed to the elements, returning his essence to the land he once roamed.

Brigid and Karnek squatted around the cold fire pit Rusk had made two winters past. They spoke quietly, and occasionally one or two of the others would join them, usually after a few words with Sorcia.

The others paced the floor or clambered over the stacks of lost cargo, chasing rats or breaking open dusty crates to examine their contents. No one could sleep.

An hour after sunset, Morrel returned with the news that a red-haired werewolf had helped free Talbot from his prison cell.

"Feena," said Rusk, with mingled ire and admiration. He glanced at Darrow to see his reaction. If he saw one, he did not comment on it.

"They'll go into hiding," said Morrel. "We must track them down."

"Yes," said Rusk, "but they will not go far. Our host has seen to that. When he goes to his servant, he will hear that his family has refused to aid him. He will have nowhere left to turn, except to me."

"You mean to Malar," said Morrel.

Rusk waved his hand irritably. "That's what I said."

Hours later, Rusk returned to the River Hall to confer with the Malveens. Darrow began to follow him, but Rusk pushed him back from the door.

"You won't be needed this time," he said.

"You'll ask about Maelin?" said Darrow.

"I have not forgotten," said Rusk, closing the door behind him.

Darrow turned to rejoin the pack, but Sorcia stood in his way. No one else was nearby.

"Do you truly believe he'll free your captive princess?" asked Sorcia.

"Why wouldn't he?"

"Because he knows you for the simpering toady you are," she said. "The only reason he lets you live is to feed his dwindling pride."

"Then why does he let you live?" asked Darrow. "He hears your whispers. He knows you question his every move."

"Yes," said Sorcia, "and so I make him stronger, so long as he can keep his place."

"Somehow, I doubt he would see it that way."

"You think you know his mind?" Sorcia asked. "What do you think he's saying to Stannis now? Is he begging permission to take your sweetheart into the pack?"

"One day you'll eavesdrop on the wrong conversation," warned Darrow.

"What makes you think I overheard you? Rusk told us all about your pathetic request. No one laughed louder than he."

"You lie," said Darrow.

"Do I?" said Sorcia. "I bow to your greater experience."

She sauntered away, glancing once over her shoulder to see Darrow standing alone by the door to the River Hall.

He clenched his fists to calm the trembling, but it did no good. His skin felt prickly cold, and he could not tell whether fear or anger was the cause. If what Sorcia said was true, he could not bear to return to the pack.

He turned back to the door and felt the latch. It was not locked. With one last look around to see that he was alone, Darrow slipped into the western wing of House Malveen and closed the door silently behind him.

He sniffed for any scent of Stannis's minions, but they were nowhere near. They must be attending the vampire and his guest on the grand promenade, he figured. His chances of approaching them undetected were practically nil, unless he ascended to the upper floors. He circled around to the servants' quarters and climbed the stairs, moving cautiously to keep the sagging floors from creaking. It took him over twenty minutes to reach the balcony at such a deliberate pace. He was rewarded with the sound of Rusk's laughter.

"For all his eccentricities, I appreciate your brother's friendship," he said. "Yet I admire your pragmatism, Radu. We are more alike than you might think."

Darrow peered over the edge of the balcony. Below him, Rusk sat comfortably in a leather chair beside the counting table. Radu stood behind it, his hands folded behind his back.

Undeterred by Radu's silence, Rusk continued in a more serious tone, "You should be more friendly. Our alliance was most profitable for your uncle, years ago. Perhaps you would like to return the baiting pit to its original purpose?"

"Mere sport is not worth such a risk," replied Radu.

"How could it be more risk than acquiring opponents for your private duels?" said Rusk. "And how can you collect wagers from an uninvited audience?"

"Bloodsport is still illegal in Selgaunt," said Radu. "And every member of an audience means another tongue to wag."

"And are you not adept at severing wagging tongues?"

"You forget that we do not own this property. Our family legacy . . . it is forbidden to us."

"Only because you let them forbid you," said Rusk. "You are too cautious, Radu. You should be bold, take chances."

"My mother was bold," said Radu. "And so were you, the night you lost that arm."

"A mistake I shall soon mend," said Rusk amiably. "You are correct, Radu. One can be too bold, and I know you wish only to protect your family. It is one of the things we have in common."

"Your pack?"

"Indeed," said Rusk. "I watch over them as if they were my own children."

"Even Darrow?"

"Sometimes children must be punished."

Darrow had heard more than enough. He crept away even more cautiously than before, slowly making his way to the other side of the grand promenade. There he listened for Rusk and Radu to leave the River Hall. When he was sure they were gone, he descended to the ground floor and slipped across to the portrait gallery.

He pressed the picture frame and went through the secret door, descending the stairs without the benefit of light. Soon he heard screams. They chilled the marrow in his bones, for he knew there was only one captive remaining in the cells. With fearful anticipation, he crept past the stands and peered over the edge of the baiting pit.

The cell gates were open, and Darrow spied Maelin through the bars of her cell. She lay across her bed, arching her back in agony while screaming her throat raw. On the other side of the cell floated Stannis, though the angle allowed Darrow to see only a fraction of his hulking body.

"I am beginning to enjoy our conversations," purred Stannis. "How good of you to give me cause to incorporate these delightful enchantments. It has been so long since I have employed them on someone other than my minions, whose screams are as street water compared to the fine wine of your delicious—"

Maelin cut him off with a searing string of obscenities. "You sick, demented monster! Just kill me and get it over with!"

"Charming to the end," said Stannis.

Whatever arcane terms he uttered, Darrow could not make out. The effects were immediate and clear, as Maelin shrieked and writhed against the unseen pain inflicted by the vampire's magic.

"Do not fret, my delicate princess. Your knight shall join you soon enough. Once he has served his purpose, you will have the chance to scream together before you dance with my brother. Perhaps he will let you face him together, like the elves. Not that you will provide much challenge in your present condition."

The thought of attacking Stannis never entered Darrow's mind. He hoped to hide long enough for the mad vampire to grow tired of torturing Maelin, then slip down and free her from her cell. He crawled along the railing of the baiting pit to find a hiding place. Before he did, a feral hiss signaled his discovery. He looked up to see one of the vampire spawn clinging to the ceiling. The thing was completely hairless, with flesh as dark and rubbery as its sire's. Its mouth opened wide and round, revealing dozens of tiny, pointed teeth. Darrow froze, transfixed by the creature's hypnotic eyes.

"What's that?" called Stannis. "Has one of my cats found a mouse?"

A new surge of fear snapped Darrow out of his paralysis. He closed his eyes against the spawn's gaze and scrambled to his feet. He ran half-tumbling over chairs and couches as he fled for the exit. Behind and above him, the vampire's spawn pursued him.

As he reached the steps, he heard Stannis call out once more. "Fetch it, my loves. Bring it back to me, and I shall punish it."

Darrow felt an unearthly chill upon his back, and the stench of undying flesh filled his nose. He transformed as he ran up the steps, falling down to four legs by the time he reached the top. On four legs he gained ground on his pursuer, racing across the grand promenade, heading toward the warehouse.

The door was open, and beyond it stood Rusk, awaiting him. The pack was at his back, and all eyes were upon Darrow. Their expressions spoke more clearly than words that he was no longer one of them.

He stopped so suddenly that he skidded across the hall, his nails carving deep scratches into the parquet floor. With the pack before him and vampire spawn behind, he fled up the stairs. He hoped his pursuers would hesitate before following, but their howls were too close behind. He had nowhere to go but up, unless . . .

Darrow ran into the first bedroom he reached, dashing across the room to leap against the boarded window. The impact cracked the wood but did not break it. Shifting into half-wolf form, he slammed the door shut. As he shoved the bed against it for support, a hairy fist crashed through and reached awkwardly for the lock.

Darrow turned his attention to the boarded window, smashing it with both his fists. It broke away in seconds, but so did the door behind him. Taking a few steps back to run, Darrow hurled himself through the broken boards, feeling their splintered ends tearing his flesh as he burst out of the darkness of House Malveen and into the pre-dawn light.

Darrow barely felt the impact of the fall as he crashed onto a stack of pitch barrels. He scrambled down the collapsing pile without looking back.

Running alone into the misty morning streets of Selgaunt, Darrow finally understood how Talbot Uskevren must feel. Now he was utterly alone, with nowhere to hide from enemies on all sides.

CHAPTER 18

TERRITORY

Tarsakh, 1372 DR

Tal woke to the sound of sparrows and the smell of fresh grass. The night's dreams evaporated in the morning air, leaving only a vague sense of contentment. His thoughts remained dreamy even as he rubbed his eyes and rose to stretch.

He was on his feet and was stretching his arms to the sky when the implications of his surroundings sunk in. He stood under a big oak tree surrounded by farmland. To the east he saw the walls of Selgaunt, their gray stone almost blue in the distance.

"Nine Hells!" roared Tal. "Where are my clothes?"

The sparrows burst from the tree, shaking down a few twigs. A big green leaf stuck to his naked chest.

"I hope these will fit," said Feena.

Tal turned to see her approach with a huge pair of home-spun trousers and a worn wool tunic obviously meant for a man much shorter and fatter than Tal. Beyond her, Tal saw a sod home and a simple barn. Between the buildings ran a clothesline with several conspicuous gaps.

The events of the previous night became much clearer in Tal's memory.

"This is the worst part of the whole thing," said Tal. "You can't take your clothes with you."

When he saw that Feena wasn't looking at his face, he plucked the leaf from his chest and tried futilely to cover himself with it.

Feena laughed so hard she dropped the clothes to hold her sides. Tal stood indignantly for a moment, then jumped at the chance to grab the clothes and put them on. Feena was still wheezing when he cinched the trousers around his waist.

"You weren't so shy last night," she said in a tone of apology. Tal only blushed more deeply.

"I'm so sorry about that," he said. "I didn't mean . . ."

"Of course you did, and don't be insulting," said Feena. She was still mirthful enough that her reprimand didn't sting. "I think we both needed it, after all we've been through."

"I mean, I just hoped you didn't . . ." said Tal, confused, ". . . that I didn't do anything . . . anything that you didn't want me to . . ."

Feena laughed louder. "It wasn't the wolves, if that's what you're trying to say," she reassured him. "It was you and I, and while I can't speak for you, I didn't do anything I didn't want to do." She laughed again at his forlorn expression, and asked, "Why do you look so glum?"

"It might sound stupid, but it feels wrong to be way out here while Chaney's still stuck in the city. I don't want him thinking I've run off to leave him to face the music alone."

"I doubt he thinks that," said Feena. "He knows you aren't running away. The man practically worships you."

Tal snorted.

"I'm serious. You should hear the way he talks about you when you're not around."

"What, you mean all the times the two of you slip off together?" It was an exaggeration, but Tal had noticed that Chaney and Feena showed up together often these days.

"Please, Chaney is just a flirt. On the other hand, he doesn't beat me away with a switch, like some people I could mention."

"I've never—" began Tal. "All right. I could have been friendlier sometimes. But you came on pretty strong. If it weren't for Maleva . . ."

As he spoke Maleva's name, Tal realized he couldn't put off telling Feena what he'd heard at the Wide Realms. He took a deep breath and steeled himself to deliver the news.

"There's something you should know," he said.

Feena sat with her head on her knees for a long time. Tal waited on the other side of the tree, wishing he could say something useful. After he'd described the fight at the Wide Realms and the taunts the pack had used to draw him out, she'd asked him to go away from her. Not knowing what else to do, he obeyed.

At last, she composed herself and told her about Eckert's brush with death and the man she caught watching the theft of the bail money.

"Radu Malveen," said Tal. "He is a dangerous man, but I never thought he was a criminal."

"According to this Darrow, he wants nothing to do with Rusk's plans for you. It's his mad brother who's behind it all."

"But why?"

"Darrow didn't say—or wouldn't. All he cares about is freeing Eckert's daughter."

"Do you trust him?"

"Not even a little."

"But do you believe what he's saying is true?"

"Some of it," she ventured. "But he did nothing to stop Radu from killing Eckert. If he really wants to save the girl, why didn't he try to help her father?"

"He didn't stand a chance," said Tal. "Radu is the best swordsman in the city. I would hesitate before facing him, too."

"Would you?" Feena said sharply. "You're probably twice as strong, now. Wouldn't you just love a good fight, a chance to prove you're better?"

"Why are you snapping at me?"

"Because you spit on everything Selûne offers, and she still gives everything to you. You don't deserve to be the Black Wolf."

"What makes you think I'm the Black Wolf after calling it a heresy for so long?"

"Your changing in the playhouse, that's something only true lycanthropes can do. Even we don't have that level of control over the transformation. Only the Black Wolf could do that."

"I thought you didn't believe in the Black Wolf."

"It's a *heresy*, you idiot! I'm not *allowed* to believe it, but that doesn't mean it's not true on some level. Maybe it has nothing to do with prophecy or fate," she said. "If there's any truth to it, then it's old mortal wisdom."

"What do you mean?"

"Maybe the 'Black Wolf' is just a metaphor for your own strength," she said.

"You make it sound like anyone could be the Black Wolf."

"Maybe anyone can," she said. "Anyone can learn to ride the moon. Maybe being the Black Wolf means you're so close to the moon that it's easy for you. It's a gift. I just never thought it would be wasted on some spoiled, conceited city boy!"

"Hey, I didn't ask for any of this," complained Tal. "Everything that's happened has happened *to* me. You're the ones who decided to keep me drugged while you decided whether or not to kill me. Rusk is the one who tried to kill me in the first place. I didn't do *anything* to you people."

" 'You people,' " she parroted. "Anybody else is 'you people' to you."

"That's not fair! I meant everyone who came looking for me, to tell me what to—"

"I can't believe Mother saw anything in you. You're spoiled and selfish! You don't see anything beyond your own desires. The Black Wolf isn't for someone like you. It should be for someone who cares about other people, someone like—"

"Like you, maybe?" Tal snapped. "You're jealous, aren't you? Well, as far as I'm concerned, you can have the Black Wolf and everything that goes with it. But Selûne didn't choose you, she chose me. All you can do is try to make me do what you think is best."

Feena balled her fists and trembled in her fury. She tried to speak but could only grimace and spit incoherent curses. Then a triumphant smile crossed her lips, and she raised her chin and looked at Tal through slitted eyes.

"What did you just say?"

"I said, all you care about is making me do what you want me to—"

"No, before that. You said Selûne chose you."

"I didn't mean . . ." Tal sputtered. "I mean . . . you know what I meant. I've got the Black Wolf in me, and you wish it were in you."

"Selûne did choose you, though," said Feena. She flexed her fingers to let the blood back into them. She took a couple of long, slow breaths before continuing. "I can't keep denying it. There is good in you; I've seen it. You're just so damned stubborn you won't let yourself accept the responsibility."

"What responsibility? A great big bloody wolf bites me and all of a sudden I have responsibilities?"

Feena laughed, as much at herself as at Tal. The sound was strained. The news of her mother's death was still gnawing at her, and she was putting on a brave face.

"I'm sorry, Tal. It's been easier for me, growing up with the wolf. I have to remember it's not the same for you." Her smile turned sad. "Mother did think a lot of you, you know. She was a good judge of character."

"Are you sure she's dead?" asked Tal, even though he too believed the pack's boasts. "Rusk isn't exactly what I'd call trustworthy, and he's cruel enough to lie about something like that."

"Rusk is many things, many bad things," said Feena, "but he's honest, in his way. He doesn't lie to others so much as he deludes himself."

"You've run into him often over the years?"

Feena hesitated before answering. "Not as often as I'd have liked."

She sounded as if there was more to tell, but she stopped talking.

"He and Maleva, they knew each other a long time," suggested Tal, hoping to encourage her to continue.

His own words triggered something in his imagination. A shape of past events was forming in Tal's mind. Feena had been born with the wolf inside her, but Maleva wasn't a nightwalker. Assuming they were rare beings . . .

"Oh," said Tal as the realization struck him.

Feena still did not speak, nor would she look at him. Tal tried to make eye contact, but she kept her gaze on the ground.

"Rusk is your father," he said.

Without raising her eyes, Feena nodded.

"Oh, no." That made everything much worse. "Oh, Feena." Tal put a big hand on her slender arm. Feena flinched but didn't pull away. "I'm sorry. It seems so obvious now. I should have realized."

Feena glanced at Tal's face, but whatever she saw there made her shy again. She turned away and hugged her arms tight to her chest. When she spoke, it was with her back to Tal.

"He roamed with his Hunt, as he called them, so we saw him only when he brought us meat every month. In the beginning, Mother was always happy to see him, and he'd stay for a day or two. When he was off again, she told me stories about him. He was her hero.

"When he was just a boy, a cleric of Malar did a divination for him. The old man said that Rusk would cast a shadow on the moon. Everyone knew that meant the Black Wolf, which the clerics of Malar hold as true prophecy. No one knew when it would happen, but everyone believed it, especially Mother. She was banished from Moonshadow Hall because she said as much to the high priestess there. She thought Rusk would be the one to put the nightwalkers back in harmony with the world.

"On holidays we'd go with him to the Feast of the Stags. Everyone knew Rusk the Hunter. He was the best tracker, the best provider. When he came to a village and promised the people meat throughout the winter, they knew they would not go hungry. We were so proud of him. I was proud to be his daughter. The Huntmaster's Daughter, I called myself. Mother didn't like that, but I thought she was jealous. I was a child . . ."

She trailed off, sniffed, and cleared her throat, but Tal could see by the set of her shoulders that she had more to tell. He wanted to touch her, to hold her perhaps. He wanted to say something to make her feel better, but he could think of nothing. He waited patiently while the autumn wind blew fire-colored leaves about their legs, their fragile edges scratching on their clothes and naked feet. After long minutes, Feena spoke again.

"The arguments began just before my first blood. Mother had begun sending me away when Rusk came, but I sneaked back and listened. Rusk knew the wolf would come with the blood, and he wanted to take me to the High Hunt that summer. Mother wouldn't allow it. She said Rusk had promised to change the Hunt. He told her change takes time, but now I think he never wanted it to be different from what it was. Do you know about the High Hunts?"

"Yes," said Tal. "I found some books in my father's library. It's what they did to me. It's when they hunt a man."

"Or a woman," said Feena. "If she evades them all night, she keeps her life and wins a boon."

"So, what? Rusk owes me a wish?"

"He's not a genie, Tal," said Feena impatiently. "He's just a man, a werewolf. A cleric of Malar. Besides, that wasn't a High Hunt. Normally, the prey is feasted and knows what's happening from the start. It was because of the High Hunts that Mother left him. She didn't want me killing people the way he did. She wanted him to be the Black Wolf and change all the ceremonies back to something that served people rather than treating them like prey."

"If it wasn't a High Hunt, why did he attack me?" asked Tal. "And not just me but a whole group of us. I'm just the one clever enough to throw himself off a cliff and escape."

Feena didn't notice his attempt at humor. "I don't know. Maybe he really did mean to kill you all. You were encroaching on his territory."

"Maybe," said Tal, "but why follow me back to Selgaunt?"

"Mother thought it was because the prophecy about Rusk was both right and wrong. The part about the shadow makes it sound like he wouldn't be the Black Wolf, but he might bring the Black Wolf into being. After their last argument about me, Mother took us both away from the woods and we hid from Rusk. She didn't want me running off to a High Hunt to become like my father."

"She protected you," said Tal. "And she was trying to protect me, too. Wasn't she?"

"She believed you are the Black Wolf, Tal." Feena turned back to look him in the face. Tal had expected tears, but her cheeks were dry. Her anger was gone, but all of its steel remained in her face. "It's been hard to accept, but I realize she was right." She looked at Tal pointedly.

"And now you want to know what I'm going to do with this 'gift'?" he asked.

"Yes. I'll help you."

"No matter what I decide to do with it?"

She hesitated only a moment. "Yes," she said. "I know you aren't like Rusk. At first I thought you were, since you both refuse to listen to anyone else. But you aren't cruel, Tal, and I think you really do care about people. You're just no good at showing it."

"I show it," said Tal a little defensively.

"You're very *polite*," said Feena. Her smile returned, or at least an echo of it. The sight gave Tal a tickling sensation just below his heart. He liked the little crinkles at the edges of her mouth, and the way her freckles wrinkled on her nose.

"And you're even nice, but that isn't enough. Sometimes you have to take action to make things better."

"Like what?"

"I thought you didn't want me telling you what to do."

"Fair enough," admitted Tal.

Now they were both smiling, and somehow they'd gotten a lot closer without Tal's realizing it. He could smell her skin and her hair mingling with the sweet scent of autumn leaves and pumpkins. He made up his mind and kissed her on the cheek. Then he took her hand and began walking back toward the city walls, drawing her along.

"What are you doing?" she exclaimed, trying to keep up without being pulled.

"Deciding what to do," he replied breezily.

In truth, he had made no decision. He had only the barest inkling of how to slip back into Selgaunt without being arrested again, and he had no idea how to clear his name after the death of the other wolf. But he felt good for the first time in days. At last he realized that he didn't have to wait for things to come to him. He could take the fight to Rusk. And while the gray wolf might have brought his wolves to the city, Tal had a pack of his own.

And Selgaunt was their territory.

They decided not to risk stealing shoes, so they walked barefoot along the Way of the Manticore and reached the city gates before noon. Normally, visitors would stop by the Outlook Inn for refreshment before joining the queue to enter Selgaunt, but they had no money, and Tal did not dare trade on his family name. He might as well walk straight up to the guards and start barking.

The Scepters at the gate were interested only in collecting taxes on goods. Tal and Feena simply walked past the men, who waved them by with only the barest glance. If their ill-fitting clothes made them conspicuous, it was only as a pair of rude country folk.

They turned left onto Rauncel's Ride and walked quickly through the stockyards. The smell of so many animals penned nearby was not normally appetizing, but Tal felt a hollow pang in his stomach and remembered that he had not eaten since the morning before. He thought a dire warning to his stomach, which growled back at him.

Tal breathed a sigh of relief when they made it to the cloth market, where they could blend anonymously into the mix of country sellers and the servants who had come to shop for household goods. It was unlikely that Tal would encounter any of his peers there.

"If I don't find Chaney at your tallhouse," said Feena, "I'll check the Wide Realms. Either way, I'll talk to Eckert and meet you before—"

"Tal!" shouted a young woman's voice.

Tal recognized it at once and winced. Before he could pretend he hadn't heard, their eyes met. Hers were such a light hazel that they appeared almost yellow at a distance. Russet hair spilled carelessly from beneath a shapeless brown scarf. The rest of her attire was just as unruly, for Larajin had never been one for primping, much less fashion or cosmetics. Nevertheless, her careless dress did little to conceal her unadorned beauty.

"Who is she?" asked Feena, craning her neck for a better view of Larajin, who was momentarily hidden in the press.

"Larajin," he said with a sigh. "One of my father's . . . servants."

Feena gave him a curious look, then tried to spot the young woman again.

"I'd better deal with this myself," he said. "Go on, and I'll meet you later."

Feena eyed him suspiciously then slipped away. Tal knew he would have some more explaining to do soon.

When Tal turned back to spot her, Larajin had already navigated the crowd and stood before him, a tall stack of parcels in her arms.

"Where have you *been*?" said Larajin, awkwardly shifting the packages. Tal took half of them from her, and she smiled her thanks.

"I spent the night outside the city," he said, feeling ridiculous in the clothes.

"I wasn't talking about your costume," she said. "I meant where have you been for the past year and a half?"

"Oh." Tal assumed she'd heard about his arrest, but Thamalon must have somehow kept the scandal from the house staff. He was good at that. "Well, I'm almost never at Stormweather."

"I've seen you there plenty of times," she said. Tal had not heard her sound so vexed since he was eight years old, and Larajin was charged with keeping him out of mischief. "You've been avoiding me, and I want to know why."

"Avoiding you? Of course I haven't . . ."

Larajin looked up at Tal's face. "Have you gotten taller?"

"What? No. I don't think so. That's not possible, is it?" He knew he had put on a lot of weight, a lot of muscle, but how could he be growing taller?

"Oh, you're standing on the curb," she said, stepping closer. Her arms pressed against Tal's hip, and he stepped away too quickly.

"What's wrong?" she asked. "I thought you'd be happy to see me."

"I'm always happy to see you," he said. As usual when he was off the stage, he sounded as convincing as a Mulhorandi rug merchant.

"Then why do you run off whenever I see you?"

"I don't . . ." Tal began, but the lie died on his lips.

"What was all that talk about our being friends if this is the way you treat me?" she said.

He remembered the conversation they'd had shortly after Rusk attacked him in the Arch Wood. Even over the buzz of the crowd, there was no mistaking the irritation in her voice.

Before he could defend himself, she went on. "The last time we talked, you scolded me for acting like a servant instead of your friend."

"No," said Tal, remembering his shame and anger after their last meeting. "The *last* time we talked, Thamalon dragged me off for a lecture on fraternizing with the help."

"What?"

"Why do you find that so surprising? Of course he'd want to keep you to himself." Thamalon had never come out and said so, but there was no doubt he was claiming Larajin as his property when he scolded Tal for being too familiar with her.

"So he told you . . .?"

"He said enough that I could figure out the rest. I'm not as thick as everyone thinks," Tal said.

"And you're upset about it."

"Of course I'm upset! Thamalon acts like some paragon of honor and integrity, but he's the biggest hypocrite in Selgaunt. I can't believe he keeps you at Stormweather, especially after he and Mother started getting along again last winter."

Larajin's chin sank. "I've often felt terrible about that," she said.

"Then why don't you leave?" he said, more harshly than he expected. He realized for the first time that he'd been as angry with Larajin as he had been with Thamalon. "Haven't you caused enough trouble? After Mother gave up her whole life for the rest of us, how can you stay in her sight? She deserves better."

Tears welled in Larajin's eyes. She tried to blink them away, but they rolled down her cheeks. "I know," she said. "I know. Often I've wanted to tell her myself, but I could never work up the courage."

"Oh, I think she knows."

"Do you really?"

"How could she not see it? I bet she's kept quiet only to save the family reputation."

"I'm sorry!" said Larajin, defiantly. "You should have said something sooner if you felt so strongly about it. I was going to tell you that last time we spoke."

"You were going to tell *me*? Did you think I'd be happy to hear it?"

"You always treated me like a sister anyway," she said.

"Like a sister? How could I think of you that way when you're sleeping with my own father?"

"*What?*"

"That makes it even worse," he said. "It's bad enough that you're his mistress without acting like you're part of the family."

Larajin slapped his face. He barely felt the blow, but it shocked him nonetheless. Larajin's eyes hardened. It was the first time Tal had seen her truly angry with him. The sight made his stomach shrink.

"How could you think that?" She dropped her packages and punched him in the arm. The crowd began to move away from them, forming a small clearing around their argument.

"*Ow!* Yes, well—"

"You thought I was his *mistress?*" She kicked him on the shin.

"*Ow!* No! I mean, obviously, you're not." He scooped up some of the fallen packages and smiled awkwardly at the people who had begun to stare.

"That's revolting!"

"I know. I thought so, too. *Ow!* Quit it!" he said, trying to use the packages as a shield.

Larajin held up both fists as if to redouble her pummeling, but then she saw the confusion on Tal's face.

"You assumed . . . he never told you!" Larajin's fury transformed to astonishment. "After all that has happened this year, he never told you the truth?"

"What is the truth?" Tal asked, keeping an eye on her fists.

Larajin watched Tal's face carefully, alert for any trace of subterfuge. Satisfied that he wasn't acting a part for her, she shook her head and smiled as she had years before, when they were children.

"I should probably leave it to Lord Uskevren to explain," she said tentatively.

"Obviously, he doesn't tell me the truth," protested Tal. "What are you talking about?"

"I'm not Lord Uskevren's mistress," said Larajin. "I'm his daughter."

Tal felt dizzy. "His what?"

"Your half sister."

Since their quarrel subsided, the jostling crowd pressed in on them again. Tal felt seasick in the tide of bobbing heads. He wanted to sit down. He wanted a drink of ale. More than either of those, he wanted to hear that he'd just misunderstood what he thought he'd heard. No matter how fantastic it seemed, it did explain some things.

Larajin seemed to read his mind. "That's why he was so upset when he thought you and I were . . ."

"When he thought you and *I* were doing what I thought you and *he* were doing."

"Yes."

Tal stood still for a few moments looking over the market crowd toward the heart of the city. In the distance, the morning sun set the spires and towers of central Selgaunt to gleaming. Dozens of family crests waved in the sea breeze, their bright colors creating the illusion of a blooming garden.

"Larajin, I don't know how to begin apologizing."

"Try anyway," she said. Indignation lingered in her tone.

"I am unutterably sorry," he began. "The fault is entirely mine." He paused, torn between inventing a more formal apology and wondering at the ramifications of what he had just learned.

"Say more things like that."

"I couldn't have been more wrong," he added. "None of this confusion would have happened if I weren't born an idiot."

"That part isn't your fault," said Larajin. "It's hereditary." She covered her mouth like a child who'd just said a naughty word in range of her parents. Then she laughed.

"At least among the Uskevren men," agreed Tal.

"Right."

Tal salvaged the dropped parcels, and they stood a while in silence as the crowd jostled them.

"Want to help me carry these back to Stormweather?"

"I . . . I can't at the moment. There are some things I have to do first."

"Like finding a set of clothes that fit?" Larajin plucked at the fabric of his stolen shirt.

"Among other things," said Tal. "Listen, there are some things happening lately . . . I have to deal with them. It means I won't be around Stormweather for a little while longer, but I'll come back soon. And I promise not to avoid you."

"Yes, Master Talbot," she said. "Whatever you say, Master Talbot."

"Oh, stop it. Even before we knew you're my sister—"

"Not so loud!" warned Larajin. "I haven't told anyone else."

"Why not? He's got to recognize you, doesn't he?"

"Maybe he is thinking of Lady Shamur."

"Oh," said Tal.

Thamalon might not be keeping a mistress these days, but Larajin was born after Tamlin. That much was obvious. Now that his parents were getting along so much better these days, Tal saw why Thamalon might choose not to disturb the past.

"But don't you deserve to be recognized as an Uskevren?"

"I thought about that," said Larajin. "Perhaps one day that's what I will want. For now, there are too many other changes happening in my life. I'm not ready to begin a new one."

"I know what you mean," said Tal. "Everything was a lot simpler when we were young."

"We're still young, you great goof. We're just not children anymore."

"Maybe that's why it used to be a lot easier."

CHAPTER 19

THE BLACK MOON

Tarsakh, 1372 DR

At first, Darrow feared he might have the wrong street. In the afternoon light, there was no question of identifying a known house, but he knew Talbot Uskevren's tallhouse only by description. Alaspar Lane seemed right, but he wasn't sure which one he wanted until he saw the guards.

He spotted the family guards first. They made no effort to hide. Two of them stood to either side of the front door of the three-story building, while two more guarded either end of the lane. Their bright blue cloaks and yellow horse-at-anchor emblems marked them clearly as Uskevren house guards. Their conspicuous locations confirmed Darrow's suspicion that they were posted more to warn Talbot off than to apprehend him.

The Scepters were somewhat subtler. Four of them stood in a cluster across the street from the tallhouse. If there were others, they were well hidden at the farthest range of a signal whistle. From the occasional glances the Scepters cast at the Uskevren house guards, Darrow saw that there was little affection between the two camps. He wondered briefly whether the guard would fight the Scepters to cover the young man's escape if he were so foolish as to show himself.

"Too bold to hide," murmured Darrow. It seemed a ridiculous motto for any of the Old Chauncel, whose successes more often depended on diplomacy and bidding wars than military conflicts.

Most house militia were simply bodyguards, but something about the proud posture of the Uskevren men made Darrow wonder just how much provocation it would take to ignite a conflict like those that had brought low both House Uskevren and House Malveen a generation earlier. Perversely, he wished Stannis Malveen were present so he could ask his opinion. Of course, Lord Malveen would never show himself in the daylight.

Unless Talbot was much slipperier than Darrow expected, there was no way he'd find shelter at his tallhouse with so many eyes upon it. There was one other obvious place for the fugitive Uskevren to take shelter. Fortunately, it was not far away.

Darrow had no reason to fear the guards, so he walked down the lane between them. Too bold to hide, he joked silently. That would make a good motto for the pack, who walked boldly through the herd here in Selgaunt. None of the lambs realized there were wolves among them, and they wouldn't—not until the wolves chose to reveal themselves.

When he arrived at the playhouse, Darrow found the outer court deserted. A sign over each entrance read CLOSED in big letters, followed by a flowery apology written in fine calligraphy. Rather than approach closely enough to read the words, Darrow walked to the tiny park nearby and found an unoccupied bench. The seat afforded him a good view of the rear entrance and one of the public entrances.

Darrow watched for almost an hour. No one entered or left the building in that time, and he saw no sign of city Scepters watching the place. That surprised him, since the playhouse seemed an obvious haven for Talbot Uskevren. Either the Scepters underestimated the strength of his connection to the place, or they considered it an unlikely refuge for other reasons. Or, thought Darrow, they had someone adept at remaining unseen watching the place.

When the sun touched the horizon, Darrow knew he could wait no longer. If Feena and Talbot had returned to the city, as he assumed they would, then he knew of no other place they might hide. If they hadn't gotten into the playhouse earlier in the day, he thought it unlikely they would try so close to dusk. The moon would rise soon after dark, and it was far more difficult to resist the call of the beast on a full moon than it was to summon the transformation on other nights. What he had to do was hard enough without his suddenly turning into the wolf.

One last look around revealed no suspicious figures, so Darrow went to the back door of the playhouse. Like the others, it bore a sign and an apology for the cancelled performances. Darrow beat on the door with his fist. He waited a moment, then banged again.

A big woman with biceps like catapult shots opened the door. Darrow recognized her as one of the players, the infamous Mistress Quickly herself. He had seen her perform in both male and female roles each time he'd come to the playhouse as Stannis Malveen's eyes in the city. She clenched a straight-stemmed pipe between her jaws. The smoking bowl bobbed as she spoke through gritted teeth.

"Closed, it says." She pointed to the sign and blew smoke out her nostrils.

"I know," he said. "I'm a friend of Talbot Uskevren. I have an important mess—"

"You thought wrong, sweetie," she said, closing the door in his face.

Darrow got a foot inside the jamb before it shut. He sniffed deeply, trying to scent past the stink of pipe smoke and the woman's garlic breath. Besides the strong smell of grease-paint and timbers, he detected the odor of human sweat and something else. Mingled among the other smells was the musk of two different kinds of animals. One was a strange smell, oily and somehow hot. The other was the more familiar musk of wolves, including one particular wolf.

"Much as I hate to bust up a potential customer," said the woman, "I'll rattle your head on the street if you don't back off."

She pushed the door open, shoving Darrow back. She was even stronger than she looked, maybe even stronger than Darrow.

"I know he's here!" he said more loudly than she obviously liked. She looked left and right. Seeing no witnesses, she cocked a fist and prepared to bludgeon Darrow.

"Is he alone?" asked someone behind Quickly. Darrow recognized Feena's voice.

"Yeah," answered Quickly. "Nothing I can't handle on my own."

"Let him in," said Feena.

"Yer kiddin', right?"

"No," said Feena. "He's here to help."

Darrow gave the red-haired cleric a grateful smile.

"Sure about that?" asked Quickly. She took the pipe from her mouth and blew a stream of smoke at Darrow through the gap in her big front teeth.

"No," said Feena, "but if he's not, it'll be better to kill him inside."

Darrow realized he had not won the cleric's trust, but the fervor with which she threatened him still scared him. He had thought Selûne was a gentle goddess. Perhaps she made an exception when one of her clerics had been slain.

"Good enough for me," rumbled Quickly. She slapped Darrow smartly on the buttocks. "Get in there, boy."

Inside, they led him out onto the stage and into the yard. Waiting in the lower gallery was a small group of men and women, along with a short, green-skinned creature with a wild black mane. The beast hissed at Darrow as he approached.

"Easy, Lommy," said Talbot Uskevren. He sat in the second row, surrounded by the others. Across his knees he held the biggest sword Darrow had ever seen. It looked impossible to wield, even in two hands. Talbot scratched the little creature behind the ears. "Go upstairs and make sure he wasn't followed." Lommy scrambled up the nearest pillar as nimbly as any monkey.

Talbot stood up and set the monstrous sword aside as easily as if it were a walking stick. He was at least as tall as the Huntmaster, and even more powerfully muscled. Darrow felt the same sense of foreboding as he did when in the presence of Rusk or Stannis. This man could kill him in a second.

"I saw you in the playhouse last night," said Tal. "You were with the white-haired elf."

"Yes," said Darrow.

Talbot looked ready to ask something else, but Feena interrupted. "Is it true what your friend said about killing my mother?"

"Your mother?" he asked.

"Maleva. He said you killed Maleva."

"Rusk said she was your teacher . . ." said Darrow. "He didn't tell us she was . . ."

"So it's true," she said. Her voice turned cold.

Darrow nodded slowly. "Rusk killed her, yes. She tried to stop us from coming to the city."

"But you helped," said Talbot. "You all killed her, didn't you?"

Darrow licked his lips. "Listen, I came to warn you—"

"Answer the damned question!" said Feena.

"I was there," admitted Darrow. "I . . . I'm as guilty as the rest."

"And you've killed before then, haven't you?" Feena spat at his feet. "You've done it yourself. You're nothing but an animal!"

This was the last thing Darrow expected. He knew they had no reason to trust him, but this badgering astonished him. "What does it matter? I'm here to help save someone, not to kill anyone."

"Eckert's daughter," said Tal. "That's what you told Feena."

"I still can't believe Eckert has a daughter," interrupted Chaney, clutching his head with both hands. "Do you know what that means? That means he's had sex. With a woman. Some poor woman had sex with Eckert!"

"Knock it off, Chane," said Tal. He fixed his eyes on Darrow. "What happened to her?"

"I don't know how she was captured, but she's been Lord Malveen's prisoner for over a year."

"There is no Lord Malveen," interjected one of the players. He was a pretty man with long black curls.

"Stannis Malveen still lives—if that's the word for it—in the ruins of House Malveen," Darrow said. "Everything that's happened to you started with him."

"Tell me everything," said Talbot.

"I will," Darrow promised, "but you've got to promise to help me get Maelin out of there."

"No promises," said Talbot, "but if you make yourself useful, I won't break your neck right now."

Darrow didn't believe the threat . . . not until he met Talbot Uskevren's unwavering eyes. They were the color of unpolished steel, dead and strong. He realized that he had put himself completely in the other man's power. He might be able to win past all the players and even Feena, if he were lucky, but he could not oppose this man that Rusk called the Black Wolf.

"Start from the beginning," said Talbot, glancing up through the open roof. "And make it quick. The moon is coming."

Darrow took a breath and obeyed. He hoped his new master would be merciful.

Talbot was quiet for a long time after Darrow finished his tale. He had told it carefully, trying not to make too much of his desire to release Maelin from captivity, but leaving unspoken his own participation in the pack's High Hunts and callous defense of their territory. Judging by Feena's steady gaze, his guilt was not forgotten, nor forgiven.

The cleric had turned away from him only long enough to say her prayers at moonrise. Having listened carefully to Darrow's tale, she called on Selûne for protections against the undead as well as spells to heal the wounded and harm the wicked. Afterward, she sat rocking slightly in a gesture that reminded Darrow of his own inner contest with the moon. She was calling to her wolf, and he had to concentrate to contain it. He had little doubt that his sudden transformation would be all the excuse Feena needed to execute him.

If Talbot felt the call, it did not show. He sat pensively, his fingers trailing the length of the gigantic sword he held on his lap. Whatever he was thinking, he did not share with the others.

Quickly lit a fresh bowlful of tobacco and broke the silence.

"Werewolves and vampires," she said. "This'll make a great play when it's all done."

Talbot began to protest, but then he sighed. "You might as well," he said. "There's no hiding it after last night."

"I want to play this Sorcia," said a slim, androgynous woman. Darrow was astonished at her aplomb.

"Sivana!" said Feena.

"Can I play Tal?" said a big, goofy looking fellow. He had the size for it, if no other resemblance to the Black Wolf.

"Not you, too, Ennis! Listen," said Feena sharply. "I know you're just trying to lighten the mood, but this doesn't help."

"Sorry," said the man with black curls. "Tell us what we can do to help."

"Absolutely nothing, Mallion," said Talbot. "I've already brought more than enough trouble to the playhouse. From now on, I'll deal with it on my own."

"Not alone," warned Feena.

"No," agreed Tal reluctantly. "I'll need your help."

"And mine," said a short, blond man who seemed some-how out of place among the players. He stood up and winced as if injured.

"Forget it, Chane," said Tal. "You've taken more than your share of lumps lately."

"It's my prerogative as the best friend," said Chaney. "I'm the—what do you call it in the plays, Quickly?"

"The male confidant," said Quickly, tossing him a wink.

"What does that make me, fifth business?" said Sivana. She twirled a polished long sword in her hand. It shone red under the light of the continual flame brands Lommy had set on the gallery support beams and the edge of the stage. "You taught us how to fight with these, Tal. It's time we returned the favor by putting them to real use."

Mallion agreed, stabbing one of the benches with his own blade. Quickly gave him a dire glance, and he pulled it out and hid the scar in the wood with his boot.

"This is not a play," said Tal. "You saw what happened last night, and that was nothing compared to what happened last time Rusk was here."

"He's got a point, dearies," said Quickly. "I was here for that, and it wasn't pretty."

"You were down in the abyss with me the whole time," protested Chaney. "Neither of us saw anything but that nasty severed arm and the mess he made of Tal's insides."

"I saw your insides right afterward," countered Quickly.

"*Quiet!*" thundered Tal. His voice resonated through-out the playhouse, and several of the players flinched at its unexpected volume. Seeing that he had their attention, he continued. "I love you all," he said. "Except you," he amended with a cold glance at Darrow. "One wrong move, and I will throttle you."

"I know," said Darrow.

"Good," said Tal. "The rest of you, I appreciate the sentiment. You're closer to me than my own family—"

"Damning us with faint praise," snorted Sivana.

"—and twice as disagreeable," said Tal. "But there's no way I can let you—"

"Tal Tal Tal Tal!" sang the tiny arboreal creature as it scampered down from the thatched roof. "They are here! They are here!"

"I knew it!" said Feena. "He led them to us."

She grasped her silver talisman and raised a finger toward him. Talbot laid a gentle hand on her arm even before Darrow protested.

"I didn't!" he said. "It's an obvious place for them to look."

"Who's here?" asked Mallion.

"Who else?" said Talbot. "Dark and empty, everyone get out of here, now! It's time I dealt with Rusk for good."

"Uh uh," said Chaney. "I'm staying."

"Me, too," said Feena.

Sivana and Mallion already brandished their blades, and Quickly adjusted her pipe and lifted a big spiked mace from behind one of the benches. "Sorry, sweetheart. You're a big, bad wolf, but this is still my playhouse. Nobody busts it up without coming through me."

Seeing the resolve in her face, Talbot gave in. "All right," he said, nodding at Darrow. "You keep an eye on this one, Sivana. That sword can kill him."

"Sugar," said Quickly, "every weapon in this house can hurt him."

"What do you mean?" said Talbot.

"After last year's 'incident,' I made a little investment. All the blades are silvered, and this is my fourth husband's enchanted mace. This pack of yours doesn't know what it's in for."

Talbot stared briefly, then plucked the pipe from the big woman's mouth and kissed her full on the lips before replacing it. She blew a smoke ring at him.

"If you're staying, then do as I say," he said to everyone. "Rusk's here for me, but we can't trust him. If he'll fight me alone, the rest of you stay back. Agreed?"

The players and Chaney nodded reluctantly, but Feena set her chin defiantly. Tal sighed but did not challenge her.

"If you beat him," said Darrow, "you command the pack."

"I'll believe that when I see it," said Tal. "It sounds too easy."

"Maybe so," said Darrow, "but they respect strength. Show them anything else, and—"

A tremendous crash shook one of the public doors.

Quickly hefted her mace and went through the lower gallery, where she could reach the bolt from the side. "Ready?"

Tal checked to make sure the others were well back. Chaney and Lommy had already slunk into the shadows of the lower gallery, and Darrow stood by himself on one side of the yard. The remaining players stood with swords in guard before the stage. They made an odd trio, giant, pretty man, and manly woman. Feena stood before them, silver talisman in hand.

Something slammed into the door again, but the bolt held.

Tal nodded to Quickly, and she stretched over the rail to grasp the latch. With a twist and a pull, she released the bolt.

The doors opened slowly, revealing the silhouettes of six massive wolves and a huge, one-armed man. Rusk's body surged with the unholy magic Darrow had seen him use so often before. Darrow noted Sorcia's absence and wondered briefly whether the Huntmaster had finally slain Sorcia and devoured her spirit to add to his own power. He could not decide whether her death should bring him sorrow or relief.

They entered slowly, not with caution but with ritual deliberation. The wolves turned to either side as they entered the yard, taking positions on either side of their leader, across from the players.

Behind the pack, the doors closed, and Quickly shot the bolt fast. No one would leave until the play was over.

As if obeying some prearranged cue, Rusk and Tal moved forward to stand in the center of the yard. Rusk's eyes fixed on Perivel's sword. "Set that aside, Black Wolf. Our contest must be decided with tooth and claw."

"I think not," said Tal. "The outcome of our last contest was to my liking. Perhaps this time I'll take a leg as well."

Rusk chuckled. "You are brave, young wolf, but I do not make the same mistake twice. Sorcia!"

Quickly shouted in surprise as a white werewolf pounced on her from the shadows. Sorcia's supple arm wrapped around the big woman's throat, the curved claws of her other hand poised to stab at Quickly's eyes.

Darrow realized at last what a fool he had been. Rusk had never done away with Sorcia because she was never truly rebelling against him. Instead, she had been manipulating Darrow into his own rebellion . . . but for what purpose, he still did not understand.

"Throw it away," said Rusk. "Or we shall begin the evening with a different sacrifice."

Talbot set his jaw and looked from Rusk to Quickly. Just as he was ready to cast away the sword, Feena called out, "Wait!" She brandished her talisman at Sorcia and shouted, "By the power of Selûne, I repel you!" A dim light gleamed on the holy symbol, then died.

The white werewolf's eyes widened briefly, then narrowed as her lupine jaws formed a long grin. She tightened her grip on Quickly's throat and drew two red scratches on the woman's brow. Quickly squirmed but could not break the grip.

Rusk's laughter filled the playhouse. "Your goddess cannot help you," he roared, pointing upward. "Look!"

The moon had risen barely above the thatched roof, but it was little more than a slender crescent.

"The Black Moon!" announced Rusk. "Malar devours Selûne tonight, and soon he will anoint his chosen avatar."

Groans of disbelief rose from the players.

"Spare me," said Sivana. "Another madman who thinks he missed out on all the fun of the Time of Troubles."

"You can't be serious," said Tal, staring incredulously at Rusk. "You think your beast god will make you his avatar for killing me?"

"Do not mock the Lord of the Hunt," growled Rusk.

"I'm not," said Talbot. "I'm mocking you, you carpet-chewing lunatic. Killing you will be a mercy." He raised Perivel's sword, but Rusk shook a finger and pointed it at Quickly.

Tal stuck the big blade into the ground, then shook his hands as if flicking water from them. Instantly, they grew wide and furred, each finger twice its normal length and tipped with a black claw.

"You *are* the Black Wolf," said Rusk. "Behold! The prophecy is fulfilled!" He sang a short prayer to Malar, and his own hand grew similarly large and wicked. Before he was finished, Talbot had moved in to attack. He stopped short at a cry from Quickly.

The white werewolf fought an unseen attacker in the shadows of the gallery. Quickly fell out of Sorcia's grasp, one beefy hand rubbing her throat while the other sought her fallen weapon. Before Talbot could react to the new attack, Rusk was upon him.

The Huntmaster lunged low, raking Talbot's thigh to leave a deep, wet wound. Before he could escape, Talbot grabbed a handful of Rusk's long gray hair and held him fast. His punch was too quick to see. All Darrow could see was a blur, the jerk of Rusk's head, and a spray of blood.

From the gallery, a thin voice cried out in terror. Lommy fled from Sorcia's grasp after distracting her. It was all the time Quickly needed to swing her mace at the white werewolf. Sorcia barely dodged the blow, leaping over the benches to seek shelter in the deeper shadows. Instead, she found another hidden lurker and shrieked angrily at an unexpected stab.

"Ha!" crowed Chaney, realizing he no longer had the advantage of surprise.

He came scrambling out of the dark gallery with Sorcia in pursuit, shifting to four legs as she came. The wound on her shoulder bled freely.

In the yard, the wolves and players alike joined the melee. Feena tried again to evoke the blessing of her goddess, and this time a wan silver light glowed briefly around her and all her allies. Even if she could not compel the werewolves to flee, she was not powerless.

In the center of it all, Rusk and Talbot rolled on the ground. Despite his missing arm and his opponent's great strength, Rusk was still the stronger. The infernal energy that coursed through his body broke every grip Talbot secured, then buffeted the younger werewolf mercilessly.

To the west, Mallion and Sivana fought back-to-back. A half dozen wolves surrounded them, darting in for quick bites before fleeing the burning points of their blades. Sivana cut out an eye and gave two other wolves searing wounds with her silvered sword. Mallion stood over the body of one he managed to pierce through the heart. The injured wolf still breathed, but it was dying.

By the stage, Ennis warded off two snarling wolves with wide swipes of his silvered long sword as Feena chanted another spell. Behind them, Chaney dashed across the stage with Sorcia at his heels. A pot of greasepaint burst just in front of the white wolf, making her veer away. Far above, Lommy hissed at her as he swung hand to hand from the open trapdoors of the heavens.

Darrow turned wildly around, unable to decide which conflict to join—or even which side to take. Rusk might consider him a traitor, even though it was clear now that Rusk had used him from the start, manipulating his fears and desires through Sorcia. Would Rusk let him live after killing Talbot? Darrow could no more expect mercy from Rusk than he could from Feena, whose mother he had helped murder.

Before he could decide, Karnek shifted from four legs to two, rising up to threaten Ennis. The distraction drew the player's eyes from Brigid, who darted between his legs and knocked him to the ground. In an instant, Karnek was at his throat, and the other wolves rushed past to overwhelm Feena.

Darrow leaped to intercept them, transforming as he flew through the air. The shift came more easily than ever before, and he landed in half-wolf form, growling a warning.

Brigid bit his leg and held fast, shaking her head to tear his sinews. Darrow smashed her head with both fists, loosening her grip but not breaking it. Before he could land another blow, Karnek crashed into him, bearing him to the ground.

"Traitor!" growled Karnek. He opened his wide lupine jaws to rip out Darrow's throat. Just as Darrow closed his eyes he felt teeth pierce his flesh, Karnek's head was knocked aside by a powerful blow. Darrow looked up to see Quickly standing above him, gripping her mace in both hands.

"Get up and make yerself useful," she said, still holding the pipe between her teeth.

Darrow tried to get up, but someone knocked him flat again. He saw a glimpse of white fur and heard Quickly scream. Feena yelled out a warning, but it was too late. By the time Darrow recovered, he saw Sorcia and Karnek both tearing at Quickly's body.

When the big woman stopped moving, both wolves turned to Darrow, their muzzles steeped in blood.

CHAPTER 20

PACKS

Tarsakh, 1372 DR

Tal heard his friends' screams, but he could not break free to help them. Rusk's single arm was charged with infernal energy, making it more powerful than both of Tal's combined. Worse yet, while Tal had only recently learned the trick of transforming at will, Rusk had known it for over fifty years. His jaws elongated when he willed, tearing into Tal's shoulders and face, only to shrink back again so he could slam his forehead into Tal's face.

If he could regain the sword, Tal had no doubt he could end this conflict in a few seconds. Rusk must have realized the same thing, for he clung to Tal even when Tal's claws pulled ribbons from his arm and chest. Instead of avoiding the attacks, Rusk tried overbearing Tal, pinning him against the ground. Despite his inhuman strength, Rusk could not maintain a hold without the use of two arms.

"Quickly!" screamed Sivana.

Tal strained his neck to see what had happened. Rusk sank long teeth into the side of his face, tearing his cheek and an ear. Tal whipped his head to turn the wolf's jaws aside, then shifted himself completely to wolf form. The transformation came so quickly that it surprised even Rusk, and Tal slipped free of his opponent.

He had only a second to look around before Rusk was on him again. In that instant, he saw Quickly's body lying ruined on the ground. Above her, Sivana and Mallion fought a losing battle against four werewolves. Nearby, Feena climbed onto the stage to avoid a trio of werewolves fighting amongst themselves.

Without looking, Tal knew that Rusk had leaped toward him again. He dropped to the ground and rolled away. The impact was nothing compared to the punishment he'd already received, but it drove his anger more firmly into his heart. He felt a fury overcome him and welcomed it. It brought no fear this time, only hot resolve to kill Rusk and all his brood.

He rolled up to his feet in half-human form just as Rusk turned to rush him again. This time Tal met his charge, both clawed hands reaching for Rusk's throat. The collision threatened to decapitate both werewolves, as their long claws sank into each other's throats.

Tal's painful grimace was mirrored in Rusk's lunatic grin. The Huntmaster's face was a mask of rapture. Tal's fingers closed more and more tightly, squeezing the breath out of him even as Rusk's own hand crushed his throat. Just as his vision blurred into a rain of red sparks, Tal felt Rusk's hand fall away from his throat just as the man's heavy body dropped to the floor. Tal almost turned away when he saw the Huntmaster's eyes move. They flicked up toward the eclipsed moon.

Tal followed Rusk's gaze to see the black disc completely obscure Selûne. For a moment, only the trailing shards were visible in her wake.

The werewolves ceased their attacks, backing away from the surviving players. Ennis clutched a wounded arm to his chest, and Mallion bled from three or four wounds, but only Quickly lay dead. Feena knelt by her body, holding her useless hands above the mortal wounds. She turned toward Tal, her face twisted with grief and helplessness. Tal realized she must be thinking of Maleva's death.

A hoarse whisper called Tal's attention back to Rusk.

"The Black Wolf prevails," he rasped. "The pack is . . . yours . . ." His whispering became too faint to hear. He beckoned weakly for Tal to lean close.

"Do it!" said a sweet voice. The white wolf had resumed her elven form. With the moon veiled in Toril's shadow, the firelight colored her pale body. "The pack needs a strong leader."

Tal looked back down at the Huntmaster. Rusk's lips were moving, but even Tal's keen ears could not make out the words. Reluctantly, he knelt beside Rusk and put his ear close to the Huntmaster's lips.

"Wait!" called Darrow. "They manipulated me into seeking you out. This is a trick!"

"No," said the elf. "Darrow wants it for himself. Hurry, before the moment is lost!"

Tal didn't trust any of them, but he began to move away from Rusk. Before he did, the Huntmaster's death rattle sounded deep in his throat, and a cold breath escaped his lips. Even as Tal backed away, he saw the breath take shape as an inky wisp more solid than any smoke. It curled and writhed toward Tal's face.

"Tal!" cried Feena. "Get away from it!" She raised her holy symbol and called on Selûne, but to no effect.

Tal stepped back as fast as he could. Two of the bigger werewolves rushed toward him, hunkered down in half-wolf form. He turned suddenly and headed for Perivel's sword. The black air moved with alarming speed. It brushed his shoulder as Tal leaped for the blade, catching it and rolling away from the werewolves.

Back on his feet, Tal swept the blade through the blackness. The stuff parted in the sword's wake, then reformed as if only blown by a breeze.

The werewolves split, one lunging for either side of Tal. He chose the one on his left, spinning backward to avoid the black smoke and smoothly turning the motion into a powerful two-handed stroke. The blade cut clear through the werewolf from shoulder to ribs. A shower of blood covered Tal as the body hit the ground with two distinct, wet sounds.

His other attacker retreated, as one of the other werewolves howled in rage and despair for her mate.

Tal felt hands on his back and heard Feena's voice. Another prayer to Selûne, he thought, as a cool sensation ran from her fingers into his body.

Whatever power she had instilled in him prevented the black smoke from coming nearer. It shied away and returned like a scorned cat determined to get inside.

Tal raised his sword, but Feena said, "Don't. You'll break the spell if you attack it."

All watched now as the angry black air curled up into itself, then fled back to Rusk's body, where it hovered over his gaping mouth. It whirled impatiently, unable to return to its ruined home.

"What is it?" asked Tal.

"Rusk," said Feena. "That's my guess. It's Rusk's own black spirit."

"Was that the plan, Sorcia?" Darrow called out to the elf. "To force his own essence into the Black Wolf?"

"You're such a tool, Darrow," said Sorcia. "You don't deserve to know."

"But I do," said Tal. He stalked toward the elf, Perivel's blade firmly in hand. "Is he right?"

Sorcia crouched, torn between running and fighting. As Tal loomed over her, she knelt down instead, hanging her head low. "It's true."

Tal cast his gaze across the other surviving werewolves. One by one, they lay themselves on the ground. Those in wolf form put their heads on their paws, while those on two legs bowed grudgingly.

Selûne formed a narrow arc as she peeked out from the shadow. As her barest light fell upon Rusk's black soul, the cloud evaporated in a high, grating squeal that hurt Tal's teeth to hear. In a few seconds, it was gone.

"It's over," said one of the werewolves. It was one of the two Tal had fought the night before. Tal had heard him called Karnek.

"No," said Tal, "not yet. The Malveens still have Eckert's daughter."

"She's probably already dead," said Sorcia.

"Shut up," said Darrow.

"No one hears you, traitor, weakling, tool!" she spat at Darrow. "Rusk used you as he did because you had already proven yourself a weakling and a toady to the Malveens." She turned her back on him and addressed the other werewolves. "With Rusk dead, there's no reason to stay here."

"Talbot is the one who killed him," said Darrow. "It's his decision, not yours!"

"You people follow whoever kills your last leader?" said Chaney incredulously. "Rusk wasn't the only one who was mad."

"You know nothing," said another female werewolf. She had twisted her blond hair into a crude braid while in human form. "We respect strength but do not follow blindly."

"It doesn't matter," said Sorcia. "We shouldn't be here. We should never have left the woods."

"Then go back," said Tal. The werewolves looked at him in surprise. "Get out of my city, and stay away. If you come here again, I'll make sure you never leave."

"But what about Maelin?" pleaded Darrow. "You can't face the Malveens alone."

"He's not alone," said Chaney. Feena had healed his injuries, and both of them stood beside Tal, staring down the pack.

Darrow watched as the pack gathered around Sorcia. They took wolf form once more before loping out into the night.

Turning back to Tal, Darrow pleaded, "At least take me with you."

"Put on your pants," said Tal, throwing the garment at Darrow's chest before collecting his own fallen clothes. After the first season at Quickly's, Tal had learned to shed his modesty with his clothes, but the constant and unintended nudity was becoming annoying.

"How can we trust you?" asked Feena. "It sounds like you've betrayed everyone you served before."

"I know how it looks," said Darrow, "but all I want is to help get her out of there."

"Do you know a spell to tell whether he's lying?" Tal asked Feena.

"Not until dusk tomorrow," she said.

"We can't wait that long. When Rusk fails to return, they'll kill the girl."

"Why not just turn this one over to the Scepters?" suggested Chaney. "He's proof that none of this is your fault. You didn't kill anyone except these monsters."

"What about the girl?" said Tal. "Even if Eckert has been feeding the Malveens information to use against me, she did nothing to deserve this. Besides, if the Malveens are behind this, I want to know why."

"It's because of your father," said Darrow. "At least, that's what Stannis says."

"What are you talking about?"

Darrow told them the story of the pirate Lady Velanna and the fall of House Malveen, along with Stannis's undying grudge against Thamalon Uskevren.

"That's the stupidest thing I ever heard," said Chaney. "What could he hope to gain by turning Tal into a werewolf?"

"At first, I don't think he had a plan," explained Darrow. "When he heard Tal escaped the werewolves, he hoped Rusk could control him and use him to embarrass the family."

"But Tal already does that. *Ow!*" He rubbed his head where Feena had rapped him with her knuckles.

"Even if Rusk couldn't control you," said Darrow, "he figured your fights with your father and brother would eventually lead to bloodshed."

"That's ridiculous," said Tal.

"Maybe not," said Feena. "Those who don't learn how to ride the moon often give in to the beast. Remember how hard it was for you to control your anger when you were newly cursed?"

"Maybe so," said Tal slowly. "Still, I have a hard time picturing Radu Malveen as part of such a scheme."

"He hated it from the start," admitted Darrow. "But you can't count on his standing aside and letting you take Maelin. He won't permit anything to hurt his family."

"Well, he should have thought about that before he helped hurt mine," said Tal.

He turned back to where Sivana and Mallion sat beside Quickly's body. They had covered her with a gold and white cloak, the one they used for monarchs in the plays. Ennis sat against the foot of the stage, his big body quivering as he wept. Tal went to kneel beside them.

"It's not your fault," said Sivana. "You're thinking it is, but it isn't."

Tal started to answer, but Mallion interrupted him. "She's right. Maybe they wanted you, but they hurt people wherever they go." He cast a rueful eye toward Darrow. "Be careful of that one."

"I will," promised Tal. "When we get back, we'll take her to the House of Song. Whatever it costs, we'll have High Songmaster Ammhaddan bring her back to us."

Sivana lost her composure at his words. "No," she said. "Quickly's will . . . she left it with me. She doesn't want us to . . . she said she liked the life she had and wouldn't want to bollocks up a second one."

Tal's breath caught in his throat. That sounded just like Mistress Quickly.

"Do you want us to come with you?" asked Mallion. Tal could tell by the tone of his voice that he hoped the answer would be no.

"Stay with her," he said. "And sing her a prayer for me."

"We'll sing a few for you, too," said Sivana. "Milil and Oghma grant you a great show. Knock 'em dead."

"That's what I intend to do."

"I have a bad feeling about this place," said Feena.

The four of them stood within the shadowed courtyard of House Malveen. The weird gargoyles watched them as they made their way toward the central building. Selûne had emerged from the eclipse as brilliant as ever, but even her silver light could not penetrate the lowest gloom.

"What kind of feeling?" asked Chaney. "Magic? Evil?"

"Yes," said Feena.

"Quiet," warned Darrow. He touched hilt of the long sword he had borrowed from Mallion, grateful that Tal had not insisted he go unarmed. "He might have set the spawn to guard the warehouse."

Tal willed his eyes to shift to wolf form. It felt as natural as squinting, and it allowed him to see light too faint for his human eyes to perceive. The details were lost, but he spotted the movement of a rat none of the others saw dash across their path.

"We need light," said Feena. Even if the three werewolves shifted to four legs, Chaney would be left blind.

"All right," said Tal, "but brace yourselves."

Feena chanted a quick orison, and her holy symbol blazed with white radiance. She cupped it in her hands to keep most of it on the ground ahead of them. They spotted the broken door, and Darrow led them through it.

Inside, the warehouse was abandoned. Tal could still smell the recent occupation of the werewolf pack, along with something salty, sour, and somehow unnatural.

"The spawn," observed Darrow, whose own nose was wrinkled in disgust. "They smell worse up close."

"If you smell them coming," said Feena, "let me cast some wards on you before you fight with them."

"Thanks," said Tal, "but once a fight begins, you stay out of the way."

"No promises," said Feena. She almost laughed at the shock on Tal's face. "I'll be careful."

"Good enough."

They navigated the crowded warehouse and found the door to the River Hall closed.

"There's no ward on it," said Feena quietly, holding her talisman before her. "At least none that I can detect."

Tal tried the handle. Locked.

"Stand back," he said, setting Perivel's sword aside.

"Wait," said Chaney. "Let me try something." He slid a flat leather pouch from his sleeve and unfurled it to reveal a selection of lock picks.

"We're going to have another chat about how you make a living, aren't we?" said Tal.

"Don't be so judgmental," Chaney said. "You're the werewolf."

"A law-abiding werewolf," Tal responded.

Chaney snorted quietly.

"Are they always like this?" whispered Darrow amiably to Feena.

Her response was a silent, icy glare. Tal still didn't like the man, but he felt a pang of pity for Darrow. The man had done some terrible wrongs, to be sure, but he seemed to crave redemption. Tal wondered how different his life might have been if Feena had not guided him through his harrowing affliction.

"There," said Chaney. "Easier than I thought. Exactly the same as the lock on Thazienne's bedchamber."

"You wish," said Tal. "You keep it up, and I'll tell her you said that."

"I take it back! I take it back!" whispered Chaney.

Tal knew they should try to remain silent, but the banter soothed his nerves. The idea of facing vampires was bad enough, but it was Radu Malveen he truly dreaded facing. Not only was the man the finest swordsman in Selgaunt, but Tal was not convinced he was a willing party to his brother's crimes. He hoped it would not come to a fight between them.

"Lead on, but go slowly," said Feena. She looked through her three extended fingers while clasping the talisman between thumb and little finger. "I'm still watching for magic."

Darrow walked slowly ahead. Watching the caution with which he set each foot on the floor persuaded Tal that Darrow was either a good actor or a man who truly did not know whether there were wards in place.

Darrow halted suddenly, crouching and sniffing. "Smell that?"

"They're coming," said Tal. Feena already had her hands on him, casting a spell that made his skin prickle all over.

"Wait," she said. "One more, for each of us."

She intoned another spell, reaching out to touch Tal and Chaney on the face before pressing a hand against her own cheek. Tal felt a cool, slippery sensation. No, it was more like a thought than a physical feeling.

"What does that do?"

"If we're lucky," said Feena, "it will hide us from these spawn Darrow described."

"What about him?" said Chaney, jerking a thumb toward Darrow.

"What about him?" said Feena coldly.

"Hurry," said Darrow, hastening toward the Grand Promenade. Tal followed, with Chaney and Feena trailing behind.

The Promenade looked empty at first glance. Tal had never seen a room more beautiful nor more bizarre. The illuminated stream cast rippling shadows on the walls and ceiling, and Tal followed Darrow's example by casting his eyes up there for any sight of Lord Malveen's minions.

"How many are there?" asked Tal.

"At least two," said Darrow, running past the inner fountains. "Maybe more. Hurry, the gallery is on the other side."

Tal waited long enough for Chaney and Feena to catch up with him, then followed. All four had just rounded the grand pool when Tal spotted a black figure running spiderlike across the wall.

"There!" he pointed. The thing scuttled away into the shadows, but then several things happened at once.

A dark, wet figure fell onto Tal from above. Even as he heard Chaney's shout of warning, a tremendous thunderclap exploded around Tal's head. All the prickling of his skin turned to hot needles wherever the thing touched his body, and a flash of light blinded him completely for a second. Tal heard his attacker fall to the marble floor nearby and moved in to strike as his vision returned.

Blinking away the stars in his eyes, Tal saw the stunned monster writhing on the floor. Once it had been human, but its clawed hands and feet were flat paddles now, with fingers half the length of a man's. Its naked skin was the darkest purple, nearly black, glistening smooth as a slug's body. Beneath round black eyes, its face consisted of nothing but a wide, lipless jaw studded with short, sharp teeth. Its mouth moved in a weak, involuntary spasm. Whatever magic Feena had cast on him hurt the thing far more than it shocked Tal.

Without hesitation, Tal severed the creature's head from its body. Perivel's blade cut through flesh and bone effortlessly, leaving a scar in the floor.

The spawn's body melted into a puddle of oily black liquid, spreading at first into a wide circle. Within seconds, it moved intentionally toward the pool, pouring itself into the clear water. Where it filled the lighted pool, darkness covered the ceiling above.

Behind Tal, Feena shouted, "Back! By the power of Selûne, I command you!"

She held her holy symbol defiantly toward another of the spawn. The monster hissed and recoiled from its place on the wall, but the talisman caused it no visible harm. Beside Feena, Chaney stood guard, his eyes searching the upper reaches of the hall for another attack.

"Over here!" Darrow called to them from an open door. Beyond it was a dark room.

Dark hands reached down from the shadows to grasp him by the head, pulling him up. Darrow screamed and struck wildly with his sword. Tal ran to help him, leaping up to catch his flailing legs as he rose into the shadows. He fell back to the floor holding an empty boot, while Darrow's screams grew louder and more frantic.

Feena sang out another prayer, her voice steady and bold. Her talisman flared more brightly than ever, shining steady rays of sunlight in all directions. The shadows flinched like living things and fled from the holy light.

The spawn within them squealed horribly and fled from Feena. One burst into flames as it fell from the high ceiling. It grabbed futilely for a long tapestry as it plummeted, tangling itself in the thick fabric and setting it alight. Another trailed smoke as it fled the River Hall. Orange light flickered in the hall where it had fled, and Tal knew it would not be back soon.

Darrow's sword clanged on the floor near Tal. Soon after, a snarling gray wolf fell heavily beside it. The beast jerked and twisted violently, still trying to bite at an opponent who was no longer there. Its red eyes met Tal's, and its nape bristled as it growled at him.

"Calm yourself," warned Tal, raising his massive sword.

The wolf whined and turned in a circle, lowering its head to the ground briefly before shifting form. The change came in awkward spurts, and when Darrow's human form crouched low before him, Tal saw the terrible wounds on his back and head. Deep black scars covered his head and shoulders, but the blood barely oozed from the wounds. The flesh surrounding them was already hardening and turning a dry, necrotic gray.

Darrow hissed and grimaced in pain. He looked ten years older, his features drawn and wan. He blinked away the tears of pain and said as bravely as he could muster, "Stings a bit."

"Feena?" asked Tal.

Before he could voice his request, she was already beside the wounded werewolf. Where she ran her fingers over Darrow's wounds, they closed under a trail of silver light, leaving only gnarly gray scars behind.

"That's the best I can do today," she said. "The life they stole will have to wait until tomorrow."

"Thank you," said Darrow. "I know I don't deserve your—"

"Don't speak," warned Feena, but her tone was less venomous than it had been earlier. "Just show us this secret passage," said Feena.

Her voice was urgent but surprisingly gentle. The fight had shaken her more than Tal realized. She had trained all her life to fight werewolves, but the undead were another matter entirely.

"That wasn't so bad," said Chaney. "Now that we're ready for them, and you have that light, this will be a snap."

"We'd better hurry," said Tal. "I smell smoke. The one who got away must have fled to the upper floors."

"Just don't be overconfident," said Darrow. "Lord Malveen is probably down there waiting for us, and he is no mere vampire."

"That makes us even," said Tal. His face was flush with excitement. Despite the horrors of the place, he had never felt so confident. "I'm no mere werewolf."

CHAPTER 21

THE BAITING PIT

Tarsakh, 1372 DR

Darrow led them through the secret panel and down the winding stairs. Years of Malveen family trophies stared down at them from the walls. The images unnerved Darrow, who found them eerily similar to the skulls mounted in Rusk's sanctum back at the lodge. He was still trembling since the attack of Lord Malveen's minion. Whatever else it had drawn out of his body, it took some of his courage with it—and he had precious little to start with.

"It's that smell again," whispered Talbot, sniffing. "Or something like it."

"Lord Malveen," confirmed Darrow. "He's down here somewhere. I wouldn't be surprised if Radu is nearby, too. Let's just hope they haven't—" Darrow couldn't finish the thought.

"They haven't," said Talbot. His confidence helped sooth Darrow's fears, but only slightly.

Chaney tugged on Talbot's arm. "I'm just going to hang back a little," he said. "But don't worry. I'll be watching your back."

"I appreciate it," said Talbot.

Feena covered her shining holy symbol in both hands, but the daylight still shone brightly through her fingers. It was too valuable to extinguish, but it meant there was no hiding their arrival in the baiting pit. As they entered, Darrow saw that they were expected.

The stone sconces all danced with green flame. In the pit below, the great iron portals were raised to reveal the cells beyond. All but one were empty. Maelin sat on the floor near the heavy bars, looking out into the dueling pit, which was empty except for a row of weapons planted in the sand and the fanged pit in the center.

On the other side of the stands, a roiling mass of shadows hovered above the floor. It was approximately the shape of Lord Malveen and half again as large.

"That's him," whispered Darrow. Talbot nodded and walked down the aisle to the edge of the ring. Darrow followed him.

Feena crossed over to the next aisle, opening her fingers to shine her daylight toward the shadowy figure. The radiance failed to dispel the shadows, but it did reveal another occupant in the room. Radu Malveen stood motionless near the door to the cells below. His reptilian eyes watched the intruders while his face remained impassive. Darrow shuddered to imagine what he was thinking.

Stannis Malveen's wheezy laughter emanated from the shadowy mass.

"You must have brought me quite a tale, dear boy. Did our friend the Huntmaster bite off more than he could swallow?"

Talbot stepped away from Darrow, fresh suspicion apparent in his face. He tried to keep his eyes on Darrow, Radu, and Stannis all at once. Darrow tried to reassure him with a quick shake of his head, but he could hardly blame the man for being careful.

Stannis seemed to be reading his mind. "How hard it must be for you to make new friends, you fickle lad, and how wicked of you to lead them back here without permission."

The shadow floated out over the ring but remained safely out of range of their weapons.

"We've come for Maelin," said Feena. "Release her, and we'll go."

"Be silent, you smelly little drudge!" spat Stannis.

Darrow had never heard such incivility from his former master. The shadows swirled, and an arm-shaped branch reached out to point at Feena. A black bolt of energy shot forth to strike her holy symbol. It smothered the daylight and plunged the room back into eerie green darkness.

Darrow's intuition told him to move the moment the light vanished. "Look out!" he cried, throwing himself over the seats into the next aisle.

The big man did not need the warning. His big sword had already caught Radu's blade as it licked toward him. He struck back with astounding speed, destroying the chair where his attacker had stood an instant earlier. Radu had already slipped away to attack from another direction.

Darrow took advantage of the fight to make a run for the cell entrance. Miraculously, it remained unlocked. He rushed down the stairs and found the portcullis closed. Cursing himself, he realized Stannis or Radu must have kept the key. He ran back up to the arena.

Talbot and Radu fought near the edge of the baiting pit, retreating and attacking by turns. Talbot bore a long slash along his face and another on his sword arm. His shirt clung to his body, sodden with perspiration. Darrow saw no wounds on Radu, who fenced with cool precision.

Feena and Stannis both hurled magic, the vampire casting forth his shadows while the cleric invoked the name of her goddess. Black tentacles erupted from the arena floor to encircle Feena's legs, pulling her inexorably down. She slashed at them with a radiant blade of moonlight, but it was a losing battle.

Stannis floated toward the struggling cleric, his armor of shadows still cloaking his bloated body. Darrow feared many things in the world, but few of them as much as the touch of the vampire's hand. He thought of what would become of Maelin should he fail, gripped his sword tightly, and ran to help Feena hack at the wriggling tentacles. With two quick chops of his blade, he freed one of her legs as she cut away another inky limb that encircled her waist.

"My sweet, reckless, feckless boy," hissed Stannis. "What a disappointment you have become. Is this how you repay my generosity?"

The vampire whispered arcane words and made a gripping gesture. Pain lanced through Darrow's body. His back jerked in uncontrollable spasms, and the sword fell uselessly from his hand.

"If only a mild lesson would suffice to correct such behavior," mourned Stannis. "It pains me to rebuke you, my dear boy. You do believe me, don't you?"

The pain became blindingly powerful, and Darrow felt he could rip Stannis's arms from his body, if only he could control his own. The spasms gripped him from head to foot, twisting every nerve and bending every sinew against his will. His own screams were deafening inside his brain, but they escaped his lips as a weak gasp.

Stannis shrieked suddenly, and through the red veil of pain Darrow saw Chaney stab again through the shadows around Lord Malveen. He had crept unseen along the inner railing, attacking from beneath as the sorcerer levitated above him.

The railing offered no protection from the sorcerer's dark magic. With a sibilant string of incantations and another violent gesture, Stannis wracked Chaney's body with waves of agony. The little man arched his back and writhed, no words escaping his gaping mouth.

"Get away from him, you revolting thing!" Free at last from the groping tendrils, Feena leaped to Chaney's defense.

Her blade cut effortlessly through the vampire's shadow armor. The flesh beneath boiled away with a sickening stench, spraying ribbons of vile ichor across the floor and down onto the sandy pit below.

"Brother!" cried Stannis. "Defend me!"

Radu did not even glance in his brother's direction. Instead, he pressed Talbot with a series of attacks to his arms and face. He was only slightly quicker than the big man, but his sword was far lighter than Perivel's war blade. Talbot used reach and retreats more than parries to defend himself. Soon he ran out of room to withdraw without stepping on Chaney, who struggled to his feet.

With his friend at his back, Chaney set his teeth against the pain and thrust again at Stannis, whose attention was fixed on Feena and her devastating blade. Chaney's blade sank deep into the vampire's flesh and evoked another shriek of pain.

The shadow sorcerer lashed his heavy tail once, then again, slamming Chaney hard enough to knock the sword from his hand. Each blow slapped the blush from his face, leaving him as colorless as rain. The last blow threw him against Talbot's back, where Chaney sank to the floor.

"No!" yelled Feena, slashing again at the monstrous vampire. "Face me!"

Talbot looked down at his fallen friend. It was the opening Radu needed. He thrust past Talbot's open guard and ran his long sword through the swordmaster's chest. The red point emerged just an inch to the left of Talbot's spine.

The big man gasped at his foe, who tried twisting the blade. The sword would not turn, and Talbot grabbed Radu's hand, holding it fast to the grip. Dropping his own weapon, Talbot grabbed Malveen's jacket and pulled him close.

Darrow saw the big man's shoulders swell and the fur sprout on his arms. For a moment he thought Radu had met his match at last, but then he remembered the real danger.

"The knife!" he cried, cursing himself silently for not thinking of it earlier. "Look out!"

The bone blade flashed at Radu's hip, striking up toward Tal's exposed stomach. Before it touched flesh, Chaney's hands closed on Radu's wrist. He mustered all of his strength to pull the weapon down, away from his friend.

Instead of struggling against him, Radu turned the point down and thrust the dagger at Chaney, who was unprepared for the sudden reversal. The slender dagger sank deeply into Chaney's throat. Hateful white light shot from the little man's eyes and mouth, showing a red skull beneath his flesh.

"No!" roared Talbot, releasing his grip on Radu's clothing to grab the hand that held the dagger.

Darrow heard the bones of Radu's arm grind and crack as Talbot squeeze his wrist and pulled the blade out of Chaney's throat.

It was far too late for Chaney. His flesh withered and collapsed, leaving only a ragged skeleton behind. Those meager remains survived only a moment longer before dispersing to the finest dust.

Still transfixed by his foe's blade, Talbot gripped Radu by wrist and throat, lifting the slender man off the floor. The motion would have seemed effortless except for the stream of blood that ran from both sides of the sword wound. With an inarticulate scream, Talbot hurled the swordsman over the edge of the baiting pit, onto the hard sand twenty feet below.

"Brother!" cried Stannis, retreating from Feena's glowing blade.

The cleric spared only one brief glance for the slain Chaney before pursuing the fleeing vampire. Stannis flew down to Radu, still dripping black ichor. Darrow looked down to see that the cell gates were open. Maelin was the only occupant, and she crouched behind the shelter of her cot when she saw Stannis arrive.

With furious abandon, Talbot grasped the sword in his chest and pushed it out in two painful thrusts, each one punctuated by a mournful howl. His face was a twisted cross between man and wolf, curved fangs protruding over a short snout, his blood-red eyes blazing furiously.

"Help him!" he cried to Feena. He scooped two big handfuls of the dust that was his friend.

Torn between rage and sympathy, Feena simply shook her head. "I can't," she said.

Talbot crouched over Chaney's remains, letting the dust sift through his bestial hands. A low growl grew in his chest, and he reached for Perivel's sword.

Darrow was afraid to speak and turn the werewolf's anger on himself, but his fear for Maelin was even greater. "Stannis has the key to Maelin's cell," he said.

Talbot's blazing eyes fell upon him, and the werewolf leaped up onto the edge of the pit. Darrow craned his neck to see the Malveen brothers below.

Stannis curled protectively around Radu, who struggled to regain his feet. The fall had finished the work that Talbot had begun. Radu's left arm turned at an impossible angle, hanging awkward and useless at his side. The bone blade lay on the sand beside him.

"Malveen!" roared Talbot in a voice that only the Nine Hells could lend him.

He leaped down into the pit and landed squarely on two feet, bending slightly to absorb the shock. His black torso gleamed with blood, but the wound had begun to close. He took one step toward the brothers, raising his massive sword.

"No!" squealed Stannis. "Spare us, I beg you! It isn't us you want."

"Be silent!" hissed Radu.

Clutching his horrid brother's chain veil, Radu pulled himself up. His left leg trailed as uselessly as his broken arm.

"Pietro!" shrieked Stannis. "Laskar! They are the ones you want. Spare me, and I will give you what you want."

"Liar!" shouted Radu. It was the first time Darrow had ever seen his former master impassioned.

"It's no good, dear brother," said Stannis. "We must make amends as best we can, even if it means acknowledging our brothers' misdeeds. Perhaps we can earn some clemency for our incidental—brother! What are you doing?"

Radu released the golden veil and snatched up the bone blade.

Talbot took a cautious step back, but Radu did not even look at him. Instead, he thrust the bone blade into his brother's wide flank.

An explosion of light dispelled the remaining shadows that cloaked Stannis. His golden veil flew away, leaving bloody wounds where the rings had pierced his face, revealing a round, gasping mouth filled with row upon row of triangular teeth. The radiance that surged from his body was tainted with wriggling strands of liquid black and red.

Still holding the bone blade, Radu was galvanized by the magical feedback. His body trembled and rose from the floor as the dark energies of his brother mingled with the life-draining magic of the dagger.

The vampire's body did not wither but flushed with power, glowing blindingly as it shook.

"Get down!" cried Feena from the rail.

Darrow heeded her warning just as an explosion shook the arena. Sand and wet matter fell all around them. The bright light was gone, leaving the baiting pit illuminated only by the flickering green flames of the braziers.

Darrow picked himself up carefully. Feena was already at the edge of the pit, leaning over to see what was below.

"Tal!" She ran her thumb across her holy symbol and spoke a word. Light shone from the talisman, revealing the aftermath of the vampire's destruction.

Radu Malveen lay on his back beside the pit. The explosion had reduced his right hand to a withered black branch. His face was also ruined, burned to the bone in some places, in others spotted with raw, weeping red wounds.

There was no sign of Stannis Malveen except for the nasty black and red stains covering every surface.

Talbot sat propped against the bars of Maelin's cell, where the blast had thrown him. Everywhere his exposed skin was burned and peeling, his hair singed and smoking.

Feena gasped and thrust her fist against her mouth, staring down at his motionless body. At last, Maelin emerged from the shelter of her overturned cot, cautiously approaching Tal. She placed a tentative hand on his neck, and he flinched at the pain.

"Oh, thank you!" cried Feena from the other side of the bars. She closed her eyes and clutched her glowing talisman. "Thank you, Lady."

Darrow ran to fetch the key from the veil. The chains were still hot, but the keys were relatively undamaged. Despite the slight bend in the shaft, the key did its job. After a few fumbling moments, Darrow let Feena into the baiting pit before releasing Maelin.

The cleric channeled the last of her power into healing Talbot's burns. The worst of them had vanished, but he still appeared groggy and weak. His burned hair stank worse than the foul odor left by the demise of Stannis Malveen.

"You're free," he told her as he opened her cell door. He mustered a weak smile, wondering whether she would throw herself into his arms or simply weep with gratitude.

She did neither. Instead, she moved into the hall, making every effort not to touch him as she slipped by. He followed her into the baiting pit. There, Maelin stood behind Feena, who knelt beside Talbot.

"Get Radu," said Tal. "Make sure he's alive. We need the Scepters to get the truth out of him."

Darrow turned to obey. First he would throw that sword into the pit, and—

But Radu Malveen was gone. Darrow searched for some trail in the sand, but there was none. He peered into the dark pit, but there was nothing but darkness as far as he could see.

"Where in the Nine Hells did he go?" thundered Talbot.

"I—I don't know," said Darrow, staring into the fanged pit. "Where does that hole go?"

" 'Somewhere worse . . .' " quoted Darrow, remembering Lord Malveen's words.

"I smell smoke," said Feena.

Darrow didn't yet, but he trusted the cleric's sense of smell. He remembered the dry timbers of the second floor and could only imagine the inferno they had ignited above.

"Dark and empty," said Maelin. "What did you do? Set fire to the place before coming down?" When she saw Feena wince, she cursed again. "Some rescue this is."

"I'll check the door." Feena ran out of the baiting pit and up the stairs.

"Where does that hole lead?" demanded Talbot, his voice thundering like that of a battlefield commander. He pushed himself up and painfully got to his feet. He looked like the walking dead.

"I really don't know!" said Darrow. Now he smelled the smoke, too. They all did. Suddenly he remembered, "The troughs!"

Maelin ran back into the hall between the cells. Darrow and Tal followed, finding her lifting the stone slabs that bordered the running water. Beneath them the trough was just wide enough for a big man to crawl through. At its end, it slanted sharply down, its bottom surface black and green with slime.

"This has to empty out somewhere, doesn't it?" Maelin said. "Probably the sewers."

"Probably," agreed Tal. He knelt down and squirmed his head and shoulders into the chute, then pulled himself back out. "It's a tight fit, but it's slippery enough."

Feena returned from the stairs, breathless. "The door's too hot to touch," she reported, "but smoke's pouring down the steps."

Darrow looked dubiously at the sewage tunnel. The thought of being trapped in there was no more appealing than the prospect of suffocating under a house fire.

"Do we have any other options?" asked Tal.

Darrow felt slightly hurt that Talbot looked to Maelin before him. Nobody had an alternative.

"Right, then," Tal said. "The sewers it is. I'm most likely to get stuck, so I'll go first."

"No," said Feena. "You're most likely to get stuck, so you go last."

Talbot started to argue but thought better of it. Before any more arguments could arise, Maelin shucked off her outer clothing.

"I don't know about you people," she said, "but I'm sick of this place." She dived head-first into the nasty chute. The rest of them followed her lead.

One by one, they slid down the chute to tumble down the slope of an enormous storm drain.

Numb after their ordeal, they picked themselves up and followed the sound of the surf until they came to a rusted grate beneath the wharves of Selgaunt Bay. Talbot grasped the bars, growled briefly as his arms grew thick and hairy, and tore their way out.

They climbed up to the waterfront and turned back toward House Malveen. The orange glow of the flames lit up the clouds from below, and they could hear the clamor of the fire brigade even at this distance.

Talbot stood with one big arm around Feena, who nestled her head against his chest. When Darrow took a step toward Maelin, she recoiled from him.

"I came back for you," he said, "just like I promised."

Maelin looked at him as if a particularly noisome rat had come too close. She skirted around Feena to keep the cleric between her and Darrow. "Stay away from me."

"Wh-what?" stammered Darrow. "I thought you and I—"

"You thought what?" she spat. "That I fell in love with you because you brought me food? The only thing I hated more than being locked down here for over a year was pretending to fancy you."

Darrow stared at her, disbelieving what he heard. "I didn't have to come back for you."

"Yes, you did," she said, "because I made you come back for me."

A cold realization slowly formed in Darrow's belly, heavy as the truth. Since he had left his home and come to Selgaunt, Darrow had done nothing but obey someone else: first Radu, then Rusk, and finally Maelin. Even when he turned against them, he had played the informant, the henchman . . . always the servant. It was all he had ever been, and he now feared it was all he would ever be.

Maelin might be free, but he was still in the cage.

CHAPTER 22

BARGAINS

Mirtul, 1372 DR

What years of quibbling among its dozen creditors could not accomplish, the second fall of House Malveen resolved in a single night. Within a tenday, salvage crews were carting away the rubble, and a new owner announced plans to build a shipyard on the site.

The inquest raged and died as quickly as the fire. Thamalon's influence combined with Darrow's cooperation spared Tal from magical interrogation, and so the secret of his curse was kept. Darrow agreed to submit to divinations that would detect any falsehood, so the magistrates relied most heavily on his testimony. Tal added his account, omitting only a few details. He reasoned there was no harm in leaving the magistrates to infer that Rusk had done away with Alale Soargyl's body when he first came to the city. Rusk was the murderer, after all, and Tal still had no idea how or where Chaney disposed of the body.

Darrow remained imprisoned pending a judgment from the mistress of Moonshadow Hall, the nearest temple of Selûne. His confessed crimes had occurred beyond the reach of Sembian law, but the magistrates deemed it politic to consult Dhauna Myritar. Justice would be hers to dispose if she so willed.

Tal couldn't decide what he thought should happen to the rogue werewolf. He had run and murdered with the People of the Black Blood, but his desire to turn away from their bloody ways seemed genuine. If asked to speak on Darrow's behalf, Tal wasn't sure what he would say. He did not want to diminish Maleva's memory by defending one of her murderers. On the other hand, what might have happened to him if Feena had not guided him away from the path of the Black Blood? He shuddered to think how close he had come to Darrow's fate.

The surviving Malveens naturally came under suspicion, but no amount of investigation, magical or otherwise, could incriminate them in their brothers' misdeeds. Tal glimpsed them at the inquest. Laskar looked stunned and confused by all the revelations, but Pietro had a peculiar smell about him, even from across the room. Tal hoped they were truly innocent of Stannis and Radu's schemes, and he wished for the thousandth time that Chaney were still around to watch his back.

Eckert's punishment was left to Lord Uskevren's discretion, but Thamalon turned the question over to Tal. Considering the circumstances, Tal couldn't bring himself to prosecute the treacherous butler. He imagined that if one of his family were held hostage, he might have done the same.

Tal found Eckert at the tallhouse and informed him of his decision.

"Oh, thank you, sir," said Eckert at the news. "I knew you would understand my dilemma. I shall redouble my efforts to serve you in the most—"

"Oh, no," said Tal. "You're definitely dismissed."

"Of course, Master Talbot," said Eckert.

"I'm still angry with you," said Tal. "While I understand why you did it, the fact is that you betrayed me to enemies of the family. But what really makes me angry is that Chaney and Quickly both died because you did not come to me sooner."

Eckert nodded soberly.

"I'm glad Maelin is safe," said Tal.

"Thank you, sir."

"Now go away," he said. "I don't want to see you again."

Quickly's funeral was held at the Wide Realms, and all the public was welcome to the feast and the play that followed. Sivana turned up Quickly's will, which included instructions that her funeral feast conclude with a free public performance of her favorite play, *The Widow of Marsember*. It was a broad, raunchy comedy filled with crossdressing and pratfalls. It went beautifully, even reducing the audience to tears in an otherwise funny scene when Ennis wept openly during the widow's recounting of her dead husband's hundred flaws and one virtue.

When the show was over, the audience left in high spirits, as Quickly wanted it. The players sat on the floor and drank toasts to their departed mistress as well as Chaney, whom they all liked. There was as much smiling and laughing as tears and comforting embraces. Everyone in the company made a point of telling Tal he wasn't to blame. Much as he loved them for the gesture, he could not stop feeling guilty both for Quickly and for Chaney.

The next night, Chaney's funeral feast was held at Stormweather Towers. The intractable elders among the Foxmantles still refused to acknowledge him, though his cousin Meena ignored the ban and attended as a guest of Thazienne. Even the players at the Wide Realms received invitations signed by Lady Shamur herself, much to their astonishment. Every one of them came, if only to see the inside of Tal's family home, to which none of them would ever have been invited on other occasions. Shamur was not only civil but quite warm to the common troupe, joking with them at the scandal she was causing among her opera circles. When she saw that the feast was going well, Shamur led Tal away from the crowd and into her parlor.

"I looked for you that night," she said. "You could have come to me."

"I know," said Tal, "but none of the other werewolves had to bring their mothers."

Shamur tried to remain cross, but her smile betrayed her. "Don't talk back to your mother."

"Why not? You're good with a blade, but I beat you last time."

"So you did know that was me? Why didn't you say something?"

"I didn't know how much you knew about my problem," said Tal, "and by the time your past came out, it didn't matter that I'd suspected something a few months earlier."

"You should keep in mind that I'm not just your mother," she said. "You can come to me when you need help."

"And become one of those mewling, spoiled children who run crying to their parents whenever they don't get their way? No, thanks."

"Then don't come to me because I'm your mother," said Shamur. "Come to me because I'm your friend."

That got Tal's attention. "Even though I've known you all my life, I still don't know you very well."

"Then let's make up for it. A new Thayvian opera opens in three days. You will be my escort."

"Why does it have to be the opera?" complained Tal.

"Because I say so, and because I'm still your mother," she said, "and you're still my son."

"Yes," said Tal. "I'm your son, but I'm not your little boy anymore. As long as you see that, and as long as the next time it's the playhouse or a bard at the Green Gauntlet, then it's a deal."

Shamur sighed dramatically. "Why is it so hard for you just to obey your elders?"

"Inherited trait, I think," said Tal.

Shamur chuckled. "You've always favored Thamalon so strongly that I never really saw it before."

"What?"

"Except for your eyes, you've never seemed to take after me," she said. "It seems obvious now why we have three willful and disobedient children."

"I don't think it's all your fault," said Tal. "Obedience isn't an Uskevren virtue, is it?"

"No," agreed Shamur. "It seems I married into the right family after all."

Tal realized the time had come for another conversation, this time with the Old Owl. "You know what *is* an Uskevren virtue?"

"What?"

"Negotiation."

Tal found Thamalon in his library, tapping his chin with one finger while studying a chess problem. He had mingled with the funeral guests for a seemly time, so no one could blame him for seeking the privacy of his retreat. Lord Uskevren looked up as his son entered.

"Care for a game?" inquired Thamalon.

"No," said Tal. "I came to thank you for Chaney's feast." Thamalon's offer to hold the event at Stormweather Towers surprised everyone.

"Very well," said Thamalon. "You may proceed."

"What?"

"It was a joke, son," said Thamalon. "Perhaps not as good as those you're used to hearing in the taverns."

"Sorry," said Tal, relieved at Thamalon's friendly tone. "I'm still an idiot sometimes."

"It's hereditary . . ." said Thamalon.

". . . among the Uskevren men," they finished together.

Thamalon's black eyebrows twitched in surprise. They were a stark contrast to his snow-white hair.

"You've been talking to Larajin," suggested Tal.

Thamalon nodded.

"Does Mother know?"

Thamalon's long pause indicated that she did not. "So she told you, did she?"

"You could have told me yourself," said Tal. "After you warned me away from her last year, I thought—Well, never mind what I thought. But it was a lot worse than the truth."

"We all have our secrets," said Thamalon, "as you demonstrated so dramatically."

"I'm glad to be rid of mine, to be honest."

"If you had come to me from the start—" began Thamalon.

"If you told me the truth about Larajin. . . ." interrupted Tal.

Thamalon pointed a finger at his son. "Challenger's point!"

Tal chuckled. "Where'd you get a sense of humor?"

Thamalon looked hurt. "Your mother gave it to me for Midwinter," he said. "You'd remember if you spent more time at home."

"I was . . . busy. Well, yes, you're right. These days I'll make more time. It'll be easier now that I don't have to worry about keeping a secret."

"It occurs to me that we might all benefit from fewer secrets—at least among the family, mind you."

"I'm not the only one—" began Tal.

"No, Talbot, indeed you are not. I'm just as much to blame."

Tal tried to mask his surprise. His father had never admitted a mistake in front of him before.

"There's another reason I wanted to talk with you," said Tal. "I have a business proposition."

By the expression on Thamalon's face, it was clear he had not expected those words. "Go on," he said.

"Quickly left her shares of the playhouse to be divided among us all," said Tal. "Only I never took a salary, so she converted my pay to extra shares. And she counted the money I gave her in the beginning as a loan, with interest."

Thamalon was nodding.

"So I'm the majority shareholder in the Wide Realms playhouse," said Tal.

"As well as the primary debtor," concluded Thamalon. "Is that it?"

"The way I figure it, the amount due each year is just over half as much as the rent on my tallhouse."

Thamalon's eyebrows jumped again. "Are you asking me to increase your stipend?"

"No," said Tal. "Hear me out. I'm offering to give up the tallhouse and asking for the money instead."

"Your mother would like having you back home," said Thamalon.

"We've already talked. I'll go with her to the opera every once in a while."

"You move back to Stormweather, or it's no bargain."

"But—" Tal tried to sound indignant without whining. The more he thought on it, the more he realized Chaney had been right about that flaw in his character. "Throw in Eckert's salary," he said. "The costumes are getting a bit shabby."

"What? You're in no position to bargain, young man."

"You want me to live at home, it's going to cost you," said Tal. "And I'll throw in fifty shares of the Wide Realms at half value."

"A hundred shares!" countered Thamalon. "With full determination rights."

"A hundred silent only . . . and only if you and mother come to twelve shows each year."

"Six," said Thamalon. "She'll never go for twelve."

"Eight—and you *don't* bring Tamlin. I want that part in writing."

"Done!"

They shook hands to seal the bargain.

Tal finished raking the playhouse yard and climbed up onto the stage for some shade from the hot summer sun. There was no one else in the yard, but he heard some of the women talking backstage. He made no effort at stealth, but he heard them long before they realized he was approaching.

". . . and Chaney if it's a boy," said Feena. She could barely contain her excitement.

"What will Tal think about that?" asked Sivana clutching Feena's arm in a girlish gesture Tal never would have expected from her.

"Tal thinks he needs to sit down," said Tal, "if I understand you correctly."

He leaned on the rake for support, for the very idea of Feena bearing his child made him dizzy. He knew it was possible, but he had hoped it would not happen so soon. Running a business was more than enough responsibility for him. Parenthood was a greater task than he welcomed.

Sivana laughed. It was a big, throaty sound that reminded Tal of Mistress Quickly. Since her death, Sivana had adopted a markedly matriarchal role among the players, playing mother to Tal's father. Tal didn't mind that, so long as it didn't cause friction with Feena or the other players. On the contrary, Sivana and Feena had become so close that Tal was beginning to worry more about their outnumbering him than quarrelling over his time and attention.

"Oh, you big goof," said Feena, wiping away her own tears of laughter. "When was the last time you understood anything correctly?"

"Well . . ." Tal knew enough that he left it there. He was too relieved to learn that he was not suddenly a father that he didn't mind the slight.

"Hasn't Lommy told you, yet?"

"Told me what?"

"Maybe you should climb up to the heavens and have a peek inside?" suggested Sivana. "But be quiet about it."

There was a ladder backstage, but it was faster to climb up the gallery rails and onto the stage roof. Both Sivana and Feena tsked at him as he took Lommy's preferred route.

"One day," Sivana always warned him, "you'll fall right through that thatching."

"Be careful up there," called Feena in a stage whisper. Tal crept along the thatching on all fours, trying to spread his weight as evenly as possible. As he approached the clarion door, he peered inside.

"Lommy?" he called softly. As his eyes adjusted, he saw the ragged outlines of the tasloi's nest. He had rarely climbed up to their lair, where Otter spent most of his time. The reclusive tasloi was virtually the opposite of his outgoing, clownish brother.

"Tal!" came Lommy's whispering voice, as did the sibilant sounds of Otter's response. Tal saw Otter curled protectively around an even smaller creature. Dark gray and wrinkly, it looked like a miniature tasloi—which is exactly what it was.

Lommy clambered over the window sill and sat on the thatching with Tal, uncharacteristically calm. Usually the little creature was a trembling spring, ready to shoot in any direction unexpectedly.

"I thought Otter was your brother," said Tal.

"Otter brother," agreed Lommy, grinning. "Chaney little brother."

"I see," said Tal, gazing fascinated at the mewling infant. While Quickly's insistence that the tasloi never improve their pidgin Common might make them more charming for the audiences, Tal never anticipated such a profound failure to communicate.

"Tal big brother," said Lommy, climbing onto Tal's shoulder and clinging to his hair. "Tal happy?"

"Oh, yes," said Tal. "Tal very happy. Dumbfounded, flabbergasted, astonished, and a few other big words, but Tal happy."

They sat together on the roof, peering in every now and again to watch Otter cradling the baby. After a while,

Lommy pulled Tal's ear affectionately and went inside to join his new family.

"It was hard enough dealing with one family," said Tal, "but now I've got three."

He and Feena lay on their backs in the yard of the darkened theater. They looked up at the waning moon as it dipped below the edge of the round roof.

"You've been with the players for years," said Feena, "you've come to good terms with your parents, and Lommy and Otter take care of little Chaney themselves. How hard can it be?"

"You have no idea," said Tal. "I just feel like I have to take care of everything these days, like I have to look out for everyone."

"And you're complaining? I thought that's what you liked best?"

Tal thought about that for a moment. "I do like it," he admitted. "It's better than having other people trying to look out for me all the time. But it's a lot of work."

"So you're whining because . . . ?"

"I'm *not* whining," he insisted. He thought of Chaney and bit his lip. "All right, so maybe I was whining just a little."

"And you'll quit it now."

"And I'll quit it now."

Feena slipped her hand into his. They looked up at the moon and the stars, dreaming their separate dreams until Tal spoke again.

"Thank you, Feena."

"For what?"

"This past year, all the time you were helping me with the wolf, I kept expecting you to come to the point and insist I join your church."

"I know I came on strong at first," she said. "You weren't the only one who had a lot of anger to face."

"Rusk," said Tal.

"And Mother, for not dealing with him earlier."

"What could she have done?"

"I don't know," she said. "Moved away, joined his bloody pack . . . something. It feels as though I've spent my whole life waiting for them to kill each other, and now it's over. I don't know what to do next."

"What do you want to do?" he asked.

"That's the problem," she said. "I've never had to decide before."

She went silent, waiting for Tal to say something. A hundred thoughts surfaced in his mind, but he pushed them back down. Every one of them seemed too perilous, too likely to add even more worries to his life. He already had his family to deal with, and now he had taken responsibility for the players as well. Adding Feena to that confusing mix could be nothing but trouble. It was hard enough keeping his relationship with her a secret from his family.

And he realized his mistake. Keeping secrets was not his virtue.

Tal turned on his side and ran a finger lightly along Feena's jaw. Even in the partial moonlight, her freckles stood out against her fair skin. She turned to face him, kissing his palm before nuzzling his hand.

"What are you thinking?" she asked.

"I was thinking," he said, "I'd like to make a deal with you."

RAVENLOFT
the covenant

ravenloft's Lords of darkness have always waited for the unwary to find them.

Six classic tales of horror set in the RAVENLOFT™ world have returned to print in all-new editions.

From the autocratic vampire who wrote the memoirs found in *I, Strahd* to the demon lord and his son whose story is told in *Tapestry of Dark Souls*, some of the finest horror characters created by some of the most influential authors of horror and dark fantasy have found their way to RAVENLOFT, to be trapped there forever.

Laurell K. Hamilton
Death of a Darklord

Christie Golden
Vampire of the Mists

P.N. Elrod
I, Strahd: The Memoirs of a Vampire

Andria Cardarelle
To Sleep With Evil

Elaine Bergstrom
Tapestry of Dark Souls

Tanya Huff
Scholar of Decay

October 2007

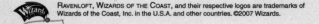